continued . . .

Also by Renée Rosen

White Collar Girl

· · ·

RENÉE ROSEN

NEW AMERICAN LIBRARY

NEW AMERICAN LIBRARY
Published by New American Library,
an imprint of Penguin Random House LLC
375 Hudson Street, New York, New York 10014

This book is an original publication of New American Library.

First Printing, November 2015

For more information about Penguin Random House, visit penguin.com.

LIBRARY OF CONGRESS CATALOGING-IN-PUBLICATION DATA:

Rosen, Renée.
White collar girl: a novel/Renée Rosen.
p. cm.
ISBN 978-0-451-47497-1 (softcover)
1. Women journalists—Illinois—Chicago—Fiction.   2. Reporters and reporting—Illinois—Chicago—Fiction.   3. Chicago (Ill.)—Social life and customs—20th century—Fiction.   I. Title.
PS3618.O83156W48   2015
813'.6—dc23   2015016495

Printed in the United States of America
3   5   7   9   10   8   6   4   2

Designed by Tiffany Estreicher

Penguin
Random
House

To John Dul. At last.

Acknowledgments

◆ ◆ ◆

When I started writing *White Collar Girl* I knew very little about the Daley machine of the 1950s and had never set foot inside a newspaper office. Thankfully, I met many kind and generous people along the way who helped bring me up to speed. Without them, I could not have written this book.

Thank you to Eric Charles May, who is not only a former reporter but also a very talented author. Meeting him was really the jumping-off point for me. It was through Eric that I met Dorothy Colin, a former *Tribune* reporter who offered further insights. Elizabeth Taylor, former *Time Magazine* correspondent and the current Literary Editor of the *Chicago Tribune*, was enormously helpful and provided encouragement early on. Her book, *American Pharaoh*, which she coauthored with Adam Cohen, is a fascinating look at the Daley machine. It was through Elizabeth that I was able to interview Barbara Mahany, a writer and former *Chicago Tribune* columnist. My friend Julie Anderson introduced me to Mark Damisch, a critically acclaimed classical pianist, lawyer and former mayor of Northbrook who gave me a crash course on the inner workings of Operation Greylord. As mentioned in my author's note, Rick Kogan gave me a tour of the *Tribune* and led me to Shirley Baugher, a historian for Old Town who shared many stories with me and her many books, which are listed in the back. Thank you also goes to Claire Dolinar for the guided tour.

Two people who went above and beyond for me are Charles Osgood, a former *Chicago Tribune* staff photographer who not only read and vetted the book for me but who introduced me to Marion Purcelli. Marion inspired more aspects of this book than I can count. Her generosity with her time, her knowledge and sensitivity to the writing process are forever appreciated. Yes, she is the girl with the attaché case and so much more.

Where would we be without friends? Thank you to Julia Lieblich, Marianne Nee, Tasha Alexander, Andrew Grant, Nick Hawkins, Amy Sue Nathan, Kelly O'Connor McNees, Karen Abbott, Javier Ramirez, Stephanie Nelson and the Sushi Lunch bunch.

Extra-special thanks go to Joe Esselin, Mindy Mailman, Brenda Klem and Sara Gruen—your friendship and support know no bounds and for that I'm forever grateful—I love you all.

To my team, starting with my amazing agent, Kevan Lyon, who has taken such good care of me and my books and has the ability to make me think I'm her only client. Thank you for all that you do and continue to do on my behalf. To her assistant, Patricia Nelson, thank you for all your feedback and the countless early reads of this manuscript. To Claire Zion, my dream editor, I couldn't ask for a better collaborator or champion. Thank you for your faith in me. I'm beyond thrilled about our future projects together. To Jennifer Fisher, thank you for your fresh eyes on the manuscript and insightful critiques. To Jessica Butler for her tireless efforts to get my books noticed. To the Penguin Random House marketing and sales teams, especially Stefan Moorehead and the one and only Brian Wilson—so very grateful to have you in my camp. You're the best.

To my family, Debbie Rosen, Pam Jaffe, Andy Jaffe, Jerry Rosen, Andrea Rosen, Joey Perilman and Devon Rosen—you have celebrated every step of the way with me and I thank you all for your love and encouragement.

And lastly, to John Dul. Thank you for coming into my life and taking this journey with me. I love you so.

"A newspaper is an institution developed by modern civilization to present the news of the day, to foster commerce and industry, to inform and lead public opinion, and to furnish that check upon government which no constitution has ever been able to provide."

—Robert R. McCormick

White Collar Girl

Chapter 1

◆ ◆ ◆

Chicago 1955

It was Voltaire and me. I stood inside the Tribune Tower and stared at his quote inscribed in the limestone: *"I do not agree with a word that you say, but I will defend to the death your right to say it."*

The elevator cars were dinging as people rushed past me to fill them, but I stood still. I needed a moment to absorb where I was and what I had to do. I thought about Milton's passage engraved out front: *"Give me liberty to know, to utter and to argue freely according to my conscience, above all other liberties."* I savored every word, letting them dissolve like something sweet on my tongue. This was a pledge, a vow I'd taken to protect and uphold.

The elevator operator held the door for me. My sweaty palms left marks on the handrails, on everything I touched. I was nervous. Excited, too. But more than anything, I was burdened by the weight of generations riding on my shoulders. It was time for me, Jordan Walsh, to carry on the family tradition. My father had been a war correspondent during World War II and before that during the Spanish Civil War, working alongside Ernest Hemingway. My mother was the daughter of a newspaperman and during the war in Europe she, too, took a job as a reporter at the City News Bureau. My brother, Eliot, named after my mother's favorite poet, T. S. Eliot, had worked at the newly formed *Sun-Times*.

Eliot was the real reason I was at the *Tribune*. All my life he'd been the push behind me, convincing me to climb the giant oak in our backyard and ride the Bobs or the Silver Streak at Riverview Park. Just because I was a girl didn't mean I couldn't keep up. He made me believe I could do anything he could do, including becoming a reporter. Eliot had been a rising star at the paper when he was killed. A hit-and-run accident that took him far too soon. All he wanted was to be a reporter, and now it was up to me to live out that dream for both of us. That was the promise I'd made to him at his funeral two years ago.

I stepped off the elevator on the fourth floor and entered an enormous open room. A sea of desks, one butted up right against the other, clustered beneath the fog of cigarette and pipe smoke. I passed by the John T. McCutcheon *Injun Summer* poster on the wall and entered deeper into the echo chamber. The linoleum floor amplified every click of the typewriters, every clack of heels walking about the room. I was surrounded by telephones ringing, portable radios murmuring, dozens of people talking and shouting. I stood invisible while conversations volleyed across the room:

"Did you get confirmation?"

"Still working on it."

"We need another quote."

Pages were ripped from the typewriters and waved in the air, followed by cries of, "Copy. Cop-py." Young boys scrambled up to snatch and deliver the stories to the horseshoe in the middle of the room. That was where the four key editors sat. They were stationed along the rim with the slot man on the inside, in the center, so he could dole out the assignments. Every inch of that

horseshoe was covered with newspapers, books, telephone directories, overflowing ashtrays and stained coffee cups. It wasn't
even eight o'clock in the morning and the frenetic energy in the
room suggested that everyone was already behind schedule, running out of time. *Welcome to the* Chicago Tribune *city room.* It
was the picture of chaos. And I loved it.

I spotted Mr. Pearson, the features editor, standing over his
desk, still wearing his fedora and overcoat as he typed away. He
hadn't even taken a moment to sit down. I hovered nearby and
cleared my throat. He didn't look up. Instead he remained over
his typewriter, pecking away, two-finger style.

To most people Mr. Pearson might have appeared rude, but I
understood newspapermen. As a young girl I had spent many a
day in the city room with my father, keeping quiet, waiting while
he banged out a story. I longed to have my fingertips up against
the deadline, my mind so consumed with facts that I couldn't
be bothered to take off my coat for fear that some detail might
escape me.

I was acutely aware that time equaled the creation of news.
Every second of every day something was happening *out there*—
maybe something sinister or uplifting, criminal or joyous. To me
news was a living, breathing entity. The facts and circumstances
were like cells that divided and subdivided. Inevitable and un-
stoppable. A story was always taking shape, evolving, and it was
up to people like me to discover it, dig down in the muck and
pull it out, roots and all.

Mr. Pearson was still typing, and I waited patiently, thinking
how this was a good time to work at the paper. There was a new
boss in town, and Chicago was in the spotlight. Richard J. Daley
had just been elected mayor, and he had promised to bring big
changes to the city. He would revitalize the Loop and build
expressways. He had plans for expanding O'Hare Airport and for

expanding the city, too, with buildings going up at record speeds and more cranes sweeping the skyline every day. Yes, it was an exciting time to call myself a member of the Chicago press.

"Who are you?" Mr. Pearson asked at last without looking up.

"Jordan. Jordan Walsh."

"Who?"

I was deflated. He didn't seem to have any recollection of our interview less than two weeks before. "I'm the new reporter. Remember? You hired me. To cover . . ." My voice trailed off when he raised his eyes, keeping his index fingers poised on the typewriter keys.

"Marie— Where the hell is she? Mrs. Angelo?" he called out. "Mrs. Angelo—Mrs.—"

"I'm right here. I'm coming." I heard the *clunk, clunk, clunk* of heels before my eyes landed on an attractive older woman, probably in her mid-fifties. She was short and had brown and silver-flecked hair that flipped up at her chin. "I'm right here," she said. "You don't have to holler."

"Come show Robin here—"

"It's Jordan," I corrected him.

He didn't care. He removed his fedora, revealing a full head of wavy white hair that didn't match his dark eyebrows, thick as caterpillars. "Show Robin here to her desk," Mr. Pearson said over the sound of his resumed typing. "This is your new society writer."

Mrs. Angelo shook my hand, firm as any man would, and introduced herself. She was the society editor and one of only a handful of women on the floor.

"Come with me," she said. "I'll get you situated."

She walked me around the floor, weaving in and around desks and down hallways. There was so much to take in, and by the end of our tour, I was discombobulated and couldn't remember which doorway led to the lavatories, the photo lab, the wire machine room or the morgue, where the archived articles were laid to rest. There were so many department desks, too, each one piled high with newspapers, books, telephones and other clutter. I couldn't recall which one was the financial desk, the telegraph desk, the cable desk or the city desk. And that was only the fourth floor.

"Oh, and don't worry about the Robin part, kid," said Mrs. Angelo as she walked me along. "He called the last girl Robin, too, and her name was Sharon. Robin was two girls before that."

"What happened to them? Did they move on to the city desk?"

She looked at me in surprise and then laughed. "You young girls are all the same. You come in here, fresh out of school, thinking you're going to be the next Nellie Bly." She shook her head. "I train you all, and what happens? You get disillusioned, get married, and then you quit."

"That's not my plan." It wasn't. I didn't even have a boyfriend. And yes, I was going to be the next Nellie Bly.

After Mrs. Angelo assigned me to a desk, she called over to a voluptuous platinum blonde seated next to me. "Hey, M— M, finish taking Jordan here around. I have to get ready for a meeting. In the meantime"—Mrs. Angelo handed me a stack of forms—"fill these out when you have a chance."

Mrs. Angelo went back to her desk across the room and M took over. She introduced herself as Madeline Miller but said everyone called her M. She was stylish, wore one of those double-breasted shirtwaist dresses that accentuated her cone-shaped breasts. She was in her late twenties, maybe early thirties, and bore a striking resemblance to Marilyn Monroe. Judging by the penciled-in beauty mark on her cheek, I realized this was no accident. She also wore enough perfume to rival the cigarette, cigar and pipe smoke in the room.

"Peter," M called to a man a few desks over who was wearing

a green eyeshade, "this is Jordan. She's starting today on society news. Peter's a crime reporter."

Peter adjusted his visor and said, "Excellent," only his voice had a squeaky-door quality to it, so it came out sounding more like, "*Ehhhx*-cellent."

"And this is Randy," said M, turning the other direction. "He's one of the staff artists."

Randy was a good-looking fellow with a long face and one of those dimples at the tip of his chin. I stole a peek at the editorial cartoon he was working on as I said hello, but he didn't bother to respond. He didn't even open his mouth other than to sing along with a jingle playing over his radio: *"Winston tastes good like a"*—*BANG-BANG*—he tapped his pencil on the desk—*"cigarette should. . . ."*

The floor began to shake and a rumbling came up from the bowels of the building. I watched the coffee in Randy's cup ripple like a calm lake that someone had thrown a pebble into. The quaking seemed to coincide with Randy's *BANG-BANG* but was completely unrelated. No one seemed concerned and that's when I realized they were used to this. *Of course.* It was only the printing presses in the basement starting to roll.

M continued with the introductions, walking me to some nearby desks. Walter Harris was a pipe-smoking, fast-talking political reporter with a jet-black flattop who grunted a hello. He sat opposite Henry Oberlin, who stopped typing long enough to stuff a handful of Frosted Flakes in his mouth while an unattended cigarette smoldered in his ashtray. He had a ring of pale blond hair around an otherwise balding head. He gazed at me and mumbled what I took to be a "hey" and went back to his story.

With each introduction I felt a little smaller. It was clear that these new colleagues had no interest in who I was, where I came from or what I was there to do. They were also all men, and frankly, I was surprised that M had bothered taking me around in the first place.

Although when she walked me over to the next desk, no introduction was needed. I recognized him right away. Marty Sinclair was a Pulitzer Prize–winning journalist who had a weekly column and whose byline frequently appeared on page one. My father knew him, but I'd never met him before and I was rapt. To me Marty Sinclair was journalistic royalty. He was a brilliant reporter and an eloquent writer, and not all journalists could be both. I took a moment to observe the great master in action, how he kept his thick black glasses propped up on his forehead just above his eyebrows and gripped a pencil between his teeth as if it were an ear of corn. His necktie was tossed over his shoulder and his shirtsleeves were rolled halfway up his hairless arms. He dropped his glasses to the bridge of his nose and looked at M for a second before his eyes landed on me.

"Mr. Sinclair"—I reached out to shake his hand—"it's an honor. I'm a huge fan." My heartbeat pounded in my ears. I could hardly believe it. *I'm meeting Marty Sinclair.*

He removed the pencil from his mouth and studied my face. I thought I detected the hint of a smile thawing on his lips, and it thrilled me.

But before he could respond, Mr. Copeland, the city editor, shouted for him from the horseshoe. "Sinclair—over here!"

"Jesus Christ. What now?" Marty shook his head.

The spell between us was broken. He shoved himself away from his desk and went to the horseshoe to talk to Mr. Copeland and Mr. Ellsworth, the managing editor, who oversaw all the desks: the national, foreign, financial and city. I kept glancing back at the horseshoe. Marty's arms were flailing. So were Mr. Ellsworth's. Mr. Ellsworth was tall and lanky with a tidy beard and enough gray in his hair to suggest he'd paid his dues in the business. Marty Sinclair may have been the *Tribune*'s star reporter, but Mr. Ellsworth was the man behind the man. He controlled the center desk, and that was the heart and soul of the paper.

Mr. Ellsworth had interviewed me two weeks before. I assumed he'd been expecting a man, because he glanced at my résumé and said, "Jordan, huh?" When he ignored my clips, I knew he wasn't interested in bringing a girl onto the city desk, especially one straight out of school. Didn't matter that I'd been the deputy editor of the *Daily Northwestern* or that I'd graduated Phi Beta Kappa from the Medill School of Journalism. Less than five minutes into our meeting, he'd sent me over to Mr. Pearson. A couple of girls in the features department had recently gotten married and quit, so Mr. Pearson had agreed to give me a break, writing for society news. During my interview I had told him that I'd like to work on some other types of stories, too.

"I have some ideas for feature stories and—"

Mr. Pearson had given me a look that stopped me mid-sentence. With his bristly brows knitted together, he said, "Society news. That's the job, missy. Take it or leave it."

I took it, having already been shot down for the city desk job at the *Daily News* and the *Chicago American*. The City News Bureau and the *Sun-Times* never called me back for a second interview. I knew what Eliot would say if he were still alive: *Just get your foot in the door. You'll work your way onto the city desk.* And that was exactly what I intended to do.

Mr. Ellsworth and Mr. Copeland were still going at it with Marty. I was dying to know what they were arguing about because I was curious by nature. Always asking too many questions, sticking my nose where it didn't belong. My father used to say, "Curiosity is the curse of a good journalist." He also used to say, "Keep your ears open. People love to tell their secrets."

The last person M introduced me to was Benny, a young general assignment reporter, who was eighteen but looked about twelve. He had red hair and freckles and reminded me of Howdy Doody. Unlike the others, he was friendly, if not downright chatty. While I got situated at my desk and filled out the new-employee forms for Mrs. Angelo, Benny told me about his breakfast that morning.

"I had a double-yolk egg." The look on his face said, *I still can't believe it.* "That ever happen to you?"

"I don't believe so. No."

"You crack open an egg and there's two yolks. I mean what are the odds? Like finding a four-leaf clover."

"Aw, shut up over there with the yolks already," said Walter.

But Benny kept going. "I think that's gotta mean something, don't you? Like today's my lucky day or something."

"It'll be your lucky day if I don't come over there and shut your trap. And yours, too," Walter said to Randy, who was still singing the Winston jingle even though his radio was blasting *Talent Scouts* with Arthur Godfrey.

A few minutes later Marty came back to his desk, muttering, "Subpoena me, my ass. . . ." He opened his top drawer and slammed it shut, knocking over the pencil cup on top. "I'm not going to jail over this, either. My word is my word."

"Hey, Marty," said Walter. "You gonna burn your source or what?"

"Fuck off." Marty shoved his typewriter stand with such force it capsized and crashed to the floor. I gasped as papers, pens and everything else went flying. Marty didn't flinch. He stepped over the carnage, grabbed his hat and stormed out of the city room.

"Is he okay?" I asked, speaking through a splay of fingers.

"Who, Marty?" Peter lifted his green eyeshade off his brow and rubbed his temples. "Oh, yeah, sure. Yeah, he's fine. Just been under a lot of pressure lately is all."

"Give me a hand with this mess, will you?" M asked.

I scampered around to the side and helped her put Marty's desk back together. Funny, but not one of the men bothered to break from their work. It was assumed that we women would do the cleaning up. Not that I minded. After all, it was Marty Sinclair's desk.

I straightened up a fan of tricolored copy paper that recorded every word in triplicate. The top sheet was white—the original. The yellow page in the middle went to the editor, and the third sheet—the pink one—went to the copy editor.

"What was that all about?" I asked M, who was still down on all fours, reaching for the pencil holder that had rolled under Marty's desk.

"Mr. Copeland and Mr. Ellsworth want him to reveal his source for some story that ran the other day."

"Can they do that?" I'd always thought sources were protected, off-limits.

"Well, it looks like he might be subpoenaed. Turns out that the identity of his source is becoming quite a news story all by itself."

I scooped up a handful of paper clips and stood up.

"Five bucks says he caves." Walter snorted as he gripped his pipe with his back teeth, struck a match and sucked the flame into the bowl.

"I don't know about that." Randy tucked a pencil behind his ear. "You think he'll give up his source?"

"Be a goddamn stupid move on his part." Walter shook out the match and dropped it in a paper coffee cup.

"Nah," said Peter. "I think you're wrong."

"Marty's a stand-up guy," said Henry, reaching into the cereal box for another handful of Frosted Flakes. "He won't burn his source."

"Five bucks," said Walter, reaching into his wallet. "Who's in?"

I was watching the betting go down when Mrs. Angelo came back to my desk and handed me a list of names. "I'll have you start by verifying these."

As I skimmed the list, my eyes landed on surnames like Preston and Vanderbilt, Crown and Rothschild.

"It's the Mortimer wedding," Mrs. Angelo explained. "That's the bridal party. I need you to check the spellings and confirm middle initials, titles—that sort of thing."

After Mrs. Angelo went back to her desk, M handed me the current copy of the Social Register.

"Here," she said. "You'll need this."

I spent the next hour verifying fourteen-karat names. There were a few stragglers—normal-sounding people—that I had to look up in the telephone book and call to confirm. Before I knew it, it was almost noon.

Mrs. Angelo came back and checked my progress, offering a nod of approval. "I'm going to lunch," she said, giving her pocketbook a snap. "We can review the rest this afternoon."

M eyed Mrs. Angelo through her compact mirror while touching up her lipstick. As soon as Mrs. Angelo cleared the main hallway and disappeared into an elevator, M dropped her lipstick and compact into her desk drawer and closed it with a hip bump. "I'm famished. C'mon, let's go eat before she gets back."

We ended up at the Woolworth's counter in the basement of State and Randolph with Gabby Jones, a young woman who, like me, was in her early twenties. She had mousy brown hair and a nondescript face. She was one of those people who blended into any crowd. She was a fellow *sob sister*, as I learned the men called us female reporters.

"They think everything we write is sentimental and coated in sugar," said M. She sat in between us and swiveled her red stool from side to side as she spoke.

"But what about the women on the city desk?" I asked. "What do they call them?"

Gabby laughed with a big toothy smile. "There are no women on the city desk."

"None?" I set my sandwich down. It felt like it was made of lead.

"There was Rita Fitzpatrick," said M with a shrug. "But she's the only one I can think of."

I really wasn't all that surprised. Others had warned me of this. Even my mother. "You're a pretty girl," she'd said. "They'll take one look at you and think beauty and fashion. Not hard news."

I wondered if I'd have to change my style. Now that I was a career girl, I'd cut my long dark ponytail and fringe bangs and gone with the sophisticated Italian cut that Gina Lollobrigida and Sophia Loren were wearing. And then there were my new clothes, which I'd spent a fortune on. The sheath dress I was wearing cost me seventeen dollars, and that didn't include the cropped white bolero jacket. I glanced at my handbag, black and white patent leather. It matched my Mary Janes. It occurred to me that if I wanted to get a real assignment, perhaps I would have to tone myself down.

I'd always known I'd have to prove myself. I wasn't looking for a free ride. But I'd thought because I was Hank Walsh's daughter, Eliot Walsh's sister, they would have assumed I was a serious journalist. I supposed my first test would be showing them what I could do with charity balls and celebrity sightings. I wasn't as confident that I'd be able to impress anyone with my recipes, which M just informed me I'd be expected to contribute for the food column.

"But doesn't Mary Meade do all the recipes?" I asked, recall-ing the byline I'd seen over and over again.

"There is no 'Mary Meade,'" said Gabby as the waitress slapped our checks on the counter. "Somebody made up the byline, and we all take turns being her."

"Oh, and don't let Mrs. Angelo scare you," said M as she draped her chiffon scarf over her hair. "She's all bark and no bite."

When we got back to the city room, Mrs. Angelo reviewed the bridal party names I'd confirmed. "Nice work," she said. "Did I mention the Carrington wedding?" She jotted a few notes in the margin of my copy. "It's this Saturday—you'll be covering it." She glanced over at Gabby and sighed deeply, letting her shoulders rise and fall. "Poor thing's drowning over there. Why don't you help her finish up tomorrow's WCG column and the write-up for the TWT column?"

The WCG—White Collar Girl—column focused on stories for career-minded women, like secretaries and schoolteachers. And TWT—They Were There—was a daily column devoted to socialites and celebrity sightings about town. They both sounded a hell of a lot more exciting than spell-checking names and con-firming hometowns.

Gabby was trying to finish her White Collar Girl column on "Gifts for Your Boss on His Birthday" and she welcomed my help. I could tell Gabby was the nervous type, the kind that got easily flustered. I noticed that whenever Mrs. Angelo walked by, she would instantly act guilty of some wrongdoing. Earlier in the day I watched her hang up on a telephone call mid-sentence and start blindly typing away, slapping at her carriage return.

She told me she was an identical twin and that when she wasn't with her sister she felt like half a person. "People always referred to us as 'the twins,' never Abby and Gabby. Everyone always asks me how Nathan and the children are. I'm not even the married one. That's Abby's family. If you're a twin, it's like you're invisible on your own. . . ."

I didn't know what to say. I hardly knew her and here she was opening up like that.

Gradually Randy, Walter, Peter and the others began to trickle back in from lunch, and I could smell the martinis, the bourbons and beers. My father and brother had told me all about the newspaperman's lunch. It sounded a lot more appealing than sitting at the Woolworth's counter.

About an hour later Marty Sinclair came back to the city room, too. He chucked his hat and jacket on the coat stand in the corner and began churning out his afternoon story. I was still curious about his piece with the anonymous source but hadn't had a chance to check his recent bylines. Instead I made excuses to walk by his desk, stealing glances over his shoulder. His workspace was littered with scraps of paper and napkins with scribbles on them. It looked like an overturned garbage can had landed on his desk.

I went back to my seat and finished the They Were There column for Gabby. She had instructed me to do a three-line write-up on Zsa Zsa Gábor and Grace Kelly, who had made the traditional celebrity visit to the Pump Room during their stopover in Chicago on their way from New York to California. There was also a mention about Jerry Lewis, who was performing at Chez Paree. All the while Randy absentmindedly continued humming that Winston jingle, which was now embedded in my brain, too. I was verifying the time of Grace Kelly's arrival at the Ambassador East when Mr. Ellsworth stood up at the horseshoe and shouted to Marty.

"Sinclair—get over here! Now!"

Marty swore as he stormed off in Mr. Ellsworth's direction.

With everyone back from lunch, the din of the city room had revved up to full volume. Given the noise emanating from the typewriters, the wire machines and telephones, it was amazing that one man would have captured everyone's attention and rendered the room practically silent, but that's what happened.

"Fuck you, Ellsworth. I won't do it!" Marty tore back over to his desk, screaming, "Fuck you, you hear me? Did you hear that?"

"Be reasonable, Marty," said Mr. Ellsworth, trailing after him.

"Fuck you all," said Marty.

"Yeah, well, fuck you, too," said Mr. Copeland. "This goddamned newspaper's looking at a libel suit, thanks to you."

I froze at my desk, watching the exchange. I couldn't take my eyes off any of them.

"I won't burn my source." Marty was sweating profusely. I could see his shiny scalp through his thinning dark hair. "I'll quit before I give up my source. I swear I will. I'll walk."

"That won't get them off your back. Or mine," said Mr. Ellsworth. "Now, maybe you don't mind serving jail time, but I do. And you're not taking this paper down with you. For God's sake, we're trying to help you here."

"I don't need your goddamn help." He started banging things around on his desk.

"Marty, just hand over your source," said Mr. Copeland.

"You know we're going to find out who it is anyway," said Mr. Ellsworth. "Christ, I'll go through your goddamn notes myself if I have to."

"The hell you will," said Marty. "I'm getting my things and I'm getting the hell out of here."

"Quick"—Mr. Copeland turned to Henry at the next desk—"his notes. Get his notes."

"No!" Marty let out a shout that traveled to my inner ear and made me drop my pen. I watched in disbelief as Marty Sinclair—Pulitzer

Prize–winning journalist—grabbed a fistful of notes off his desk and shoved them into his mouth.

"Holy crap!" Mr. Ellsworth pulled off his glasses as if his lenses were not to be trusted. "He's eating his goddamn notes."

"C'mon, now, Marty," Mr. Copeland said, shaking his head. "Get ahold of yourself, for God's sake."

Marty's eyes bulged as he shoved more wads of paper in his mouth. I'd never seen anything like it. Tears ran down his cheeks as he chewed and crammed the notes into his mouth.

"Marty, relax," Mr. Ellsworth said. "Let's talk about this."

Mr. Ellsworth took a step toward Marty, who groaned and flung his coffee cup at him. An arc of brown liquid seemed suspended in the air for a beat before it sloshed down, barely missing Mr. Copeland and Mr. Ellsworth. The two men kept coming, and that's when Marty really lost control. I shrieked as he threw his dictionary and his stapler, followed by the Rolodex and a radio. People ducked, taking cover under their desks, but I stood transfixed. Mr. Copeland and Mr. Ellsworth tried to rush him while Marty hurled telephone books and tape dispensers, paperweights, his chair, the trash can and anything else within reach. My pulse jumped each time Marty went for a new piece of ammo. When he hefted up the typewriter and hurled it at Mr. Copeland, Walter and Randy grabbed him from behind. I let out a loud gasp. Watching my journalistic hero kicking and screaming made my heart drop to my stomach.

It took four of them to restrain Marty, and eventually they had him on the ground, on his stomach, clawing and yelping like a wild animal. Walter was planted on his rear end, pinning down his arms while Randy had him by the legs. Peter and Henry were down on all fours, trying to make eye contact with him and get him to calm down, but Marty only screamed and cried, spitting out bits of chewed-up paper.

Ten minutes later the ambulance arrived. Mrs. Angelo, Gabby,

M and I were all huddled in a cluster, and I winced when the medic knocked Marty out with an injection to the hip, driving a two-inch needle straight through his trousers. Within moments the fight had drained out of him, but my heart still hammered as I watched them strap Marty Sinclair onto a gurney and wheel him out of the city room.

"Okay, everyone." Mr. Ellsworth cupped his hands, yelling into them like a megaphone. "Get back to work. The show's over."

Chapter 2

. . .

A fter work that night M, Gabby and some of the others were going for drinks at Boul Mich over on Grand and Michigan Avenue. No one extended an invitation to me, but Benny shot me a glance as he reached for his hat. "Aren't you coming with?"

I was in no hurry to head home, so I grabbed my handbag, tucked a stack of newspapers under my arm for later reading and went to join them. After all, drinking was an industry tradition. I'd grown up knowing that. My mother kept a list tacked up on the kitchen wall with telephone numbers for Radio Grill, Riccardo's, Twin Anchors, Mister Kelly's and my father's other favorite bars, along with the numbers for the doctor and the fire department.

By the time Benny and I arrived at Boul Mich, everyone else was huddled together at the bar, talking with Red Maupin, the bartender. Their ashtrays were already full and the nut bowls nearly empty.

Mr. Ellsworth was telling everyone about when he first met Marty Sinclair. "There was nothing that guy wouldn't do to get a story. . . . He'd never let a little thing like ethics get in the way of him and a byline. . . ."

People listened, nodding as Mr. Ellsworth spoke. I could tell everyone was still bewildered over what had happened.

"Let's face it," said Henry, speaking to the group. "The guy was between a rock and a hard place. He tried to take on the Mob, for Christ's sake."

"Henrotin Hospital's probably the safest place for him right now," said Peter.

The others agreed.

Earlier that day, after Marty had been carted off and things had quieted down, I'd taken a few minutes to pull Marty's story from the morgue. Apparently his source was a gangster, an underling to Anthony "Big Tony" Pilaggi, a lieutenant in the Chicago Outfit. Six months ago Pilaggi had been on trial for murder and got off after his mistress testified that he was with her at the time of the murder. There was some bad blood between Marty's source and Big Tony, something to do with promises made and broken, so apparently he had gone to Marty and told him that Big Tony's mistress fabricated the alibi. He knew this for a fact, because Pilaggi's mistress had been with him the night of the murder. Marty reported the story, but had refused to reveal his source, so the information couldn't be used in a court of law. That's why he was under so much pressure now.

Walter banged his pipe against the ashtray on the bar, cutting into my thoughts. "If Marty gave up his source," he said, "they probably could have put Big Tony away for life."

"Yeah, and Marty would be six feet under right now," said Randy.

"Why Marty?" asked Benny.

"C'mon, think about it," said Peter, giving Benny a light clip on the ear. "Marty's source, whoever the hell the guy is—and let's not get started on that guessing game. Could be any one of a hundred lugs out there gunning for Big Tony. But one thing we know is that whoever it was would have been a marked man for ratting out Big Tony. The source wouldn't have been too happy with Marty about that, either. And then you got Big Tony, who would have put a hit on Marty for opening up the murder case again."

"I still thought he'd cave," said Walter.

"You're crazy," said Randy. "And if you ask me, Marty was crazy for dredging up Big Tony's murder case again in the first place."

"Yeah," said Henry. "But you know Marty. He's fearless when it comes to chasing down a scoop."

"The real shame is that he tried to do a good thing," said Benny. "Marty just wanted to get to the truth and expose the real story, and look where it got him."

There was a lull in the conversation, and I pondered what Benny said. On one hand, as a reporter you have a responsibility to reveal the truth. But on the other hand, in doing so, you could wind up in jail, or worse—dead. If I'd been in Marty's shoes, I didn't know what I would have done.

"How long do you think he'll be in the hospital?" asked M.

"Do you think they're going to give him electric shock treatment?" asked Gabby. "I had a cousin once who had a nervous breakdown and they gave her electric shock. She was never quite right after that. She couldn't remember to do things like turn off the stove or the faucet in the bathtub."

"I wonder if he'll come back to work," said Peter.

Walter was ready with another wager. He bet five bucks that Marty wouldn't. Henry said he would.

Mr. Ellsworth snapped and told them to knock it off. "Marty Sinclair's one of the best goddamned reporters I've ever worked with. Even with a bolt of electricity shooting through his skull, he could still write circles around any of you." He looked at Walter as he said this.

That resulted in another lull in the conversation, but thanks to Randy, I still had that Winston cigarette jingle playing inside my head. I couldn't shake it, the words and melody looping through my mind.

Gradually the guys started talking again, changing the subject, going on about other things, more comfortable topics. It was almost seven thirty, and by then Benny, M, Gabby and some of the others had already left. No one was talking to me, so I finished my drink, collected my newspapers and said my good-byes. The men didn't break from their conversation when I was leaving.

"See you all in the morning," I said anyway, speaking to the air.

It was only Peter who looked over and said, "*Ehhhx*-cellent."

I still lived at home with my parents in Old Town, and on a salary of sixty dollars a week it would be a while before I could afford a place of my own.

I took a shortcut and came up the back way, slipping through the fence. I walked up the pathway, aware of my mother's missing flower beds. Normally by now her tulips and crocuses would be in bloom. But it had been two years since she'd planted any flowers. She'd lost her passion for gardening and had let her flowers perish after her son died. Since then my father had built the fallout shelter where the flower beds once stood. I drew closer and saw the shelter handle poking up from the grass. It was attached to something that looked like a garbage can lid. I'd been down in the shelter only once, and that was to help my father load it up with canned goods and powdered milk. It was dank and musty, but it could sleep three adults and even had a toilet. If the Russians were coming, my father would be ready.

I went around the pathway to the front of the house. The porch lights were on, guiding my way up the stairs. I was warm, perspiring from the walk home, and I noticed that the ink from the newspapers tucked beneath my arm had bled onto my jacket. I was hoping I hadn't ruined it as I fished inside my handbag for the keys. Our house was an old Victorian Painted Lady, pale blue and gray with a dusty rose trim. It looked like a dollhouse, but there was a stark contrast between the outside and the inside.

It was dark when I entered the foyer except for the wedge of light coming from the living room, running a triangle across the hardwood floor. I smelled Lucky Strikes in the air and that faint stale scent that comes from a house filled with books. My parents were voracious readers and had long since run out of space on their shelves, so now the overflow was stacked on tables and on the floor in the hallway, teetering in piles that stood here and there, crooked spines three and four feet high.

In the distance I heard the *tap, tap, clack, clack* coming from my father's typewriter in his office at the back of the house, off the kitchen. As I expected, my mother was in her chair in the living room. She had a book in her hand; another one spread facedown, hanging over the lace-doilied arm of her recliner. Dust motes swam in the light above her shoulder.

"You're home," she said, using her index finger to mark her place in the book. "How was it?" She reached for her glass, leaving a circle on the table that was already so blemished with water rings she no longer bothered with a coaster. She raised her nose toward the ceiling. "Do you smell that?"

"CeeCee," my father called out from his office. "Something's burning."

She sprang out of her chair and sprinted through the swing door into the kitchen with me following closely behind. My mother wasn't much of a cook, especially when she got absorbed in a book, so it was no surprise that three of the four pots on the stove top were spitting and hissing, smoking away.

"Oh, would you look at this?" She shook her head, swatting at the smoke with a potholder.

"Did you hear me out there?" my father called again from behind his closed door. "Something's burning."

"I know, Hank. I know."

I went to the window and opened it all the way. My father's typewriter got going again.

My parents made for an interesting couple. The two of them were writers. Up until the time Eliot was killed, my father worked at the *Daily News*. Before that he'd been at the City News Bureau and then the *Tribune* for a brief stint. He knew Mr. Ellsworth and Mr. Copeland and some of the others, including Marty Sinclair. Even though my father had been a hard-core newsman, he made no secret about wanting to be a novelist.

After we lost Eliot, my father resigned from the paper to focus on his own writing. When the money got tight he wrote magazine pieces to keep the household afloat. Thankfully, my mother's family had money, and I was aware of the checks that arrived every now and then and how my mother would get on the telephone, the cord coiled about her wrist. "Yes, we got it. It arrived today. . . . Yes, thank you. . . . What? No, he's not here. You just missed him," she'd say, looking at my father, who'd be looking everywhere else. "Yes, I'll be sure and tell him you said so. . . ."

My father never did get along with my mother's parents. And the fact that he wasn't Jewish was the least of their problems with him. Hank Walsh was a rebel and an Irishman from Chicago to boot. Their CeeCee was a nice Jewish girl from the Upper West Side who was supposed to settle down in New York with a nice Jewish boy. They should have known better than to expect such obedience from their daughter.

While my mother tended to the stove, I made room at the

kitchen table, moving a stack of books to the far end, where she used to sit back in the days when she bothered setting the table for dinner. I got down three plates and three glasses and a handful of silverware. I told my mother about lunch with M and Gabby and how we were labeled sob sisters. I was saving up the Marty Sinclair story for my father. That would give us something to talk about.

"Sob sisters, sheesh." My mother shook her head. "Sounds like not much has changed since the days I was in the business."

"Do you ever miss it? Do you ever regret leaving the City News Bureau?"

"Oh, heavens no," she said, waving a dish towel above the stove, still trying to clear the rising smoke pooling up near the light fixture. "It was fun, exciting and all, but I never really wanted to be a reporter."

"But you were good," I said. I'd read her clips. They were impressive. "I think you would have been a really great journalist. You had an eye for detail. You knew how to turn a phrase."

"Well, honey, that's because I'm a poet."

Her voice was tinged with pride, and I was surprised by her choice of tense. She hadn't composed a poem since Eliot's death. Now she was prone to spending an entire day in her reclining chair, reading, while letting the housework go to hell and occasionally dinner, too.

My mother cautiously lifted the lid, peering inside the pot to see what had survived. I watched her, thinking how much better she was with a pen than with a spoon. Back in the days when she wrote, her poetry was brilliant and finely wrought. She taught in the writing department at Columbia College. A woman ahead of her time, she was known for her daring, risqué prose about sex, drugs and rebellion. Running around Greenwich Village as a teenager exposed her to a wild, untamed world, and her pen had captured and committed those experiences to paper. On a bookshelf in the other room were four volumes of poetry with her name embossed in gold on the spines. Three were published by Doubleday and the most recent one by Scribner. She was exacting about her words, and I'm not sure if my father was jealous or in awe. Maybe a little of both.

My mother liked to shock, and she reached and strained for every word. She was a perfectionist when it came to her work. I could remember finding her hunched over her writing desk, her head down, her face lined with angst because she couldn't articulate a nuance, couldn't pinpoint the essence. The very word she needed didn't exist, hadn't been conceived, and the inferior ones at her disposal would not cooperate.

"It's killing me," she had said one day.

"Why do you write if it's so painful?" I'd asked. I was young. I didn't get why she did it.

She had looked at me, her cheeks flushed. "Because I have to. I can't *not* write." She brushed a few stray hairs off her face with the back of her hand. "Even if no one ever published another word or paid me another dime for my poems, I'd still have to write them."

So why not now? But I knew why she'd stopped writing. Even if she didn't understand it herself, I knew. It was obvious to me that she was too afraid to write for fear that everything she'd been suppressing about Eliot's death would come rushing to the surface. And that terrified her. My brother's death had put my mother and her poetry on pause. She read everything she could get her hands on but hadn't written a word since Eliot died.

My father was the opposite. All he did was write. His writing and the need to write were ego-driven. He sought the kind of celebrated success his friend Hemingway had found. My father had written one novel, which had been published after he returned from covering World War II. It sold only about a hundred copies, and he'd been struggling ever since to write another one.

Hemingway had read my father's first book but hadn't liked it. I, however, thought it was exceptional. *Among the Trees* was an allegory about a boy raised in a forest by a family of trees. My father made the fatal mistake of showing Hemingway the first draft of his second book. Evidently Ernest had shredded it. Amazingly enough the two men remained friends after that. Even more surprising, my father, undeterred, started working on a third novel, although he hadn't let anyone else read it—not even my mother.

Their current struggles aside, my parents were very much regarded as an intellectual, literary couple. I remember Eliot and me sitting at the top of the stairs, eavesdropping during their many dinner parties. Everyone who was anyone had sat at our dining room table: Nelson Algren, Simone de Beauvoir, Saul Bellow, Ben Hecht and Studs Terkel. Then there were the poets like Carl Sandburg, Delmore Schwartz and Karl Shapiro. Given that crowd, was it any surprise that my parents' dinner parties often turned into drunken bashes that lasted till the wee hours? My brother and I would wake up the next morning to get ourselves ready for school, stepping over the empty whiskey bottles and an occasional guest on our way to the kitchen.

But that was years ago, and so much had changed since then. What happens to people after life takes its shots at them is heartbreaking.

The smoke cleared from the kitchen. My mother put a cigarette in her mouth and bent over to light it off the burner as my father came out of his office to fix himself a fresh drink. He was tall and lean with a jutting Adam's apple and a crew cut. People said he looked like that actor whose name I could never remember, who always played the daft friend of the leading man. My brother and I both took after my mother. She was a dark-haired, blue-eyed beauty, and everyone said she was far too pretty for my father. I do believe that Hemingway had a thing for her, though she hadn't returned his affections. She was more taken with Fitzgerald. Or with his talent, I should say. As far as I knew, she'd never met him, but oh how she loved his writing. For the longest time I thought I was named after Jordan Baker, who wasn't an admirable or likable character. But my mother assured me that I was named after her favorite uncle. When I complained that people thought I was a boy, my mother said she'd done that on purpose. She wanted me to have a powerful name, one that would open doors for me, not hold me back.

"CeeCee? What the hell was burning in here?" my father asked, lifting a lid, inspecting what was in the pot.

"What do you think was burning?" My mother drew a final puff from her cigarette before extinguishing it beneath the dripping faucet. "C'mon now, before it gets cold."

We took our seats as my mother placed the smoking pot roast on the table. It was charred and looked like someone had dropped a bomb on it. Any part that wasn't burned was full of gristle. She'd overcooked the green beans, too. Boiled the life out of them so that the color had faded to the shade of lima beans.

"What's that on your jacket?" my father asked, pointing at me with his fork.

"Oh—" I twisted about in my chair, looking at the ink on the fabric, feeling ridiculously pleased that he noticed something about me, even if it was a flaw. "That's just newsprint ink. Think it'll come out?" He tended to respond well to questions. But this time he only mumbled in response, so I tried a different approach. "Guess what happened today."

"What happened?"

"I watched Marty Sinclair have a nervous breakdown."

"Sinclair?" My father hiked up his eyebrows. "No fooling? Really? That's surprising."

"It was awful. You should have seen it."

"But he's such a gifted reporter," said my mother.

"What the hell happened to him?"

"They wanted him to—"

"Jesus Christ, CeeCee"—my father was staring at his pot roast—"is there a piece in there that doesn't look like the bottom of a shoe?"

"Here"—my mother took a slice off her plate—"try this one. It's not as well-done." My mother turned to me. "Go on, now. About Marty Sinclair."

"So anyway, the editors wanted him to reveal his source. But he refused because his source is in the Mob. They said he might get subpoenaed and then he—"

"Aw, Christ." My father pushed his plate away. "How do you expect me to eat this? I can't eat this."

"Fine. Then don't eat it. You know, you were right there in your office, Hank. You smelled it burning. Would it have killed you to get up, walk two feet and check the stove?"

My parents glowered at each other. There was a time when their behavior would have upset me, but sadly, I was used to this sort of thing now. They were sparring partners and seemed to take comfort in sniping at each other. It was familiar, and they never held on to the jabs. An insult here and there was a flesh wound compared to everything else they'd been through.

"Like I was saying," I continued in an effort to defuse their tussle, which was my job. The peacekeeper. I often worried about how they'd resolve their tiffs after I moved out. "So he had a nervous breakdown. Right in the city room. He started eating his notes. I mean he literally put wads of paper in his mouth and started chewing them."

"Probably tasted a hell of a lot better than this." My father dropped his fork and knife to the plate with a loud clank.

That's when my mother got up and pulled his plate away from him.

"Hey—what are you doing? CeeCee—"

"You don't want to eat it, then fine. Don't eat it." She stepped on the foot pedal of the wastebasket, and when the mouth flipped open, she dumped the whole thing. She came back to her seat, picked up her knife and fork and proceeded to saw through her pot roast.

"Did you ever give up a source, Dad?" I asked, hoping to distract him.

"Who, me? Never. You never want to burn a source," my father said, reaching for a dinner roll. "Your mother here—now, she'd burn just about everything else, but never a source," he teased. This was his way of saying he forgave her for throwing out his burned dinner. "What the hell else is there to eat around here?"

My mother just shrugged and continued chewing, letting him know that he was on his own. She was going to eat every bite of meat on her plate even if it killed her. I labored through mine as well. I didn't have much of an appetite but felt I owed it to my mother to suffer the roast along with her.

My father got up to fix himself another drink. "How's Ellsworth and Copeland?" he asked.

"I guess okay. I didn't really talk to them."

"Ellsworth was a hell of a reporter. Christ, I remember when we started out together at the City News Bureau. A couple of punks was what we were. I covered my first story with him." My father laughed.

"You did?"

"Sure, sure." He laughed some more, enjoying his reverie. The scotch must have kicked in.

"What was the story, Dad? What were you two covering?"

He took a sip and studied the melting ice in his glass. "Ah, that was a long time ago." He sat back down at the table. "Any of that tuna casserole left?"

"Help yourself." My mother's jaw was working back and forth on the meat.

My father wiped his mouth, tossed his napkin aside, and when my mother refused to look at him, he pushed back from the table. Without another word, he went into his study, shut the door and started clacking away on his typewriter.

My mother reached for her napkin and spit out whatever she was chewing on.

Chapter 3

◆ ◆ ◆

I couldn't sleep that night. My mind was still back in the city room, my head full of typewriters plinking, telephones and news chatter. After an hour of staring at the ceiling and watching the headlights that shone through the parting of the drapes each time a car passed by, I got up for a glass of water.

There was a light on downstairs in the living room, casting a shadow that crept up the stairs and reached the tips of my toes. From the landing I saw my father in a chair, his chin resting on his chest, eyes closed, an empty glass in his hand. The radio was on low, tuned to *Man on the Go*. I recognized the murmuring voice of Alex Dreier.

I was reminded of all the nights, especially those first few months after Eliot was killed, when I helped my father to bed, all his weight leaning on me as we tackled the stairs. The next morning, miraculously, he'd be dressed, shaved and showered, without the slightest hint of a hangover. There seemed to be no consequence to his drinking and, therefore, no reason not to get drunk again that night and every night thereafter.

I knew I should have left him in his chair, left his neck to kink up, his shoulders to stiffen, his lower back to lock up, but I couldn't have done that to him then any more than I could now. And silly me, somehow I thought he'd appreciate it.

I went over to his chair and jiggled his shoulder. "Dad? Dad—time to go to bed."

He shifted with a start. "Jesus Christ, you scared the hell out of me."

"I'm sorry. I didn't mean to—"

"What are you doing sneaking around the house at this hour anyway? Christ, if there's one thing I can't stand, it's someone sneaking up on you. . . ."

The booze made him angry, made him ready for a fight. "C'mon, Dad," I said, tugging at his arm. "Time to go to bed."

He pulled away from me. "Let me be, dammit." There was such finality to his voice. I knew better than to challenge him then. I'd give him another twenty minutes or so and try again.

In the meantime I went back upstairs, and as I passed by the bedroom that had once belonged to Eliot, I had a strong urge to go inside. I wanted to plunk myself down on the foot of his bed and talk to him like I used to do.

Eliot was five years older and many, many years wiser than me. Sure, the two of us had our times, like any siblings, when we'd fought over silly things like hogging the bathroom or the telephone line. But at the end of the day, we were friends, confidants. I wanted to share my first day of work with him.

I was still standing in the hallway, remembering Eliot's first day at the *Sun-Times*. It was 1948 and the *Chicago Sun* had recently acquired the *Chicago Daily Times*. When Eliot landed that job, you'd think he'd landed on the moon. My parents were *that* proud. I went with my mother to Dinkel's Bakery up on Lincoln Avenue that day and picked out an enormous devil's food cake for him. My father gave him a bottle of Cutty Sark with a red bow taped to the label, drooping like a wilted rose. We sat around the table that night listening to Eliot impersonating his city desk editor. My brother was a natural-born mimic, able to imitate just about anyone. I used to get so mad when he'd do me, slapping at his arms and begging him to stop exaggerating my laugh or the way I used to reach up and pat down my bangs. That night he was impersonating his boss, who apparently had a propensity for trying to stifle yawns and belches in mid-sentence. He had us laughing until tears oozed from our eyes. We always said if he hadn't been a journalist, my brother would have made a great stand-up comic.

After his first day my parents started keeping a scrapbook, cutting out and pasting every one of Eliot's stories that ran, no matter how small or insignificant. But Eliot's pieces didn't stay small for long. The *Sun-Times* recognized what they had in him and the promotions quickly followed. Eliot had started as a general assignment reporter, and by 1953 he was being groomed for the position of city desk editor.

At the time of his death Eliot was working on a big story, an exposé, and I always wondered if one had something to do with the other. He was hit near the subway station about nine o'clock on a Tuesday night—June 9, 1953. We got the call sometime after eleven. The police couldn't tell us much. There were no eyewitnesses, only a man saying he heard tires squealing moments before he turned around and saw my brother down on the sidewalk. Eliot died less than an hour later, while in surgery.

After the shock wore off, I found myself questioning the police investigation, which seemed cursory at best. Why weren't they looking for more witnesses? It was right by a subway stop—someone had to have seen something. Why hadn't the police combed the area again, looking for evidence, maybe a stray hubcap or a piece of the grille? As far as I could see, the police weren't doing anything to try to catch the guy.

I went from being numb to being outraged, thinking that my brother's killer was going to get away with it. I wanted answers and justice. I wanted the police to delve deeper. I mentioned this to my father, thinking that a seasoned newspaperman, not to mention the victim's father, would challenge the investigation. Instead he grew livid with me for even suggesting we raise concerns over how the police had handled it.

"Haven't we been through enough? Leave it be, dammit."

I could only suppose that the thought of investigating his son's death was too much for him to deal with at that point. And ever since then I hadn't been able to question the circumstances of Eliot's death without starting a battle, especially with my father. But I knew I wouldn't find any peace until the person who killed my brother was caught and prosecuted. I grew silent, as did my parents. We didn't talk about Eliot's death. We didn't talk about Eliot. Hell, my father and I hardly talked about anything at all.

God, how I missed my brother.

Everything was so different now with him gone. It was as if everything we knew and trusted had been stripped away and we were starting from scratch. I felt lost. We all did as we struggled to reinvent our family, still trying to figure out how we were supposed to do something as simple as set the damn kitchen table. And what about holidays and birthdays? Who was going to go in on gifts with me now and help me pick out the perfect cards? It was the little things that left the biggest holes in my heart.

And it wasn't that I'd lost just Eliot. I'd lost my parents, too. They were never the same afterward. Day by day I watched them withdrawing, and I felt abandoned, orphaned and lonely. Maybe

I was jealous that no one had rallied around me for my first day at the *Tribune*—no cake, no bottle of scotch. No nothing. I shouldn't have been surprised, though. My father told me a newspaper was no place for a woman to work. And that incensed me, which led to a host of other arguments. He did his best to discourage me from getting a job with the press, but at the end of the day, I was my father's daughter, just as stubborn as he was.

Now that I'd been hired as a journalist, I felt compelled to finish what Eliot no longer could. I wanted to become the reporter that he was meant to be. I also wanted to be both daughter and son for my parents, convinced that if I could fill the void my brother left behind, I could bring my parents back. Back to me. Truly, in the end, it was a selfish endeavor. But that's why I had my eye on the city desk.

I placed my hand on the glass doorknob and gave it a minute, drew a deep breath before stepping inside. Eliot had still been living at home when he died, saving his money for a trip to Europe that summer. Besides, he liked being here—it was a different home back then and my parents were the modern type. He could do anything in their house that he'd do on his own. He could smoke, drink, bring girls around—as long as they weren't prostitutes. That was where my mother drew the line.

His room was just as he'd left it when he'd left this world, preserved like a shrine. It had been two years, and still my parents—especially my father—couldn't bring themselves to clear out his things. The hint of a gray sweater still stuck out of the chest of drawers where he'd stuffed it inside. His shirts, trousers and suits hung like ghosts in the closet above the mass of shoes, a loafer with its heel smashed down in back, probably kicked off in a hurry. There were books and record albums that I would have loved to read and listen to that sat idle now, collecting dust. And then there was his typewriter, a brand-new IBM electric resting on the desk. It was green, the color of plastic toy soldiers, and I coveted it. I'd never seen anything like it, and when he turned it on it hummed as it *rat-a-tat-tat*ted while he typed. He'd promised to give it to me when he got a new model. I never had the courage to ask my parents for it, but I wanted it. Oh, how I wanted it.

Chapter 4

• • •

It was the end of June. Six weeks had passed since I'd started at the *Tribune*. I was eager and always among the first to arrive at the paper. I'd get to the city room before seven, just as the night men were finishing up their shift. Everything was different in those early hours—the air was clear of cigarette smoke, the typewriter racket was minimal and there were fewer telephone lines ringing, fewer voices to be heard. The sunlight seemed more translucent then than at any other time of the day.

I was told that Marty used to be one of the first ones in, too. Last I heard he was still in the hospital. No one knew when or if he was coming back to the paper. His wife had stopped by a few weeks earlier to get a sweater left behind, an extra pair of reading glasses and a book from his bottom drawer.

I was at my desk that morning in June, reading the day's headlines with a cigarette in one hand and a cup of coffee in the other. Benny came in and slapped his cap onto his desk and moaned as if in agony.

"Can you believe this?" he said, holding out the morning edition.

"Believe what?"

"Walter's piece on the mayor's latest appointee. Daley made an ex-con the head of one of his departments. And Walter says right here that the guy has no qualifications, no relevant training for this job whatsoever."

"That guy doesn't need to have qualifications," I said. "He's from Bridgeport. That's all the credentials he needs." I turned back to the front page and scanned Walter's article: "Daley Appoints Ex-Convict."

"But Jesus," said Benny, clearly outraged. "The guy's been in prison."

"Oh, but only for two years," I said mockingly as I continued to read. "And according to what Walter says here, the ex-con's father went to high school with Daley."

"That makes it even worse."

I let my paper dip so I could get a good look at Benny to make sure he wasn't joking. He wasn't. "Oh, Benny, Benny, Benny," I said, setting my newspaper aside. I knew he was young and that his cousin in sales had gotten him the job, but plenty of reporters got their start right out of high school. Not everyone went to journalism school like me. But still, the things Benny was questioning wouldn't have been taught in a classroom anyway. If the others suspected how green he really was, they'd never let him live it down. "Let me explain this to you. Don't you know that everyone on the city's payroll under Daley is there by design?"

"Well, yeah, sure," he said with a shrug, as if to suggest he knew more than he did. "But still—"

"*But* nothing. Almost everyone in City Hall is either Irish or from Bridgeport or both," I said. "They're all old pals from the neighborhood, and they've all got cushy patronage jobs now that their buddy is the mayor. They're all part of the machine."

"I know all that, but . . ." He didn't finish his thought because he couldn't. He didn't know what he was talking about.

"Think of it like this: there are thousands of people work-ing for the city of Chicago—from the street cleaners to the city councilmen—and that means there's plenty of jobs for Daley to give his friends. He's got his people sprinkled all throughout the system and some are in key places. Each one is a cog, or a lever, or a gear that's connected to Daley. All those gears and levers and cogs turn according to what Daley and the Democratic Party say. That's how Chicago works. That's the machine. It's how this city has always operated, going as far back as Mayor Cermak and Big Bill Thompson and even before that. And don't forget about the Mob. The mayor's office has been in bed with them since the days of Capone. You got it?"

"Yeah, yeah, I know all that stuff. Of course I know that stuff. I was just saying that, cripes, the guy's an ex-con. . . ." He muttered and went into the kitchen for coffee.

One by one the other reporters began trickling in for work. I watched M touch up her lipstick at her desk while Henry opened a fresh box of Sugar Smacks and Peter adjusted his eyeshade. Walter came in with Randy, who was already whistling. Slowly the din of phones ringing and typewriter keys striking copy paper picked up steam, while the cigarette and pipe smoke rose toward the ceiling. By a quarter past eight, the floor began to rumble from the presses. The start of a new day.

Not an hour later, Mr. Copeland came up to Walter and said, "I just hung up with the mayor's office. You gotta ease up on Daley."

"What do you mean, ease up? I've been easing up."

"Apparently not enough. He's upset about today's paper. He doesn't like what you said about him. Says you're intentionally trying to hurt his image."

"Well, too bad." Walter laughed.

This wasn't the first time Daley's office had telephoned to complain about the paper's coverage. After all, the *Tribune* was a

Republican paper. Still, Mr. Ellsworth and Mr. Copeland couldn't afford to antagonize the mayor and had to walk a fine line between letting their reporters do their jobs and pacifying Daley's ego.

Later that afternoon Mrs. Angelo called me over to her desk. "I've got a wedding for you to cover this Sunday."

"Another wedding?" I blew out such a deep breath it fluttered my bangs. "Maybe I could work on something a little more challenging."

"Oh, yeah? What'd you have in mind, kid?" She'd taken to calling me kid, and I didn't know if she meant it as a term of endearment or a put-down. Try as I might, I couldn't get a bead on her. She gazed at me and tapped her pencil on her desk. "Have a seat."

I knew I wasn't going to want to hear this, and reluctantly took the chair opposite her desk, staring into the Baccarat crystal paperweight on top.

"Let me tell you something, kid: if you want to work in this business, you have to be patient. I started here in 1923. My father got sick and I had to go to work to help support my family. My uncle knew someone at the *Tribune* and he put in a good word for me. I was seventeen—the first time they ever hired a copygirl. They paid me five dollars a week. I went and got coffee for the fellows, ran out and got their lunches, their cigarettes and even did their Christmas shopping. But I also did their fact-checking, routed their copy books and most important," she said, accenting the point with her pencil, "I got to watch them in action. I learned the newspaper business by watching those men. I didn't get to write a word for the first three years I was here. Worked my rear end off and fought like hell to get promoted to the morgue. Spent five years there before they made me a listing girl. I listed every radio program for the paper. I did a good job, so they kept me there for another five years. Eventually they moved me to the Sunday Room to help put together the Sunday edition, and then finally, *finally*, they gave me some assignments for society news and eventually made me the editor.

"I've known most of the guys in here from the time they were pups," she said. "Marty was just sixteen when he came to work here as a copyboy. Walter wasn't much older. Same is true for Randy. I remember Henry had a full head of hair when he started in the mail room. So do you see what I'm saying? It doesn't happen overnight, kid."

"But . . ." I wanted to say, *But look where they are now and look at what you're stuck doing.*

"Nobody said this was going to be fair, kid." It was as if she'd read my mind. "And I'm telling you for your own good, for your own peace of mind—don't expect too much too soon. Or at all."

I was still staring into the spiral swirls of her paperweight. It was all circles within circles within smaller circles until there was nothing but a solid dot in the center. I hadn't been able to take my eyes off the paperweight, for fear I might start to cry.

And I almost did. But then something shifted inside me. I got mad. And then I got smart. I realized I'd been looking at this all wrong. After all, the most influential people in the city were attending the weddings and balls I was covering. They were the force and power of the city—the newsmakers. They were the very people I needed to know if I was going to make it as a reporter.

So one week later I attended another wedding, wearing a strand of pearls I'd borrowed from my mother along with her favorite Milore leather gloves. Usually I sat in the shadows, taking copious notes on flower arrangements, dresses and menu items, but at this wedding I had another agenda. The groom was a second cousin of

Mayor Daley and the bride was the daughter of the 1st Ward alderman, John D'Arco, one of the most powerful men in Cook County.

I arrived at the reception and entered the banquet hall in Bridgeport. It was filled with long aluminum tables covered with paper tablecloths and plastic flower centerpieces. A nearby bulletin board boasted flyers for yard sales, local plays and picnics. There was a small dance floor in the center and a three-foot-high platform stage where a band in white ruffled shirts and green bow ties performed.

Given that half the Daley administration was there, I'd been expecting something more elaborate and classy, but I had to remind myself that there was nothing fancy or sophisticated about Mayor Daley or his circle.

I spotted Paddy Bauler, the 43rd Ward alderman, over by the band, doing a little soft shoe, letting his three-hundred-pound body jiggle like gelatin.

When he was done I applauded with everyone else and made my way over to introduce myself. "Perhaps we could talk sometime about your thoughts on reform."

He rested his hands on his belly and laughed. "Haven't you heard, little lady? 'Chicago ain't ready for no reform yet.'"

"*Everybody's* heard you say that," I said, letting him know that I was well aware of his famous saying. "That's why I was hoping—"

A group of loud men interrupted me mid-sentence and whisked Alderman Bauler off to the bar. He never looked back. It was as if I'd never said a word to him.

I scanned the room, looking for other familiar faces. The guest list was teeming with local politicians, who, for the most part, looked like they could have been street vendors who'd put on a suit for the day—including Earl Bush, Daley's press secretary.

I waited while he posed for a photo. Round-faced and balding, he seemed open and approachable, so I introduced myself. As soon as I mentioned that I was with the *Chicago Tribune* he frowned and said under his breath, "Not here. Not now." He excused himself and I stood watching him sift through the guests until my eyes landed on the mayor himself.

It was the first time I'd ever seen Daley in person. He had thick jowls and a double chin that rested on his collar as if he had no neck at all. He was shorter in person, too, or maybe he seemed so because the man standing next to him was so tall—six three or four. I watched the mayor, knowing that he hated reporters even more than his press secretary did. While I observed Daley, I felt the tall man's eyes still on me. My fingers protectively fluttered toward my open collar, and I held his gaze until he turned his attention back to the mayor.

Moments later I found myself standing next to Danny Finn, the assistant chief of police. He was in his early thirties, tall with a strong, sturdy build. He wasn't my type, but I was certain that plenty of women were taken with his rugged, dark looks. I reached inside my purse for a cigarette, a prop I used as an excuse to ask him for a light. I thanked him as I leaned in to his flame, aware of him eyeing me up and down. I extended my hand and introduced myself.

"Tell me something," he said, rubbing my gloved fingers. "Is there a ring underneath there?"

I ignored his question. "I'm with the *Chicago Tribune*," I said.

"Well, you sure are a hell of a lot prettier than Peter," he said with a laugh.

"Maybe we could talk sometime?"

"Sure. We could talk any old time you'd like."

"Maybe we could talk about the Peterson-Schuessler murders?"

His smile morphed into a smirk. "We've told the press everything we know."

"Oh, c'mon now." I didn't believe him. The Peterson-Schuessler murders had been front-page news all week. Three young boys had been found dead and the city was on edge, holding its breath while the police conducted their investigation. If I could get even one new detail out of Finn, I'd have something to run with. "There must be something you can tell me. Some new piece of information that just came in."

"Honest, we've already told the press everything we know."

"Listen," I said, "how about if I come see you down at police headquarters?"

"Come down and see me anytime," he said, his smile coming back. "But don't shoot me down for a drink if I don't have any information for you."

"Then I'll be seeing you down at headquarters." I shook his hand again before I went to my table to sit with the other female journalists—my fellow sob sisters from competing papers like the *Daily News*, the *Sun-Times* and the *Chicago American*.

We'd all met before at various weddings and charity balls and had become friendly enough to share notes and make sure we all got the dinner courses right, the correct spelling of who was officiating the ceremony and the details on the wedding dress. I doubted that sort of camaraderie would have existed among our male counterparts. Because of the public figures at the wedding, there was a good deal more fact-checking needed than usual. One of the girls, Muriel from the *Chicago American*, knew I was up on politics, and during the reception I found myself fielding her endless string of questions.

"So who's that man over at the bar with the groom?" she asked.

"Fred Roti," I said. "He's also from the 1st Ward. Big pals with D'Arco. Rumor has it he's part of the Chicago Outfit. They both are. And the one next to him with the mustache"—I pointed discreetly with my pen—"he's the 1st Ward precinct captain. And see that man over there with the red carnation in his lapel?

See him? He was the former alderman of the 42nd Ward. He was defeated in a big Republican upset."

"How do you keep all of this straight?" she asked.

For me it was easy. I grew up in a family that followed politics. My father had been covering the machine dating back to the days of Cermak and Kelly. He'd reported on Mayor Kennelly, too. We'd sit around the table, listening to my father read his articles aloud.

I looked over at Muriel. Her head was bent, her chin tilted down as she wrote the names and wards in the margins of her notebook. I was surprised that a reporter from the *Chicago American* wasn't better versed on her politicians.

"What about that other man?" Muriel asked. "See the tall one who keeps looking over here? He's been watching you all afternoon," she said. "Do you know him?"

"No, actually, I don't." I didn't know who he was or how he was connected to Daley. Or what it was about me that he found so interesting.

The reception wore on, and the bride and groom made their way from table to table, collecting thick white envelopes in exchange for hugs and handshakes. The cake had been served and the bouquet had been tossed. I had what I needed but not what I wanted. I spotted the tall man again over by the bar, and I excused myself from our table and headed toward him.

"Do we know each other?" I asked.

"I don't believe we do. I'm Richard Ahern."

"Jordan Walsh."

"So, Jordan, are you here for the bride or the groom?"

"Neither. And I'll bet you already knew that, since you've been watching me all afternoon."

"Aw, you caught me."

Something about this man made the hairs on the back of my neck prickle, and I went out of my way not to reveal how uneasy he made me. "Actually," I said, placing a hand on my hip, "I'm here for the *Tribune*. And you?"

"The city. Actually." He offered a cryptic grin. "I work down at City Hall."

"I see. And what exactly do you do down at City Hall?"

"My but you're curious. Aren't you supposed to be asking me about the hors d'oeuvres and what I think of the bride's dress?" He laughed and gazed around the room before his eyes locked onto mine.

"I'm a reporter. It's my job to be curious."

He took a pull from his drink and set the empty glass down on the bar. "Well, it's been nice meeting you. I'll be looking for your byline, Jordan Walsh."

Chapter 5

• • •

The next day, after I finished the wedding write-up, I began working on a piece inspired by Muriel at the reception: a sort of women's primer for Chicago politics.

"What's that?" Mrs. Angelo asked, coming up behind me, looking over my shoulder. "Precinct captains? Patronage jobs?"

"It's a piece on Chicago politics."

Mrs. Angelo pursed her lips. "I can tell you right now they're not going to run a piece about that."

"But they should."

"Damn straight they should, but that doesn't mean they will."

"I think women want to know how our local government works. I just covered the D'Arco wedding with a woman—a woman *reporter*, no less—who didn't know how Chicago fits into Cook County or that this city has fifty wards or that the power in this town all comes down to who can produce the most Democratic votes for their precincts and wards on Election Day."

"Do me a favor—work on the stories I assign you. Nobody has time for this sort of thing, and they won't run it anyway." She pulled the copy sheet from my typewriter and fisted it up. "Get back to work, kid. Gabby's going to need a hand with her piece on the Jimmy Durante sighting at the Hi Hat Club."

I did as I was told, but it wasn't long before I was glancing at the row of clocks mounted on the wall with *Injun Summer*: *Los Angeles. New York. London. Chicago.* It was only half past noon Central Standard Time and the hands on the clocks seemed to be moving in slow motion, making my eyelids heavy. I was about to get a cup of coffee when my desk phone rang.

"Jordan? Is this Jordan Walsh?"

I didn't recognize the voice. I had the phone cradled between my ear and shoulder. "Who is this?" I was absentmindedly playing with a paper clip, bending it back and forth.

He paused for a moment. "I'd rather not say."

I sat up a bit straighter. Reporters like Marty, Walter and Henry were always getting cold calls from people claiming they had a tip or some burning scoop. But me? No one even knew I was on the paper unless they were reading about debutante balls and wedding receptions.

"Okay, well, what can I do for you?"

"I think I have some information you could use. Meet me in an hour—"

"Wait a minute—wait a minute." I shifted the phone from one ear to the other. "You have to give me more than that."

"Let's just say I have some information that any young, hungry reporter would be interested in."

I dropped the paper clip. "Where are you?"

"I'll be outside the main entrance at Wrigley Field. Meet me there in half an hour."

"How will I know who I'm looking for?"

"Don't worry. I'll find you." Before he hung up he said, "Trust me. I'll make this worth your while."

I was mildly rattled when I placed the receiver down. I knew most of these calls went nowhere, but every now and then a few turned out to be legit. I had nothing to lose in meeting this guy, and I understood that he was trying to be discreet. But still, I didn't appreciate him being so cryptic.

I grabbed my things and headed to the el. It was unseasonably warm and felt more like August than the middle of June. I hopped on a packed train, holding on to the ceiling strap as the car shimmied over the tracks, nothing but hot air blowing through the windows. The train hadn't thinned out much by the time we got to Addison.

There was a game that day: the Cubs were playing the Brooklyn Dodgers. The sidewalks up and down Clark Street were congested with fans, and I was pacing back and forth outside the main entrance among the vendors selling T-shirts, baseball caps, pennants and stuffed animals. A big roar came from inside the stadium. The Cubs must have done something right.

As I checked my watch, I heard the voice, recognizing it from the telephone call earlier. "Jordan Walsh?"

I turned around and fought to keep myself in check as a rush of adrenaline flooded me. It was Richard Ahern, the tall man from the D'Arco wedding. I knew nothing about him aside from his working at City Hall, but that was enough for me.

"Nice to see you again," I said.

He didn't extend his hand, and when he explained that he was one of Mayor Daley's special aides, I did my best to conceal my excitement.

He gestured with a nod toward a vendor selling snow cones. "Cherry or grape?" he asked.

"I'm not hungry, but thanks." I followed him over to the vendor. "So what was it you wanted to see me about?"

He ignored my question and turned to the man behind the cart. "Give me two cherries." I felt like I was being handled and I didn't like it, but I was at his mercy. He had me on the hook, and we both knew it. He gave the vendor a dime and handed me one of the snow cones. I followed him down the street, away from the stadium, the giant red Wrigley Field sign looming behind us. We were surrounded by horns honking, people shouting, the rumble of the el in the distance. The snow cone was melting, so I took a bite and licked at the syrup running over my knuckles. The light changed to red, and we paused and looked at each other. He had me pinned down with his eyes, and it unnerved me.

"So," I said, breaking the silence, trying to sound casual, "what exactly is this all about?"

"You're dripping." He pulled a handkerchief from his breast pocket and handed it to me. "Let's just say I think you and I are in a position to be of great service to each other."

"Okay, well, you've certainly got my attention." I dabbed away the syrup and returned his handkerchief.

"I *have* information. You *need* information."

"Information about what?"

"Information that belongs on page one." He took a bite of his snow cone and tossed the rest in the trash can on the corner.

My senses kicked into high alert. I squinted at him, trying not to appear too eager. "And why would you want to share that sort of information with me?" Any reporter, except for the rare Marty Sinclairs of the industry, always had to ask, *Why me?* Out of all the reporters in this city, why would a source come to them with their scoop? This was especially true in my case. I wrote for the women's pages, and if Ahern's information was as good as he said, he could certainly have found a reporter to get him better coverage than I could.

When he didn't acknowledge my question, I pitched my snow cone and locked eyes with him. "So, what are you looking for in exchange? Because I'll tell you right now, I won't sleep with you for information."

He smiled as if this were thoroughly amusing. "I wouldn't expect you to."

I lowered my chin, looking down at my shoes, hoping he wouldn't notice my face was burning red. "So what is it that you want, then?"

"A mouthpiece. And, of course, total and complete anonymity as your source. I'll need that from you before we go any further. And speaking of which, I'm sure you're wise enough not to mention this little meeting to anyone."

I straightened the strap on my handbag and pressed my lips together, trying to regain some ground here. Even though I was dying to know the information he was sitting on, I cautioned myself to be smart, methodical. Professional. Maybe I was thinking about Marty Sinclair and his source, but something about this didn't feel right. There was something off about Ahern, something sinister. I had to know a whole lot more about him in order to figure out if I could trust him.

"I don't know," I said. "Let me think it over."

"Sure." He served up another cocky smirk. "You think it over while you're writing about bridal bouquets and taffeta gowns."

"Don't underestimate me, Mr. Ahern."

For the first time he laughed—really laughed—and it sounded genuine. "I know better than to do that." He started to walk away, and then turned around. "You let me know whenever you're ready to talk. You can reach me down at City Hall."

Later that day I sat at my desk revising a fashion piece on "Tricks to Keep Your Slip from Showing." I was thinking about my meeting with Ahern when M stretched her very shapely leg out from under her desk.

"Oh, darn it." She pointed her toe while hiking up her skirt, turning her ankle this way and that. "I got a run in my stockings."

"Don't you just hate when that happens?" said Henry with a chuckle as he batted his lashes.

"Hey, sweetheart," said Walter. "Bring that gorgeous gam over here. I'll fix you right up."

M giggled along with the rest of them.

I liked M, but at times like this I wanted to go over and shake her. Did I have to remind her she had a brain? I feared it was women like her who convinced men like Walter and Henry that we were all half-wits, and that kept the rest of us stuck. But nothing sank my heart more than seeing that morning's edition of White Collar Girl with my byline beneath an article entitled: "What a Tidy Desk Says About Your Work Ethic." I didn't know how much longer I could go on writing those kinds of pieces. They weren't getting me any closer to my goal of the city desk.

Maybe Ahern was the answer. I knew that my own attempts to get myself off the women's pages had gotten me nowhere. I'd toned down my style of dress, hoping to be taken more seriously, opting for plain skirts and simple blouses with Peter Pan collars. I left my earrings and bracelets in my jewelry box and limited my makeup to a touch of lipstick and rouge. None of that seemed to help the situation. I still got patted on the rear end, still was referred to as *little missy*, *sweetheart* or *honeybuns*.

I had recently pitched an important story to Mr. Ellsworth about the infant mortality rate inside Chicago's orphanages. I had spent my nights and weekends working on it, had met with a doctor from the city's Board of Health and had ventured into shady pockets of town to interview former orphanage employees. I wrote and rewrote and polished the entire article, and when it was ready, I showed it to Mr. Ellsworth. He had a way of stroking his beard while reading your work that said he was unimpressed and that you were wasting his time. I remember he was stroking his beard that day just before he set my piece aside.

"But you didn't finish reading it," I said.

"I didn't need to finish it."

"But it's a good story."

"It's a story that I have no interest in running."

"All I'm asking for is a chance. Can't you give me a break? I just want to be helpful."

Mr. Ellsworth gazed at me and rubbed his chin. "You really want to be helpful?"

"Yes."

He reached for the mug on the corner of his desk. "Then go get me a cup of coffee. Black."

After that I vowed not to pitch another article to Mr. Ellsworth, Mr. Copeland or even Mr. Pearson until I had something so big, so enticing that they would have to run it.

All this was going through my mind as I went to the morgue and began digging for information on Richard Ahern.

I could still hear the commotion from the city room, seeping in through the doorway as I glanced around. Naked bulbs swung overhead in a room lined with filing cabinets that stood five feet tall. There were heavy wooden drawers along with rows and rows of flat files that squeaked each time I pulled one out. When I stopped to think about what the morgue housed, the history of the paper and of the city, it was mind-boggling. If there was something written about anyone or anything, it was lurking in that room. And that's when I decided to take a moment and locate the archives from June 1953.

My fingers worked through the files, running over tattered labels and rumpled folders while I searched for anything reported on my brother's death. I harbored a foolish hope that the answers

I sought—some tidbit of information that would lead to my brother's killer—were tucked inside these archives.

I pulled a folder dated June 10, 1953:

REPORTER KILLED IN HIT-AND-RUN

Sun-Times reporter Eliot Walsh was killed in a hit-and-run late last night on the corner of State Street and Grand Avenue. Walsh, twenty-five, was struck at approximately nine p.m., presumably on his way to the subway. Authorities say there were no eyewitnesses. However, a passerby, Adam Javers, heard the squeal of tires and then saw the body on the sidewalk and called for an ambulance. Walsh was rushed to Henrotin Hospital, where he later died at eleven fifty-three p.m., during surgery. . . .

I finished that article and checked through the rest of the folder, going through his obituaries and other reports about the accident in the *Chicago American,* the *Daily News* and the *Sun-Times.* I'd already read all those articles when they first appeared back in '53. By the time I'd looked at the last one, I was drained and agitated. There was nothing new to be found. I slapped the files shut and slammed the drawer closed. Even after two years my anger was still raw.

I took a step back and leaned against another file cabinet, clenching and unclenching my fists until the frustration left me. Or maybe it just subsided, because really, it never fully disappeared. Afterward I cleared my throat and got busy looking for what I'd come for in the first place.

I spent the next couple hours in the morgue concentrating on Ahern, and when I surfaced, I had clips that had been cross-referenced five or six times. I returned to my desk and abandoned a set of revisions for my "Slip Trick" article and began reading through the files.

Turned out Ahern had graduated law school from the University of Chicago in 1947. He'd worked for the former mayor, Kennelly, and after three years had accepted a job as one of Daley's special aides. He had a young wife named Suzanne. There was no mention of children. Thirty minutes later, after shuffling through the clips, I had turned up nothing that would suggest Ahern's motive for leaking information to the press.

As I was about to close the file, something did jump out at me. Just a minor mention, not more than three column inches long. It stated that Ahern had wanted to run for the state senate but that Daley had backed another candidate, Paul Douglas. That right there could have been enough, but it seemed thin. I got the feeling there was something else about Ahern that I wasn't finding here. And I was still questioning why he had come to me of all people.

A million ethical questions raced through my head, everything I'd learned at Medill about fairness, anonymity, confirming a source's motivation. I closed the folder and leaned back in my chair, making the joints squeak. I knew I was right to question Ahern's motives, but I also had to recognize an opportunity when it was standing right in front of me.

I packed up all the clips and carried them home with me, along with the day's papers tucked under my arm. Yes, I was desperate to get off society news, but was this the way to do it? I felt like Faust about to make a pact with the devil.

Chapter 6

◆ ◆ ◆

After a night of fitful sleep, I awoke just as conflicted as I'd been the day before. I stumbled to the bathroom, squinting to avoid the burst of light from the overhead fixture. My vision took a moment to adjust, and once I could see, I looked in the mirror and brought my hands to my face, my fingers pulling on the skin beneath my eye sockets. I looked like a basset hound. What happened to jumping out of bed before the alarm went off? Was I already beaten down? All I knew was that I was dreading the day ahead, filled with recipes for the Mary Meade column and a write-up about a Tony Curtis sighting for They Were There.

I splashed water on my face, and as I reached for the towel, I caught ahold of myself. What was the matter with me? Those pieces were supposed to be a stepping-stone, not the be-all and end-all. I was Hank and CeeCee Walsh's daughter. Eliot Walsh's sister. I'd made a promise to my brother and to myself. What was I waiting for?

At that moment I knew what I had to do.

I hurried back to my room. Sitting on the side of the bed, I rolled on my stockings and fastened them to my garters before slipping into the same dress I'd worn two days before. I hardly even bothered to do my hair, not that it mattered much since my cut was already growing out, losing its shape. With a slice of toast in hand, I said a quick good-bye to my parents and headed down to the paper.

As soon as I got into the city room, I telephoned Ahern. The back of my neck grew clammy as I dialed and held my breath waiting for him to come on the line.

"Let's talk," I said. "I'm ready."

We met two hours later at an out-of-the-way diner west of the Loop. He was waiting for me at a booth way in the back. The place was quiet. We were there between the breakfast and lunch crowds.

"Tell me one thing," I said right off the bat. "How did you feel about Daley backing Paul Douglas for state senate instead of you?"

He smiled and began absentmindedly stacking sugar cubes on the table, one on top of the other. It was as if he were building an igloo, or maybe a skyscraper. "I see you did your homework. Not many people remember that I wanted to run for office."

"Well?" I waited while he carefully set another sugar cube in place.

"Let's just say I wasn't happy about it. But I'm a loyal servant of the city. I only want what's best for Chicago."

I tried not to roll my eyes.

"Anything else you need to know?"

"I'm still wondering why you came to me. I know you have your reasons. I just don't know what they are."

"Maybe I didn't want someone as jaded as a Walter Harris or a Marty Sinclair."

"Maybe so." I didn't believe a word of that and pursed my lips to keep from saying more. No point in pressing for an answer he clearly wasn't ready to give. "All right then, let's cut to the chase—what have you got for me?"

He rubbed the excess sugar granules off his fingertips and pulled a document from his breast pocket, creased in a trifold. "Why don't you take a look at this and tell me what you see?"

I unfolded the document and began to read. "City council meeting agenda?" I glanced up at him. "This is public record. There's no scoop here."

"Keep going."

My eyes scanned down the list of proposed ordinances and new appointments all put forth by Alderman Frank O'Connor, the city council chairman. Nothing stood out to me. I looked up again and shrugged.

"Stop when you get to the fourth item under Miscellaneous Number 25."

I read silently to myself: *Miscellaneous Item Number 25 (4). Orders authorizing the payment of hospitalization and medical expenses of police officers injured in the line of duty.* "So? They risk their lives every day. The city should pay for their medical needs."

"I wholeheartedly agree."

I looked at him. I didn't get it. "Am I missing something here?"

"Yes, as a matter of fact, you are." He reached into his other pocket and produced an envelope. "Here's a report with a list of the officers' names, their injuries, their doctors and the amount of their claims."

I opened the report and glanced at the list of about seventy-five names, neatly typed in uniform columns.

"Now, I don't know about you," said Ahern, "but I think there's something mighty suspicious about all this."

I looked at the list again. The first thing that struck me was that several of the officers were from one district. "Looks like a lot of the injuries happened in the 35th District."

"You're getting warmer."

The second thing I noticed were the staggering dollar amounts—
$825, $900, $1,150, $2,165—all being paid to one doctor: Dr. Stu-
art Zucker. My pulse began racing because I knew. I knew I
was onto something. They don't teach you this in journalism
school. It can't be taught, but there's a feeling you get in your
gut—pure instinct. "This is major insurance fraud we're talking
about, isn't it?"

"You didn't hear me say that, did you?" Ahern gave me a thin,
rigid smile. "Oh, and Miss Walsh, I'm not trying to tell you how
to do your job, but you may want to take down some of that
information, because I'm not about to leave that list with you."

Heat crawled up my neck and cheeks as I reached inside my
bag and pulled out a pad of paper and a pen, scratching down
names and dollar amounts as quickly as I could.

"I'm sure you know what to do from here," he said.

I continued to write, and when I set my pen down, he plucked
the list from my hand and folded it up, tucking it back in his
pocket as if it had never existed.

"Trust me, Walsh. This is a house divided." He picked up his
knife and sliced it through the igloo, sending the sugar cubes
crashing down.

I reached for a cigarette, struck a match and watched it burn
between my fingers.

"You think you can do something with this, Walsh?"

I gave him a nod and lit my cigarette, the flame still flickering
in my grip.

The first thing I did after I left Ahern was talk to Mr. Ellsworth. I found him at the horseshoe, slashing someone's
copy with his red pen. "Yes?" he said, striking out an entire paragraph. He didn't bother to look up.

"I just spoke to someone about a possible insurance-fraud case," I said. "It involves the Chicago City Council and the police department."

"Where are you getting this from?"

"I have a contact. A source inside City Hall."

He looked at me as if this were all so amusing. "Okay, fine. Let Peter, or better yet, let Walter know—give him the information on your source. We'll have him follow up on it."

There was no way I was just going to hand over this lead to Walter. Or Peter. So I kept my mouth shut, and the next morning I paid a visit to the District 35 Police Station on Superior Street. I wanted to see if Commander Graves could explain why so many of his officers had been injured. It was midmorning and the station was quiet. I was one of three people there; the other two were seated on folding chairs before a table covered with newspapers and magazines. I smelled burnt coffee coming from a little pot on a hot plate off to the side.

While I waited to speak with Commander Graves, I smoked a cigarette and studied the beat map pinned to the bulletin board. District 35 was sandwiched in between Lake Michigan and the Chicago River and encompassed the Gold Coast and a section of downtown called Streeterville—not exactly the roughest neighborhoods in the city. They had a sign that read 35TH DISTRICT MOST WANTED on their bulletin board. There were two photographs: one of an elderly man wanted for indecent exposure and one of a teenage boy wanted for a purse snatching outside Bonwit Teller on Michigan Avenue.

It was nearly an hour before Commander Graves emerged from the long hallway and was willing to talk to me. His office was at the end, cramped and windowless. He kept his cap parked on the edge of his desk next to an ashtray that needed emptying. A portrait of Mayor Daley was mounted on the wall behind him.

"So I understand you're with the *Chicago Tribune*. What happened to Peter? He's the one who always calls on me."

His reaction didn't surprise me. Peter was a crime reporter. I
was a nobody. And a woman. "Peter isn't working on this story. I
am," I said with as much authority as I could muster. "I wanted
to ask you a few questions about the number of officers in your
district that have been injured on the job."

"What is it you'd like to know?" He leaned forward on his
desk and laced his meaty fingers together.

"There appears to be a disproportionate number of injuries
from District 35 as opposed to the other districts—even districts
with a higher crime rate—and I—"

"I don't know what you mean by *disproportionate*." He cut me
off. "My officers put their lives on the line every day. There's
bound to be injuries."

"Yes, I agree. But I'm wondering if you could verify that the
following officers have been injured?" He didn't object, so I showed
him the names that I had jotted down during my meeting with
Ahern.

He looked at the list, twisted up his mouth and slid the paper
back across the desk toward me. "Yes, I recall they were all
injured." His face relaxed, went expressionless. He cleared his
throat and pushed himself back in his chair. "Now, if you'll
excuse me, I need to get back to work."

I walked away that morning with nothing and returned to the
paper with more questions than answers. While Mrs. Angelo and
Mr. Pearson were in a meeting, I went to the morgue and pulled
anything I could find on robberies, shoot-outs, anything in the
District 35 neighborhoods that mentioned those police officers.
And when I was done with that, I called Dr. Zucker's office.

"I'm afraid Dr. Zucker's in with a patient at the moment."
When I said I was with the *Tribune*, his nurse sighed into the

telephone and covered the receiver, muttering to someone in the background. "I'll have him call you back when he's free."

I gave her my number, and rather than waiting on a call that I knew probably wouldn't be returned, I focused on the files I'd pulled from the morgue. They were filled with articles about vehicle thefts, aggravated assaults, armed robberies and larceny, but there were no reported injuries involving any of the officers on Ahern's list. There was, however, one document that was particularly helpful: the Chicago Municipal Code

According to sections 3-8-190 and 3-8-200 of the document, the city council finance committee, chaired by Sean McCarty, was in charge of appropriating moneys for treatment, rehabilitation, even the hospitalization of officers injured while on duty. Furthermore, it was up to Sean McCarty to provide a report on the costs of this care and the specifics of each officer's condition. I realized that was the document that Ahern had shown me. The municipal code also stated that before any moneys could be released, the Chicago Police Department's chief physician, Dr. Edgar MacAleese, had to verify McCarty's reports and confirm that the medical treatments and costs were appropriate given their doctors' diagnoses.

It was complicated. There were a lot of parties involved, but at least I now understood who the main players were and how the city handled reimbursements for medical treatment when they were footing the bill.

I was blurry-eyed from reading through everything. I needed a break, but I also had to finish up a piece I was doing for White Collar Girl on Gloria Harper, the secretary to the president of Morton Salt. I had eight column inches devoted to Miss Harper answering Sterling Morton Jr.'s phone, making his lunch and dinner reservations, reminding him of important anniversaries and birthdays. I'd met her only once, during our interview, but I felt sorry for her.

Mrs. Angelo was still in her meeting when I finished my story, so I went back to the police reports and the city council municipal code. I stared at the pages, hoping something new would leap out at me. It didn't.

That night I hardly slept. It was like I had a bee buzzing inside my brain. It circled over and over again, coming back to the same spot. Something wasn't right. Ahern knew it and he was making a believer out of me, too. But first I had to figure out what it was and then I'd have to prove it.

Chapter 7

◆ ◆ ◆

The next morning I telephoned Zucker's office again, and when the doctor still wouldn't take my call, I went down to his office in the Pittsfield Building at 55 E. Washington Street.

The thirty-eight-story building was ornate, a combination of gothic and art deco with a gold-coffered ceiling and giant spangling chandeliers. It looked more like a dance hall than an office building. I was in a daze as I checked the building directory, anticipating what I was going to say to Dr. Zucker. I knew better now than to tell him I was from the *Tribune*. That approach had gotten me nowhere. I was running all this through my head when one of the cleaning women in a blue uniform started mopping the floor near me, swishing the thick gray strings over the marble. "You mind stepping aside?" She shook her head as I moved toward the elevators, clearly annoyed with me as she went back to her mopping.

I rode up to the seventeenth floor and entered a modest-looking office with a few plants here and there and various diplomas on the wall. A plastic runner stretched from the doorway to the waiting room comprised of three upholstered chairs. Dr. Zucker's receptionist was an older woman, in her mid-forties, early fifties. She had brown teased-up hair and a big, toothy smile. The nameplate on her desk read MRS. CARSON. She was the woman I'd talked to over the phone the day before. She greeted me, and I felt a twinge of unease when I introduced myself as Gloria—the first name that popped into my head. I was no saint. I'd told my share of little white lies and not so little lies, but this was the first time I could recall ever looking into someone's eyes and blatantly deceiving them.

"And how can I help you, Gloria?" Her smile seemed so genuine. It made this moment all the more difficult for me.

"I have an appointment with the doctor," I said.

"Well, let's see now . . ." Mrs. Carson consulted the scheduling book, her lacquered nail tracing the columns. "Gloria, what's your last name?"

"Smith." Again I went with the first name that popped into my head.

"Well, let's see now." Mrs. Carson furrowed her brow. "I'm not seeing you in the book here. Are you sure your appointment is for today? With Dr. Zucker?"

The telephone rang, and I waited while she took the call, looking all around the office, thinking how I was going to play this.

"Yes . . . Uh-huh . . ." Mrs. Carson jotted something down on a pad of paper. "Let me just check our files for you. Would you mind if I put you on hold?" She pushed a button on the phone and turned back to me. "I'm sorry, Miss Smith. This will just be another minute."

"Take your time. I'll wait."

While thinking of a way to get some information out of her, I watched Mrs. Carson turn to the wooden file cabinet behind her desk. Five drawers, the top one packed with manila folders, presumably filled with patient information. It struck me that everything I needed was probably inside that cabinet. It was right there, just three feet away, but I had no idea how I was going to get to it.

After she finished her call, she examined the scheduling book again and clucked her tongue. "Now, you're sure your appointment was for today? With Dr. Zucker? When did you set it up?"

"Oh, dear, maybe it's not with Dr. Zucker. . . ." I went into a scatterbrained act, looking frantically inside my handbag before I launched into a string of apologies. "I'm so sorry. I don't know how I could have been so confused. . . ."

I thanked Mrs. Carson for her time and went back to the city room, where I began working on my assignment for that day, a story about a kitten rescue. The only reason I'd gotten that story was because one of the Neighborhood News reporters was out sick and they needed someone to cover it. I should have been more grateful that they'd given it to me at all—even if out of desperation on their part—but I was too preoccupied with the insurance fraud. After I turned in the rescued-kitten story to the copy desk, I went down to City Hall to see the finance committee chair and the chairman of the city council. Sean McCarty was conveniently unavailable, but Frank O'Connor was willing to meet with me.

In addition to being the council chairman, Frank O'Connor was the 42nd Ward alderman, overseeing the Gold Coast, the Loop, Streeterville and River North. The first thing he did was ask why he was talking to me and not Walter. Just as I'd explained to Commander Graves yesterday, I told him I was covering this story. Not Walter.

He smiled, offered me coffee, tea, a glass of water, a dish of pralines. I thanked him and got to the point. "At a recent city council meeting you had an agenda item about medical reimbursement for policemen injured in the line of duty."

"That's routine procedure. The sort of thing that goes through the council for approval."

"And were all the medical expenses approved?"

"I assume they were." He pressed the pads of his fingertips together before bouncing them off one another. "I couldn't say for certain. That sort of thing gets approved by the finance committee, so I'd have to go back and check."

"And would it be Sean McCarty who approves payment?"

"Yes. That would fall under the finance chair's discretion. Of course, that's after he's reviewed each case."

"And would that be after Dr. Edgar MacAleese reviews the report from the physician who treated the injured officer?"

"Well, I see you've already been looking into this." He smiled and made a notation on his calendar that I sensed had nothing to do with our conversation.

"Were you aware that the majority of injuries filed came from District 35?"

"I'm sorry, Miss—Miss . . ."

"Walsh. Jordan Walsh."

"I'm sorry, Miss Walsh, but I'm afraid I'm going to have to cut this short."

"I just have a few more questions."

"Oh, and I do wish I could stay and answer them." He smiled again, even wider, with the teeth of a Doberman. "I have an appointment that I'm running late for, but I'd be happy to speak with you again. You just call my secretary. And tell Walter he owes me a drink." He laughed as he held his office door open.

Moments later I found myself standing outside on the sidewalk wondering what just happened to me. I'd never been more abruptly or politely dismissed in all my life. I glanced at my watch. I still had some time before I needed to get back to the paper, so from there I went down to police headquarters at 11th and State. The building had thirteen floors, an unlucky number. Danny Finn worked on the sixth floor.

"Well, well, well," he said when he looked up from his desk. "To what do I owe this nice surprise?"

Ever since we'd met at the D'Arco wedding, I'd been keeping in touch with him. Every few weeks or so I'd drop by and grab a drink with him, see if he had some scoop for me. So far he hadn't offered me anything other than invitations for dinner.

That afternoon we went down the street to a bar on Plymouth Court. Danny smoothed his hands down the front of his uniform and placed his hat on the edge of the table. I reached for it and put it on my head.

"How do I look? Think I could cut it as a police officer?"

He smiled. "You'd definitely be the best-looking one on the force."

I smiled back and removed his hat, setting it back on the edge of the table. I took a sip from my drink and I told him what I was up to.

"And here I thought you came to see me because you missed me."

"Oh, but it goes without saying that I missed you," I said teasingly. "But c'mon, tell me if you know *anything* about this."

"Wish I could help you." He picked at his beer label. "One of these days I'm bound to have something for you. Something big." He winked and took a pull from his beer.

Over the next few days I met with one of McCarty's aides and with Dr. MacAleese. The aide was polite but guarded and shed no new light on the documents produced by the finance committee, and all Dr. MacAleese did was confirm that McCarty's reports were accurate.

I tried to focus on my regular assignments from Mrs. Angelo, but each time I took a break, my mind went back to the insurance fraud, going over and over the facts. It was like a tangled chain I was trying to work through.

One morning at breakfast I asked my father for advice. "What did you used to do when you were investigating something and you hit a dead end?" I immediately regretted my choice of words, but he didn't seem to notice.

Without looking up from his newspaper, he said, "Depends on the story." He reached for a slice of toast, his eyes still on his paper.

"I'm looking into a possible fraud case."

"Uh-huh." For the first time he set the paper aside.

I sat up straighter, wide open and eager to receive his wisdom.

"CeeCee," he said, "where's the jam? There's no jam on the table." He reached for his paper again and began reading. "Another burglary on the North Side . . ."

I couldn't hide my disappointment. Yes, I had sincerely wanted his help. But I had also hoped he'd be interested in what I was working on. Once again I was on my own to figure this out.

My gut told me I needed to back up and try a different angle. So when I arrived at the city room, I reviewed the list of names I'd copied down from Ahern and took a chance. Starting with the first name, I went through the telephone book and called the officers' homes. Aside from a housekeeper who didn't speak English, a party line and a couple busy signals, all I got were brush-offs, a few hang-ups. It was clear to me that no one was interested in talking to a reporter. Going legit wasn't working, so I called upon the help of my new alias, Gloria Smith. It was awkward and I fumbled on the first few calls, so aware that my coworkers, who probably weren't paying any attention, could hear my every word.

Eventually I got an Officer Geck on the line.

"This is Gloria Smith from Illinois Mutual Insurance?" I paused, holding my breath.

"Yes."

"I just wanted to review your claim from your recent visit to Dr. Zucker."

"Dr. Zucker?" He paused for such a long time I almost thought he'd hung up. "I don't know any Dr. Zucker."

A ping of light shot through my head and I nearly gasped. "Is this Officer Ralph Geck?"

"Yes, that's me. Who did you say you're with?"

Shit! Who was I with? I consulted my notepad. "Illinois Mutual Insurance."

"Yeah, well, I don't know any Dr. Zucker."

I'd been nervously doodling on my notepad, and now I wrote out *Geck doesn't know Zucker.* I underlined it three times and put a question mark. He could have been lying. "So you didn't have an appointment with Dr. Zucker last October?"

"Not me. You must have the wrong person."

I kept my hand on the receiver after we'd hung up. My fingers were shaking. My entire body was pulsating. I was sure that everyone could see it. It was like I had an electrical current running through my veins. Now I knew beyond a doubt that I was really onto something.

I made a few more calls posing as Gloria from Illinois Mutual Insurance, expecting to find another Officer Geck. But I was back to hang-ups, wrong numbers and brick walls. I dialed the next number, and just as I was about to hang up, a woman answered.

"Messner residence."

"Is this Mrs. Messner?"

"Yes. Who's calling?"

"Gloria. Gloria Smith." I was amazed at how much easier it was to say that now. "May I speak with Officer Messner?"

"He's not home right now. . . ." There were children screeching in the background, and she seemed distracted.

"I'm calling from Illinois Mutual Insurance and—"

"The insurance company?" She hushed the children and cleared her throat. "Is there something *I* can help you with?"

I gave her the same preamble I'd used with everyone else Gloria had spoken to and followed it up with, "I understand your husband, Officer Messner, is a patient of Dr. Zucker's."

"Well, he was. But he hasn't seen Dr. Zucker in at least a good year or so."

"And was that for his ruptured disc?"

"Ruptured disc? No, no. He had an upper respiratory infection. You remember when that bad flu was going around? He was in bed for more than a week. . . ."

I'd been doodling on my notepad again and pressed so hard, the lead tip on my pencil broke off. A rush of heat shot through my body. "Was your husband ever injured in the line of duty?" I asked.

"Thank heavens, no. But don't think I don't say a prayer each time he walks out that door."

The air was trapped in my chest. "Mrs. Messner, has your husband ever been treated for a ruptured disc?" I cradled the phone between my ear and shoulder, reaching for another pencil and writing so fast I nearly tore the paper in half.

"No, like I said, it was just that upper respiratory infection. Turned out to be bronchitis."

"And was Dr. Zucker his regular physician?"

"No, no. Dr. Louie is our family doctor. But my husband didn't want him to come to the house and I couldn't get him to go see Dr. Louie. My husband hates going to the doctor, but he was so sick—like I said, he was in bed for more than a week—they finally made him go. They were the ones who sent him to Dr. Zucker."

They? Who's they? Another flash of heat coursed through my body. "Do you remember who referred your husband to Dr. Zucker?"

"I believe it was his boss down at the station."

"Commander . . ."

"That's it. Yes, it was Commander Graves."

I continued to shake long after I hung up the phone. I felt like I'd guzzled a gallon of coffee. Everything inside me was alert, wide-awake, buzzing. I looked over my notes again and knew I couldn't work the rest of this from my desk. I had to get closer, as close as I could to the heart of this story.

The next morning, armed with a list of names and addresses, I went one by one to the officers' homes and rang their doorbells and spoke to anyone who would talk to me. And by me, I mean Jordan Walsh. I was coming face-to-face with police officers who were used to doing the interrogating, and posing as a secretary from an insurance company wasn't going to cut it. Neither was the truth. Or at least not the whole truth. It was something I'd have to play with, and it made me nervous as hell.

When I arrived at Officer Pratt's home in Rogers Park, I found him lying on the ground in his driveway, his legs sticking out from under the body of his Buick. His wife stood on the front porch, calling to him. "Will? Willie, someone's here for you."

Officer Will Pratt scooted out from under his car on a creeper. I introduced myself while he stood up and pulled a rag from his back pocket, wiping motor oil from his fingers.

"So what does a woman from the *Tribune* want with me?"

"Well, first off, I'm a reporter," I said. "And I'm doing a piece on police officers injured in the line of duty. I understand you were injured while on the job."

"Yeah, so . . ." He looked back at his wife, who was now standing on the bottom porch step.

"So I understand you're one of Dr. Zucker's patients?"

"What the hell's this all about?"

His reaction was too strong. My question had put him on the defensive. I drew a deep breath and wiped my sweating palms down the front of my skirt. "We're looking into some recent claims you filed."

"And why would you be doing that?" He took a step forward, and it took all my will not to back up.

"I think you know." I held his gaze with everything I had.

"What the . . . ?" He squinted and gave me a look like he was drilling down through my skin.

"And I know Dr. Zucker didn't treat you for a ruptured disc." For all I knew his claims were legit, but I was putting on my best poker face. "Would you care to make a comment?"

"About what?"

I could hear the irritation in his voice and hoped he couldn't hear the fear in mine when I said, "We're talking insurance fraud. This isn't the first time Dr. Zucker's been accused of falsifying medical records. I'm giving you a chance to explain your role in all this. A chance to say you had nothing to do with it."

I expected him to explode, but instead he scratched his head and lowered his voice. "Look, I just saw Dr. Zucker the one time. That was it."

My pulse quickened. I couldn't believe it; he was softening. "So why did you see him if it wasn't for the ruptured disc?"

"They told me to go see him, so I did. It was just a routine checkup. I was flat broke at the time, and they said they'd give me twenty-five bucks for my troubles."

"Who's they?" I reached inside my bag for my pad and pencil. "Do you mind if I take down a few notes?"

He looked back at his wife, standing on the edge of the lawn. "I—I really—I can't talk about this." He stuffed the rag back in his pocket. "I don't want to say nothing more without my lawyer here."

I was still firing off questions as he lay back down on the creeper and disappeared beneath his Buick.

I stood in the driveway writing everything down: *Someone paid him twenty-five dollars to see Zucker. Mentioned his lawyer.* I called to Officer Pratt again, but he refused to come back out from under his car and finish our conversation.

Next I tracked down Officer Nelson. It was his day off, and his wife said I'd find him over at the school playground, shooting baskets with his son. Shooting baskets when my notes said that he had ruptured his fifth lower lumbar and was in acute chronic pain.

I found another officer right where his precinct said he'd be, in uniform, directing traffic at Lake and LaSalle. According to Ahern's records, this officer was listed with a broken jaw after being pistol whipped. When the light turned red, I rushed up and introduced myself. The records said Zucker had wired the officer's jaw shut just three weeks before, but there was no evidence of that now. He went on conducting traffic the whole time we spoke. If he was listening to anything I said, he didn't indicate it.

"I see your jaw has healed rather quickly."

"My jaw?" He stopped with his hand gestures and looked at me. "What are you talking about?"

"You were treated by Dr. Zucker for a broken jaw. You had it wired shut."

"Lady, I don't know what you're talking about." He blew his whistle and resumed his work. "I've never broken my jaw, and I've never heard of Dr. Zucker."

I was stunned. My feet were glued to the pavement as cars whirled past me. It wasn't until someone laid on their horn that I made it back to the safety of the sidewalk. I was light-headed; my whole body was swaying along with the buildings. Everything was moving. Nothing felt solid just then. No doubt about it, a pattern was taking shape.

I darted to the pay phone on the corner. My heartbeat pounded inside my ears as I pushed a nickel through the coin slot and dialed Ahern's number. While I was waiting for the switchboard operator to connect the call, I pulled out my notes, trying to make sense of my hurried handwriting. The claims were as recent as three weeks ago, and some of the officers said they hadn't seen Dr. Zucker in more than a year. Others, like the man I'd just spoken to, claimed they had never heard of Dr. Zucker. Still there was the officer who'd been treated for a dislocated shoulder and another for a double hernia that both sounded legit. Honestly, I didn't know who was lying and who wasn't. But despite that, I found at least ten officers with ruptured discs or back injuries, and yet when I went to see them, I discovered they were out golfing or playing basketball or lying on a creeper.

Ahern came on the line.

"I need to meet with you," I said.

Thirty minutes later we were at a hot-dog stand outside of Grant Park. "A lot of these guys aren't injured," I said to Ahern, declining his offer for a hot dog. "Some of them claim they never saw Zucker, or saw him once for something besides what's on this list. Do you think MacAleese is working with O'Connor? Do you think McCarty and MacAleese are in cahoots together?"

He took a bite of his dog. "All I can tell you," he said with his mouth full, "is that someone's getting rich here—and it's not those police officers. They may have thrown a couple of them a few bucks to get them into Zucker's office, but that's pocket change."

"I don't know where else to turn. I got nothing from MacAleese or McCarty. O'Connor wasn't much—"

"Zucker," he said.

"I tried to talk to Zucker. I've already been to his office. I can't get past his receptionist."

"Try again." He dabbed a bit of mustard off his mouth. "Go back. Check again, Walsh. Dig a little deeper this time."

After meeting with Ahern, I stayed and roamed through Grant Park to clear my head and think of how I was going to get this story. A cluster of pigeons on the pathway burst into a flurry of flapping wings and took flight as I approached Buckingham Fountain. I knew there was something wrong going on, and now I was going to have to do something wrong myself in order to prove it.

Chapter 8

◆ ◆ ◆

By the next morning I had a plan. It had come to me sometime after midnight, and even though I thought it was a viable idea, it didn't sit well with me in the darkness and felt no less uncomfortable in the light of day. In fact, the whole idea made my stomach ache. But it was the only way I could get this story.

I was so preoccupied that morning I was already zipping my skirt before I realized my sweater was inside out. By the time I made it to the kitchen, I was clammy and out of sorts. I made a pot of coffee, grateful that no one else was up yet. I'd never done anything this gutsy before, but I'd weighed the consequences and the risks and determined that it was worth it to get the scoop. I reminded myself that Marty Sinclair would have done anything to get a story. What I was planning to do was probably nothing compared to the lengths he'd gone to. I told myself that if it was okay with Marty, then it would be okay with me.

Marty Sinclair . . . I wondered how he was doing. I'd heard that his lawyer had challenged the subpoena. And because Big Tony had recently been arrested on another murder charge, it appeared that the state's attorney no longer needed Marty's testimony. They had Big Tony and that was all they cared about. I was thinking all this when my mother came into the kitchen and startled me.

"Oh, I'm sorry, love. I didn't mean to scare you."

I reached for a towel and dabbed up the coffee I'd just spilled.

"Did you eat breakfast already?" she asked.

I shook my head. My stomach was too jumbled and I couldn't have forced anything down. My mother was chatty that morning. I nodded, I spoke, I may have even asked her a question or two, but later that day I couldn't recall a single thing we talked about. I only remembered leaving my coffee untouched and going straight to the city room, acting as if it were business as usual.

I checked the assignment book, said hello to the slot man and Higgs, the rewrite man coming off the night shift. I spent the morning working on a few celebrity sightings for the They Were There column and a piece on "Boardroom Etiquette" for White Collar Girl. I'd also begun doing some work for the fashion department along with society news and was finishing up a piece on "The Smart Way to Wear a Pencil Skirt and a Peplum Top."

M and Gabby invited me to lunch, but I begged off and instead went to Norm's Diner around the corner by myself. The thought of food was still unappealing, and I couldn't be in their company. I needed time alone to brace myself.

I took my seat at the counter and ordered a cup of coffee. The stools were set close together and the woman next to me accidentally elbowed me as she removed her cat-eye glasses, setting them on the counter while she read the menu. She smiled, apologized and placed her order. I went back to thinking about my plan, thinking that it wasn't too late to back out. And if I did, then what? The fraud would continue and I would be stuck writing about skirts and sweaters, celebrities and secretaries.

The woman next to me accidentally elbowed me again as she reached in her purse and put on her sunglasses. It wasn't until she was done paying the cashier that I noticed she'd left her other pair of glasses on the counter. I picked them up, about to call out to her just as she pushed through the front door. I realized then that I was holding more than her glasses in my hand. I was holding my disguise. After a quick glance around the diner, I slipped them into my handbag.

I went back to the city room, my stomach gurgling from too much coffee and nerves. I watched the clock, time moving in slow motion through the day until finally I was ready to leave.

I went on foot and made it to the Pittsfield Building at a quarter past four. People filtered through the lobby, filing out of the elevators, rushing to catch trains and hail taxicabs. The cleaning crew was out in full force. Blue uniforms were everywhere, emptying wastebaskets and ashtrays, polishing the banisters on the stairwell. I needed the place to thin out, so I went to the newsstand and bought a package of Juicy Fruit to pass the time inconspicuously. My hands were shaking as I placed a dime on the counter. I wiped the sweat from my palms down the front of my skirt and tried to steady my breathing.

When I was ready I rode up to the seventeenth floor and waited until I saw one of the cleaning women heading down the hallway. Surprisingly I calmed down. It was showtime. It was as if a switch had kicked on inside me, and I moved into action, knowing exactly what I had to do.

I followed the cleaning woman and in the midst of her sweeping, she stopped, startled. "Can I help you?"

I approached with my heart in my mouth, but said as evenly as I could, "How would you like to make five bucks?"

Her eyes hardened, and after what felt like an eternity, she said, "What would I have to do?"

I began to breathe again. I knew I had her. "I need to borrow your uniform. And your office keys."

Five minutes later I was dressed in a blue smock, carrying a bucket, a mop and some cleaning supplies. I pinned up my hair and put on my pilfered glasses. The woman they belonged to must have been blind as a bat because I felt like I'd just entered the fun house at Riverview Park. The walls and ceiling were distorted, moving with each step I took. Because I couldn't see straight, I was walking like a drunk and heard the water sloshing about inside my bucket. I hoped I wasn't leaving a trail behind me.

I worried the ring of keys in the pocket of my uniform as I approached Dr. Zucker's office. I saw a figure moving about behind the frosted-glass window. The door was still unlocked, and my hands were clammy again as I turned the knob, my breathing shallow. I could only hope I didn't look as guilty as I felt.

Mrs. Carson looked up from the receptionist's desk. "You're new."

"Yes, ma'am," I mumbled, busying myself with the mop and bucket to avoid making eye contact. Despite the pinned-up hair and glasses, I was worried that she might recognize me from my previous visit. I kept my head turned away, but in my peripheral vision I saw her pull her handbag from beneath her desk and then lock the file cabinet behind her before dropping the key into the top drawer.

"Make sure you remember to water the plants," she said, snapping off her desk lamp.

As soon as she was gone, I checked the examination room and made sure no one else was there, including Dr. Zucker. I went back out front and locked the door and listened to the building breathing and creaking, the water running through the pipes from the lavatories. Everything else was quiet.

I opened Mrs. Carson's desk and retrieved the tiny key for the file cabinet. I couldn't see a thing with the glasses on and flung them off, giving my eyes a moment to readjust. The first drawer was

marked 1954–To Date. I found the patient files, all neatly alphabet-
ized. It was so easy, almost too easy. I had a handful of folders
out when I heard the *ding* of the elevator car. I froze. My heart
hammered. *Footsteps.* There were footsteps coming closer, growing
louder, louder, louder . . . and then soft, softer, softer as they moved
past Dr. Zucker's doorway and down the marble hallway.

I calmed myself as I quickly went through the first stack of
folders. Everything appeared in order: claims, diagnoses, billing.
There was nothing new in there. Next I searched for folders of
the officers who had told me they'd never heard of Dr. Zucker,
or else hadn't been to see him in more than a year. I couldn't find
them. I pulled open the second drawer and found nothing, and
nothing in the third drawer either. I was beginning to think I'd
taken this risk for nothing.

In a last-ditch effort, I opened the bottom file drawer, expecting more of the same, when several familiar names leaped out at
me: O'Connor, Graves, McCarty, MacAleese, Messner, Nelson . . .
A jolt rushed through my body, making even my scalp prickle. My
fingers trembled as I sifted through the first folder. Contact information. *Date of birth: 11.28.1918. Home address: 678 Franklin Ave.
Chicago, IL 60610. Wife's name: Trudy.* Dammit. Nothing out of
the ordinary. There was a tattered red ledger in the way back of the
drawer listing the insurance payments along with canceled checks,
tucked into a side pocket, made payable to O'Connor, Graves,
McCarty and MacAleese. None of this looked good for Dr. Zucker
and the others, but it didn't necessarily *prove* fraud, either. Still it
was all I had, so I went to the Photostat machine, flipped the on
switch, and while it warmed up, I dug around some more and
found a series of notes in another file. Cryptic messages, like *Xbudi
zpvs tufq. Uif Gjobodf Dpnnjuuff jt btljoh rvftujpot* . . . I realized it
was some sort of cipher and there was a little square of paper
clipped to the top page that said *Use this* and was underscored

three times. I studied the pages for a moment, knowing I'd never have time to decipher them. The Photostat machine was ready. I held my breath and broke out into a full-on sweat while making copies of everything I'd found.

My hands were still shaking even as I returned the folders and locked up the file cabinet. I set the key back inside Mrs. Carson's desk drawer, and as I reached for the cat-eye glasses, I noticed a scrap of paper on the floor. *Use this.* It must have fallen out of the folder while I was making the copies. I was getting antsy, wanting to get out of there before I got caught, so rather than unlock the cabinet, I slipped the note into my pocket. Before turning out the lights and locking the door I did remember to water the plants.

On my way home I approached Norm's Diner and contemplated going inside and slipping the cat-eye glasses back onto the counter. I truly did want to get them back to the woman who'd left them behind, but I was reluctant. Perhaps I was overthinking the situation, but I *had* committed a crime—breaking and entering, or maybe it was criminal trespassing. I didn't know what I'd done exactly, but I knew I'd crossed a line. It was probably far-fetched, but what if someone had seen me take those glasses at the diner earlier? What if someone in the Pittsfield Building had seen me wearing them when I was up on the seventeenth floor?

I passed by Norm's Diner and looked in through the picture window. The lights were out, the chairs flipped upside down, perched on the tabletops. I was grateful that they were closed and that the dilemma of returning the glasses had been taken out of my control for the night. I told myself that I'd tried, and had no choice but to console myself with that for the moment.

I went home, changed from my work clothes into a sweater

and a pair of ratty old pedal pushers. I sat at the kitchen table with all my photocopies spread out before me. I was reading over everything and picking at some leftover meat loaf when my father came out of his office.

"How's the writing going?" I asked, watching him reach inside the refrigerator for a handful of ice, dropping it cube by cube into his empty glass. "You making good progress on your novel?"

He curled down his lower lip and raised his shoulders. "Who knows?"

"Well, I'm sure it's brilliant. I can't wait to read it."

"Your mother still up?" he asked.

"She's in the living room. Reading *The Deer Park*."

"*Auch*, Mailer." He shook his head, uncapped the bottle of whiskey on the counter and poured himself another drink.

"You're not going to believe what I'm working on right now. It's a big piece on insurance fraud," I said, pushing my plate aside. My desire to reel him in overrode the concerns about my investigative methods. "And I think it goes all the way to City Hall."

"Insurance fraud, huh? That's good. Good." He nodded and looked toward the hallway. "Tell your mother not to stay up too late, will you?"

I was going to tell him more about the fraud, but he turned and said, "Mailer, Christ . . ." Then he went back into his office and closed the door. I stayed at the table, trying to make sense of the material I'd photocopied. I couldn't look at the ledger numbers anymore. The columns were blurring together, and even though what I found was suspicious, it wasn't enough. I glanced at the note that had fallen on the floor in Zucker's office. I smoothed my fingers over the handwritten letters: *Use this.* I could tell it had been torn from a pad of paper, because some of the gummy adhesive was still stuck to the top. I didn't even know who'd written it or whose notepad it had come from. All

I could make out were impressions on the paper, left behind from whatever had been written on the previous page.

I looked again at the ciphered messages. I'd never be able to crack this code. My God, there were cryptologists who did this for a living. To me it was just a jumble of letters, so I set it aside and got up to fix myself a cup of coffee. It was getting late, and I needed something to keep me awake.

While the percolator gurgled and burped, I thought about the little note that had been attached to the ciphered pages. For some reason I was reminded of a game Eliot and I used to play called Secret Message. We would take a pad of paper and write each other a note and then tear off the top page and throw it away. The other person would take a pencil and run it over the indents on the paper and try to make out the words.

Make out the words. Make out the words!

I raced over to the table and grabbed a pencil and gently ran it back and forth over the indents on the page until stroke by stroke, letter by letter and word by word the previous message revealed itself: *Alphabet shift one.*

That didn't make any sense either. It could have meant anything. Could have been meant for something totally unrelated. I gave up, left everything on the table and decided to go upstairs and get ready for bed. I was brushing my teeth with the words *alphabet shift one* repeating over and over again with each stroke. Up, down, up, down, *alphabet shift one, alphabet shift one, alphabet shift*—wait a minute. I spit out a mouthful of toothpaste and raced back downstairs.

I reached for one of the coded pages and scrutinized the first word: *Avdlfs.* Alphabet shift one would mean the *A* either was a *Z* or a *B* and the *v* would either be a *u* or a *w*; third letter had to be *c* or an *e*. *Awe* didn't hold much promise, but *Zuc* had to be the start of *Zucker,* which meant the alphabet shift was one letter backward. I looked at the message before me:

Avdlfs: Xbudi zpvs tufq. Uif gjobodf dpnnjuuff jt btljoh
rvftujpot. NbdBmfftf upme NdDbsuz up gjy uif sfqpsu. Dibohf
uif svquvsfe ejtd up b cpof gsbduvsf. Gps opx lffq bmm
qspdfevsft voefs $300 fbdi. Qfpqmf bsf hfuujoh tvtqjdjpvt.
Dbo'u bggpse up cf tmpqqz.

—Gsbol

This was going to take forever. I got up and poured myself a fresh cup of coffee and started in. Figuring out the message was painfully slow at first. But when I worked out the first sentence a chill went through me. It said, "Zucker: Watch your step." This spurred me on, and after a few more words I got the hang of it.

An hour and a half later, I had it worked out:

Zucker: Watch your step. The finance committee is asking
questions. MacAleese told McCarty to fix the report. Change
the ruptured disc to a bone fracture. For now keep all
procedures under $300 each. People are getting suspicious.
Can't afford to be sloppy.

—Frank

There were more encrypted pages—pages and pages full of incriminating statements about fudged diagnoses, fake procedures, false claims. I translated a few more passages, then stopped. There were still more to decode, but I had what I needed.

I went back up to my room and stayed up late working on my article. My mind was racing as I typed. The coffee on my desk had turned cold and still I was wide-awake because now I knew

I had it. This was the scoop I'd been waiting for. This was the one story my editors wouldn't be able to turn down. So I kept working as if Eliot and my parents were sitting there in the corner, watching me, prodding me on. My father had hardly said two words to me that night. My mother couldn't pull her nose out of Mailer's book. I told myself that if I could land this piece in the paper, maybe they'd get excited about something again. Maybe it would lure them out of their grief.

I glanced at the clock. It was a quarter past two. The initial rush had faded and by now I was so exhausted I almost dozed off in the middle of typing a sentence. But I had to keep going. I had to do this for my mother and father. And for me, too.

By eight thirty the next morning, I was pacing in front of Mr. Ellsworth's desk, waiting while he jotted down something on the corner of his blotter. I hovered until he finally raised his eyebrows and said, "What can I do for you, Walsh?"

"I've got something," I said. "And it's big."

He gave me a look that said *why the hell are you bothering me with this stuff?* "Tell Mrs. Angelo about it. And for the love of Christ, quit going behind her back and coming to me. Pearson's, too. You work for society news, remember?"

"But this isn't society news. This is city news."

He sighed, scratched at his whiskers. I could feel his patience wearing thin. "Okay." He leaned back in his chair and folded his arms. "Let's have it."

I gave him my copy and watched as he stroked his beard and gave me that blank stare of his that I was all too accustomed to.

Eventually he said, "You want me to run a story about Alderman O'Connor—the *chairman* of the city council—and some crooked doctor committing insurance fraud?"

"And don't forget Commander Graves. You can see for yourself. It's all right here."

"Walsh, we've been through this. You need proof."

"Oh, I have proof. Here—" I showed him the encrypted pages.

He shuffled through them and shot me a look. "What is this, some kind of joke?"

"It's in code, but I figured it out. Here's the decoded messages. Take a look." As a backup I handed him the Photostat copies from Zucker's files.

He ran a hand down his face, pausing to massage his jaw. "How'd you get your hands on all this information?"

I knew this was coming and I was so conflicted about my methods, all I did was shake my head and say, "You don't want to know."

He glanced at the copies and back at me. "And you stand by what you've got here?"

"Absolutely. You're looking at the photocopies of the doctor's files yourself."

"Walter—" he called out. "Walter? Get over here."

"Walter?" I dropped my hands to my thighs. "I don't need Walter."

"Well, I do. And I need legal to look this over, too."

Walter appeared, pipe gripped between his teeth. "What is it?"

"Walsh has something here. I'll have legal take a look, and in the meantime, run it through the typewriter again—fill in the holes."

"There are no holes," I said.

Mr. Ellsworth gave me a look that shut me up. He wasn't interested in discussing the matter.

I followed Walter back to his desk. "I'm on deadline," he said, tearing the copy from his typewriter. "I really don't have time for this kind of nonsense right now." But once he started reading, his face took on a different cast. He looked up at me, stunned. "I don't believe it. Holy fucking crap, Walsh—how the hell did you get this?"

I didn't say. Instead I paced while he typed, stopping now and then to look over his shoulder. Essentially all he'd done was retype my story. He used my same lede and ended up changing only a handful of words. Reversed the order of two paragraphs toward the bottom. That was it.

Half an hour later we were back at the horseshoe. I stared at a spot on the ceiling while Mr. Ellsworth read. I heard him grunt here and there before pulling out his dreaded red pen. He made one mark before he said, "If it gets past legal, we run it."

"You will?"

"I will." Mr. Ellsworth chucked his pen onto his desk and stood up, leaning into a stretch. As I turned away, he patted me on the rump. "Nice work, Walsh." Then he turned to Walter and gave him a nod.

Despite the little ass pat, I was pleased. I felt like a different person returning to my desk after that. I pushed out my chest and threw my shoulders back. I was a member of the team. This was my first real news story—and it was a big one. Finally, a byline to be proud of.

First thing the next day, before I'd even gotten dressed, I raced downstairs and opened the front door. Pinching my bathrobe closed, I grabbed the newspaper that the paperboy had folded and flung onto the porch. I couldn't wait to show this story to my parents, picturing how their boozy, bloodshot eyes would open wide and their mouths would curve into smiles. We'd talk about it over breakfast, and I'd tell them what I'd done to get the scoop. My mother would clip the article, and unable to wait until Sunday, when the long-distance rates were lower, she'd call her parents in New York just to tell them what I'd done. It would be like old times, and Eliot would be right there, sitting on my shoulder.

The pages were chilled from the morning air, and I was filled with anticipation as I stood in the foyer and began to read. My eyes raced across the front page and I saw my headline: "City Council Chairman Linked to Insurance Fraud." But then I saw something that drop-kicked my heart to my stomach: "by Walter Harris."

With my insides shaking, I read the article, thinking maybe Walter had rewritten it again. Maybe some new development had come in. But no. It was my article, all right. I could feel my cheeks growing flushed and the rage surging inside me as I stormed upstairs and dressed in such a harried rush, I didn't notice until I was on the el that I'd missed a button on my blouse.

I was still spitting mad as I marched into the city room and started toward Mr. Ellsworth at the horseshoe.

Who in the hell did he think he was, giving my byline to Walter? Did he think I was some silly little schoolgirl that he could push around? I didn't care if he was the managing editor. I wasn't about to be treated like this.

He saw me coming, and as soon as our eyes met, the words boiling inside my head began to dissipate, vaporizing into nothing but a blank stare. I couldn't go through with it. I caved and turned and went back to my desk. How was I going to explain this to my father? I'd already told him I was working on a big story about insurance fraud. He read the *Tribune* every day. He'd see this story and he'd see Walter's byline on it instead of mine. I was seething, and the anger started blistering up again inside me. I heard Walter laughing on the telephone, and that did it. I grabbed the newspaper, shot back up and made a beeline for the horseshoe.

"Mr. Ellsworth." I cleared my throat. "I need to speak with you about something."

"I'm busy, Walsh." He didn't bother looking up.

I flapped the paper down in front of him. "That was *my* story. *My* reporting. *My* investigating."

"And it was *your* first piece. I put a more seasoned reporter on it."

"Walter added nothing to this story. Absolutely nothing."

"I'm not going to sit here and explain myself to you. I don't care who your father is, or where you went to school. You have a lot to learn about the newspaper business." He handed back my paper.

"But—"

"I think we're done here." He picked up his telephone and dismissed me without so much as another glance.

I went back to my desk and dropped into my chair, still clutching the newspaper. I needed a drink. As I unzipped my handbag, I saw the cat-eye glasses lying inside. I pushed myself away from my desk and rushed downstairs and back over to Norm's Diner.

I went up to the cashier, a middle-aged woman with a lopsided bun and a coffee stain on her blouse. I set the glasses on the counter. Now that my name was nowhere on the article, I no longer feared anyone tying those cat-eye glasses to me. "I think one of your customers left these here."

To this day I think about that woman and hope that she went back and got her glasses.

Chapter 9

• • •

I was not okay after my story ran without the byline that I'd worked for and earned. I hadn't just been marginalized. I'd been eliminated from the equation. And it stung. I thought about giving up, accepting my role as a sob sister, but to do so went against my nature. I wasn't raised to be a quitter.

Every other newspaper in town jumped on the story, and Walter did all the follow-up reports and had a cryptologist decode the rest of the messages. I didn't even try to get involved. There were indictments and firings and resignations, and I couldn't bring myself to read about any of them. Try though I might, I couldn't keep the anger and resentment hidden from my voice whenever I spoke to Walter or Mr. Ellsworth.

"Is there a problem, Walsh?" Mr. Ellsworth had said to me on more than one occasion.

"No. No problem." I'd swallowed it down, moving out of his way before I snapped.

With Walter I was less restrained. One morning, about a month after he stole my byline, I stood in the kitchen nook, watching him pour the last of the coffee into his mug before placing the empty pot back on the burner.

"You killed the coffee," I said, sounding much more exasperated than the offense warranted.

"Yeah, so?" He looked at me as if it were no big deal, which made it an enormous deal to me. This was not about coffee. This was about my pride, my ego. He still had his hand on the pot.

"So I suppose you expect me to make a new pot," I said.

"Well, I guess you'll have to if you want a cup of coffee now, won't you?"

I ripped the percolator from his grip, accidentally dislodging the basket of coffee grounds, sending brown specks all over the counter. I slammed the pot down, while Walter laughed, waltzing past me. I was fuming, every bit as mad at myself as I was with him. I had just confirmed his belief that a woman was too emotional to cut it in the city room. On top of that, now I had to clean up the mess *and* put on a fresh pot of coffee.

I went back to my desk, broke down and made the one telephone call I didn't want to make. I'd been hoping instead that the call would have come to me. But it had been a month since I'd heard from Ahern. We spoke briefly after the article ran. He said he was heading into a meeting and would call me back. He never did, and I'd been too proud to call him again. Until now.

When Ahern answered the phone, I practically begged him to meet with me. An hour later I was waiting for him outside the monkey house at the Lincoln Park Zoo. I sat on a boulder and watched a group of schoolchildren across the way, holding hands, skipping, laughing, so happy with their simple lives, not a care in the world.

I was getting antsy, wondering where Ahern was and if it was really wise to get in any deeper with him. There was something about him that I didn't trust, but still, he was the only man who'd been willing to take me seriously.

And besides, I had tried making my own contacts. I'd gone out of my way to meet the right people at those society balls and weddings. I'd sent flowers to Daley's private secretary for her birthday. I went down to police headquarters and bought raffle tickets for their kids' schools, brought them cookies and cakes, even got drunk with Danny Finn and the others. I considered Danny a friend, but the rest only wanted to see if I'd let them slip their hand up my skirt beneath the table.

I had just glanced at my watch, thinking Ahern wouldn't show, when I heard footsteps coming up the pavement. It was him, tall and slender, perfectly groomed and so out of place at the zoo. We exchanged hellos and went into the monkey house. It was cool inside and dimly lit and smelled like wet dog. The monkeys watched us from their cages, some swinging down on ropes to get a closer look.

"So what is it you needed to see me about?" he asked as he checked his wristwatch.

"We never really got a chance to talk again after the story ran."

He folded his arms and leaned his tall frame against the cage where the sign read: Do Not Lean on Cage.

"And I wanted to explain why it ran without—"

"Explain what? Why you gave the story to Walter Harris? Listen, that's your business." He unfolded his hands, raising them in surrender. "I can't tell you how to do your work. Frankly, I'm just glad someone put the brakes on that insurance racket."

"But it was my piece. My reporting. I did all the investigating—not Walter." It was the same defense I'd given to Mr. Ellsworth. One of the monkeys began jumping up and down. It startled me, and I backed away from the cage. "It was all me," I said. "You have no idea how far out on a limb I went to get that story."

"Relax, Walsh. There'll be other stories. Bigger stories."

"When?" I shuddered at my desperation.

"When I have something to give you. Nothing's cooking right now."

"Nothing?" I didn't believe him. I always got the feeling that there was something he wasn't telling me. There were times when he wouldn't look me in the eye, and it frustrated me. But I was at his mercy. No one else in this town was going to give me a tip.

Another monkey swung down from a rope, landing with a thud and kicking up a plume of dust.

"There's nothing I'm in a position to share with you at the moment." He gave me a smug look. "Patience, Walsh. You need to have a little patience."

"So you're not going to give me *anything*? Not even a crumb? C'mon, you wouldn't have met with me today if you didn't have something."

"I came here as a favor."

"Funny, you don't strike me as the type that does favors."

"Well, then, you don't know me very well." He frowned as if genuinely hurt and turned to walk away.

"Hey, Ahern? Ahern, c'mon, don't leave."

With his back to me, he waved and disappeared out the door. I was left standing there, dumbfounded and wishing I hadn't said that to him. Another monkey swooped down, pressing his face to the bars, watching me. I had the feeling I'd just alienated the one person who was on my side.

I left the monkey house drained and achy like when you're coming down with something. All the frustration and upset of the day had collected in a band of tension stretching down my neck and across my shoulders. I was convinced that I was going to be stuck writing for the women's pages the rest of my career. I would have liked nothing better than to crawl into bed and shut the world off, but instead I forced myself back to the city room.

I sat at my desk, staring at the little red crescent moons, the index tabs on the side of my dictionary. I was unable to concentrate, distracted by Henry, who was on the phone with his wife.

"Calm down, Mildred. Jesus, just calm down and take the damn dog to the vet. . . . Well, you're not helping matters with your hysteria. . . . Just tell Bobby his dog's gonna be okay and hang up now and get him to the vet. . . ."

When he got off the phone, I looked over. "Everything all right?"

"Christ." Henry shook his head. "Fucking maniacs out there." He reached for the phone again, dialing with the eraser end of his pencil. "They think they can get away with murder. But I'm gonna teach that bastard a lesson." He adjusted the receiver. "Yeah, get me Sergeant Tessler." He turned back to me and said, "You can't fuck with a member of the press." He reached for the box of cereal on his desk and shoved a handful of Frosted Flakes into his mouth. "Yeah, Gil," he said into the phone, "it's Henry over at the *Trib*. Need a favor. Some asshole just hit my kid's dog with his car and kept driving. Broke the dog's leg. . . . Yeah, happened right in front of the house. . . . Just happened, so the son of a bitch is probably still driving around on the North Side. . . . Mildred said he was driving a green DeSoto. And it's a big dog, a golden retriever, so I wouldn't be surprised if there was some damage to the grille. . . . Yeah, thanks. I owe you one. Let me know when you find him." He hung up the phone and said, "I'm gonna teach that son of a bitch a lesson—you can't fuck with a member of the press."

When he said that for the second time, something clicked inside my brain. I came alive inside. I was reminded that I too was a member of the press and I had tools at my disposal that the average person didn't. I felt a surge of control and hope. If Henry was able to use his connections to track down a driver who'd hit his son's dog, I could certainly do more to find the man who killed my brother.

Just thinking that some coward was still out there on the

loose stirred my anger. Someone had robbed my family of its only son and they had robbed me of my parents. I wanted justice. I wanted someone to pay for what they'd done to Eliot. I had the means to investigate what happened, and I'd be damned if I wasn't going to use everything at my disposal to get to the truth.

I remembered the articles I'd read in the morgue, and the name Adam Javers popped into my head. He was the closest thing we had to a witness. Along one wall we had rows upon rows of telephone directories from every city across the country, around the world. I went and pulled the one for Chicago, riffling through the tissue-like pages until I reached the *J*s, and from there I looked up Adam Javers.

The next day I was sitting beside him, a middle-aged man with thinning gray hair and narrow-set eyes. He was wearing a sweatshirt and had a whistle hanging about his neck. We were in the bleachers at the Wendell Phillips High School gymnasium. He was in the middle of coaching basketball practice while I spoke with him.

"Could you tell me what you remember about that night?"

"That was a while ago," he said. "I don't remember much other than what I already told the police. Hey—hey now—" He twisted about and yelled to a few of the boys on the court.

I waited patiently until he turned back around and faced me.

"Well," he said, "I remember I heard those tires screech, and I turned to see where they were coming from. At first I didn't see anything, but then I noticed something across the way and I realized it was a man—lying there along the curb. It took another minute before I realized what happened—you know, that he'd been hit." He blew his whistle—the shrill chirp ripped through my chest.

"Do you remember seeing the car that hit him?" I asked.

He shook his head. "Like I said, I just heard the tires. I didn't see the car."

"Was anyone else around?"

"It was right by the subway stop down on Grand and State. It was late but not *that* late. I'm sure there were other people around. You talk to anyone else? Maybe someone else remembers seeing the car."

I thanked Coach Javers and walked away broken. Of course there had to have been other people around. I'd always questioned that right from the very beginning. How could the police have said there were no witnesses?

I went to a pay phone and called my buddy Danny Finn down at police headquarters. I told him I was investigating a hit-and-run that happened in 1953.

"Can you help me with this?" I asked. "Can you pull the report?"

Before I had the chance to explain that the victim was my brother, he said, "I can try. But c'mon, Jordan, we're talking more than two years ago. Nothing new is going to turn up."

I went silent, listening to all the chaos in the background on his end, people talking, other phones ringing. Then I began to focus on the buses and taxicabs going by. My heart was sinking. All the hope I'd harnessed after watching Henry in action had dissipated. I felt worse now for having even tried to find the person responsible for my brother's death.

Chapter 10

• • •

It wasn't that I stopped looking for Eliot's killer, but after talking to Danny Finn that day, I had to acknowledge that I might never find the person responsible. Still, it was hard to let it go because I felt like I was turning my back on my brother. But I knew I had to accept that he was gone. I had to let it go, let *him* go. I didn't want to end up like my parents. It was time to start living for me.

That afternoon, during my lunch break, I went to look at an apartment in a six-story walk-up. There was a bulb burned out overhead. It was dark and musty smelling. As the landlord and I headed down the hallway where the light was better, I saw that he was wearing a sleeveless undershirt with ribbing that widened over his gut. A heavy chain attached to his belt held about a dozen keys, and it took him two tries before he got the right one.

"This for you and your husband?" he asked as he threw open the door.

I should have expected this question. I'd already seen three other apartments, and each time the landlord had asked the same thing. "No. Just me." I dared to look inside. It was a dump. Less than seven hundred square feet, and every inch smelled of cat piss and the carpet had the urine stains to prove it.

"Just you, huh?" He grunted and, without blinking, told me the place had been rented.

"Then why did you bother showing it to me?"

"Listen," he said, "I'm not renting to you single girls, okay? Half the time you can't pay your rent, and I ain't got time to listen to your hard-luck stories."

"But I have a job." I never would have taken that apartment anyway, but now it was a matter of principle.

"I don't care if you have a job. You dames are nothing but trouble. You can't even change a lightbulb. I get calls every time the toilet won't flush 'cause you broads keep putting your damn pads in there and none of yous knows how to use a plunger. . . ."

I argued with him for a few more minutes before realizing it was futile. All the single girls I knew either lived at home or in crowded rooming houses for women. Except for M. She had her own apartment and it was nice. Far nicer than anything I could have afforded.

"How'd you do it?" I asked once while we were taking a coffee break.

"What do you mean?" M was waiting for the saccharin pellets to dissolve in her cup while leafing through a movie magazine.

"How did you get your landlord to rent your place to you? And how did you get the price down so you could afford it? All the landlords I've met with won't give me the time of day."

"Well, actually," she said, closing her magazine, "it's not in my name. My father rented it for me."

Well, that explained it.

My head was still spinning after I'd left the apartment building and boarded the el car. The train was full, and I was standing until a woman in shorts got up and I took her spot. The wicker seat had left the backs of her thighs looking waffled.

When I got to my stop and stepped out of the train, I spotted a familiar face on the platform. Scott Trevor. *Well, my oh my.* There was a nice symmetry about it, seeing as we'd met on the el some four years earlier.

Scott had been studying business law at Northwestern when I was a freshman at Medill. He lived in Evanston but had night classes at the downtown campus. I lived in the city but had classes up at Evanston, so we commuted into the city together in the evenings. If we had time, we'd grab a beer.

He was wearing a suit and tie now. A far cry from the law student I used to see leaning against the platform wall, striking a James Dean pose. I could still picture him with the heel of his shoe butted up against the brick and his thumbs tucked inside his blue jeans pockets. He used to notice me, too, saddle-shoed, Peter Pan collared and bobby socked, clutching my book bag. I don't remember who spoke to whom first or how we started sitting together on the el, but during his last year of law school, that's what we did.

Scott looked up and came rushing over as soon as he saw me, the two of us embracing on the platform like reunited lovers in a movie. But we were not lovers, only friends. There was a time when I'd desperately wanted him to ask me out, but he'd had a steady girlfriend. And if there's one thing I learned about Scott Trevor, it was that he was a stand-up guy. He never would have cheated on his girl. It was just one more thing you had to love about the guy.

We stood at the base of the stairwell and continued talking.

Once again I noticed that I had newsprint smeared down the side of my tunic dress. Scott noticed it, too.

"Ink," I said, trying to rub the stains away. "It's an occupational hazard. I'm at the *Tribune* now."

"The *Tribune*, huh? Well, good for you. Looks like your journalism classes paid off. How do you like being a reporter?"

I laughed. "I don't feel like much of a reporter. They've got me on the society pages, and once in a while when I'm *lucky*, they let me do something for the features department. Lots of weddings and fashion shows, cook-offs and home-decorating tips. The one time I actually had a real story, they gave my byline away."

"Give it time," Scott said. "You'll make your mark."

I smiled. Eliot would have said something like that. I looked into his eyes, and my heart lifted in my chest. I felt light inside. God, it was good to see him.

Scott glanced at his wristwatch. "Listen, I have to be in court at three, but I have time for a quick cup of coffee if you do."

We went to Jimmy's just a few doors down, tucked under the el. Even inside you could hear the trains roaring overhead. We sat in a corner booth beneath the Coca-Cola clock that chimed a little "Refreshing" chorus on the quarter hour. I glanced at Scott, thinking he was still as handsome as I'd remembered, one of those chiseled types with a strong chin and a genuine smile. He wore his dark brown hair brushed back off his forehead in a high quiff. I noticed he didn't have a wedding band, but he wasted no time telling me about his girlfriend, Connie. I smiled extra wide, hoping to mask my disappointment.

"She's a secretary," he said. "We work together in the state's attorney's office."

"Oh, really." I gave an approving nod. "You did it."

"Yep. I'm an assistant state's attorney now."

"You always said you wanted to do that. So, tell me, are you putting all the bad guys away?"

"Hardly." He pulled a pack of Chesterfields from his pocket and offered me one. "Not that I haven't tried." He lit our cigarettes and dropped the match in an ashtray that said, *This was stolen from Jimmy's.* "Maybe I was a fool, thinking I could make a difference. I've been in and out of so many courts, prosecuting everyone from prostitutes to drunk drivers to murderers. I should have won. They were open-and-shut cases. I should have put the defendants away for years, but instead they ended up walking. After that happens enough times, you start thinking you're an incompetent lawyer."

I propped my elbow on the table, my chin resting on my knuckles. "I can't imagine *you* being incompetent at anything."

"I got so discouraged I thought about quitting." He pinched the cigarette filter between his fingers before taking another drag.

"Really? You were going to quit?"

"Thought about it." He nodded. "I felt like a failure—like I wasn't cut out for this kind of work. Eventually though I started to wise up. I realized that something fishy was going on."

"Fishy?" My reporter's ears perked up.

"I know it sounds crazy, but I have reason to believe that the defense lawyers are paying off the judges. They're on the take. That's why their clients are getting off."

"Wow—that's huge. Are you sure?"

He nodded.

I leaned forward, not wanting to miss anything. "What can you do to stop it?"

"Apparently nothing. I've moaned and bitched about it, and

all they do is move me to another court system, where the same damn thing happens. If there's one thing I hate, it's a corrupt lawyer, and I feel like this city is crawling with them."

I couldn't help but smile. Everything inside me had come alive. Adrenaline pumped through me, and I was already composing the lede inside my head: *Several Cook County lawyers and judges come under scrutiny for allegedly taking bribes. . . .*

I leaned forward even further and lowered my voice. "Would you be willing to go on the record with that?"

"Whoa, Jordan," he said with a laugh. "I'm talking friend to friend here. That's all this is. I'm just venting."

"I know, but you have a story that needs to be told."

"Maybe. Maybe someday. But not now. Besides, I've got no real proof. It'd be my word against theirs."

I stubbed out my cigarette. "Okay, but let's just say I wanted to do a piece on this—on the corruption inside the Cook County courts. Would you be willing to give me a quote?"

He shook his head more emphatically this time. "No way. You can't use my name."

"Okay, okay."

"Jordan?" He gave me a searching look.

I held up my hands. "I won't. I promise." I thought for a moment, my mind still racing. "What about an anonymous quote?"

"You know damn well that no paper would run a story like this with nothing more than an anonymous quote."

"I know. I know. It's just that I need a story. A *real* story." I was getting desperate.

The desperation stayed with me. All I wanted was to get closer to the action. I had some free time the next morning, so I took myself down to City Hall, flashed my credentials and

entered a packed conference room where Mayor Daley was holding a press conference.

I was there strictly as an observer and hid out in the very last
row, one of the only women in the room. The reporters from the
radio stations were all clustered together with the fellows from
the AP and UPI. Men from the other papers were scattered
throughout the room. I recognized Walter in the second row and
saw the pipe protruding from his mouth each time he turned
profile.

Daley took to the podium and began talking about the city's
plans to crack down on slumlords. "Our citizens can rest assured
that their homes will be properly heated with working toilets
and plumbing. . . . We won't stand up for their negligent standard complaints. . . ."

Everyone exchanged puzzled looks while Daley kept blather-
ing. No one had any idea what he was talking about. But this was
typical of a Daley speech. Walter was always coming back from
press conferences laughing over some blunder the mayor delivered, his favorites being "Alcoholics Unanimous" and "We shall
reach greater and greater platitudes of achievement."

For someone who supposedly hated members of the press,
Daley certainly did spend a good deal of time with them. And
for someone who was so challenged by the English language, he
seemed to love to get up in front of a roomful of reporters who
were there to capture his every flub.

A political writer from the *Daily News* stood up and challenged the mayor, asking what kind of scrutiny would be practiced in order to ensure compliance.

"Scrutiny?" Daley took offense. His face went bloodred, and I
half expected to see steam rising from his ears. "What else do you
want? Do you want to take my shorts? Give me a break. How
much scrutiny do you want to have? You go scrutinize yourself!

I get scrootened every day, don't worry, from each and every one of you. . . ."

When the press conference ended several reporters approached Earl Bush, Daley's press secretary, for clarification on several of the mayor's statements. I was standing right there when I heard Bush say, "Don't print what he said. Print what he meant."

Chapter 11

◆ ◆ ◆

The following Friday afternoon the guys in the city room were clowning around, ganging up on Peter. Someone hid his eyeshade and he had worked himself into a state trying to find it.

I was on deadline for a fashion feature on self-belted Bermuda shorts. And this was one of the more exciting assignments I'd been given lately. I had ten column inches for this piece, a lot of space to fill with seersucker versus linen, plaid versus solid.

I was trying to focus when Randy started singing *"See the USA / In your Chevrolet. . . ."* Meanwhile, Walter and Henry were passing around the new issue of *Playboy* and debating who had the better centerfold, Jayne Mansfield or Bettie Page.

"But did you see the jugs on Mansfield?" said Walter, banging his pipe against the ashtray. "I'd take a sultry blonde with a pair of jugs like that over a brunette any day."

"Oh, I don't know." Henry laughed and whistled through his teeth. "I wouldn't kick Bettie Page out of bed. She's got a sweet pair. . . ."

"Guys—" I looked up, exasperated. "Do you mind saving the locker-room talk for later?"

"What's the matter, Walsh?" said Walter as he fired up his pipe. "Are we offending your delicate sensibilities?"

"Oh, fuck off, you asshole."

"Whoa!" Henry laughed. "She told you."

The fellows were still giving me a hard time when Mrs. Angelo interrupted, calling me over to the features desk by waving a piece of copy above her head.

"Come here, kid. What's this piece all about?" She held up the copy for me to see. "The first human trials for a female contraceptive?"

"It's an article about Margaret Sanger and—"

"Yes, I can see that." Mrs. Angelo pursed her lips. "Mr. Pearson said you submitted it to him earlier this morning."

"I was—"

"Why would you take it upon yourself to write an article like that without discussing it with me first? Or Mr. Pearson, for that matter."

"Because I knew you probably wouldn't have let me write it."

"And you would have been correct." She fisted up the copy in her hand and pitched it in the wastebasket. "From now on stick to the assignments you're given. Understood?"

"But this is important. We're on the verge of a major breakthrough for women."

"Uh-huh . . ." She left her desk with me trailing behind her down the center aisle.

"And I bet most women don't even know that this is possible."

She spun around. "I'm only going to say this to you once more—I appreciate what you're trying to do. I get it. I do. But you're paid to write about subjects that you're assigned to, and right now that's taffeta and calla lilies. Not contraception, kid."

Henry, Walter and the others laughed while Mrs. Angelo reprimanded me.

"Hey, Walsh," said Walter with a snort as I made my way back to my desk, "how's that calla lily exposé coming along?"

"Why don't you take your little *Playboy* into the men's room and do something useful with yourself."

"Whoa!" Henry pounded his fist against the desk and laughed along with Benny, Randy and the rest of them. Even though I was disappointed that Mrs. Angelo killed my article, I joined in, knowing that the guys got a kick out of me. They weren't used to working with a woman who could take her share of razzing and dish it back.

I glanced up at the row of clocks over the horseshoe. It was half past four and I was beat. It had been a long week. I was putting the cover over my typewriter when M came up to my desk. Her butterfly-rimmed sunglasses were propped on her nose, and her Kelly bag, which must have cost a small fortune, was hanging off her forearm just above her charm bracelet. She looked very Marilyn-like.

"Come on," she said. "I think you and I could use a cocktail."

We headed over to Riccardo's, a bar near the *Tribune*, tucked away behind the Wrigley Building, down the stairs on Rush Street. Riccardo's was a legendary watering hole. From as far back as my father's day, it was where the newspapermen went for lunch and for drinks after work. A lot of advertising types went there, too, which made for an interesting dynamic because everyone knew that the copywriters made more money than the reporters but that the reporters were better writers and worked harder. So the ad guys stayed on one side of the bar and the reporters on the other.

I remember my father telling my brother and me stories about Riccardo's back in the days of Prohibition, when it was a speakeasy. He and Ben Hecht used to sit at the back table and

have their martinis and shoot the bull. When Eliot started working at the *Sun-Times*, he and his buddies went to Riccardo's, too.
It was a journalistic rite of passage.

Now it was my turn to join the newspaper drinking tradition,
only I was a woman and my male coworkers didn't see me as a real
reporter. I'd been working alongside them for the past two months
and they knew damn well that I was tougher than the typical sob
sister. They knew I'd been around a city room all my life. But still,
I was a girl, assigned to society news and therefore relegated to a
table with the other female journalists while the guys sat at the
bar, backs turned as if they hardly knew us.

M, Gabby and the others paid them no mind. They were
engrossed in their own conversations, talking about plans for the
weekend. We were sitting with Eppie Lederer and some other
girls from the *Sun-Times*.

Eppie wrote an advice column. Millions of women read her
faithfully, but when it came to us, her friends, she rarely offered
an opinion. You'd ask her about a specific concern—maybe you
were having problems with your fellow or you were in a jam at
work—and she'd look at you and say, "How the hell would I
know what you should do?"

"Because you're Ann Landers!"

"Only on paper."

Mr. Ellsworth and Mr. Copeland came inside and brushed
past us on their way to the bar. M excused herself, and on her
way to the ladies' room, she got detoured. I watched as she stood
before the men at the bar, hip jutting out, laughing, basking in
their attention.

No sooner had she returned to our table and placed a cigarette in her mouth than one of the ad guys swooped in from
across the room and offered her a light. She thanked him with a
long, luxurious exhale and a smile. He snapped his Zippo shut

and stood there, waiting for an invitation to join her, but she dismissed him with another cool exhale.

It was going on seven o'clock and Eppie, Gabby—who rarely stayed for more than one drink—and the other girls had already left. I was about to go myself when M asked me to stay for one more.

"Please? Just one."

She seemed lonely, and I was surprised that a beautiful woman like her wouldn't have had a date on a Friday night. Certainly enough men at Riccardo's would have loved to take her out. I sat back down and ordered another vodka tonic.

"So what are you doing this weekend?" she asked.

"I have to go interview an anthropologist down at the University of Chicago for a story I'm working on."

"You never stop. You really love this business, don't you?" M said, giving her drink a swirl.

"Don't you?"

"Nah, not like you. I've been at the *Tribune* for five years— that's four and half years longer than I expected. I started out as a copygirl, and that's only because Mrs. Angelo took pity on me. She was standing behind me one day at Logan's Luncheonette and I came up ten cents short on my check. She gave me a dime and a job. I had just moved here from Milwaukee after my father died. I was lost without him. I couldn't stay back home with my mother. She was insane. When I was little she used to chase me around the house with a broom, swatting me with it. My father was the only one who could keep her in line. He protected me from her, and once he was gone, I had to leave too. So I came to Chicago—didn't know anyone. I was flat broke when I met Mrs. Angelo. . . ."

M continued talking, but I was stuck on *after my father died*. Hadn't she told me that her father was the one who'd rented her apartment for her?

". . . I never thought I'd become a journalist," M was saying. "Never wanted to be one. I really thought I'd be married and raising a family by now." She smiled with a certain sadness in her gaze.

I wanted to say something about her apartment but Mr. Ellsworth and Mr. Copeland stopped at our table.

"Good night, ladies," said Mr. Ellsworth with a tip of his fedora.

"See you Monday morning," said Mr. Copeland.

"My goodness," I said as they walked away. "They actually acknowledged us. Do you believe it?"

"Aw, the two of them are okay." M watched as they left, her eyes trained on the door long after they'd gone.

Before I could steer the conversation back to her apartment, M excused herself to talk to a table of cigar-smoking men from Leo Burnett and I found myself sitting alone. A few seats opened up at the bar, so I dared to join Walter, Henry, Benny, Peter and Randy, saddling up beside them. They gave me an amused nod, as if to say, *Isn't she cute*, and went back to their conversation.

At one point Walter turned to me and said, "You really want to be one of the boys—don't you, Walsh? How about doing a shot with us?"

The others leaned in, watching me, expecting me to refuse.

"Sure," I said. "Why not?"

Walter snickered as he packed tobacco into his pipe, tamping it down. "Johnny," he called over to the bartender. "A round of Canadian Club over here." Walter struck a matchstick and set his bowl flaming before extinguishing the blue tip with a shake of his wrist.

The bartender poured six shot glasses of whiskey and dealt them out like a hand of cards. The others laughed, thinking I'd pack up my handbag and head home. But this was my moment to prove that I was as tough as any of them. I picked up my shot, clanked my glass against theirs, and with my eyes locked onto

Walter's, I threw it back. The heat spread through my chest while the vapors rose up to my sinuses. I felt the burn of the whiskey behind my eyes. The others watched me, waiting, expecting me to cough, to wince, to grimace. Instead, I slammed my empty glass on the bar and said, "Johnny, set 'em up again."

"Holy Christ," said Henry.

There was a burst of laughter.

"*Ehhhx*-cellent," said Peter.

"Now you're talking." Randy scooted up closer to the bar.

"I'm serious," I said, still looking at Walter. "Set 'em up."

There was a round of howls as they clapped, and Henry signaled to the bartender for the bottle. We all held up our next shot, did a toast and knocked them back. The second shot went down easier. I had just set my glass down and barely gotten a cigarette lit before Benny called for a third round.

We took our time with that one. I got lost in clouds of cigarette smoke. The jukebox was stuck on *Mr. Sandman*, playing it over and over again. I had no idea who ordered the next round, but before I knew it, half the men at the bar had gathered around us, eager to see if the little lady could keep up. Apparently the gauntlet had been thrown.

I became vaguely aware of a man, about my age, standing behind me. He leaned over and touched my shoulder. "Are you okay?" he asked.

I nodded.

"You don't have to do this," he whispered.

"Oh, yes, I do." I turned and looked into his eyes, blue-green and drooping slightly at the outer corners.

I was woozy and could tell that the shots were getting to the fellows, too. They eyed me, trying to see if I was weakening, getting ready to cave.

"Another round," I said. "On me."

Onlookers banged on the bar top, making their drinks jump while chanting, "Go, go, go. . . ." I could feel the whiskey churning in my stomach. I didn't think it was possible to down another shot, but I had to. If I couldn't keep up with them, they'd never let me live it down. So I drew a deep breath and took the next shot. When I turned the glass over, the others cheered, applauding.

I was prepared to have another go at it when Walter stood up, peeled off a few bills from his money clip and said, "It's getting late."

"Aw, c'mon," said Benny, swaying on his stool. "One more."

Walter didn't take his eyes off me. I couldn't tell if he was impressed or insulted. "I've got dinner waiting at home." He dropped his money onto the bar and left without so much as a good-bye.

Henry and Peter followed shortly after, and the crowd began to disperse. I stayed at the bar, trying to get my bearings, and the guy who'd been standing behind me earlier ended up on the stool next to me. He reached into his pocket and pulled out a fistful of papers, one of which dropped to the floor. Amazingly, despite being drunk, I managed to bend down and retrieve it.

"Here you go." I handed it back to him. It was covered in scribbles, front and back. "You dropped this."

He thanked me, deliberately letting his fingertips brush against mine. He caught my eye and smiled, exposing two imperfect front teeth, both slightly turned inward. Maybe it was the whiskey shots, but I found him more attractive than he had been just moments before. He sorted through the napkins and scraps of paper, lining them up on the bar. When he drew a heavy sigh, I looked over again. There was something about him, the sort of thing that snuck up on you. He was not the kind of man you looked twice at, and yet I did. I did look twice, because he'd put his hand on my shoulder while I was doing shots and because he had sighed again. Louder this time.

"Something wrong?" I asked.

He held up a scrap of paper. "I can't read my own damn handwriting. Is that an *f* or a *t*?"

I tilted my head and scanned his scribbles. It didn't look like either one to me. "I don't know. But you spelled gubernatorial wrong. It's with an *e*, not an *a*." I pointed out his error.

He looked over at me and flashed his imperfect smile. "How can you spell after you just drank those guys under the table?"

"Aw, years of practice." I grinned and propped my chin on the heel of my hand.

Benny came over and tapped me on the shoulder. "Want me to walk you home?"

I glanced back at the man next to me. "Nah, I think I'll stick around for a little while."

Benny looked at the man and stepped in between us, leaning forward to whisper in my ear, "You've had a lot to drink. You should really let me take you home."

I smiled and patted Benny's boyish, freckled face. "Don't you worry. I'm a big girl."

Benny nodded and reluctantly went back to his seat.

"He's mighty protective of you."

"Oh, that's just Benny."

"I think he has a little crush on you."

"No. You think?" I glanced back at Benny, who was still looking my way, a hopeful smile surfacing on his face.

"He's got good taste," said the man. "You're the prettiest woman in this bar."

I laughed. "Even prettier than ol' Marilyn over there?" I gestured over at M.

"Is that who she's supposed to be? I've seen her in here before and I've always wondered."

"Watch it. She's my coworker. And my friend."

He laughed and squinted at me, as if trying to size me up. "Who exactly are you anyway?"

"Jordan Walsh."

"I'm Jack. Jack Casey." He held out his hand. "I'm with the *Sun-Times*."

"I'm over at the *Tribune*."

"What do you do there, Jordan Walsh?"

"I write for society news. And do a few features. And you can stop right there," I said, holding up my hand. "It's temporary. I'm going to get on the city desk if it's the last thing I do."

"Well, then, here's to the city desk." He raised his glass to me.

About forty-five minutes later M left with one of the Leo Burnett guys, and Peter, Randy and Benny left, too. Though Benny did make one last plea to see me home.

Jack reached over for a lock of my hair, rolling the strands between his thumb and index finger. "I'm starving," he said. "Are you starving?"

"Food?" I smiled. That was all I could do.

I don't remember much after that other than walking out of Riccardo's with Jack helping me up the stairwell. We ended up at a greasy joint at State and Lake, where we had burgers and ate french fries off each other's plates. He fed coins into the jukebox, and we listened to the music he selected: *Rock Around the Clock, Maybelline, Blue Velvet.* As we lingered over coffee I began to sober up.

Jack was a talkative guy and volunteered all kinds of information about himself. He was raised in a strict Irish-Catholic family. His father was a judge. His mother took care of his five younger brothers.

"Six children?" I couldn't imagine. "That's a big family."

"And that's not counting the cousins and aunts and uncles. My father had six brothers and sisters and my mom had seven.

Relatives are always dropping by my parents' house. You never know who's going to turn up for dinner."

"And your mother's okay with that?"

"Are you kidding me? She loves it. You should see her around the holidays. My folks will have fifty or sixty people over for Thanksgiving and Christmas."

I set my coffee cup down. I was jealous. Or maybe it was more a sense of longing I was feeling. The last time we celebrated a holiday with my relatives was before Eliot was killed. Not surprising that my grandfather had a problem with our Christmas tree. You can see the scowl running across his face in the pictures we took that year. He and my father sat at opposite ends of the table, arguing about the nuclear bomb tests in Nevada. They were both opposed to the testing but still they had managed to turn it into an argument. That was two years ago, and now my parents didn't even bother with the holidays. We tried the first year. My grandparents arrived from New York and left the next day after a blowup with my father. In the meantime my mother had brought out the menorah that we never lit and my father had hauled a tree home that we never trimmed. I remember it stood untouched in the corner, bound in twine, slumped up against the wall, its pine needles dropping to the floor until we threw it out sometime in January.

"And what about you?" Jack asked. "What about your family? You're Irish-Catholic, too."

I didn't want to get into religion with him. I dragged a cold fry through a pool of ketchup, stalling. "My parents are both writers," I said.

"Really?" I could tell he was impressed.

I nodded. "My mother's a poet. My father's a novelist."

"Would I know their work? What are their names?"

When I told him, his eyes went wide. "Hank Walsh? The reporter?"

"Yep."

"That's your father? I didn't know he was a novelist."

"He's working on a new book now."

"And your mother is CeeCee Walsh? I can't believe it. I used to date a girl who was obsessed with her poetry. She wanted to study with your mother at Columbia College but then she stopped teaching. She must be a fascinating woman."

"She's definitely not your typical mother type."

"I'll bet. And what about brothers? Sisters?"

I shook my head. "No." It was true. I had no brothers or sisters, so I wasn't lying. I just couldn't bring myself to tell him about Eliot. Jack must have been new at the *Sun-Times*. Otherwise he would have made the connection and figured out that Eliot was my brother. And if I told him that Eliot was dead, he'd have questions that I wasn't up to answering. No, a dead brother didn't make for good first-date conversation. That was, if this was even a date that we were on.

"I'm not ready to go home yet," I said after he paid the bill. "We should go dancing."

"Dancing?"

"Oh, c'mon. It's early."

"It's not early. It's late." He glanced at his wristwatch and turned it my way. "It's after midnight."

"It's a Friday night. Just one dance. Please?"

He looked at me with those eyes and I knew I had him. I could have told him I wanted to go canoeing and he would have said yes.

Half an hour later we were uptown at the Aragon Ballroom. GORDON JENKINS & HIS ORCHESTRA was on the marquee, and people lined the sidewalks of Lawrence Avenue and Broadway. It was a perfect summer evening with just enough of a breeze to keep it comfortable. Everyone was dressed for a night on the town, the younger girls in poodle skirts and the older ones in halter-style cocktail dresses that flared at their hips. The fellas wore their best drainpipe trousers and winklepickers. Despite the heat, a few of them were doing their best Brando, wearing rolled blue jeans and leather jackets that would most likely get them turned away at the door.

I loved the Aragon. Walking into the ballroom was like stepping into an elegant city with a sparkling starlit sky on the ceiling. Couples twirled to the big-band sounds, and when they began to play *My Foolish Heart*, Jack reached out his hand.

"This is our song."

"Is it?" I placed my hand in his. "I didn't know we had a song."

"Well, we do now."

He pulled me onto the dance floor, and he smelled of cigarettes and Vitalis. It had been a long time since I'd been held, and I'd forgotten how much the body needs to be touched. I liked the feel of his shoulders, strong and sturdy. When he drew me close, I dared to rest my head on his collarbone.

And that was how it started.

Chapter 12

◆ ◆ ◆

We'd been seeing each other only a few weeks, but by the end of July I knew Jack Casey was the kind of guy I could get serious with. And that terrified me. I was fighting it even as I kissed him. Even as I ran my fingers through his hair and along the muscles in his back, I pushed against the feelings welling up inside. I wasn't ready. He'd come along too soon, or at the wrong time—I wasn't sure which. And yet I couldn't resist him. I loved the way he laughed and how his smile was just off-center, with those imperfect front teeth, a flaw that somehow made him all the more handsome to me.

The other thing that frightened me about Jack was that I'd come to depend on him. The last male I'd depended on had been my brother, and when he died, I was lost. Helpless. It took nearly a year for me to figure out how to be on my own. If something happened to Jack, I wasn't sure I could endure that lesson again.

But still I didn't want to let him go, because the truth was he made life better for me. Easier, too. It was the silliest things that melted my heart. Like how he drove me places and carried bags, or pulled out chairs and opened doors. He stroked my hair in a way that no one else ever had and liked to tuck a strand behind my ear. And he listened. He listened when I complained about the guys in the city room and commiserated with me when it was needed. It was even Jack who found me an apartment. A friend of a friend knew someone who was moving out of a cheap, safe building in Lincoln Park. It was a walk-up above a Polish bakery on Clark Street. Nothing fancy, but it was mine.

My mother came with me the day I signed the lease, and by the time she made it to the third-floor landing, she was panting. "No elevator, huh?" She wrinkled her nose at the yeast smells wafting up from the bakery. The neighbor across the way had a baby carriage parked outside the door. I noticed a couple cans of Campbell's soup tucked inside, resting on a pink blanket.

My apartment was small but cheery with a stream of sunlight coming in from the windows. The wallpaper in the bedroom had been hung upside down, the flowers and butterflies all pointing toward the floor, but I didn't care. My mother noticed that the hot and cold knobs in the bathroom were reversed and that the tub was on a slant going the wrong way.

"The water won't drain out."

"So I'll get a squeegee."

"You're going to squeegee your tub?" She smiled and went back into the kitchen. "Oh, the things the young will do to get away from their parents."

"I'm not trying to get away from you," I said.

My mother opened one of the cupboards and looked at the empty shelves. "Of course you are, but I'm glad. I think it's good for you. You have a boyfriend now, and you're entitled to your privacy. Not that you and Jack couldn't do whatever you wanted to back at the house. You know me. I wouldn't object. You're a grown woman, after all."

"So you're really okay with me moving out? I thought you'd try to fight me on it."

"Nah. Not me." She closed the cupboard and leaned against the counter. "I remember I wanted to get my own place down in the Village, but Grandpa wouldn't let me. He was afraid I'd get myself into all kinds of trouble. And that was before I'd even met your father. No, I'm all for you moving out. Not that I won't miss you. Heaven knows I will miss you dearly. I don't know what your father and I will do in that big house without you."

"I doubt Dad will even notice that I'm gone."

"Don't say that. Why would you say a thing like that?"

"Because it's true. He hardly ever talks to me."

"You know how your father is. He's not a talker. Not even with me."

"He used to be. Before Eliot died we used to talk all the time. About everything." I hadn't planned on going down this path, but now that I'd taken the first step, I kept on. "We used to be so close, and now—now he just hides in his office and ignores me."

My mother pushed away from the counter and went into the main room. "You know what I was thinking?" she said, keeping her back toward me. "Remember that table down in the basement? The one with the glass top? That would be just perfect right over here. What do you think?"

"I don't want to talk about a table."

She looked at me from over her shoulder, her eyes narrow and turning glassy. "You won't change him. He's been broken, don't you know that?"

I did know that. I knew it because I had been broken, too. We all had.

That conversation with my mother stayed with me throughout the day and infuriated me. It wasn't that I was angry with her or even with my father. I didn't know the person I was mad at, because he was a faceless coward who had never come forward. But out there somewhere was a stranger who had taken my brother from my parents and my parents from me.

That night I lay in bed, trying to imagine this villain. What did he look like? How old or young was he? Had I ever passed him on the street? What was he doing right at that very moment? Had he ever confessed to anyone? Did he have nightmares like I did? I hoped that he was rotting from the inside out, his guilt eating him alive.

About a week later, on a drizzly summer day, Jack helped me pack up the last of my things, including the Emerson television set that I'd saved up for. It was too heavy for me to lift, so I waited for Jack to move it. The two of us took turns carrying the other boxes to his car parked out front at the curb.

I'd just dropped off a carton of books and was coming up the front steps for the next load when I heard my father say, "What are you doing with that?"

Jack was on the porch, backing out the front door. At my father's words, he stopped, his shoulders up, frozen in place. I knew what he was holding.

"It's okay, Dad," I said, coming onto the front porch. "I'm taking that with me."

"The typewriter? What do you need with the typewriter?" My father had a drink in his hand. Bourbon. I could smell it from across the porch, lingering in the damp open air. "You already have a typewriter."

"Not an electric one. And he always said I could have it."

"What else have you picked through and taken?"

I held my tongue, reminding myself that he'd been drinking and that it was best to let it go. I brushed past him, about to head back inside for the next load, but he grabbed my arm.

"I asked you a question. What else have you taken? Like a little thief, you go in snooping around and taking things that aren't yours. Never were yours."

I twisted out of his grip. "Go ahead, take it out on me. Call me whatever names you want. It's not going to change anything. It's not going to bring him back."

My father raised his hands, shook his head and turned his back to me.

"Sure—that's right, walk away. You know, it happened to all of us. Not just to you."

My father turned back around, his eyes focused on me for the first time. "You want to move out—so hurry up already and move out. But you leave that goddamn typewriter here." My father went back inside the house and slammed the front door.

I wanted to run after him, but my feet wouldn't move. Didn't he know how hard I was trying? Didn't he know that I was exhausted and scared and that he was part of the reason why I pushed myself like I did? Didn't he understand me at all?

Jack was still holding the typewriter, a bewildered look on his face. "So is this going with us or what?"

"No." I shook my head and told him to take the typewriter back upstairs to the spare bedroom. I no longer wanted it.

"So what was all that about with your dad?" Jack asked, as we carried the last two boxes out to the car. It had started to rain harder, and the sidewalk was slick and shiny with plastered leaves that had fallen. We were dripping all over the place as he put the car in gear and we eased away from the curb.

I lit a cigarette and cracked the little triangular vent window.

"Well?" He turned and looked at me. "What just happened

there?" We were stopped at a red light. The radio was playing *Ain't That a Shame*. I drew down hard on my cigarette. He turned and looked at me.

"It's about my brother, okay?" There. I'd said it. It was out in the open.

"I didn't know you had a brother. How come you've never mentioned him before?" The light changed. The car behind us honked. "Jordan? How come you never told me about him?"

The air inside the car shifted. The windshield fogged up. "He's dead. He died. He was killed." I took a final drag off my cigarette and shoved it out the window.

Jack pulled over to the side of the road and turned to look at me. "I'm so sorry. I had no idea. Why didn't you tell me?"

"I couldn't."

"What do you mean, you couldn't? What happened to him? How'd he die? My God, I don't even know his name."

"It's Eliot. It *was* Eliot."

"And how did he die?"

I looked out the fogged-up window and reached for another cigarette.

"Jordan, tell me."

"I can't—I can't go into it right now."

He smacked the top of the steering wheel. "Jesus, when are you going to let me in? When are you going to trust me?"

"This has nothing to do with you. This isn't about not trusting you. This is about me. About my family."

We both went silent. Jack pulled back into traffic and the only sound was that of the tires rolling over the wet pavement. I was watching the raindrops collecting on the windshield when I finally spoke. "It was a hit-and-run, okay?"

"Jesus. Jordan, I'm sorry. Did they catch the guy?"

"No."

"Jesus," he said again.

My vision blurred as I watched the wipers clear away the rain, wanting them to clear away the past, too.

"I wish you would have told me about your brother. How could you keep something like that inside and not tell me?"

"Because, goddammit, I come from a family where we don't talk about it." I hadn't meant to snap at him, but I couldn't help it, and I couldn't keep from doing it again. "Don't you get it? We don't talk about him." I was glaring at him, fighting to choke back the tears. "My mother was a poet before Eliot died and now she won't write because she's afraid of what's going to come out. And my father—*all* he does is write. But neither one of them—*none of us*—talk about it."

After Jack and I arrived at my new place, at least the two of us had started talking again. And the rain had stopped, but it was muggy inside and out. Opening windows did little to circulate the moist air, and I couldn't remember where I'd packed the fan.

Together we emptied out the car and Jack helped me sort through boxes, hang pictures and rearrange the bed and dresser so there was room to open the closet door. When we finally got the furniture in position, it was late, and we took a break, moved out to the living room and opened a bottle of wine. I settled in on the couch while he plugged in the television set and adjusted the rabbit ears so we could watch Steve Allen.

"Not a bad picture," he said, coming back to the couch.

I glanced over at him. The blue light coming off the TV danced across his cheek and forehead. His skin looked smooth, his jaw square and strong. I found him especially handsome that night. I studied his profile, gazing into the dark tunnel of his eardrum, wondering what was going on inside that head of his. He must have sensed my staring, because he turned and faced me, locking eyes with me.

"What?" I brought my fingers to my mouth.

He smiled and reached over to tuck a strand of hair behind my ear. "I know it hasn't been that long, but, well, I've never known a girl like you before. You're different from the other women."

"Different? How so?"

"C'mon, don't you know?"

I shook my head. I honestly didn't.

"You're strong. And smart. And you're beautiful. And, selfishly, I think you're good for me."

I stared into my hands resting in my lap, fingers tangled together. Though I loved hearing every word, his confession made me uncomfortable. I wasn't used to anyone, let alone a man, being so effusive. I didn't know how to respond, so I didn't.

"You don't have to say anything. But I want you to know that I think I'm falling for you."

My eyes stayed fixed upon my hands. I couldn't look him in the eye. I was stunned.

"No," he said, catching himself. "I don't think I am. I *know* I am. I love you, Jordan. I do."

I finally gazed at him and he gave me that imperfect smile. I wanted to say, *I love you, too,* but the words wouldn't come. Here was a man who listened to me, who put me in the center of his universe, who made me the priority of his days. I couldn't remember the last time anyone had made me feel so special. He filled me with raw emotion that rushed to the surface, pushing, pushing, pushing, wanting to get out. And if I did let these feelings out, what then? Would he leave me? Would he go and die on me?

Would he take his love away? It frightened me that a man I'd known for only two months had twisted up my thoughts like this. When I wasn't looking, he had come into my world and stirred things up. I stared into his eyes, wanting to tell him all this, but all I could do was lean forward and kiss him while the *I love you, too*s piled up inside my head.

We didn't speak about love again that night, but about a week later, on a balmy July evening, Jack came by my place with a bouquet of roses. I was touched by the gesture, but I was ever practical, and as I arranged them in a vase, all I could think was that in a few days the water would turn and start to stink. Jack was the romantic, not me. But he was also a handyman, and he changed a lightbulb that had burned out in my closet. Instead of replacing it, I'd worked around the problem, learning by touch alone to find exactly what article of clothing I was looking for in the dark.

As I set the roses on the table I watched him reach into the refrigerator for a bottle of milk. He unscrewed the cap, smelled it, scrunched up his face and, without saying a word, poured it down the drain. The milk was spoiled, but the moment, it was sweet. I can't tell you what that did to me. Such a simple act. Some women might have been offended by it. But not me. Instead, an overwhelming feeling of being cared for bubbled up inside me.

"I love you," I said, going to his side, kissing him deeply on the mouth as I reached for his belt buckle.

"Whoa." He placed his hands on mine.

"It's all right," I told him. "I want to. I'm ready." I kissed him again, deeper, tugged on his belt, harder. I wanted to show him how much I cared. "Really, it's okay. I'm not a virgin."

He looked shocked. And disappointed. How could I explain

that that's what happens when your mother sends you to college with a fistful of rubbers and tells you to *go experience life.* "It's not like I was loose or anything," I said. "There was only one man. He was my—"

"Jesus, Jordan." He dragged his hands through his hair, stopping when they reached the top of his head, and blew out a deep breath. "Did he love you? Did he want to marry you?"

"Don't you want to know if *I* loved *him*?"

He released his hands and let them drop to his sides. "I don't know."

"Well, I did. I did love him. I wasn't *in* love with him and he wasn't *in* love with me. But in his own way, he loved me. So yes, in answer to your question, there was love there."

Jack shifted away from me and shook his head. "I can't—I don't want to hear any more about this."

I went silent and thought about the other man. He was older than me, nearly old enough to be my father. He was my journalism professor. It had started out innocently enough, with me staying behind after class to discuss his lecture or ask about something. That progressed to coffee, which progressed to drinks, which led to his apartment. I had no illusions about a mad love affair or a future we might have together. I knew exactly what I was getting myself into and that it would be over when I graduated.

He said I was very mature for my age, but that's what happens when you're forced to grow up on the spot. When your parents are so distraught that you have to deal with the police, when you end up making the funeral arrangements, choosing the casket and selecting the cemetery plot that wasn't supposed to be needed for another fifty or sixty years.

Jack leaned forward and brought his hands to his forehead. His cheeks were red and flushed. "I wish you hadn't told me."

"Would you rather I'd lied? Or lied by omission?" I reached over and stroked his face.

He stopped my hand with his. "I wanted you, you know."

"And what—now you don't?" I leaned back, exasperated. *Just tell him. Tell him you've never felt this way before. Tell him that the other man was nothing compared to him. Tell him that he's everything to you.* The words were right there inside my head, but I couldn't get them out. I made my living off of words, and now they failed me. All I could do was lean in and kiss him, pulling his body close to mine. "It's okay. It's okay." I kept saying that, pressing the words into his lips over and over again until he couldn't fight it anymore.

He was shy and anxious as we burrowed through each other's clothes, and before he would shed his boxers, he reached over and turned off the light. I knew he wasn't a virgin, but I could also tell that of the two of us, I was the more experienced one. To me this was something beautiful and natural, but even in the dark I could see the anguished look on Jack's face. It was as if he were doing something wrong and had to hurry and get it over with before he was caught.

"Open your eyes," I said. "Look at me."

He was breathing hard and fast. I could feel his heart pounding against my chest. His eyes were still closed.

"Relax," I said. "Slow down. We have all night." I cupped his face and kissed him slowly, softly, and guided him the rest of the way. I took the lead. "It's okay. This is all okay."

We moved awkwardly at first, him going one way and me the other, until we found a shared rhythm. Then we were together. Then it was good. I wrapped myself around him and held on. He opened his eyes and looked at me in wonder before he squeezed them shut and let himself go.

An hour later, as we lay naked on the bed, *The Star-Spangled Banner* began playing in the other room as the TV prepared for its nightly sign-off. While drifting to sleep, I thought about the evening and what had led up to our lovemaking. It was the milk that did it. In the weeks and months and years ahead, I would forever link a quart of milk gone bad with my falling in love with Jack Casey.

Chapter 13

• • •

It was hot. I was sweating badly. The condensation slid down my glass just as surely as the sweat trickled down the side of my face and the back of my neck. It was the end of August, the dog days of summer, and there wasn't a window in sight. The choking plumes of cigarette smoke didn't help.

Jack was with me that night, along with the gang from the *Tribune*. We were gathered at a couple of round tables near the front of the stage, the red tablecloths brushing across our thighs. It was a Monday night and most people were home watching *The George Burns and Gracie Allen Show* or *Caesar's Hour*. Not much of a crowd came out to hear an unknown performer.

All day long Randy had been singing *"Turtle Wax builds a hard shell finish . . ."* and now there he was standing before the microphone, crooning *Vaya con Dios* followed by *Rags to Riches*. Closing my eyes, I could have sworn I was listening to Desi Arnaz one minute, Tony Bennett the next. I never thought I'd use the word *charismatic* to describe Randy. Handsome, yes, but charismatic, no—and yet that's what came to mind when I saw him on that stage, gripping the microphone, running his fingers up and down the stand and making eyes at all the women.

Earlier in the week, when he'd invited us all to the Gin Club's Amateur Night on Rush Street, we razzed him pretty good. "What are you gonna do—serenade us with 'Brylcreem, a little dab'll do ya'?" Walter had run his fingers through Randy's hair, knocking the pencil lodged behind his ear to the ground. We all laughed then, but now we were watching Randy with our mouths hanging open. We had no idea.

"*Ehhhx*-cellent," said Peter, applauding full force.

"And to think I thought his only talent was drawing," said Henry.

"He's what you call a triple threat," said Benny, beaming as if he were in some way responsible for Randy's masterful performance.

"Aw, shut it." Walter reached for his fedora and swatted Benny on the head. "You don't know what you're talking about. A triple threat can sing, dance and act." He counted them off his fingers, one, two, three. "Gene Kelly—now, he's a triple threat."

I pressed my leg against Jack's beneath the table. That was my signal for him to bookmark this for a later discussion. After telling him stories about the people I worked with, I was glad to point to hard evidence, as if to say, *See? I told you.* He tangled his fingers in my hair and I leaned in closer, letting our shoulders touch. It gave my insides a flutter.

We all stuck around until the end of Randy's set. It was hot as an oven inside the club and we spilled onto the sidewalk, hoping for a break from the heat, but to no avail. Walter, Henry and the other fellows walked with their neckties loosened, shirtsleeves rolled up and suit coats draped over their shoulders. We passed by people standing in the doorways of buildings, trying to cool themselves, electric fans propped up on the windowsills. A blue Studebaker, honking like mad, cruised by slowly with six or so men leaning out the windows, whistling and calling, "Hey, sweetie." M expectantly looked over, smiling, but the men's heads were turned the other way, looking at the buxom redhead across the street. I saw the smile slip from M's face. Those boys were far too young for her, but she was bruised just the same.

As she raised her hand to hail a cab, Mr. Ellsworth called to her. "M"—he gestured with a nod—"I'll give you a lift home." He glanced at Benny, who was asking Jack and me to join him for a nightcap. "C'mon, Ben," said Mr. Ellsworth. "You too. I'll drop you on the way."

The others dispersed after that. It was ten thirty and we all had to get up for work the next morning. Jack walked me back to my place. He had hold of my hand, the moisture collecting between our palms, our fingers laced together, sweating. We walked like that in silence for half a block.

We stopped at a light and he turned to me. "I'm telling you that redheaded guy has a thing for you."

"Who? Benny?" My voice sounded surprised, though I supposed he was right. Benny was always stealing glances my way, inviting me to lunch, out for drinks. "Don't tell me you're worried about him."

Jack laughed. "Hardly." But he turned quiet again.

"Is everything okay?" I asked.

"Yeah, yeah." He nodded. "Just thinking about the O'Hare expansion piece. . . ." He'd been working on a feature about the airport and his editor had already made him rewrite it twice. As we neared my apartment he came right out and asked if I would read his story and give him my opinion.

"Of course." I loved it when he asked for my help.

While I keyed in, he reached into his back pocket for his story, folded into quarters.

The neighbor's baby stroller was in its usual spot, but the canned goods were gone, replaced with a hammer and a pipe wrench. I still hadn't met this mysterious neighbor of mine.

Once inside my apartment, Jack and I sat side by side on the couch. Resting the paper on my knees, I read, sensing his anxious eyes on me.

"Well?" He cocked his head to the side. "What do you think?"

I raised my index finger while I finished the last paragraph. It was a fine, solid piece of writing. I looked over and smiled. "It's good. Very good."

"You think so? Really?"

"Absolutely. My only suggestion would be to flip your second and third sentences. It gets the commissioner's name in faster and it's stronger."

He reached for the paper and scanned it, letting a deep line furrow along his brow. "But what about the whole 'expected delays'?"

"That can come right after."

He thought for a moment. "I don't see how that's any stronger than what I have now."

"Okay. Then keep it the way you have it."

"Don't get mad."

"I'm not getting mad. You asked me what I thought and I told you. You don't agree, so that's fine." I meant it as a simple statement, no hidden meanings at all, but still he questioned me.

"You're not jealous, are you?" he asked, folding the paper and tucking it back inside his pocket.

Jealous? I turned and looked at him. Honestly, until he'd said that, it hadn't occurred to me to be jealous. I knew my place in the pecking order. I'd spent half my day fact-checking a five-hundred-word piece on ten ways to tie a scarf. I wasn't happy about that, but I wasn't done yet. I wasn't rolling over. I was still chasing down stories wherever I could. And sometimes, when the guys were too busy, Mr. Ellsworth or Mr. Copeland would give me a shot at something meatier. Just earlier that day Mr. Pearson sent me down to City Hall to see what I could find out about some building code violations. I had even cornered Earl Bush, Daley's press secretary, in one of the corridors.

"Can you tell me what the mayor's thoughts are on all the criticism the city's getting for not enforcing the building codes?"

"No, I can't tell you." He had kept walking.

I jogged up beside him. "But don't you think people have a right to know?"

He had stopped and adjusted his eyeglasses, shooting me an unnerving look. "What you reporters need to get straight is that you and me—we're not on the same team. We're not buddies. I don't owe you a damn thing. And if the mayor don't want to talk about building codes or anything else, then don't come running to me thinking I'm gonna tell you something." He brushed past me, shaking his head as he disappeared down the hallway.

"Listen," Jack said, interrupting my thoughts. "I'd understand if you *were* jealous." He leaned over and kissed my neck, letting his hand slip down the front of my blouse.

I knew what was coming next. He was predictable in this department, and for someone who had initially resisted sex with me he was now the aggressor. He stood up and led me to the bedroom. There was only one tiny window in the corner, and it felt ten degrees hotter in there than the living room. He unbuttoned his shirt and hung it by its collar on the doorknob while I worked myself out of my skirt, unrolled my stockings and slipped under the covers. The top sheet was sticking to my damp skin even before he climbed in next to me. It was stifling, and all I could think was how I couldn't wait to sit in a cool tub as soon as we were done.

Chapter 14

◆ ◆ ◆

Thursday nights became bowling night. We formed a league that fall and took on rival newspapers and ad agencies in town. Once a week we'd go to the King Pin Lanes on Grand Avenue dressed in our blue *Chicago Tribune* bowling shirts. For a quarter we got a lane and for a dime we got shoes. There was a cocktail lounge in the corner with neon lights flickering, luring us in with flashing J&B signs and promises of ice-cold Schlitz. The jukebox never sat idle, and you'd see couples occasionally jitterbugging right there in an empty lane. The King Pin had recently switched from manual pinsetters to an automated system with mechanical claws that came down, grabbed the pins and set them back up for the next bowler. It was fascinating and a little eerie to watch.

The *Tribune* had two teams going. M and I were the only girls who bowled along with Walter, Henry, Peter, Randy, Higgs and Benny. Gabby sat back and nursed her one Manhattan of the evening and rooted us on. M probably should have sat out as well. She confessed that she was only there to meet men and was more concerned about not messing up her manicure than her score. In between rounds, she'd thrust out her hip, pull out a nail file and fix up any snags.

We were bowling against the *Sun-Times* that night. There was a new guy with them, a skinny chain-smoker who introduced himself as Mick, but I'd later heard the fellows calling him Mike and then just Royko. He wrote for the *O'Hare News* but was hoping to get a job with the City News Bureau. In the meantime, he was bowling for the other team.

I couldn't help noticing that my coworkers each had their own bowling styles. Walter never once removed his pipe, and you could see the way his jaw clenched down on the stem after he released the ball. Peter was a terrible bowler but had great form. He'd stand expertly holding his ball just below eye level, sizing up the lane, and when he was certain the moment was right, he'd make his approach, throwing the ball with a great flourish, his arm extended high above his head, his back foot raised a good two feet off the ground. It was the pose of a strike, despite knocking off only a pin or two. Henry had a solid command of the game and threw a respectable number of strikes and spares. Randy hummed his way down the lane, and afterward—whether he threw strike or a gutter—he'd burst into song, singing, *"It's Howdy Doody Time. . . ."* The first time he did it we all looked at Benny.

"What?" Benny looked at us, oblivious. He was the spitting image of that puppet.

Jack was showing off that night, getting cocky after his first throw nailed a strike. He did a little dance and gloated as he reached for his beer. The evening stretched on. It was a close game, and when Jack had a split on his next turn, he clasped his head in anguish and let out a string of *shits* and *goddammits*. I thought he was clowning at first. I'd never seen him take the game so seriously before, but suddenly the tension ratcheted up and each time the *Tribune* team landed another strike or a spare, Jack groaned or hissed. After a seven-ten split in the third game, Jack spun around. "Jesus Christ, did you see that? There's too much wax on our lane. The ball's not hooking right." He ended up clipping the tenpin, but still it was his turn that lost it for the *Sun-Times* with a final score of 1,863 to 1,865.

Jack was still questioning the conditions of the lane while the other players were shaking hands, slapping one another on their backs. Everyone was packing up their bowling bags and changing their shoes before heading to the lounge for a nightcap when Jack grabbed his coat and said he was leaving.

"What do you mean, you're leaving?" I stood up. "You're not even going to say good-bye to me?"

"I'll call you tomorrow," he muttered, and turned away.

"Oh, c'mon, man," Royko called to him. "Stay and have a drink."

But Jack wasn't interested. I watched him disappear through the glass doors. I was embarrassed by his behavior and found myself making excuses: He was tired . . . on a deadline . . . hadn't been feeling well. . . . No one really cared that he was a sore loser. They just took their seats in the lounge and ordered their drinks.

Two hours later everyone was saying their good-byes, but I didn't feel like going home. I was still upset about Jack, and after the others left the King Pin, I called my buddy Scott and asked if he'd meet me for a drink at Twin Anchors.

Twenty minutes later I saw him walk into the bar, and I was taken aback. Scott had lost a good deal of weight since I'd last seen him, and his trousers were baggy, his belt fastened on the tightest notch. His handsome features were hidden beneath the shadow of a haggard complexion and he had dark circles under his sunken eyes. He looked tired, and I detected a slight tremor in his hand as he shook a cigarette from the pack of Chesterfields on the bar.

"Hey," I said, reaching for his arm. "Are you doing okay?"

"Is it that obvious?" He grinned and struck a match. "Been a rough couple of months," he said, lighting his cigarette. "Connie and I split up."

"Why didn't you call and tell me?"

"I didn't want to bother you with my love life."

"Well, I'm really sorry."

"Yeah. Me, too." He drew down hard on his cigarette and nodded. "Me, too. But that's not the problem. Not the real problem anyway."

"What is it? What's wrong?"

He picked at a fleck of tobacco on his tongue. "I quit my job."

"What? When did you quit?"

"Few weeks ago."

"Why didn't you say something earlier?" Scott and I talked all the time and he never mentioned it. "What are you going to do now?"

"I got another job." He paused and examined his cigarette before taking a drag. "I'm a defense lawyer."

"You're a *what*? How can you of all people go from being a prosecutor—an assistant state's attorney—to being a defense lawyer?"

"Once I made the decision, it was easier than you'd think."

"What kind of clients are you representing?"

"Oh"—he forced a laugh—"your usual brand of thugs and criminals. Let's see, I've taken on a prostitute, a drunk driver, a guy who allegedly assaulted his boss. And please don't look at me like that, Jordan. I feel guilty enough as it is."

"Then why are you doing this?"

He shrugged and hung his head. "I figured if you can't beat 'em, join 'em."

"Really?" That was all I could say. It didn't sound like Scott Trevor at all.

"At least I've won my last three cases." He smirked. "That's more than I could say for being a prosecutor."

I pulled out a cigarette and leaned forward while he lit it for me. His eyes shone through the flame, and I found myself transfixed, unable to look away. There was something there, something between us—at least on my part—and I needed to extinguish it. Fast. I leaned forward and blew out the match. We finished our drinks, paid the tab and went outside.

"So have you lost all respect for me?" he asked, his hand in the air, signaling a taxicab for me.

"Not *all*. Well, not quite." I winked and rose up on my tiptoes to kiss his cheek before I slid into the backseat of the cab.

When I got home that night I was still thinking about Scott when I found Jack waiting for me. He was sitting outside my door, across from the baby carriage, his back flush with the wall, his knees up close to his chest.

"I was beginning to think you weren't coming home," he said, his joints cracking as he eased up off the floor.

"You put on quite a show tonight," I said, fishing my house key out of my bag. "I hope you're proud of yourself. Since when are you such a sore loser?"

"Can we let this one go? I didn't come here to fight with you." I didn't respond.

"I just came by to say I was sorry. I'm apologizing. Okay?"

"Okay."

"So you forgive me?"

"Yes. I forgive you." He didn't pick up on my tone or else chose not to.

He followed me inside and pulled me close for a kiss. I was still angry with him and didn't feel like having sex, but I knew that's what he wanted. That was what he'd come for, more than to apologize to me.

So we made love that night and it was surprisingly satisfying, given that I was unhappy with him, that I hadn't been in the mood. Afterward we lay in bed. All was dark except for the light coming in from the streetlamp outside my window and the hot ash at the end of my cigarette.

Out of the blue, Jack asked me what parish I belonged to.

"What?" I leaned up on one elbow, my cigarette ash moving through the darkness like a tracer.

"Your parish? My mother was asking."

I laughed and situated the ashtray on the bed between us. "I don't belong to a parish."

"You don't? Are you serious? What about your parents?"

"They don't belong to one either."

"But you're Irish-Catholic. You have to belong to a parish."

"Not if your mother's Jewish and your father doesn't believe."

He sat up in bed and hugged his arms about his knees. "So what does that make you? Are you Jewish?"

I thought for a minute. "I'm not anything."

"But you have to be something. Everybody's *something.* Either you're Catholic or you're Jewish."

"Technically, I guess a child is the same religion as the mother, but I'm not a practicing Jew. Neither is she."

"And your father is what?"

"Atheist."

"Jesus!" He released his knees and clasped the sides of his head. "Do you even believe in God?"

"I do when things are going my way."

"God's not conditional," he said. He reached over to the nightstand and turned on the lamp. "I can't believe you never mentioned this to me before. I thought you were—you know, not super-religious maybe, but at least Irish-Catholic. You knew I was falling for you. How could you not say anything?"

I propped my pillow up against the headboard and gave him a blank stare. "I never really thought about it. I guess the whole thing's not that important to me. I didn't think it would matter."

"Of course it matters. I come from a strict Irish-Catholic family."

"So what would you like me to do about this?"

Without skipping a beat he said, "Convert."

"Convert? To Catholicism?" I laughed and ground out my cigarette.

"Yes. I mean if we were to get married, I'd need to know that—"

"Married? You want to marry me?"

This seemed to have surprised him as much as it did me. He yanked playfully on a fistful of my hair and laughed. "Yeah. Yeah, I do. I do want to marry you."

"So is this a proposal?"

"Sort of. I mean we'll get a ring and everything. And we'd need to meet my family, but yeah. Would your parents let you marry me? I mean, would they be okay if you converted?"

I thought for a moment. "Probably." I figured they wouldn't object. After all, my mother had walked away from her religion when she married my father, much to her own father's dismay. And while my parents may have been alcoholics, they weren't hypocrites.

"Well, okay then. So, ah, yeah." He smiled. "This is a proposal."

"How romantic." I laughed.

He laughed, too. "I do love you—you know that, don't you?"

"Yeah. I do know that." And I did. We weren't perfect. We had our differences, our quibbles, but we were in love. I rolled onto my side until our faces met in the middle and then our lips.

And that was how Jack and I decided we were getting married. I had no idea what converting entailed. I didn't yet know that I'd have to enter the catechumenate and attend Mass every Sunday. I didn't know I'd have to be baptized and confirmed and would have to jump through a host of other holy hoops. I didn't know that it could take up to a year before the church would even deem me worthy of marrying one of their own.

But before I could think about passing the church's test, I would have to pass the Caseys' scrutiny.

The lipstick was too much. Too bold. I looked in the mirror and wiped it off with toilet paper, leaving my mouth a peculiar shade of red. I considered changing my sweater again, too. I was meeting Jack's parents that day and had been second-guessing everything, rehearsing lines inside my head. They didn't know about our plans to marry. Jack thought it was important for them to meet me first and I agreed.

When he came to pick me up, one of the first things he said was, "Now, remember, don't say too much about your mom and dad—especially your mom—if they ask."

"About what? Her poetry or her religion?"

"Both."

He had already warned me that his parents—especially his mother—were very conservative and that, given my last name, they were expecting a nice Irish-Catholic girl, not a girl whose mother was a salacious Jewish poet and whose father was an Irish atheist.

"I'm going to break it to them gently, when the time is right," he said.

"Wow. I didn't realize I was such bad news."

"What? Bad news? No, I didn't mean it like that." He reached across the seat to squeeze my hand. "My parents are going to love you. It's just that they're old-fashioned. That's all I meant."

I wasn't convinced and what he'd said sat a little funny with me, but I let it go. I didn't want to get into it right before I was meeting his family.

It was an overcast day when we drove up to the Caseys' home. The giant oaks that flanked their tree-lined street in Bridgeport had already begun to change colors, and the air smelled of hickory, signaling that winter was around the bend. The Caseys' home was nothing like my parents' and certainly nothing like the other, more modest bungalows in Bridgeport, including Mayor Daley's, which was just around the corner on Lowe Street. No, the Caseys' house was enormous—five bedrooms with dormer windows along the top floor and two redbrick chimneys.

Inside, it was spotless and bright, as if the sun rose from within its walls. Mrs. Casey had decorated everything in buttercup yellows and mint greens. There were fresh flowers on the polished end tables and clear plastic coverings clinging to the couch and chairs in the living room. The wall of portraits confirmed that this was a home that celebrated family. Baby pictures, graduation pictures, birthday pictures, pictures with the Christmas tree, and huddled around their Norman Rockwellian Thanksgiving turkey. At my parents' house you found photographs by Ansel Adams in the hallway and a caricature by Al Hirschfeld hanging over the fireplace in the living room. But nowhere would you find a family portrait or even a photograph of my parents' wedding day resting in a silver frame. There were no embarrassing pictures of Eliot and me in diapers, no pictures of us, period. They didn't even bother with photographs posing with Hemingway and their other famous friends.

"Why, she's darling, Jack," said Mrs. Casey, taking my hands in hers and swinging them side to side.

I was worried my hands were sweaty—that's how nervous I was.

"Just darling," she said again. Her blond hair was perfectly coiffed and she wore her apron like a beauty-pageant banner.

"She sure is." Judge Casey gave me a hug that I wasn't expecting. He was a jovial man, the type who always had a smile. He was tall and had probably been handsome in his youth, like Jack.

The five other boys were handsome, too. They lined up and one by one rattled off their names. After a few more pleasantries were exchanged and Judge Casey offered me a drink, I followed Mrs. Casey into the biggest kitchen I'd ever seen. It was color coordinated like the rest of the house with yellow canisters on the counter and a row of cookbooks parked between two book-ends shaped like giant lemons. She even had a yellow telephone mounted right on the wall. I'd never before seen a telephone like it. I watched her move about the kitchen, doing all kinds of things as if she had magical powers: I could almost picture her opening a can of vegetables with one hand while beating a bowl of egg whites to perfect peaks with the other.

The first hiccup came when I asked if I could help with any-thing because that's just what you do when you're a dinner guest.

Mrs. Casey hesitated with a thoughtful finger pressed to her chin. "Well, I suppose you could set the table." She pointed to a stack of china on the counter and a collection of water goblets and wineglasses turned facedown on a monogrammed dish towel.

I went out to the dining room, and after placing the plates all around, evenly spaced, I separated the various forks, spoons and knives she had waiting on the buffet and arranged them before each place setting. I folded the napkins and tucked them under the fork to the left of each plate. I stood back, thinking the table looked rather nice, until Mrs. Casey stepped into the room.

"Oh my," she said. "What have we here?"

My face burned red as she laughed and went from plate to plate correcting my work, moving the napkin to the plate and switching the order of the forks, the spoons and the glasses. Apparently I managed to get the knives right.

I was still apologizing for my faux pas back in the kitchen while she pulled a roasted goose from the oven.

"No harm done," said Mrs. Casey, basting the potatoes and roast. "Thank goodness we caught it before everyone sat down." She laughed and changed the subject, asking about my family. "Jack tells me your mother is a poet."

"Yes." That was as much of an answer as I was allowed to give.

"I'm afraid I'm not much of a reader."

"That's a shame." I couldn't imagine. Reading was like breathing to me.

"Well, who has time? So much to do around the house and then there's the boys to look after." She smiled, slinging a dish towel over her shoulder.

Mrs. Casey and I continued to make small talk until Mr. Casey called me out to the living room.

"Jack's smitten with you," he said. "And I can certainly see why." He raised his glass to me and winked. "So tell me, did you grow up here in Chicago?"

I sensed that this would be the first of many personal questions and so I got out in front of him and turned it around. "Did you always know you wanted to be a judge?"

"Absolutely." He smiled and went on to tell me how he'd put himself through law school and paid his dues, working his way up to the bench. "I believe in the system. I truly do. In this imperfect world of ours, I believe that our justice system is worth upholding. You know what makes this the greatest country in the world? It's not our standard of living—it's our constitution." He thrust his finger in the air and nodded. "That's the backbone of our society and we owe a debt of gratitude to our founding fathers. What courage, wisdom and foresight they had." He spoke with such pride. It made me feel patriotic. "I wanted Jack to go to law school, too, but he's got that reporting bug. I guess you have it, too, huh?"

"It runs in my family," I said with a smile, grateful that we were called to dinner before he could ask me to elaborate.

I took my place at the table with the rest of the family, and as I looked around the room, something caught in my chest. Something bittersweet. Jack and I hadn't officially become engaged yet, but still, it struck me that this was my future family. There was so much to live up to. In my mind, the Caseys were perfect. The judge no doubt helped his young boys with their schoolwork after supper while Mrs. Casey darned their socks and tucked the younger ones in for the night with bedtime stories. They were wholesome and innocent, and no one drank too much or used curse words or isolated themselves in their office. I couldn't see how my parents and I fit into this picture. But I knew I wanted to try.

I was admiring them when without warning all members of the Casey clan joined hands, bowed their heads and said grace.

"O heavenly Father," began Judge Casey, "we give thanks for the blessings you are about to bestow upon us. . . . We praise your grace and mercy. Thank you for all the fruits which we are about to enjoy. Amen."

I joined the others and I meant it. *Amen, amen, amen.*

As plates were passed and spoonfuls dished out, Judge Casey and I entered into an interesting conversation about the political rift between Mayor Daley and his former friend and primary opponent, Benjamin Adamowski.

"Now, now," said Mrs. Casey, dabbing the corners of her mouth with her napkin. "No politics at the dinner table."

"You know"—Judge Casey continued anyway—"there's talk about Adamowski leaving the Democrats and joining the Republican Party."

"So I've heard. A friend of mine told me that Adamowski is going to run for state's attorney."

"A friend?" Jack gave me a look that said, *So when were you and Scott talking about this?*

"It's a long shot," I said, touching my thigh against Jack's to reassure him.

"Daley'll never let him get elected," said Judge Casey. "Adamowski would be out to clobber the machine. Can you imagine if Adamowski won? The last thing Daley needs is his enemy in a powerful position like that. Adamowski would be a real thorn in Daley's side."

"C'mon now," said Mrs. Casey, lightly slapping the table. "Enough political talk. We're having dinner."

I smiled and went back to my roast. I didn't see what the problem was. All my family usually talked about over dinner was politics and I enjoyed talking with Jack's father. It reminded me of the conversations I used to have with my own father and it was comforting even though it made me homesick for him. Homesick for what we had before we lost Eliot.

Since our uproar over Eliot's typewriter I'd stopped by the house several times, and each time my father had mumbled his usual hellos. This told me there was no permanent damage done to our already fragile bond. Or else he'd been so drunk the day I moved out that he'd blacked out and didn't remember a thing we'd said. Either one was possible.

Chapter 15

• • •

One morning in mid-October, I arrived at the city room early and shot the breeze with the slot man while I checked the assignment book. I saw that Mr. Copeland had me covering a piece for Neighborhood News about an expansion for Kiddieland, a theme park for toddlers. Not exactly hard news, but it was better than weddings and charity balls.

So I went out to Melrose Park and met with Arthur Fritz, who had opened the theme park back in 1929 with half a dozen ponies. The park was closed for the season now, and all the rides were dismantled, their frames covered by heavy tarps to protect them from the winter. I sat in his office while he showed me plans for the new Ferris Wheel and the Roto Whip coming that summer. The whole time he spoke, I was looking for a bigger angle, but two hours later, it was clear this was about the expansion of a wholesome little theme park for tykes and that was it. There was nothing sinister, nothing scandalous to report. It was just Kiddieland.

When I got back to the city room I began writing up the piece, and as I was about to pull the copy from my typewriter, Ahern telephoned, wanting to see me. Right away.

"And bring a sharp pencil with you," he said.

I met him at the Museum of Science and Industry in front of the Corliss steam engine exhibit. He gazed around the area while I looked at the chambers and levers before I followed him to a coffee shop around the corner overlooking Lake Michigan. I hadn't even known the place existed. We sat at a picture window with half curtains covering the lower panes of glass.

"I was surprised to hear from you," I said.

Ahern lit a cigarette, cupping the match with his hands. "Well, I saw your piece the other day on the 'Origins of Trick or Treating' and figured you could use some help."

"So is that what this is about? You helping me?"

"This is about us helping each other." He dropped his match to the ashtray, sending up a ribbon of smoke.

"So what do you have for me?"

"Get out your pad and pencil. You're gonna want to take this down."

I did as he said and reached inside my handbag. "Okay, shoot."

But he didn't say anything. I cleared my throat. Still nothing. He was making me wait while he *tap-tap-tapped* his spoon to the rim of his coffee cup. At last he said, "How quickly do you think you can get a juicy story out about a crooked politician who's about to be subpoenaed?"

"That depends on who the crooked politician is and what he's being subpoenaed for."

"Let's start with the 1st Ward."

"D'Arco?" John D'Arco was the 1st Ward alderman and in thick with the Outfit. He *was* the Outfit. Everyone knew that.

"You didn't hear this from me, but the state's attorney is going to subpoena him first thing tomorrow to appear before a grand jury."

"For what?"

"Faking automobile accidents. And with government cars."

"Excuse me?"

"*Allegedly*, D'Arco hired a group of crooked insurance appraisers to fake a string of auto accidents for city vehicles. He ended up collecting close to $70,000 in false claims from a dozen different insurance companies."

"How do you know this?"

His smile was a sly one. "I have friends in the state's attorney's office."

I sat up a little straighter. Scott was no longer working there, but I wondered if Ahern knew him. I was tempted to ask but knew I couldn't. Ahern was supposed to be an anonymous source. No one was supposed to even know I was speaking with him. I couldn't let my friendship with Scott jeopardize this arrangement with Ahern, so I kept my mouth shut.

"It was really a brilliant operation D'Arco had going," said Ahern. "They'd take a perfectly fine automobile and dismantle it, bang it up good so that it looked like it had been totaled. They could get about six or seven claims off one staged smashup."

I asked a few more questions and jotted down my notes.

Ahern reached for my notepad and scribbled down a name and telephone number. "That's who you need to talk to. He's in the state's attorney's office. He'll talk to you, but you can't use his name in the piece. He has to remain anonymous. That's the agreement." Ahern slid the notepad across to me. "No names. We're clear, right?"

"No names."

"And you need to move quickly on this if you want to break the story," he said as he stood up. "I don't know how much longer they can keep it quiet, and you know as soon as word gets out it'll be all over the place." Ahern dabbed his mouth with his napkin and turned up his collar. The bells above the door chimed when he walked out.

As soon as he left, I stubbed out my cigarette, rushed to the nearest pay phone and called the number Ahern had given me. I spoke to the contact, assuring him that I would not print his name. In exchange he spoon-fed me the story. With the receiver cradled between my ear and shoulder and my pad pressed to the phone booth's wall, I wrote upside down and sideways. He gave me the real license plate numbers and the fake plate numbers, too. He gave me the names of the crooked adjusters and the insurance companies they had swindled.

I made more calls until I ran out of change for the pay phone. But by then I had spoken to an insurance adjustor who corroborated everything my first source said. I was still looking for more backup and had left messages for everyone I could think of. No one wanted to talk, and those who did, didn't want their names mentioned. By four o'clock I was waiting on one of the insurance adjusters to call me back. Another fifteen minutes and I knew I couldn't hold out any longer. The clock was ticking and I had to get the story out before D'Arco was subpoenaed and this scoop would become yesterday's news. I raced back to the city room, fed the typewriter a set of copy sheets and cranked out the story.

It was a few minutes after five and Mr. Copeland was already gone for the day, so I went straight to Mr. Ellsworth, catching him just as he was reaching for his coat and hat. "Wait—don't go."

"Excuse me?"

"Here—wait." I held out my copy to him. "You have to take a look at this."

He tossed his hat onto the horseshoe and unbuttoned his overcoat. "This better be good. I have dinner reservations at Fritzel's tonight." With one hand stuffed in his pocket, he stood next to the desk and read, his head nodding every few minutes. He read some more and muttered to himself before he looked up and said, "So D'Arco is about to be subpoenaed by a grand jury for operating a fake auto-accident insurance ring?"

"Involving city automobiles."

He nodded again. "This is a good start. Get another quote and we'll take a look at it tomorrow."

"Tomorrow? No. Tomorrow's too late."

"No?" He gave me an indignant look.

"If we wait until tomorrow, this story is going to be all over the place. If we run it now, we can be the first. We can have it out in the bulldog edition."

"No, we can't." He chucked the copy onto his desk and said, "I need another quote and if you get that, we'll take another look at it tomorrow."

"But we'll miss our window."

"Walsh, do you feel that?" He indicated the rumble beneath our feet. "The presses are running. The story will be there tomorrow."

"Tomorrow when it's old news."

"Even if I were going to stop the presses, which I'm not about to do, there's not enough here. It's too thin. You need another quote."

"But I have two sources."

"Still not enough."

"But didn't you see the quote I have?"

"Yeah. I saw it. 'An unnamed source inside the state's attorney's office . . .' Hell, Walsh, you might as well have spoken to the cleaning woman."

"But they confirmed the $70,000 worth of fake claims. That's rock solid. And what about the fake license plates and the multiple claims for the same car?"

"Says who? Who's your source?"

I knew this was coming. "I can't say. But what about the insurance adjustor?"

"He doesn't have a name either." Mr. Ellsworth reached for his fedora. "Tomorrow, Walsh. Go get me another quote. And not from an anonymous source this time and we'll look at it tomorrow." He turned off his desk lamp and squared his hat on his head. "Now, if you'll excuse me, I have dinner plans tonight."

I worked until ten that evening trying to get another quote, but it was late and no one was at their desks. I tried home telephone numbers, too, but I couldn't reach anyone. By eleven o'clock I had no choice but to accept defeat.

The next morning Ahern telephoned, and I cringed when he asked what happened. "Where's the story?"

"My editor wouldn't run it. I tried. It was too late. The presses were already running." I couldn't bring myself to tell him that Mr. Ellsworth thought the piece was too thin.

Ahern sighed into the receiver. "I'm doing what I can to help you, Walsh, but I'm afraid you blew it this time."

Later that morning I saw that very same story on the front page of the *Daily News*. As soon as I started reading the article, a tightness settled into my chest as the blood rushed to my face. I was consumed with jealousy. The *Daily News* had that extra quote I had so desperately needed. What's more, they had documented $120,000 in fake claims, not just $70,000. Their reporter had scooped me.

Ahern was right. I had blown it. I should have worked smarter, faster. I shouldn't have waited around for callbacks. I should have moved on and found other sources. I should have gotten in front of Mr. Ellsworth sooner. After I beat myself up, I promised that I'd never let something like that happen to me again.

Chapter 16

• • •

About a month later, I was working on a piece for White Collar Girl about "Popular Lunch Spots for Busy Secretaries." Mrs. Angelo had just made her rounds, causing Gabby to hang up in the middle of a phone call with her sister so she could make believe she was working.

Gabby had been on the phone with her sister all morning. From what I could gather, one of the kids had a fever. She must have spoken with her sister half a dozen times that day.

It was almost five o'clock and I was about to pack up when the wire room bells sounded. Those bells meant a news bulletin was coming in. Something was happening. Something big. A shooting, a fire, something overseas. You never knew what it could be. The peal of those bells reverberated throughout the city room, getting everyone's heart racing. I stopped packing up my things and froze in place, waiting.

Even before Mr. Ellsworth rushed over, we heard the news crackling over Peter's police radio: *"El car derailed. In the Loop. Lake and Wabash. Fatalities expected. Ambulances en route."*

All eyes were on Mr. Ellsworth. He was scrambling, looking

for people to send to the scene. He ran a hand through his hair before he held his arm straight out and snapped his fingers. "Peter, Henry, Benny, get down there. Take Russell and another photographer with you. If you need more cameramen let me know. And you"—he looked at me—"Walsh, go talk to the victims."

Half a dozen of us raced out of the city room and headed toward the Loop. It was snowing and blustery cold that day. One of the first accumulating snows of the season. Raw energy pumped through me as we rushed over the bridge at Wacker and Michigan and headed another two blocks to Lake Street. Before we'd reached Wabash, just a few blocks to the west, we heard the sirens barreling down the street. You think you're immune to that sound. After all, sirens were the melody this city danced to. But just then those sirens sent a chill through me, far more penetrating than the wind. I stuffed my hands inside my pockets, gripping my fountain pen nestled against the lining.

As we turned the corner, I let out a gasp. An el car was hanging off the overhead track, swinging back and forth. Another car had jackknifed, and the one behind it had uncoupled and crashed, bottom-side-up on the street below. A fourth car had reared into another and was folded up like an accordion.

We picked up the pace, going from a jog to a full-blown run, traversing the patches of ice on the sidewalk. There was black smoke billowing up from the cars that had caught fire. Rows of people crowded in, gawking, crying. Victims were walking around with blood gushing from the gashes on their foreheads, their arms and legs. The ambulances were just arriving on the scene, and fire workers were using crowbars and blowtorches, trying to free passengers still trapped inside the cars. People were down on the sidewalks, lying in the street, groping for someone, anyone to help them. A few doctors, nurses and Good

Samaritans jumped in to help treat passengers who had been thrown from the train.

Mr. Ellsworth said I should talk to the victims, but I was looking for anyone I could get a statement from—riders who'd been on the train, people who'd been walking by and had seen it happen, workers in nearby buildings who'd witnessed it from their office windows. Anyone.

"I was just standing there," said a woman who'd been in one of the front cars. "I was waiting for a seat to open up. We were going around the curve and I felt a jolt. I lost my balance. So did everyone else. Then people started screaming. . . ."

I tried to get to the conductor and the motorman, but both had been too badly injured and had already been taken to the hospital. The site was filled with police and investigators. I ran into Danny Finn, but he had no information for me. Said he'd just gotten there himself. Everywhere I looked I saw reporters from the other papers and the wire services as well as the radio stations.

Finally the chief of police made an official statement to the press, saying: "We're going to conduct a thorough investigation as to how and why this tragedy occurred. . . ."

There was a flurry of questions as reporters vied for the chief's attention. I was the only woman in the pack and couldn't even get him to make eye contact with me. I was invisible.

I went through the crowd then, talking to cops and ambulance drivers, trying to get a count on fatalities, but all I had were conflicting reports. An AP stringer was saying two dead and another stringer from UPI was saying at least thirteen. The whole downtown area from Madison to Kinzie and State to Michigan was blocked off. Ambulances came and went and circled back to get more victims.

After I'd exhausted the crash site and had spoken to everyone

I could find, I called Higgs, the rewrite man at the city desk who worked the night shift. Mr. Copeland eventually got on the phone.

"Get your butt over to the hospital, Walsh. Talk to the victims and bring me back some stories."

I'd been afraid he was going to say that. I hated hospitals, especially Henrotin Hospital. The last time I'd been there was the night Eliot died.

"And make sure you take a photographer with you, Walsh."

I hung up with Mr. Copeland, found a cameraman and went to Henrotin over on Oak Street where the victims had been taken. Mr. Copeland had sent me there to get the human side of suffering, and like it or not, that's what I had to do.

As soon as we arrived, Charles, the photographer, went about getting pictures. I headed into the waiting room and found families of the injured sitting around, looking like they didn't know what day it was. Waiting in that room to hear of a loved one's fate was nothing new to me. I'd been in their shoes. The tiled walls, the harsh overhead lights, the row of blue chairs, their upholstery torn from having been worried by those waiting—it was still haunting to me now even two and a half years after I'd lived out my own tragedy in this very room. But now it was my task to bring back the sob stories. I had to talk to these people, pry the gut-wrenching details from them that would tug at the readers' heartstrings. I found the task repulsive. I felt like a vampire feeding off their blood.

I remembered when Eliot was in surgery. My mother had stood before that same vending machine—where an older man now leaned. She had bought cups of coffee because she didn't know what else to do. My father had sat across the room, in that very chair where a woman was now with her sleeping child in her lap. He had smoked his Lucky Strikes down to their last puffs and tapped his foot to the floor while I alternated between picking at my mosquito bites and chewing my cuticles. None of us spoke to one another. We needed each other then more than ever, but we were already separating, retreating into our own worlds. Forty minutes later, the doctor had come out to speak with us. Forty-five minutes later we walked out of the hospital in a state of shock, my father carrying a bundle wrapped in heavy brown paper and tied with string: Eliot's personal effects. It was all we had left of him. We'd lost one of our family members, and it was like having an arm cut off.

"Come sit down," someone said.

The words pulled me from my trance. I looked up and there was a woman speaking to me, patting the chair next to her.

"You have to be strong at a time like this. Don't let your mind run wild on you," she said.

I nodded and accepted the seat.

She continued talking. "My son was on that train," she said. "He'll be nine next month. First time he ever rode the el by himself. He wanted to ride down on the train to surprise his grand-mother."

I looked at her and clutched my heart.

"Don't worry for him. Harley'll be fine. That's just all there is to it. So whoever you're here for, don't worry; they'll be fine, too."

"I'm not waiting on anyone. No one in particular," I said. "I work for the *Tribune*." I was ashamed when I explained why I was there.

"Well, everybody in this room has got a story for you."

"I just don't want to intrude at a time like this."

She chewed the inside of her cheek and said, "For some of us it helps to talk. I know it does for me."

"Does it?" Coming from a family that never talked, this was a foreign concept to me.

"What is it you want to know?"

So I took out my notebook and took down her story. Her full name was Harriet Jackson and her son's name was Harley Jackson Jr. The man next to her, Alfred Paine, overheard me asking questions and he chimed in with a story of his own. His brother was visiting from Indianapolis and Alfred was on his way to meet him at the Clark and Lake Street stop. He got as far as Wabash and saw the whole thing happen.

"At first I thought my eyes were playing tricks on me," he said. "And then I knew it was happening. The first car was coming off the rails and I just started praying. . . ."

I sat with Harriet Jackson and Alfred Paine, listening more as a fellow human being than as a reporter. I was right there with them when the doctor came out in his bloodstained gown.

"Harley Jackson? Anyone here for Harley Jackson?"

Harriet raised her hand like she was in a classroom. The doctor came over, and before he'd said a word, his face told it all. Harriet let out a shriek and began to cry.

"We did everything we could," said the doctor. "I'm sorry."

All I could do was put my arms around her and let her weep onto my shoulder. Other people in the waiting room, strangers up until then, huddled around her, too. When I felt I couldn't breathe, I slipped away and let the others comfort her. Charles was in the thick of it, taking pictures. I turned away, unable to watch. My collar was still damp from the tears of Harley's mother.

With my heart in my throat, I returned to the city room after eight that night and worked until eleven, confirming notes and quotes, facts and fatalities with Higgs and the copy editor in order to make sure we were ready for the morning edition.

I went home at a quarter past midnight but sat up in my living room with a glass of bourbon until well after two. I had telephoned Jack earlier, but he hadn't answered. So I called Scott. We talked for almost an hour. He'd offered to come over, but I said no; I was okay. And yet I was still upset, even after we'd hung up. How was I supposed to sleep after all that? It was hard to get the faces out of my head, to separate the facts from the lives that had been lost or shattered in an instant.

But wasn't life just like that? When I think back on all the stupid things I've worried about and fretted over, wondering if I'd forgotten to sign my rent check, or if Mrs. Casey had given me a weird look, or if I'd be fined for a late library book—silly things that never came to pass or amounted to much—and then the one thing you never expected, that you never saw coming, like an el car derailment or a hit-and-run, blindsides you and changes your life forever.

Chapter 17

◆ ◆ ◆

The week before Christmas Jack and I officially became engaged, with his grandmother's ring to prove it. The stone was modest but still it glinted and sparkled with every move of my hand.

The day after the proposal I was getting a cup of coffee when Gabby noticed my ring in the way that only other women of a marrying age notice these things. She squealed, hugged me and summoned M and the other sob sisters into the galley kitchen. They circled around me, taking turns reaching for my hand, *ooh*ing and *ahh*ing over the stone.

"Have you set the date yet?" Gabby asked.

"Where are you going to live?" asked M.

"Who's going to be your maid of honor?"

"What about the honeymoon?"

"Did you find a dress?"

They were asking things I hadn't yet contemplated. Honestly, I didn't care about the dress or the honeymoon. All I knew was that I wanted to spend my life with Jack Casey. He wasn't perfect. He snored like a freight train and sometimes drank the orange juice straight from the bottle. But he had come into my world and filled in all the thin spots, all the places that weren't whole. And it wasn't just him. It was his family, too. I'd lost mine, but his was there, ready to embrace me. They showed me what my future could be—birthdays, anniversaries and holidays would be celebrations, and I longed for that. I wanted to have children with Jack and raise a family of our own. Oh, how I wanted a taste of that Casey lifestyle for myself.

Mrs. Angelo appeared in the doorway of the kitchen and made an exaggerated point of looking at her wristwatch. "Don't you ladies have some work you should be doing? By the way," she said, grabbing hold of me with her eyes, "congratulations."

We dispersed and went back to our desks, back to writing about our recipes and celebrity sightings and secretarial tips. Thankfully, I was working on a series of small follow-up articles about the el derailment.

The investigators had determined that the accident was caused by human error. The motorman was reportedly going twenty miles per hour over the regulated speed limit. He was consequently fired and was now facing manslaughter charges. The total number of fatalities had climbed to thirty-four, and the funerals and memorials were held back to back.

The derailment had happened nearly two weeks ago, and since then the city had moved on, but I couldn't. I was beginning to think I was the wrong person to have covered this story. I couldn't stop thinking about those thirty-four lives lost and the thirty-four families for whom Christmas would be torture this year. And for every year going forward.

Later that day I visited Harley's mother. Not to write anything more about her, but just because I couldn't stay away.

"Look at this," she said, walking me into his bedroom and pointing to a glass beaker, test tubes and a microscope. "This was his science-fair project for school." She traced her fingertips over the surface of each item on his dresser. "He'd been working on it for more than a month." She smiled faintly.

I knew this was the exact type of story Mr. Ellsworth wanted me to get. He would have had a photographer there in an instant, taking pictures of the deceased boy's room. It would have been a nice piece for me, but I wasn't going to exploit a mother's grief. No, unfortunately, there was no shortage of other stories to write about from the derailment.

"He was so close to finishing his science project," said Mrs. Jackson. "And now it's just been left undone forever because"— her voice cracked—"I can't finish it for him. You can't imagine what that feels like. Having that unfinished edge left hanging in my mind."

Oh, but I knew exactly how that felt. At the time my brother was killed, he'd been working on a big scoop. I didn't know all the details, just that there was a racket in Chicago passing off horse-meat as beef. He had been working on it for nearly two months and was close to piecing it all together. He said he'd never eat another hamburger again in this town. And that was true. He didn't. He was killed, run down before he got to finish his article. No one at the *Sun-Times* picked up on the story and attempted to complete the investigation, which I always thought was a shame. But for whatever reason they let the whole thing die right along with my brother.

A few days later, I sat at my desk, finishing up a piece on the best festive holiday centerpieces. *Oh, the things you could do with pinecones and cranberries.* The city room was caught up in its usual buzzing.

Walter was puffing on his pipe, shouting out of the corner of his mouth at Benny, who was frantically trying to track down some information for his afternoon story about a citywide air-raid test with simulated H-bombs. Immediately following the sirens, every TV and radio station would switch from their regular programming to the CONELRAD system created to broadcast civil-defense information. Meanwhile Randy was humming *Winter Wonderland* and I was just about to rip my copy from the typewriter when I got a telephone call.

"Jordan? Jordan Walsh?"

"Yes."

"Oh, I'm sorry. I was expecting a man."

I rolled my eyes. I'd lost count of all the people who thought Jordan was a man. And they always seemed so disappointed. So much for my mother's theory. I was used to this reaction, only this time it was coming from another woman. A woman who didn't want to give me *her* name.

"So what can I help you with?" I was skimming over my copy, but as soon as she said she was with the Chicago Transit Authority, I gripped the phone tighter. I could hear the trepidation in her voice. "Hello? Hello? Are you still there?"

"I'm sorry," she said. "I shouldn't have bothered you." *Click.* She hung up.

I was still staring at the telephone when it rang again.

"It's me," she said. "I didn't mean to hang up. Well, maybe I did. I just didn't realize you were a female reporter," she said again. "You see, I've been following the articles you've written about the el derailment and . . ."

I switched the phone to my left ear and covered the right one to block the background noise. "Go on."

There was a long pause. "Do you think maybe we could talk? Over coffee? I'd rather do this in person."

We agreed to meet at a Wimpy's on State Street in the Loop, not far from Wabash and Lake where the accident had occurred. It was cold and snowing that day with the kind of biting wind that got right down inside your bones. The weather didn't deter the holiday shoppers though. They packed the streets, scurrying in and out of stores, their arms loaded down with packages. The el track had been repaired, but it still gave me an eerie feeling each time I was near the site where so many people had died. I turned up my collar and stuffed my hands inside my pockets, fingering an ever-growing hole in the lining.

It was quiet when I stepped inside Wimpy's. The lunch crowd was already back at work. Other than a couple of waitresses behind the counter and two ladies surrounded by green Marshall Field's bags, I didn't see anyone who could have belonged to the voice on the telephone. I slipped into one of the booths along the side for privacy, ordered a cup of coffee and smoked a cigarette to pass the time.

Finally a woman appeared inside the doorway, hovering next to a life-size cutout of Popeye's friend Wimpy with a caption that read *I'll gladly pay you Tuesday for a hamburger today.* The woman was a bit heavyset and had light brown hair that rested on her cheeks, curving upward like two fishhooks. She looked to be in her mid- to late forties. She clutched her pocketbook with both hands and scanned the room. When we locked eyes I gave a slight nod, and she came over and slid into the booth.

"I'm sorry I'm late. I—I had to make sure no one was following me." She glanced around the restaurant.

"Who would have been following you?"

"Could have been anyone from work. I just can't take any chances." She was nervous, curling and uncurling her paper napkin as she spoke. "I'll get fired if anyone finds out I'm talking to the press. And I can't afford to lose my job. My husband passed two years ago and I have three small children to raise."

I knew she was reluctant to speak to me and somehow I had

to put her at ease. She didn't say another word in the time it took the waitress to pour her coffee and refill my cup.

I reached for another cigarette. "So, you wanted to talk about the derailment?"

The woman looked at me, on the brink of speaking but still hesitating. I thought there was a chance she'd change her mind, get up and leave.

"I won't quote you," I said. "I won't even allude to you. I can keep you out of this—whatever it is. I promise."

She bit down on her lip and her voice cracked. "I can't take it anymore. I can't keep quiet." She shook her head as the tears ran loose. "All those people who died—I tell you it's eating me up inside, and I have to come forward and tell someone." She dabbed her eyes with a napkin and went silent again, as if rethinking her decision to meet with me.

Again I feared she might back out. "Okay," I said. "Let's start at the beginning. You work for the Chicago Transit Authority, right?"

She nodded and fiddled with the buckle on her pocketbook. "I'm a secretary to Anthony Briar, the Senior Director of Infrastructure and Maintenance."

I lit my cigarette, waiting for her to continue.

"Someone needs to look into what happened," she said eventually. "What *really* happened."

"They did an investigation. They said it was human error."

"I know for a fact that that's not true. It wasn't human error." The tone of her voice and the look in her eyes set off alarms inside my head.

I exchanged my cigarette for my pen.

"The motorman didn't do anything wrong," she said. "The train wasn't going too fast. The problem was in the tracks. I tell you it was an accident waiting to happen, and they knew it, too. Take my word for it—it won't be the last one, either." Now that she'd started speaking, she couldn't stop. It was as if she was purging herself of weeks of guilty silence. The details came gushing out, and I had my notepad out like a bucket to capture it all.

"The CTA has a subcontractor—J.T. Porter and Company. They do the routine inspections and conduct the maintenance on all the tracks. They've been doing it for the past ten years—for as long as I've been working there. During their last round of inspections, they had some concerns about the condition of the tracks in certain locations. They sent the directors a series of reports, recommending they shut down the track for maintenance. My boss, Mr. Briar, called a special meeting that afternoon, and by the end of business that day, they had fired J.T. Porter. And that was after ten years of service."

"Did they say why they were firing them?"

"They were afraid they'd lose too much money on rider fares if they shut down the tracks."

"I see." My father used to describe that moment for a reporter when they knew they'd landed something big, like a fisherman who's hooked into a shark. I had that feeling now, so much stronger than I'd ever felt it before. My pulse pumped as fast as my pen would write.

"So they hired another firm," she said. "Unger Brothers Iron and Rail. They said they were going with them and that they weren't closing down the tracks. I wondered how they were going to make the necessary repairs without doing that. My husband was an engineer, so I knew how these things worked. Then I happened to get a look at the Unger Brothers' bid. It was $7,000 more than what the other company charged."

"So Unger was charging more than J.T. Porter?"

"That's the thing. It didn't make any sense—especially since they were worried about losing money. But then I realized that the owner of this new firm, this Lawrence Unger, was my boss's brother-in-law. I'm not stupid. I knew right then that this company—this Unger Brothers—was going to do a fraction of the work that J.T. Porter did and that Mr. Briar and his brother-in-law were going to pocket the difference."

While she spoke, I wrote, not wanting to miss a word. In the back of my mind, I could hear Mr. Ellsworth asking for the quotes, the facts, the proof. I had a frightened woman before me who wouldn't go on the record with her name. I knew I was going to need more than that.

"I couldn't keep quiet anymore," she said. "All those innocent people died for no good reason. And now the motorman is being blamed for something he didn't do. I saw the article in your paper yesterday about charging him with manslaughter and negligence. It's just not right. Those monsters inside the CTA are going to let an innocent man take the fall for this." She paused, looking away. "And there's more."

More? My pen froze in place. What more could she possibly have?

"I wasn't even going to say anything about this, but with you being a woman and all . . ." She bit down on her lip again, pinched open her pocketbook and pulled out a trifold of papers. Without a word she passed the documents to me.

I shuffled through the pages and looked up at her, stunned. "How did you get these?"

"They were sent to my boss and all the department heads."

I was holding a series of memorandums and reports from J.T. Porter and Company dated November 8, 1955. Less than a month before the derailment. It was page upon page of track inspections and maintenance recommendations. Each one was stamped URGENT . . . TRACKS IN NEED OF CRITICAL REPAIR. . . . HAZARDOUS CONDITIONS . . . RECOMMENDATION: CLOSE TRACKS IMMEDIATELY. . . .

Holy crap. I swallowed hard.

"Mr. Briar told me to gather all the memos that had been distributed to the department heads and destroy them."

"He what?" The hair on the back of my neck stood up for the umpteenth time. "Anthony Briar? The Senior Director of Infrastructure and Maintenance for the Chicago Transit Authority told you to destroy these?"

She nodded. "Only I didn't. But I didn't mean to disobey him. I had a dentist appointment after work that day and I was rushing to get out of the office on time. I put the memos in my drawer and figured I'd destroy them the next day, but then there were meetings and well, I—I plain forgot. In fact, I forgot all about them until the derailment. And it's been eating me up alive inside ever since."

"Have you spoken to anyone else about this?"

"God, no." She shook her head. "No. I've been too afraid. I'm hoping that enough other people in the office saw that memo that they won't be able to trace it back to me. Do you think they'll figure out it was me who told you?"

I didn't answer her question. I couldn't say. "All I can tell you is that I think you're doing the right thing." I studied her face. The color was gone from her cheeks. "Why didn't you go to the police with this?"

"I was too afraid. I called you at first because of your articles, but then I lost my nerve. That's why I hung up. But when I realized you were a woman—I figured I could trust you. That's why I decided to meet with you. I'm showing you this now because

I'm hoping you'll understand my predicament. Do you understand what I'm up against and why I can't lose this job?"

"I do. I do understand."

She looked at the memos in my hand. "You can keep those if you want. I made copies for you. I'm figuring I can trust you not to use my name—you know, on account of you being a woman reporter and all."

It was the first time that my gender had ever worked to my advantage.

I raced back to the city room and stood over my typewriter while I knocked out a quick memo and then rushed over to Mr. Ellsworth at the horseshoe.

He read it and puckered his mouth. "Christ, Walsh. Where'd you get this from?" He turned to me, fingers in his beard. "Wait—don't tell me, you *can't tell me.*" He set the memo down on his desk and shook his head. "You're accusing the directors of the CTA of blatant criminal activity, and without a shred of evidence."

"Oh, I have evidence, all right."

"Well, let's have it."

I hesitated. My hands were sweating. My heart was pounding.

"Well?" He hiked his eyebrows up on his forehead.

"I have the evidence. Hard evidence. And I have an exclusive. But before I show it to you, I need something in return."

He chucked his pen onto the desk. "What the—"

"I'm sorry, but you can't cut me out of this piece like you did with the insurance fraud. You can't have me doing all the work and then hand over my byline to Walter or Henry or anyone else."

"You got some nerve, Walsh. You do realize that you're talking to your managing editor."

"I do realize that, sir, but with all due respect, I also realize what I'm sitting on and that any managing editor in this city would jump at the chance to run this story."

"I don't like your tactics, Walsh, I can tell you that right now. This scoop of yours better be as big as you say it is."

"So do we have a deal?"

He folded his arms and gave me a look that seemed to be equal parts contempt and surprise. He didn't think I had this kind of fight in me. I didn't know I had it, either. The din of the city room seemed muted. It was a showdown between the two of us.

"Okay, Walsh," he said eventually. "We have a deal."

I nodded and handed over the memos from J.T. Porter and Company.

Mr. Ellsworth glanced at them and sprang up from his chair. "Hey, Copeland," he called out, his eyes still on the memos. "Get over here."

Mr. Copeland came over and stood next to Mr. Ellsworth, reading over his shoulder before glancing at me, dumbstruck. "Where the hell did you get these?"

"From someone who works for the CTA."

"Does this someone have a name? A title?"

"They work under one of the executives." That was all I was willing to say.

"Can you get more information from this guy if we need it?" asked Mr. Copeland.

"That won't be a problem." I found it reassuring that they assumed my source was a man. I hoped for the woman's sake that others would draw the same conclusion.

Mr. Ellsworth and Mr. Copeland finished shuffling through the memos. Mr. Ellsworth tossed his pencil onto his desk and rubbed both hands over his face as if he were scrubbing it clean. He turned to Mr. Copeland. "Do we have any art for this?"

"I'll have Russell pull something from the photo lab."

Mr. Ellsworth looked at me and said, "Well, what are you waiting for, Walsh? I need your copy on my desk by four o'clock, in time for the page-one meeting."

The page-one meeting was *the* meeting where all the editors hashed through the top stories and mapped out the next day's edition, including what would appear on the front page.

"Did you hear what I just said?" He gave me that impatient look of his.

I was still stunned. "Yes, sir. You got it."

I hurried back to my desk and spread my notes out, sorting through the napkins and scraps of paper. My hands were shaking as I spun the copy paper into my typewriter and started crafting my lede. I never thought that doing what I always wanted would make me so nervous. But it came with the burden of responsibility to protect my source and to get it right.

At four thirty I paced back and forth while the page-one meeting was underway inside the glass cocoon of a conference room. Plumes of smoke collected above their heads as the men questioned and scrutinized every item the other editors presented.

When Mr. Ellsworth emerged, I pounced on him. "Well?"

"Well, what?"

"Are you going to run my piece?"

He seemed surprised that I'd asked such a thing. "Hell, yes, we're running the piece."

"I meant *my* piece. With *my* byline."

"You'll get your byline. Front page. Above the fold." Then he reached over and squeezed my shoulder. "Good work, Walsh."

It was the first praise I'd ever received from him in the seven months I'd worked there and the first time since I'd stepped into that city room that I felt like a real reporter.

Chapter 18

• • •

The day my story ran I met Jack for lunch, plopping the *Tribune* down on the table between us. My byline was right there in black-and-white. While he read through the article, I glanced about the coffee shop, looking at the Christmas decorations, the fake snow on the windows that spelled NOEL, the sprig of mistletoe above the cash register.

Meanwhile, my leg was anxiously bobbing beneath the table. When I couldn't take it any longer, I asked, "Well? What do you think?"

"It's—it's great." Jack folded the newspaper and slipped it onto the seat beside him. I think if he'd had a fish with him, he would have wrapped the thing up in my story.

"That's it? That's all you have to say?"

"I told you it's great." He opened his menu. "Really great. No, I mean it." Which of course meant he didn't. He motioned over the waitress. "We should probably hurry up and order. I have to get back to the paper soon. I'm on deadline and I want to get out of there early today. I'm going to Mass with my parents later, remember?"

Of course. It was Christmas Eve. I'd almost forgotten. Jack had made excuses and got me out of attending Mass with the Caseys but warned that next year I'd be expected to go.

I glanced at the menu while Judy Garland sang over the speakers, telling us to have ourselves a merry little Christmas. The lyrics made me melancholy. Would there ever be a time when the holidays were not an aching, painful reminder of what and who was missing from our lives?

I closed my menu and ordered the meat loaf even though I wasn't hungry anymore. I shouldn't have brought up my article again but I had to. So after the waitress disappeared, I leaned forward and said, "So that's *really* all you're going to say?"

"About what?" He seemed truly puzzled, which was even more upsetting.

"That's a huge story I just broke, and all you can say is 'Great. Great job'?"

"It *is* great. You *did* do a *great* job. I told you that."

"You don't seem all that happy for me."

His shoulders rose and fell as he sighed. "Honestly, I'm just a little surprised you didn't tell me about it before it turned up in the paper, that's all."

"Because it all went down in a matter of hours. You know how this business works."

"I know, but you could have at least told me you had a source inside the CTA."

"Jack, you work for a competing newspaper. If the situation had been reversed, would you have told me? And you, better than anyone, know how hard it's been for me to get my work noticed. I had an exclusive—not to mention that I was working with an anonymous source. Was I supposed to hand all that information over to you because you're my fiancé?"

He shook his head, defenseless. "You're right. I'm sorry. I'm proud of you. I am. I guess I'm just not used to competing with you."

"Don't think of it like we're competing with each other. The derailment story is my first real break. It was a lucky break for me, and I got it at the cost of other people's lives. That part doesn't make me very proud." For the sake of soothing his ego, I found myself diminishing the importance of what I'd done. And to make sure he still felt superior to me as a reporter and as a man, I felt compelled to add, "And it doesn't mean that Mr. Ellsworth and Mr. Copeland are going to move me off of society news. In fact, I'm pretty sure they won't." As soon as I'd said it, I worried that it was true. I got a sick feeling in my stomach, like my innards were radiating heat. I couldn't afford to lose what ground I'd just gained. I was already hungry for my next big piece. *My editors can't expect me to go back to covering the women's pages. Can they?*

"I know it's going to take more than one story to get you off society news." He leaned forward, reached for my hand and kissed it. "I'm sorry I was such a jerk. I really am proud of you. You know that, don't you?"

After we finished lunch, he rushed back to the *Sun-Times*, but I still had a little time to kill and decided to wander around the Loop. Snow had started to fall, leaving behind a picturesque dusting on the sidewalks and streets. I cut east and walked past the holiday windows at Marshall Field's on State Street. Animated snowmen and elves were gliding about on an artificial skating pond. Enormous boxes with oversize bows were stacked on top of one another. Candles shimmered, tinsel sparkled and people crowded in on the sidewalk to get a closer look.

As I passed by the windows I remembered all the times my parents had taken Eliot and me to see the giant Christmas tree and sit on Santa's lap. Even as we grew older there was the traditional family brunch we had each year in the Walnut Room. Back then we were like a normal family. Not like the Caseys, maybe, but still normal enough. My father would come into our rooms and wake us up early, urging us to get dressed so we could hurry down to State Street. My mother would wear one of her best dresses, like the blue satin or my favorite, her green velvet with the lace trim and pearl buttons. My parents never failed to know other people who were there with their families, and while we waited for our food, my father would get up and go from table to table, like he was hosting the whole event.

But that was long ago and those were bittersweet memories. I felt aimless now, like a snowflake floating downward, looking for a place to land. Here it was the day before Christmas and I hadn't bought a single gift for anyone, not even for Jack. The stores were filled with shoppers and Christmas carolers were on the corners. People everywhere were caught up in the holiday frenzy, and I was hoping it was contagious and that I might catch their spirit.

I went inside Marshall Field's and stood before the display of wristwatches. I was reminded how Ernest Hemingway, in a rare show of compassion, had taken off his wristwatch after Eliot's funeral and placed it in my father's hand.

"Time is the only thing that helps," he'd said, curling my father's fingers around the watch.

My father wore Hemingway's watch every day after that until six months later, when it stopped keeping time. He never bothered to get it fixed and he hadn't worn a watch since. Even though I didn't really have the extra money, I bought my father a Timex. For Christmas. So that time could begin moving forward again for him.

Before leaving Field's, I settled on a sweater for Jack, a necktie for his father, some dusting powder for Mrs. Casey, and a bottle of Shalimar for my mother. The snow had started to pick up, and with the winds gusting off the lake it set the flakes blizzarding sideways. I made one more stop on my way back to the paper and popped into Kroch's & Brentano's on Wabash Avenue, where I picked up a copy of *The Man in the Gray Flannel Suit* for Scott.

With my shopping bags filled, I fought against the weather and walked over the snow-covered sidewalks, making my way back to the Tribune Tower. The lobby had a Christmas tree in the center with a cloth of white snow skirting around the bottom. A radio at the front desk was playing *Jingle Bells*. It felt like Christmas when you stepped inside.

But not so up on the fourth floor. The city room didn't stop for the holidays. Deadlines were deadlines, and accidents, murders, earthquakes and other tragedies halfway around the world were still happening and needed to be covered. I still had a story due that afternoon myself.

I was working on a follow-up piece on the CTA scandal, mostly about the reaction from the CTA spokesman, their lawyer, William Lynch, and someone from the mayor's office. Earlier when I'd called around, asking questions, I'd gotten a lot of *No comments*. They were caught off guard. I was sure they'd never expected any of this to leak out. Already people were calling for the Senior Director of Infrastructure and Maintenance to resign.

But still, even as we continued to report the news, we managed to have our own pathetic sort of holiday party. There was whiskey and scotch on the counter in the galley kitchen, along with a case of Schlitz. M had brought in a plate of cookies and Henry's wife had made a fruitcake. Someone's radio was playing *White Christmas*, but that didn't stop Randy from singing, *"You can trust your car to the man who wears the star. . . ."* M wore a

Christmas-tree brooch on her ample bosom. Peter came to work that day wearing a Santa Claus cap along with his green eyeshade. That was the extent of our festivities.

People would go to their desks, write up their stories, call for the copyboys to retrieve their work before rejoining the party. Mr. Ellsworth leaned against the wall with his red pen out, marking up Walter's piece. Mr. Copeland had a scotch in one hand, red pen in the other, doing the same to Henry's work.

"You trust your source on this?" asked Mr. Copeland.

Henry drew down hard on his cigarette. "Absolutely."

"And did you get confirmation on that second quote?"

"Check."

Mr. Copeland grumbled and glanced again at the copy. "And you're sure about the dollar amount?"

"Completely."

"You've got art?"

"Yep."

Mr. Copeland capped his pen, shoved it in his breast pocket and handed back the copy. "Nice work. Get it to the composing room."

It was late in the day. The sun had long since dipped below the horizon, making it officially Christmas Eve. One by one I watched my coworkers finish up their work, bid the rest of us good night and head home to their families. Mrs. Angelo was going to her sister's house in Hyde Park; Gabby was going to her sister's; Benny was catching a train bound for his childhood home in South Bend. M went into the ladies' room and came out a few minutes later dolled up for her date that night in a sequined dress with her hair teased high and her lips painted a shade darker. Mr. Ellsworth nearly dropped his drink when he saw her. Randy sang *I Wanna Be Loved by You*, and Walter whistled through his teeth

like a sailor. Before long it was just Mr. Ellsworth, Walter and me
left behind. The night shift was already at their desks, picking up
where we left off.

Walter drained his drink, crumpled up the paper cup and
pitched it off the rim and into the wastebasket. "I gotta head home."
Firing up his pipe, he gave his fedora a Sinatra-like tilt. "My wife's
holding dinner for me." Much to my surprise, he reached over and
squeezed my arm. I was touched. It was the friendliest gesture he'd
ever made toward me. "Merry Christmas," he said, slapping Mr.
Ellsworth on the back.

Mr. Ellsworth turned to me and said, "What the hell are you
still doing here, Walsh?"

I didn't have an answer. Jack was going to Mass with his family, and I knew my parents wouldn't be doing anything special to
celebrate. I was in no hurry to head home and be alone in my
apartment.

"C'mon," he said. "Let me buy you a Christmas drink."

That was one invitation I couldn't pass up. Ever since the CTA
scandal, I felt like Mr. Ellsworth was slowly letting me into his
circle. Even though my approach had ticked him off, I could tell he
respected me more now for having done that. After that he'd
acknowledge me when he passed me in the city room. He'd even
stop by my desk to ask what I was working on. One night when the
whole gang was at Radio Grill he sat next to me and clanked his
glass to mine. I knew these were crumbs, but I savored each one
because I sensed that I had challenged everything Mr. Ellsworth
believed about sob sisters and what it took to be a good reporter.

So we went over to Riccardo's and sat at the bar, just a regular
reporter and her editor.

"M sure was dolled up tonight," he said, working his way out
of his overcoat and tossing it on the empty stool next to his.
"Wonder where she was off to."

"A date," I said.

"Well, good for her." Mr. Ellsworth nodded. "Good for her." He turned to the bartender and ordered two scotches before proceeding to tell me how he'd become a newspaperman.

"I started straight out of high school as a copyboy working for a small press that went out of business before you were even born. Then I went over to the City News Bureau. Met your father there. Good ol' Hank Walsh. Together we worked our way up from copyboys to reporters. The City News Bureau was a hell of a place to cut your teeth. We were all so green. None of us went to school back then to learn how to write for the newspapers—not like you kids nowadays. No, it was the rewrite men who taught me how to be a journalist. You think I'm hard on your work—let me tell you, they ripped everything I wrote to shreds. They questioned everything, made us verify every single word. They used to say, 'If your mother tells you she loves you, check it out.'" He rattled the ice in his glass and took a sip.

"I don't care what other people say, the City News Bureau was the nerve center of Chicago. I was there. I know. Every newspaper in town looked to us because we had three different teletype wires." He nodded to punctuate the point. "Anything happening in the city, in the country, in the world, came to us. . . . I remember I was working on the desk when we first heard about the murders on Clark Street—the St. Valentine's Day Massacre. I don't think I slept for three days trying to keep up with that story. . . ."

Normally Mr. Ellsworth could hold his liquor, but that night the scotch was getting the better of him. He was slurring his words, rambling and repeating himself, confessing things he never would have said had he been sober.

"Do you know I met my wife just two weeks before that massacre happened? She was younger than me. Still is." He laughed.

"People probably thought she was my daughter. I was supposed to take her out for Valentine's Day." He sat back and laughed some more. "Marjorie should have known right then and there that the paper was always going to come first. You're getting married to a newspaperman yourself, aren't you?"

I glanced down at my ring. "Yes. Jack Casey. He's a general assignment reporter over at the *Sun-Times*."

"Well, I hate to be the bearer of bad news, but trust me on this, Walsh"—he raised his finger—"marriage and newspapers don't mix. I've got a wife and a son, and you know where they are right now? They're with my wife's family. If I show up—if I make it there before dessert—they'll be shocked. But that's an editor's job. He puts his paper to bed." Mr. Ellsworth took a long pull from his glass. "Yep, the editor puts his paper to bed. Walsh, always remember that marriage and newspapers don't mix. Will you promise me that?"

I didn't promise and he kept on talking.

"I know I haven't been a saint. Haven't been the best husband, the best father, but I've been the best damn newspaperman I could be."

The bartender leaned in, running his damp, dingy towel over the surface. "Last call, Stan."

"Last call? It's early."

"It's Christmas Eve. We're closing at ten tonight. So what'll it be?"

I didn't really want another drink and I knew Mr. Ellsworth didn't need one, but we were like two orphans—alone on Christmas Eve with no place to go. So I had another scotch with him, and twenty minutes later, he paid the bill and we stood outside Riccardo's while one by one the lights went out around us. The sidewalks were empty. No one was riding the bus, and we hadn't seen a car go by in five minutes. It was so quiet we could hear the el roaring over the tracks in the distance. Eventually we walked up to Michigan Avenue and stood in the street, hoping that sooner or later a taxi might turn up on Christmas Eve and transport us to a happier place.

Chapter 19

. . .

On Christmas morning I stopped by my parents' house to give them their presents before going on to the Caseys'. The Caseys had invited all of us to their house for Christmas Day, and much to my surprise my parents had accepted. My mother and father liked Jack and they seemed pleased about our engagement, but this would be the first time they'd meet the Caseys. To say I was nervous about bringing our two families together was an understatement.

I let myself inside the Painted Lady with my spare key and removed my slush-covered boots, leaving them on a rubber mat in the foyer. The house was quiet and dark as usual. There was no tree in the bay window where we used to put it and no wreath on the back of the door, nothing to suggest that it was Christmastime.

Not living at home for the past few months had enabled me to see everything with fresh eyes. I knew it was not a happy home, not the same home I'd grown up in, but I wasn't prepared for it to be this oppressive, this sorry and sad. It wasn't that the house was dirty. There were no dishes piled in the sink, no dust bunnies in the corners, but still the place suffered from neglect. Nothing felt loved or cared for. I was painfully aware of the sealed windows, the closed doors and the isolation that was the house itself. The walls needed to breathe as much as the people who lived there.

We were leaving for the Caseys' in an hour and my parents were still in their bathrobes at the kitchen table, having their coffee, reading the morning papers as if they had all the time in the world. My mother had kicked off her slippers, keeping one bare foot tucked beneath her rear end.

"Shouldn't you be getting ready?" I asked.

My mother glanced at the clock above the stove. "Oh my goodness, you're right. She's right, Hank. We should go get dressed."

But neither one bothered to move, so it seemed like as good a time as any to give them their presents.

"Ho, Ho, Ho," I said as I handed my mother a gift-wrapped box. My father stayed hidden behind his newspaper.

"Oh, Jordan," my mother said. "What have you done? You know we don't exchange gifts anymore."

"I know. But I wanted to get you something. And this isn't about exchanging. It's about giving."

"Well, now you're going to make me feel bad." But she didn't hesitate to open her box of Shalimar. "Isn't that lovely. Look, Hank—that's lovely."

My father let a corner of the paper droop down, revealing one eye. He nodded before he snapped the pages back up.

"And here, Dad." I set a small gift box down before him.

"What's this?" The paper flopped forward again.

"For you. For Christmas."

He looked bewildered for a minute, as if I were pushing something poisonous on him. Reluctantly he traded the paper for the box, holding it in his hands, turning it over and over like a Magic 8 Ball about to reveal an ominous answer.

"Well, c'mon, open it."

He muttered as he worked his way through the gift-wrap and

lifted the lid. "A watch." No inflection whatsoever. I didn't know
if he liked it or hated it. He mumbled a *thank you* as he put the
lid back on the box and reached for his Lucky Strikes.

"Aren't you going to put it on?" I asked.

"Sure, yeah, sure," he said, fishing a cigarette from the pack.

"I thought this could replace the watch that Mr. Hemingway
gave you."

"What watch was that?"

He couldn't have forgotten. "The watch. You know. He gave
you his watch. Remember?" I couldn't bring myself to remind
him of the when and why.

"Oh, oh, yeah . . . that one." He nodded, muttered another
thank you with his cigarette propped between his lips. He struck
a match and pushed the box aside.

I turned to hide my disappointment. *Is there no way to reach
this man?* What a fool I was to think there was something I could
do to make him smile, to make the light return to his eyes. Why
did I do this to myself? It would have been easier to let him keep
slipping away, but I just couldn't let him go. He sat there and
smoked his cigarette before he excused himself and went upstairs.
A few minutes later, I heard the bathroom faucet kick on.

My mother reached over and patted my hand. "You should
really return that," she said. "Get your money back. You know
he won't wear a watch."

"That wasn't the point."

She looked at me as baffled as my father had been earlier.

I shook my head. "Never mind."

An hour later, we found ourselves at the Caseys' along with
their forty-some relatives. Christmas carols were playing,
eggnog and fruit punch were being ladled out of crystal punch
bowls and presents were placed around their magnificent tree.

When we first arrived, Mrs. Casey came bounding from the kitchen, untying her floral apron. I noticed that she had removed the plastic seat coverings from the good living room furniture. Bustling over to my parents, she hugged and kissed my father and then did the same to my mother. I didn't come from a family of huggers, and open affection wasn't something we practiced, so imagine the look on my father's face when Judge Casey pulled him in close for an embrace. My mother nearly froze when he took hold of her, pressing his cheek to hers.

My sweaty palms always gave me away. I was a nervous wreck. I wanted my parents to love the Caseys and had a vision of us all getting along, becoming one big happy family. I thought the Caseys were the key to restoring the connection and closeness we'd lost. After Judge Casey welcomed us inside, the five younger brothers, ranging from eight to eighteen, lined up in the hallway to greet us. My father wasn't good with kids, but he made an effort, limply accepting each well-mannered handshake. My mother propped her cigarette in her mouth as she said hello, waving with just her fingers. Next came the extended family and, then, the matriarch, Grandma Casey.

Grandma Casey had clear blue eyes, a face full of wrinkles and ankles thick as tree trunks. I'd met her twice before, and both times she'd smelled of mothballs and cinnamon. She sat on the radiator, atop an overstuffed cushion, and had a box of chocolates on her lap, which she fed to the children, giving them out like dog treats whenever they came over to her.

Thankfully my mother was trying to make a good impression. She joined Mrs. Casey in a glass of punch, but when she set her glass down on the coffee table, Mrs. Casey swooped in with a coaster. I don't think my mother noticed. My father had his usual whiskey while Jack and his father had a couple of Pabst Blue Ribbons.

There was picture taking and toasts, and later that day Judge Casey was walking around wearing the necktie I'd given him despite the fact that it didn't go with his shirt or sweater.

"Come with me," he said, leading me over to Grandma Casey. "It's time the two of you got better acquainted." He gestured to the empty cushion beside her on the radiator.

She held out her box of chocolates. "Frango mint?"

"No. No, thank you."

"Why not? Don't you like chocolates?"

"No. No, I do, but I just don't care for any right now, thank you." I was aware of the radiator heat rising up through the cushion. Her chocolates were sweating, on the verge of melting.

"I see." She helped herself to a Frango mint. "Good," she said as she chewed and licked her fingers. For a second she seemed to drift off, but I knew better. Jack told me Grandma Casey was sharp as could be. Never missed a thing, like she had eyes in the back of her head.

"I remember when I first met Jack's mother," she said. "When Jack's father brought her home and told me this was the girl he was going to marry, I asked Katie why she loved my son. And now I ask the same of you. Why do you love my grandson? Why do you want to marry him?"

I couldn't believe it, but I went completely blank. I was never good at expressing my feelings, but of all the times to freeze up, why now?

"He's a good boy, you know," said Grandma Casey, as if prompting me.

"Yes. Yes, he is. And he's kind. And smart." I wished I could have been more articulate, more specific. I knew I loved Jack, but I couldn't come up with the reasons why. "He's a good, loyal friend, too." My backside was roasting on the radiator.

"And don't forget, handsome," said Grandma Casey.

I smiled. "And yes, he is handsome. Very handsome."

She nodded and looked at Judge Casey, who had appeared at my side. "I like her," she said. "Here, have a chocolate. Take it for later." She handed me a mint and turned to her son. "And for goodness sake, Patrick, take off that ridiculous tie—it looks terrible with your sweater."

Judge Casey removed my necktie and walked me across the room. "You passed with flying colors," he said, putting his arm around me. "Sweetheart, as far as I'm concerned, you're already a member of this family."

His genuine warmth made my heart swell as we joined my father on the couch. My father, ever the reporter and not one to tolerate small talk, launched into a series of questions for Judge Casey.

"So how long have you been on the bench?" he asked.

"About ten years now."

"Circuit court?"

Judge Casey nodded.

My father pressed his lips together and reached for a cigarette. I could tell that he didn't like Judge Casey, but I wasn't sure why. It could have been as simple as Mr. Casey's gold pinky ring or his brand-new Lincoln in the driveway. Or maybe he was jealous of the bond that I'd formed with Jack's father.

"What sort of cases are assigned to you?" my father asked as he struck a match.

"I'm a municipal judge."

"So traffic court and city ordinance violations, eh?"

Judge Casey nodded. "For the 1st District."

My father lit his cigarette, but the match was still burning. Just when I thought it would scorch his fingers, he shook it out, dropping it in a crystal ashtray that was probably just for show.

Mrs. Casey called to me, "Jordan, dear, would you give me a hand here in the kitchen?"

My mother and I exchanged puzzled looks as if to say, *Me, help in the kitchen?*

I headed through the swing door. "Is there something you need?"

Mrs. Casey—perfect, smooth and crisply pressed Mrs. Casey—wiped her hands on a towel and said, "I just wanted to have a word with you. In private. We haven't really had a chance to talk since you and Jack became engaged, and after all, we're talking about a mixed marriage here." She gave me a look that I hadn't seen from her before. She had an edge to her. It threw me, and like with Grandma Casey, I found myself standing there speechless once again.

"Naturally, Jack's told us all about your plans to convert to Catholicism. As you know, it takes a long time, so we're going to speak with the bishop and see if he'll grant you permission to be married in the church before you've completed your Christian Initiation."

"That—that would be—"

"I'm assuming you haven't been baptized."

"Well, no, I haven't, but I'm—"

"Now, I realize you're making an enormous sacrifice here, but I hope you're ready to embrace your new faith. I'd hate to think you were doing this just for the sake of getting married and for the sake of the children. And I'm sure you'll have more time to meet with the parish priest once you stop working."

I didn't know how to tell her that I wasn't planning on quitting my job. Or having children right away.

I was still thinking of how to respond when she said, "And by the way, we haven't said anything yet to Jack's grandmother about you converting. We think it would be best if she got to know you a little better before we tell her that you're really a Jew. Or I guess technically you're only half-Jewish, aren't you?

Grandma Casey's old-fashioned when it comes to these things. We wouldn't want to upset her."

"Of—of course." I didn't know what to say. I felt dirty, and for the first time in my life I felt Jewish and felt the urge to defend my roots.

Just then my mother joined us in the kitchen.

"We're terribly excited about this wedding," Mrs. Casey said to my mother as she leaned over the oven, poking a fork into her Christmas roast.

"So are we. Jack's a wonderful boy."

I expected Mrs. Casey to say something similar about me, but when it became obvious that she wasn't going to return the compliment, my mother brushed imaginary dust off her hands.

"So, how can I help? What should I do?"

"Why don't you slice the bread?" said Mrs. Casey as she stirred a rich-looking sauce on the stove. "There's a serrated knife in the top drawer."

My mother was a lefty and a serrated knife in the hands of a southpaw could be lethal. With a cigarette propped between her lips, she sawed into a log of Mrs. Casey's homemade bread. When Mrs. Casey wasn't looking, I wiped away the cigarette ashes that had fallen onto the countertop.

"Jack tells us you write poetry," said Mrs. Casey, looking on while my mother mutilated the bread. "Here," she said, stepping in. "Let me give you a hand there. . . ."

Fortunately, the bread slicing derailed any further discussion of my mother's poetry.

When it was time for dinner, we took our places at the dining room table and Mr. Casey asked us to all join hands while he led us in saying grace. My father cleared his throat and cocked an eyebrow as if to say, *Jesus Christ, you've got to be kidding.* My mother squeezed his hand, a warning that said, *Just go along with it.*

"Dear Father, our God, our Lord and savior . . ." began Judge Casey.

I dared to open my eyes and saw that Mrs. Casey was watching me.

After dinner, while everyone relaxed in the living room, Mrs. Casey was back to being her saccharine self and brought out an oversize book that turned out to be her wedding album.

"I thought you'd like to see this, dear." She sat between my mother and me on the couch and took us through the album page by page. ". . . And this is the church you'll be married in. Isn't that a beautiful altar?"

"Church?" My mother's voice took on a strange quality. "I know Jordan said she'd be willing to convert, but—" She couldn't finish her sentence because a gasp filled the air as everyone looked at Grandma Casey, their mouths hanging open.

"Well, of course they'll have a church wedding," said Mrs. Casey, sharpening her smile.

"Convert? Who's converting?" asked Grandma Casey.

"Don't worry about it, Mother," said Mrs. Casey.

"Hank and I were married down at City Hall," said my mother, clearly trying to stir the pot.

"What does she mean Jordan's converting?" asked Grandma Casey again. "What's she converting from?"

"Been twenty-eight years." My father piped in from across the room. "Seemed to do just fine for us."

Grandma Casey raised her voice louder than I would have thought possible. "Would somebody tell me what the hell's going on here?"

"It's nothing," said Judge Casey. "Everything's fine."

"I'll tell you right now," said Grandma Casey, "my oldest grandson is not getting married down at City Hall. Over my dead body he will."

I sank down on the couch and felt the tension rush to my temples. This evening was not going the way I'd hoped and there was nothing I could do to turn it around. My dream of one big happy family was slipping away. The judge and several relatives were at Grandma Casey's side, reassuring her that it would be a church wedding. Meanwhile, Mrs. Casey announced that the house at the end of the street was for sale and it would be just perfect for Jack and me.

By the time we left the Caseys' house, I couldn't get out of there fast enough. As much as I longed to be a part of their family, I now saw that there was a price to pay. It was assumed that I would quit my job at the paper, raise a family and make a home in Bridgeport for Jack, who would go on to live the life I'd been planning for myself.

Chapter 20

◆ ◆ ◆

After the New Year, in January of 1956, Marty Sinclair returned to the city room. He was a bit thinner than before but otherwise none the worse for wear. One thing I did notice was that he now kept a copy of the Bible on his desk. I'd see him crack it open, read a passage or two and close his eyes as he'd press the book to his chest. I wondered if he was praying for protection from Big Tony. He'd been sentenced to life in prison, but even behind bars, a guy like that still had men on the outside ready to carry out his orders.

There was lots of whispering about Marty going around the city room. I'd walk by a cluster of people and overhear them saying things like, "He seems normal to me. . . . He's not doing anything strange that I can tell. . . ."

For the first two weeks or so, Marty turned the guys down each time they invited him out for lunch or to grab a drink after work. But gradually he began coming out with us, staying for one and tossing his dollar on the bar even before he'd finished his beer. After a couple more weeks, though, the beer progressed to whiskey, and by the time he returned to the bowling league, good ol' Marty was back in the swing of things.

One night we were back at the King Pin, going up against the City News Bureau. Jack and the *Sun-Times* were a few lanes over, taking on the *Chicago American*. I was sitting with Mr. Ellsworth, who'd surprised us by showing up even though he couldn't bowl on account of having a bad back. Mrs. Angelo, Benny, Gabby and a few others were there as spectators. Afterward we went into the lounge and the losers bought the winners drinks and then the winners bought the losers a round. Everyone was crowded in around the bar. Mr. Ellsworth was holding court, talking about his days at the City News Bureau, when I noticed M sitting alone in a banquette off to the side. She kept looking over at us, and I excused myself and went to her.

"What are you doing back here all by yourself?" I pulled up a chair and sat down.

She looked at me in a boozy haze, her eyeliner smudged beneath one eye. "Do you even know how lucky you are? My God, you've got everything." She pointed to my engagement ring.

"Just because I'm getting married doesn't mean I have *everything*. I'm not crossing the finish line, you know."

"Trust me, that's close enough."

But was it?

I remember my parents questioning me after they met the Caseys at Christmas. We'd barely made it to the car before they started in.

"Is this what you want?" my mother asked. "Don't get me wrong. We love Jack. He's terrific. And the father's not so bad, but that mother. Sheesh."

"And what about that saying grace business? Are we going to have to do that every time we sit down to a meal with those people?"

"*Those people?*" I looked at him. "Those people are going to be my in-laws."

"She's right, Hank," said my mother. "We need to try to make an effort."

"I'll make an effort. I made an effort tonight, didn't I?"

"Yes, dear. You were on very good behavior."

"I'll say one thing—they sure as hell have a big family." My father leaned closer to the steering wheel, no doubt calculating the costs of inviting them all to the wedding.

I was thinking about all this as I watched M finish her drink. She stood up and worked her way into her coat.

"Well, if you ask me, Jordan, you've got it made." She left without saying good-bye to anyone.

One snowy morning I arrived at the city room and went over to the horseshoe like I always did, said good morning to the slot man and checked the assignment book. Even though I was still working on the women's pages, every now and then, when the other reporters were too busy, Mr. Ellsworth gave me a shot at some bigger stories. He had me covering accidents and fires, that sort of thing. He said I was good with human tragedies.

I ran my finger down the first column, looking for my name, not knowing if I'd be reporting on a ribbon cutting that day or a six-car pileup. I took on whatever they threw my way, believing that each story got me closer to the city desk.

That day I was assigned another car crash, this one involving an elderly man who'd driven his car into the side of a building. The driver was pronounced dead on the scene. I went to my desk to read through the autopsy report, which said that the driver had suffered from a heart attack moments before the impact. I was always amazed by the information we got back from the coroner's office and the forensics lab and the things they could gather from a victim's shirt or a seemingly random piece of scrap metal. Trace evidence came in the form of everything from gunshot residue to blood-splatter analysis. It made me wonder about Eliot's personal effects, which we'd been given the night he was killed. I imagined everything would have been blood-soaked, torn and covered in dirt and gravel from the pavement. Could those items have filled in some of the gaps of information missing from Eliot's accident?

"Whatcha working on there, Walsh?"

I looked up, startled, thrown out of my thoughts.

Marty Sinclair was standing over my shoulder, reading as I typed. "Oh, it's nothing," I said, splaying my fingers over the page so he couldn't see.

"C'mon, show me."

"It's an accident. Car hit a building. Poor driver died. I guess Benny didn't have time to do it."

"Well, let's have a look." Marty pulled up a chair. "I read your piece about the art gallery fire. It was good, but it could have been stronger." He reached over and adjusted the carriage return so he could see the whole page.

I chewed the inside of my cheek while he read.

"See now, right here"—he pointed to the second paragraph— "you want to keep hitting the reader with the facts. Front-load it. You're going soft on them too early. . . ."

I glanced back at him. So obvious. Of course. He was right. That's what made him Marty Sinclair.

"Let me have another look before you turn it in," he said as he stood up.

"Really?"

"Really." He offered a subtle wink.

I felt anointed and very aware of Henry and Walter and some of the others overhearing this exchange.

A few days later, Marty stopped by my desk again and gave me some pointers on a story about a funeral parlor with unscrupulous burial practices. Apparently the doorway in the back of the funeral home was too narrow for the caskets to pass through, so they always turned them on their sides before loading them into the hearse. The thought of people's deceased loved ones being tossed about like fruit salad made me sick, but as Marty said, "It makes for good copy." The following week he helped me on another piece about a suicide jumper in the Loop.

"What's up with you and Marty?" Randy asked one night over cocktails. "We're starting to think he has a thing for you."

Jack had thought that as well, but there was nothing of the sort going on. But one day, after Marty had been working with me, I did finally ask him myself.

"Why *are* you doing this? Why are you helping me?"

"Because you're hungry and you're good. But"—he raised a finger—"you could be great. That's why." He pointed out a few more things about my piece and said, "So when are you getting married, Walsh?"

I was surprised that Marty of all people would ask me that. But then again, that was the question everyone had been asking lately. Usually I'd tell them "soon" or perhaps more accurately, "next year."

I thought about the night Jack asked me to marry him. Despite his discovering that I wasn't Catholic or Irish, that conversation had gotten us ahead of ourselves. Jack had said things that night that he hadn't really thought through, and it forced our hand, accelerating everything. I loved him. I did. And I wanted to marry him. Someday. But the truth was that I wasn't ready yet and neither was he.

We had set something in motion and there was no calling it back. This all came to me like a streak of lightning, illuminating everything for an instant before disappearing, leaving me in darkness once more. Only a vague uncertainty remained.

What I told Marty and others was that planning a wedding took time and converting to Catholicism took even more time—

time that I couldn't spare. Especially now that I was getting some real assignments and I had Marty's support. I was making strides at work and I didn't want to lose my momentum.

"So tell me the truth?" Marty said. It was just the two of us, huddled over our scotches, waiting for the others to join us at Riccardo's. "You getting your fill of car crashes and gas explosions?"

I laughed. "I can't believe I'm saying this, but I'm starting to see that it really doesn't matter if it's a debutante ball or a five-alarm fire."

He smiled. "The news is the news, isn't it?"

"It's so true. You get down the facts and your who, what, where, when and why and then you write it up."

"Pretty much," he said, giving the scotch a swirl in his glass. "But don't be discouraged. There are still bigger stories out there. One day you come across a story that's never been told, or something sticks in your craw and you want to bring it out to the public, or you want to right a wrong. When you come across a story like that, then"—he raised his glass—"then it's a whole new ball game. That's the kind of reporting that wins you awards and recognition and gives you the freedom to write whatever you want."

"But how do I get those kinds of assignments in the first place?"

"You do exactly what you're doing. Don't wait for the assignments to come to you—you go out and find the stories yourself. Keep your eyes and ears open. And keep writing. Keep digging. You'll get there."

"You'll get where?" I heard someone say. I turned around and there was Walter with the others.

Marty and I didn't talk any more about my reporting that night, but his words stayed with me. And so, in addition to the fires and crashes, I used my spare time to cultivate my own stories.

Right away I started working on an article about female

inmates in the Dwight Correctional Facility. What I'd learned so far was that behind every convicted woman there was a man to blame. One woman told me that her boyfriend brought her along on robberies because he was too fat to fit through the windows and had her crawl inside and unlock the door. Another woman told me she forged checks for her husband because he was illiterate and couldn't do it himself. I spent nearly two weeks meeting with the inmates and writing down their stories.

People, especially M and the other ladies at work, thought I was crazy taking on extra assignments in my free time.

"I don't understand why you don't just hurry up and get married," said M.

"I'm too busy right now."

"Doing what?" M shook her head. "I don't understand you at all sometimes. And I really don't understand what we're doing here."

We were at the Berghoff on Adams near State Street. They operated a men's-only bar, and I was working on a feature to see if they'd wait on me. It was the middle of the afternoon and the bar was fairly empty. Still, the few men sitting there scowled when they saw us, and one of them complained to the bartender who was now making his way toward us.

"They're going to throw us out, you know," said M.

"You're probably right." I sat on a barstool and patted the one next to me for M. "But if they do, that'll make for a better story, won't it?"

"Ladies," the bartender said, wiping out a glass, "we only serve men here."

"We just want to order a drink," I said.

"I'm afraid you'll have to do it somewhere else." He slung the towel over his shoulder and folded his arms across his chest.

"I'm Jordan Walsh with the *Chicago Tribune*. I'm doing a story about why you won't serve women in this bar."

"I don't care who you are and where you're from. The rules are the rules, ladies, and this is a men's-only bar."

I pulled out my notebook and pen. "Would you care to make a comment?"

"I said, we don't serve women in here. That's my comment. Now, I've asked you nicely, but if you and Blondie don't leave quietly, I'm going to have to make you leave. You understand?"

Less than a minute later, M and I were outside on the sidewalk. It was the middle of March, and Daley had the lampposts all over downtown done up in shamrocks and green tinsel in preparation for his St. Patrick's Day parade.

"Let's see if there's a side door," I said.

"Why? They're not going to serve you. What are you trying to do, get us arrested?"

"I'm trying to get a story."

"Oh, Jordan, why don't you just stop this?"

"Stop what?"

"Chasing down stories. Looking for your big break." She reached inside her pocketbook for her compact. "You should be focused on converting and planning your wedding now. That's what you should be doing. What are you waiting for? I swear sometimes you act like you don't even want to get married."

"That's not true. I do want to get married. I just—I'm—"

"Poor Jack," said M as we drifted away from the Berghoff. "You're making him wait all this time. I hope he's as patient as you think he is, because I'm warning you, one of these days you're going to have to stop putting your job first."

Putting my job first was something I learned when I was sixteen, before I even had a job. My parents were having one of their dinner parties. Nelson Algren was there that night with Simone de Beauvoir. He'd just published *The Man with the Golden*

Arm, and the English version of de Beauvoir's book *The Second Sex* was coming out. Mr. Algren had given a lecture at the University of Chicago earlier that evening. There was another couple there that night, along with the poet Gwendolyn Brooks.

I remember the adults were sitting around the dining room table, a haze of cigarette smoke lingering over their drinks. I said good night and went upstairs to do my homework. Eliot was away at college then. The hour was growing late, and from my room I heard the conversation below me getting louder. Algren and de Beauvoir were arguing.

"You could not even so much as mention my book tonight," came the thick French accent. "An entire auditorium filled with people and you could not so much as mention my book!"

"And why should I have?" said Algren. "When the University of Chicago invites you to come speak, you can talk all you want about your book."

"You're not taking my work seriously," de Beauvoir said. "It is men like you who are the very cause of the oppression I write about."

The volume escalated and soon everybody was speaking over each other. Next I heard something break—sounded like glass shattering—followed by high heels coming up the stairs. A moment later my bedroom door swung open.

"Oh, pardon," said de Beauvoir in her chic French accent, tears clouding her eyes. She was stylishly dressed with her dark hair parted in the center and pulled back in a silk turban. "I thought this was the powder room."

I sat up straighter and put my book aside.

"It's down the hall, Simone," my mother said as she came up behind her, the two of them fitting neatly inside the doorframe. "Are you all right?"

De Beauvoir was very drunk and very beautiful despite the

tears streaming down her cheeks. "No. I am not all right," she said as she took a step forward and dropped down on the corner of my bed, resting her elbows on her knees and her head in her hands. "From this man I will never recover." She was pure drama, from her words to her accent.

My mother came inside my room, and I scooted out of the way, closer toward the headboard, so she could sit beside de Beauvoir.

"You can't let him get to you like this," my mother said, draping her arm over de Beauvoir's shoulder. "You know how he is. How all men are. Did you really expect him to mention your work tonight?"

When de Beauvoir raised her head, her eyes were bloodshot and the tip of her nose was red. "Men are such bastards. Selfish bastards, each and every one of them. I have two men, and they both take and take and take and give me nothing in return. It's all *me, me, me,*" she said, beating her fist to her chest. "It is like I am not important. Not *as* important. Is he so threatened by me that he cannot give me the credit I deserve? The respect I have earned?" She paused, and her shoulders sagged, broken. "Oh, but my heart, it loves him. So I do for him whatever I can, things I didn't even think possible. But even that is not enough. I give and I give and I give and still Nelson wants more. I lose a part of my soul each time I give my heart to him. I don't know how to love that man without hating myself for it. I regret all that I've done for him and I resent him for making me abandon myself." Her eyes flashed open wide, and she clasped a hand over her mouth just as she collapsed and sobbed into my mother's arms.

"See what love can do?" de Beauvoir mumbled to me, her eyes growing heavy. "It can destroy. It can ruin lives. . . ."

I'd never seen a grown woman crumble like that. It frightened me to know that it was possible to feel that kind of pain.

And over a man. While she went on crying, I scooted out of the
way and let my mother help de Beauvoir into my bed, slipping
off her shoes and pulling the covers up to her shoulders. Just
before de Beauvoir passed out, my mother said something to her
in French. De Beauvoir smiled sadly and nodded. *"Oui, oui."*

Afterward my mother and I went down the hall to Eliot's
room, where I'd be sleeping that night. "What did you say to
her?" I asked. "In French?"

"I reminded her never to put a man first. Ever."

That conversation I'd witnessed between my mother and Simone de Beauvoir in my bedroom took place five years ago, but
I was only now realizing how true her words were.

Chapter 21

♦ ♦ ♦

In June the Caseys met with their bishop and received special permission for Jack and me to be married in the Catholic Church. After that we were off and running. A date was set: November 10, 1957. It still seemed far enough off and slightly unreal despite that the invitations were being printed and the guest lists pondered.

Around this time my mother and I went looking for dresses. We were not natural-born shoppers when it came to this sort of thing. While we could spend hours in bookstores, we usually only shopped for clothes under duress. I had dragged her along when I bought all those outfits for my new job, both of us irritated and snapping at each other by the end of the day. I remember how buying back-to-school clothes each year was an arduous task that we put off until the last minute.

This time we decided to get a head start on things and went to the bridal department at Marshall Field's. We were such novices as we stepped off the escalator, landing in an enchanted forest of white silks, satins and taffeta. As we sorted through a rack of gowns, my mother's attention was diverted to my blouse, peppered with ink from the newspapers I always carried under my arm.

"You're ruining all your clothes," she said.

"I don't know what to do about it." I shrugged. "It comes with the territory."

The shopgirl patiently waited on us, bringing out a series of wedding dresses. My mother and I selected half a dozen flowing white gowns to try on, each embellished with beading and embroidery and satin and lace. Some were tea length, and some hung to the ground with mile-long trains. One dress was more glorious than the next, and soon I was standing on a riser before a three-way mirror wearing a gown that cost more than two months' salary.

"Don't worry about that right now," said my mother when she saw me looking at the price tag. "I can always get Grandpa to pay for it."

It had been more than a year since I'd seen my grandparents. They'd been aloof about my engagement, especially when they learned that, like their daughter, I wasn't marrying a Jewish boy. I wondered if they'd even bother to make the trip in for the wedding.

"You know I didn't wear a wedding dress when your father and I got married. I didn't even wear white. It was a powder blue suit with a sable collar. It was a Christian Dior. But it was no wedding dress. And we weren't married in a fancy church, either."

"Are you trying to make me feel guilty?"

"Oh, God, no. It's just that the Caseys are making such a big deal over this."

"Excuse me. Some would argue that a wedding *is* a big deal."

"Of course it is, but did you see their guest list? They're practically inviting the whole city."

"And I think that's *just* their relatives."

She laughed and fluffed out the train on my dress. "There—" She came and stood beside me, and I felt absolutely giddy as she squeezed my shoulders. To see myself as a bride was both exhilarating and terrifying.

"Well?" I set my hands on my hips. "What do you think?"

"I love it."

"I do too." I turned to the left and then the right.

"Oh, wait a minute." My mother frowned. "The fabric's puckering in the back here." She tugged on it, inching it this way and that. "Nope. It's still doing it."

That was enough to make us fall out of love with it.

The next dress, an ivory silk, was too low-cut.

"*Oy.* Can you imagine what *Grandma Casey* would say if she saw this?" my mother said in a mocking tone.

I laughed. "You really don't like the Caseys, do you?"

"It's not that I don't like them. I actually love Jack. But those people? That mother and the granny—*Oy gevalt!*"

I laughed but immediately felt guilty for doing so.

By the time I'd tried on the next dress, it was getting warm inside the fitting room. The overhead lights were bouncing off the mirror, glaring back at us. The salesclerk was too persistent, repeatedly knocking on the door, asking if we needed anything else. I was getting cranky and so was my mother.

Now she looked at each price tag and added commentary.

"That's ridiculous."

"That's a bit much."

"You've got to be kidding me."

With each new dress our spirits sagged a bit more. It was like a balloon steadily losing air until it reached the point where we looked at the dozens of buttons on one dress and decided that was too much work and moved on. But even as I pulled the next gown over my head, I knew I wouldn't like it. The moment had passed, and now my mother and I were only going through the motions.

We were like cutouts of ourselves, a mother-daughter duo look-ing for that perfect dress. But finding it just wasn't all that import-ant to us, and by the time the salesgirl brought in another round, we were done. We felt burdened and put-upon and we were still dragging even as we left the flowing, glittering bridal department and made our way to the escalators.

We didn't begin to feel like ourselves again until we reached the first floor and my mother suggested we look at the handbags.

"We should find you something that's big enough for all your newspapers so you don't keep ruining your clothes."

I agreed and so we revived ourselves while looking at the Korets, the Wilardys and, of course, the black quilted Chanel 2.55 bags that were so popular. From there we moved on to the more moderately priced leather bags, alligator bags, knit bags and bags made of cloth. None of them were big enough to hold all my newspapers and magazines, my notepad and everything else that I schlepped to and from the city room each day. We had about given up and were working our way toward the Wabash Avenue exit when something caught my mother's eye.

"Aha! Come with me." She headed toward a display of sleek leather attaché cases in the men's department. "How about some-thing like this?"

"An attaché case?" I started to laugh. I thought she was kidding.

"Why not? It's perfect." She snapped open the brass latches and ran her hand across the suede interior. "Isn't it lovely? Feel this. It can hold everything. You can even carry an umbrella and your lunch. A change of shoes."

"But, Mom, it's an attaché case. They're for men."

"Says who? Who's to say you can't carry one as well?"

And so that afternoon, instead of a wedding dress, my mother bought me an attaché case. Actually it took little convincing on her part as soon as we zeroed in on the right one. It was quite handsome, made of soft brown leather with brass buckles and a combination lock for safekeeping.

Beyond the practicality of it, I didn't give it much thought. But the next day, as I stepped onto the el, I couldn't help noticing the looks my attaché case was attracting. The same was true on Michigan Avenue, when every businessman I passed eyed my briefcase, sizing it up to his own. Even the doorman in the lobby of the Tribune Tower gave me a quizzical look. And when I entered the city room the fellows were all over me about it.

"Whose is that?" asked Benny, pointing to my case.

"It's mine."

"What do you mean, it's yours?" Walter burst out laughing. "Hey, look everyone. The boss lady's here."

"That's some lunch box," said Marty with a chuckle.

"Whatcha sporting in there?" asked Henry. "A machine gun?"

"Or better yet, maybe it's a body," said Peter.

They all laughed while I set the briefcase on my desk and snapped open the brass buckles. I'm sure they were disappointed to see that it was filled with just newspapers and magazines. And that extra pair of shoes that my mother thankfully suggested.

As the day progressed, the others continued to razz me about my attaché case. Even the girls were taken aback and seemed almost offended when I brought it along after work and set it on the empty chair at our table at Riccardo's.

"It's just not the sort of thing a lady carries," insisted Gabby.

"Aren't you worried that it makes you look too masculine?" asked M.

"I'm worried that the rest of you don't want to start carrying one yourselves," I said. "It's much easier than trying to cram everything inside your handbag or trying to carry everything in your arms. And besides, there's no law that says these cases are for men only."

"She has a point," said Eppie Lederer. "Still, I don't think it's for me. I can't see me carrying that thing. It's too bulky and then what would I do with my handbag?"

"I agree," said Gabby. "And I still think it's off-putting to men."

"But she doesn't need to worry about what men think," said M. "She's already got a man. She's engaged, remember."

"And how does Jack feel about your carrying that thing?" Eppie asked with a laugh.

I looked at her, baffled. I couldn't tell if she was joking or not. Were my mother and I the only ones who didn't think it was a big deal for a woman to carry an attaché case?

I continued to carry my attaché case despite judgmental looks from strangers on the el and from men and women passing me on the street. Not to mention the ongoing mocking from my coworkers, whom I thought would have been more concerned about preparing for the upcoming Democratic National Convention.

Chicago was a steam bath that August, with temperatures in the high nineties. The humidity crept onto every surface, finding its way into every fold of fabric and crease of skin. Oscillating fans were perched on top of the desks in the city room trying to cool everyone while we revved up for the convention. There was a steady influx of updates coming in on the wires and announcements of candidates and delegates arriving.

I was polishing a piece on "Planning the Perfect Picnic" for Women's World Today when Mrs. Angelo, Mr. Ellsworth and Mr. Pearson called me into one of the conference rooms. I was a bit uneasy as I stood in the doorway. It was unusual to meet with the features editor and the managing editor together. And having Mrs. Angelo there only concerned me more. I was certain they were going to reprimand me or possibly even fire me for doing everything in my power to move off the women's pages.

"Come in, Robin," said Mr. Pearson. Even after I'd worked in his department for a year and three months, he still didn't know my name. "Have a seat."

I took the chair next to Mrs. Angelo. Mr. Pearson sat at the head.

Mr. Ellsworth paced back and forth, his fingertips caressing his whiskers, as was his habit. "We've got a special assignment for you, Walsh."

"We're putting you on the convention coverage," said Mr. Pearson.

"What?" At first I thought I hadn't heard right. "But what about Marty and Walter?"

"What about them?" Mr. Ellsworth planted his hands on his hips. "Marty's still covering the convention. So is Walter. Relax, you're just covering the women's interest stories there. Mrs. Angelo will give you your assignments."

I left the meeting trying to decide if I was pleased that they were letting me cover the convention or disappointed that I'd been relegated to the women's stories. That night I was home at a reasonable hour, washing my stockings in the bathroom sink and planning what I'd wear to the convention center the next day. I was squeezing out the excess soap when I heard a pounding on the front door.

With my hands still dripping water, I looked through the peephole. Jack was standing in the hallway. When I opened the door, he was staring at the baby stroller, filled with black socks and one discarded sneaker. I let him inside, and with my sudsy hands held up like a surgeon's, I leaned in to kiss him, but he pulled away.

"What's wrong?"

"Goddamn fuckin' assholes."

"Whoa." I'd never heard Jack talk like that before. "What happened? What's going on?"

"My fucking editor reassigned the convention."

"What does that mean?" I reached for a kitchen towel and dried my hands.

"It means I'm not covering the goddamn convention—that's what it means."

"But why not?"

"He says he's got enough men on it. He needs me to stick with the zoning story. A goddamn zoning story when there's a national presidential convention in town."

"Can't you do both?"

"I told him I could. I told him I'd sleep at my desk if I had to. He wouldn't bite."

"I'm sorry." I brushed my fingers through his hair, but he shrugged me away. I raised my hands in surrender. "I'm just trying to help."

"Forget I said anything." He went over to the fridge and surveyed the shelves. "What happened to all the beer?"

"We drank it."

"Terrific." He slammed the door shut.

"There's some vodka in the cupboard." I retrieved a bottle, but then he was upset that I didn't have any ice. He drank it warm anyway.

"Why do you keep vodka in the cupboard anyway? You're supposed to keep it in the freezer."

"I'll make a note of that."

He leaned up against the refrigerator and made a face as if to say I didn't understand.

"What's really bothering you?"

"I'm damn frustrated is all. I wanted to cover the convention."

"I know you did." I went and wrapped my arms around him from behind, butting my chin up against his shoulder. "It's not fair. You would have done a brilliant job." I tightened my hold around his middle and drew a deep breath.

"Oh, before I forget, my mother needs to talk to you. Something about flowers or menus or something. I don't remember what. And she said to remind you about your meeting with Father Greer on Wednesday."

"Okay. I know."

He looked at me with little confidence.

"I know," I said, this time louder. "I have it on my calendar and don't worry, I'll call your mother first thing tomorrow. Okay?"

"Okay."

It wasn't okay. Not with me it wasn't. There were so many more important things on my mind just then, like figuring out how I was going to tell Jack that I would be covering the convention. Even though I'd been assigned only to the women's stories, I knew it was going to sting.

After Jack drank half his vodka, he said, "Listen, I'm in a shitty mood and I don't want to end up fighting with you about the wedding." He jangled his keys in his pocket and turned toward the door. "I've had a lousy day. I'm tired and—"

"You're not leaving, are you?"

"I gotta go."

"No. Don't. Stay."

But he put his hand on the doorknob. "I'll—I'll call you later."

Chapter 22

◆ ◆ ◆

I hardly slept that night, and the next morning I woke before my alarm to the steady sound of raindrops pelting my bedroom window. It was one of those gunmetal-colored days. Everything was gray and gloomy, and I could see the clouds moving overhead with nothing behind them except for more bleakness.

By the time my attaché case and I headed down to the International Amphitheatre at Halsted and 42nd Street, the drizzle had changed over to an ominous downpour filled with thunder and lightning. It was as if the city were rebelling against this onslaught of delegates with their bad suits and their convention-eer antics.

The first morning Mrs. Angelo had me do a piece on the convention organist. He was a young man from Palos Park. Just twenty-two years old. When I interviewed him, he told me he had memorized more than two thousand political songs and military marches.

"Before this convention is over," he said, "I bet you'll have played *Chicago* from *Pal Joey* at least two hundred times."

As soon as I finished that up, I moved on to the next assignment: the eighty switchboard operators in the convention telephone center. Political warfare was going on inside the amphitheater, and here I was, down the hall, talking to a roomful of women in matching blue uniforms. They had undergone hours of special training for this with Illinois Bell, which included speech and elocution classes. The supervisor explained that their main responsibilities were to place calls, connect incoming calls and take messages for the delegates. How Mrs. Angelo expected me to make an interesting piece out of this was beyond me.

Next I was scheduled to interview the New York governor's secretary for White Collar Girl. The rewrite desk was standing by back at the city room. Higgs was working 'round the clock, awaiting updates so he could knock out the stories as they were called in. He had to have been as bored with my topics as I was.

I finished up early for the day and so I flashed my credentials and sat in on a press conference. Marty and Walter were sitting across the way, looking at me as if to say, *What the hell are you doing in here?*

"I'm not trying to step on anyone's toes," I explained afterward. The three of us were standing in a crowded hallway. Reporters and photographers were chasing down the press secretaries, hoping for statements. "I just had some free time and was curious. . . ."

"Spare me." Walter stuffed his pipe in his mouth, shook his head in disgust and walked away.

"Walter, c'mon—"

He ignored me and kept walking.

"Aw, don't worry about him," said Marty. "He'll cool off."

"Honestly, I don't want to cause problems. I just wanted to sit in and listen. That's all."

"Then be smart. Watch how you go about it. That's my only advice."

After Marty left, I went to a pay phone and called Jack,

asking if we could meet for a drink. Twenty minutes later I found him waiting for me in a dark corner of Marge's Pub, a dive up on Sedgwick. Marge, the owner, and her husband lived above the bar. They both waved to me when I came in.

"Sorry about last night," Jack said, pulling me toward him for a kiss. "I was just so damn ticked off about the convention."

"I know. And you have every right to be upset about that."

"I knew if I stayed last night you were going to try to make me feel better, and I didn't want to feel better."

I reached for his glass. "What is this?"

"Scotch."

I took a sip because I needed a shot of courage. What I was about to tell him would definitely not make him feel better. But I had to say something before he saw my byline in the next morning's paper. And he would see it because Jack and I followed each other's work, read each other's pieces. He even read my recipes in Mary Meade's column. I took another sip of his scotch and called to the bartender for another.

"So I need to talk to you about something," I said after I brought my drink back from the bar.

"What is it?"

"Well, I was going to tell you last night, but I just couldn't. It wasn't the right time."

"What's going on? Are you all right?"

"Yeah, yeah, I'm fine. It's just that, well . . . My editors had a little meeting with me yesterday afternoon and . . . well"—I reached for his hand and shook my head—"God, I hate to tell you this. But see, they asked me to cover the convention. But"—I watched his jaw open as his eyes closed—"but I'm only covering the women's stories. Just small pieces. Nothing big. Nobody's probably even going to read them." I heard the words leaving my mouth and it hurt. It was just like Simone de Beauvoir. It was a betrayal of the self. I wasn't raised to downplay who I was and what I was capable of. If anything, it was just the opposite, especially being a girl and having a strong mother. But I didn't want to hurt Jack. "Please"—I looked at him—"say something."

He slapped the table. "That's—that's great. I'm happy for you." He grabbed his drink and gulped it.

"Please don't be like that. I know it's weird for you, but . . ."

He looked around the bar and then leaned his head back and scratched his neck. A thin sheen of perspiration had collected on his brow. "I don't want to talk about this right now."

"I don't want you to be mad at me because my editors gave me—"

"I said I don't want to talk about it."

"Okay, fine. We won't talk about it." I reached in my handbag for a cigarette and waited, expecting Jack to offer me a light. When he didn't, I leaned over the candle. "So tell me about your day." I exhaled toward the ceiling.

"I don't want to talk about it."

I exhaled again, harder this time. "Okay, fine. So you don't want to talk about the convention. You don't want to talk about your day. What *do* you want to talk about?"

"Nothing."

"Jee-sus. C'mon, Jack."

But he wasn't talking. So we sat in silence and finished our drinks. When we were leaving, we said good-bye to Marge and Mindy, one of the regulars who was at the bar, the two of them doing shots.

The rain had temporarily stopped, but the air was thick and smelled of earthworms. Jack and I started down the street, traversing the puddles. I assumed he'd be coming home with me like he normally did, but instead he stopped, stepped into the road and raised his hand to hail a cab.

"What are you doing? Aren't you coming with me?" I asked.

He waved his hand in the air. "Nah, I'm tired. I need a good night's sleep."

He barely kissed me before he got in the taxi and drove off.

I t was drizzling again the next morning when I made it to the amphitheater. I sat down in the entryway to wait for Mrs. Bernice McCray to arrive. Mrs. McCray was Governor Averell Harriman's executive secretary, and I was scheduled to interview her for White Collar Girl.

While I waited on her, I ran into an acquaintance who was with the AP.

"Come with me," he said. "I just got the results from last night."

I followed him down the hall and ended up being among the first reporters to get the overnight polls. When you're one of a handful of people who know something that the rest of the world is waiting to hear, it's a powerful feeling. Everything inside me came alive as I rushed to the bank of phone booths. They were all taken—probably by other reporters calling in their scoops. I couldn't wait and let this chance pass me by, so I darted outside and found a phone booth around the corner and called back to the city room. The windowed panels of the booth were pelted with raindrops, like a Coca-Cola bottle pulled from an ice bucket. After a brief hold, I got Higgs on the phone. I swore the man never slept, always on the rewrite desk.

"I've got the overnight polls," I said, standing in a phone booth, covering my ear to drown out the noise on the street.

There was a long static pause, and for a second I thought we'd lost the connection.

"Hello? Higgs? You there?"

"Yeah, yeah, I'm here." There was another pause before he said, "Shouldn't I be getting this information from Marty or Walter?"

"They don't have it yet. And I do." I knew Marty and Walter would be good and sore at me for making this call. But I had the information, and at the end of the day, editors didn't care who delivered the news as long as they got it. And got it first. It would have been irresponsible not to have called it in.

"Now, take this down," I said, switching ears. "Stevenson just picked up three more votes, so right now he's got 690 dele-gates. . . . Yeah, he's basically got it wrapped up. . . . No official word yet on Kennedy's votes for vice president. We should have confirmation soon. But here's the real news. Harriman's not back-ing down. I know he's only got 228 votes . . . but they say they've talked to Truman and they're still in the fight. But everything indicates it's going to Stevenson on the first ballot and—"

"Jordan, that's Marty calling in on the other line. I have to go."

"But wait—"

"Marty's holding for me. I—I gotta go."

"I'll call you back as soon as I've got something else." I barely got the sentence out before Higgs hung up.

I tried calling Jack after that, but there was no answer, so I went back into the amphitheater and waited for Mrs. Bernice McCray and the Roll Call of States. Meanwhile, I spoke with more delegates and the campaign and press secretaries.

Later that day I bumped into Marty and could tell right away he was upset with me.

"I thought I told you to watch how you went about this," he said.

"Marty, I had the information. I had to call it in."

He planted his hands on his hips and narrowed his eyes. "I've been good to you, Walsh."

"Of course you have, and I really appreciate—"

"I don't give a goddamn what you do to Walter, but don't think you can waltz in here and try to show me up."

"I would never. Honest. That's not what I'm—"

"I'm a nice guy, Walsh, but if you ever go behind my back again, I'll mop the goddamn floor with you."

"Marty—"

"We're done here." He adjusted his hat, turned and walked away.

I called after him, but he kept walking, disappearing into the crowd. I was thrown off-balance after that. I felt stunned and misunderstood. I hadn't done it as a personal affront to Marty, just as a means to help myself.

I stopped into a café for a cup of coffee and a smoke, hoping to shake it off. It was crowded inside, and I got one of the last seats at the counter. I didn't make eye contact with anyone and stared into my steaming cup as if there were something there to see, like tea leaves, perhaps. I took a sip of coffee. It burned a hole in my gut.

When I returned to the convention hall, I saw Marty again. He had his thick glasses propped up on his forehead while he jotted down some notes. I sheepishly wandered over to him. "I'm really sorry about what happened earlier."

"Aw, shrug it off, Walsh. Shrug it off." He smiled and gave my shoulder a squeeze. "You know me. I don't stay mad for long. But watch yourself. The others won't be as forgiving."

And that was it. He seemed fine again. Normal. All was well and I was relieved. After that I was able to concentrate and finish the interview with the governor's secretary. It was getting late, but knowing I had Marty back on my side, I took a chance and went over to Stevenson's law office on LaSalle. I thought it was an ingenious move, and apparently I wasn't alone. There was a handful of reporters already standing around in the lobby, hoping to get information from his campaign manager or his press secretary. I figured that if I ran into Marty or Walter there, I'd offer to team up with them.

The hour grew later, and one by one the other reporters drifted home or to their hotel rooms. I toughed it out mostly because it was raining again, coming down hard in sideways sheets, and I'd left my umbrella back at the amphitheater. I didn't want to stand in the downpour trying to hail a cab along with every other stranded Chicagoan, so I sat on a hard wooden bench and waited it out. That was really the only reason I stayed behind, but it was a good thing I did.

Twenty minutes later one of Stevenson's aides came down and went over to the vending machine. I recognized him from earlier in the day, when he'd been standing on the stage next to the candidate. He was alone now. We were the only two people in the lobby. He was patting down his pockets, searching for change.

"Need a dime?" I rushed over and held out my hand with a few coins resting in my palm.

"Oh, thank you." He slipped a dime into the slot and pulled out a Coca-Cola.

"Long day, huh?" I said.

He nodded. "You can say that again."

"So what's going on up there?" I gestured toward the elevators, expecting him to give me the brush-off. But he was young and inexperienced. He didn't ask if I was a reporter.

He uncapped his Coke, took a long guzzle and began talking. "Stevenson's up there working on the nominating speech with the senator."

"The senator?"

"Yeah. Senator Kennedy." He took another gulp of his soda pop.

"So you're saying that Senator Kennedy's going to give the nominating speech?"

I probably should have masked the shock in my voice. That tipped him off, making him nearly choke on his drink. The aide realized then that he had said too much. But it was too late. If what he'd just told me was true, it meant that Kennedy would not be the vice presidential candidate. The party never let a running mate deliver the nominating speech.

"I need to get back up there," he said, chucking the bottle in the wastebasket as he punched the elevator button.

As soon he disappeared, I rushed to the nearest telephone booth and called back into the city desk.

"Jordan," said Higgs, "I've just hung up with Walter. I'm going to finish this up and—"

"But Walter's not at Stevenson's office and I am. And I've got word that he's working on his nominating speech at this very minute and get this—this is . . ."

I heard some muffled voices and scuffling on the other end of the line before someone else came on the phone. "Walsh—" It was Mr. Copeland. "What the hell are you doing now? Stick to the goddamn stories you've been assigned to and stop messing with—"

"Kennedy's not going to be the vice presidential nominee."

That stopped him from shouting at me. "What? How do you know?"

"I spoke with one of Stevenson's aides and the party's asked Kennedy to nominate him. And you know that if Kennedy delivers the nominating speech, he's not going to be on the ticket."

I heard Mr. Copeland exhale into the receiver. He sounded exasperated when he said, "Get a confirmation on that and then call us back. And, Walsh?"

"Yes?"

"Nice work."

He hung up on me, but I didn't care.

The next day the editors brought Gabby in to cover the rest of the women's stories for me and I began working the convention, sharing a byline with Marty and Walter. Marty seemed okay with this change. Walter, of course, was not. But too damn bad. It was a personal victory, and I wasn't going to apologize for that.

I wanted to tell Jack what had happened but feared he'd be even more upset than he'd been about me covering the women's stories. Besides, we'd hardly spoken the past few days, and when we did talk, the conversations weren't good. We were too polite and stiff or else we were snapping at each other. I carried a dull ache around with me each time we hung up.

And then the next day I received a telephone call from Judge Casey.

"Does a busy gal like you have time for a quick lunch? I can come meet you down by the amphitheater. There's a place over on Halsted, not far from the convention. I need to talk to you about something privately. Just the two of us."

The restaurant was the Sirloin Room inside the Stock Yard Inn. It was a fancy place with white tablecloths and brass-accented leather banquettes. They were known for their meat and had this gimmick where you'd pick a raw steak and watch while your waiter seared your initials right into the meat.

I had no idea what Judge Casey wanted to see me about, and I was nervous until I saw him coming through the revolving door with that ever-present smile on his face. He greeted me with a big hug and playfully rapped his knuckles against my attaché case.

"How's my girl doing?" he asked. "I haven't seen much of you lately."

"I know. I'm sorry I missed Mass on Sunday and—"

"Oh, don't apologize. I know you're busy. I just wanted to see how you're doing."

"Oh, me? I'm fine."

He gave me a doubting look, as if he could see right through me. "Listen, I know Jack isn't always the easiest person to get along with."

"It's just that he sees this as some sort of competition between us. I don't want him to resent me because of my job."

"No, no, it's not that. But you have to understand, he's not used to you career types. His mother never worked a day in her life. This is all new to him. And Jack's a proud young man. He wants to be the big shot, the breadwinner. Someone you can look up to and respect."

"But I do. I do respect him." I rested my head in my hands. "I just—I don't know how to make this work with him."

"Can I give you a little fatherly advice?"

"Yes. Please." I was starved for some fatherly advice and my own father had checked out of that department.

"You're a strong woman. I knew that the first time Jack brought you home. And I know strong women because I was raised by one. Grandma Casey is tough as nails. Why do you think everyone in the family's scared to death of her?" He laughed, and as his smile receded, he leaned in closer and cleared his throat. "Jordan, I don't mean to pry, and I hope you know that I only want the best for you, but . . ."

"But what?"

"I know you and Jack love each other, but I see you struggling with all this and I have to ask—are you prepared for what is expected of you?"

"What do you mean?"

"You're going to convert to a whole new religion and a whole new way of life. You're entering into a mixed marriage, and it won't be easy. I just want to make sure your eyes are wide open. I want you to make sure this is right for you. Is this really what you want? To become a Catholic? To become a housewife? A mother? And understand that I won't judge you either way."

I couldn't speak just then. These choices had caged me in. I ran my hand along my collar and opened the top button. I needed air.

"You know I want you to be happy. I want Jack to be happy, too. I don't want to see anyone get hurt. But if this isn't right, then you both have to recognize it. Doesn't mean you don't love each other, but converting just to pacify Jack and the rest of us won't be good for the marriage or for the children."

I heard myself sigh as a knot of tension that I didn't even know I'd been harboring began unraveling inside my chest. Someone understood. Someone was giving me an out.

"Do you get what I'm saying?" he asked.

All I could do was nod.

I had been working eighteen hours a day covering the convention, and when it was finally over, the Democrats had nominated Adlai Stevenson and Estes Kefauver to go up against Eisenhower and Nixon.

I was tired to the bone and could have easily gone home, taken a bath and crawled into bed, but I wanted to follow up on my story about the close of the convention. I went back to the city room and stood with Higgs at the rewrite desk, reading over his shoulder, adding in last-minute facts and scouring my notes for the best quotes. After we finished, we ran it by the night editor, dropped the copy into the capsule and sent it through the pneumatic tube to the composing room on the third floor. I followed the story down, not wanting to leave anything to chance.

The composing room always fascinated me. I remember the first time I was down there. It was an enormous place, noisy, hot—even in the wintertime—and filled with a pungent scent of ink and newsprint. This was where dozens upon dozens of men— bank boys, Linotype operators and proofreaders—dressed in heavy leather aprons brought the paper to life each day. With ink-stained fingers they set our stories letter by letter and had the uncanny ability to read type upside down and backward, to proof a story reading it right to left. I had no idea how they did this, and it fascinated me.

When I came back up from the composing room, I ran into Mrs. Angelo.

"What are you still doing here?" I asked.

"Rewriting all of Gabby's stories from the convention. She's no good being out in the field. Makes her a nervous Nellie. I told them so, but did they listen to me? No." She sat down at her desk and started typing like a madwoman.

"Is there anything I can do to help?"

"Yeah, come back to society news."

"Mrs. Angelo, I—I . . ."

"Oh, never mind. I'm just giving you a hard time. It'll be faster if I do it myself." She pressed her lips together tightly and shook her head as she typed.

I went back over to my desk and telephoned Jack. I held my breath, listening to the phone ringing. I could picture the sound echoing off the bare walls in his apartment, his black rotary phone no doubt on the floor by his bed, the cord tangled in a pile of discarded socks and blankets. I was about to hang up when at last he answered.

"Will you meet me at my place?" I asked. When he didn't say anything, my voice cracked. "Please? I need to see you."

By the time I got to my apartment, Jack was waiting for me outside. I kissed him hello and felt his hand lightly stroke my back. I tried to look him in the eye, but he wouldn't have it yet. We stood in the hallway of my apartment building. The stroller was still there, a broken lamp lying on the quilted blanket. With my attaché case in hand, I fumbled through my handbag for my keys while Jack and I made small talk about the rain and the humidity. It was a ridiculous conversation, and painful.

When I got the key in the door, I turned to him and said, "How long are we supposed to pretend that you're not upset with me for covering the convention?"

"That's not what I'm upset about."

"If that's not it, then I'd love to know what's bothering you."

"You want to know what's bothering me? All right, I'll tell you. You said you were covering the women's stories—not Kennedy's nominating speech. Why didn't you tell me the truth? Why would you have lied about it?"

"Lied? I didn't lie about it." I turned the key and heard the lock trip. "I didn't even know I was going to cover that. I was covering all that other crap. I was bored to tears. Believe me, Mr. Ellsworth did not assign the nominating speech to me. I went out and got that story. I saw an opportunity and I took it. You would have done the same thing if you'd been me."

I watched him run his tongue along his crooked front teeth, making a sucking sound. "You need to get your priorities straight," he told me.

"What the hell's that supposed to mean?"

"Do you want to marry me or what? The bishop already gave us permission to be married in the church—even though you haven't done anything about converting."

"Oh, God"—I dropped my briefcase to the floor—"now you're starting to sound like your mother."

"Well, either you're ready to convert and get married or you're not. It's just that simple."

"So this is all on me now—is that it?" I was appalled, and my mind shot back to my lunch with Judge Casey. I had to ask once again if this was the right decision for me. "What's really bothering you?"

"I can't get five minutes alone with you to discuss anything."

We both knew that wasn't true, and I was getting tired of apologizing for my drive, for my wanting a career.

"What are you trying to prove anyway?" he said. "You're running around town with that ridiculous briefcase—trying to act like you're a man." He gave my attaché case a shove with his foot.

"That's funny, because we both know that if I *were* a man—if the situation were reversed—this conversation wouldn't be happening. We'd be celebrating my success, and instead you're punishing me for it. This was a big story I was working on and you know it. Just admit it: this isn't about us getting married. This is about me covering the convention and you being pulled off of it."

"That's bullshit."

"Is it really?"

We were standing in the living room. I hadn't bothered to turn on the light, and the streetlamp's slow coming in through the window was casting a shadow over his face. We weren't saying anything. We had reached a standoff. I heard the kitchen faucet dripping and I went over to tighten the knob. He came up behind me at the sink and wrapped his arms about my waist, letting his chin drop to my shoulder.

"Just tell me one thing," he said, his breath rushing in and out against my neck. "Do you *need* me? Do you even want me around?"

"Oh, God, Jack." I groaned and pulled away from him. "Why do you always have to say things like that?"

"Because I never know how you feel about me. About us. You never tell me. You never show any real emotion."

"That's not true."

"Your family has really made a mess of you. You think *they're* cold and unfeeling. Take a look in the mirror sometime. You're like an iceberg."

He glared at me, and in that moment I felt my stomach knotting up even as I discounted what he'd said. I was strong. I had to be strong. I couldn't go to pieces and start blubbering every time I hit a bump in the road. Didn't he understand that?

I stared into his eyes, my body shaking. "How dare you stand there and criticize my family? You and your perfect little family have never had a problem in all your lives. When we lost Eliot, we lost everything. You have no idea what we've been through. You don't understand a damn thing about it."

"You're right," he said. "I don't. I don't understand your family, and I sure as hell don't understand you."

Jack had just confirmed everything I'd been questioning for weeks and months. All my doubts had been resolved. The ground beneath us was shifting. I felt it, and he had to have too. There was no going back.

"I love you," I said with the words crowding my throat. "But we're not good for each other. You know it and I know it." Excruciating silence followed. "We could blame it on religion. That's the easy out. But I think we both know there's more to it than that. I can't have a husband who's not on my side."

"I am on your side."

"Not when it comes to my work, you're not. I've been nothing but supportive of you and you can't do the same for me. You know what the problem is, Jack? You love me because I'm smart. And you resent me because I'm smart."

He leaned forward and held me closer. He didn't deny it.

"You can't have it both ways," I said. "Let's face it, this isn't going to work. We're only going to end up hurting each other." I reached down and tugged on my finger until the ring slid past my knuckle. "I'm sorry, but we can't do this to each other anymore." I held his grandmother's ring in the palm of my hand.

He didn't fight me on it. Didn't try to persuade me to change my mind. He accepted his ring back and nodded as he tucked it in his front pocket. He knew I was doing the right thing and that he didn't have the guts to do it himself.

"I love you," he said. "I wish we could have made this work." He held me for a long time before he made it out the door. I could still feel his breath on my temples and the side of my neck even after he'd gone.

Chapter 23

• • •

After Jack left I had a good cry, mostly to prove his theory wrong and convince myself that I was not a cold, unfeeling woman after all.

Once I'd calmed down, I reached for the telephone, thinking I'd call Mr. Casey so he could hear the news from me. But I lost my nerve and tried Scott instead. There was no answer. That made me cry even more. I knew better than to call M. She'd only tell me to patch things up with Jack so finally, I composed myself enough to call my mother.

She came over an hour later with a bottle of brandy and a box of chocolates. As soon as I saw her I had another good cry. I supposed I was more upset than I'd thought. After I calmed down, we sat on the couch with an ashtray and a box of tissues planted on the cushion between us. We opened the brandy but didn't bother with the chocolates.

"You know, I almost called it off with your father."

"You did?"

She nodded, contemplating a cigarette. "I thought there were too many hurdles in our way. Grandpa didn't like him. And

Grandma—well, you know how she is—she just went along with whatever Grandpa said. And I was a New Yorker. I wasn't sure I wanted to move to Chicago. I wasn't sure I could see my life here."

"So what made you go through with it?"

She struck a match and held it, the flame less than an inch from her cigarette. "Because I loved him." She inhaled deeply and shook out the match. "I realized that no matter how difficult it might be, I didn't want to be without him."

I took a sip of brandy. "I don't feel that way about Jack."

"I know you don't." She smiled. "But you had to figure this one out for yourself. And I knew you would. I told your father you'd come around."

"So Dad didn't like Jack, either?" I was surprised that my father even had an opinion on this at all.

"It's not that he didn't like him. He just didn't think he was the right man for you."

I took another sip of brandy. "Do you think Eliot would have liked him?"

She leaned her head back and let a faint smile play upon her lips. "You know Eliot. He liked everyone."

When she said that, an unexpected flare of resentment shot through me. *Eliot, the perfect, favorite child, the golden son and fair-haired boy who loved everyone and everyone loved him.* My reaction caught me off guard. How long had that been festering? I immediately felt guilty for thinking that way, but I couldn't help it. Eliot had been canonized, and I couldn't compete with the dead.

"God, I miss him," I said, mentally backpedaling. "There's so much I wish I could talk to him a—"

My mother placed her hand on mine. "Don't." Her eyes were

closed, cigarette smoke curling up around her cheeks. "I can't," she said. "I can't talk about it."

I didn't want to break her, but I couldn't *not* talk about it anymore. "Sooner or later we're going to have to."

"I know. I know." She squeezed my hand. "But later, okay? We'll talk about it later."

I met Scott the next day for lunch and misted up when he took me in his arms. He held me longer than he normally would before guiding me over to a table. After we were seated, he reached across and ran the back of his hand along my cheek. I leaned in to his touch like a purring kitten.

"So how are you doing with all this?" he asked.

I covered his hand with mine and sniffed away my tears. "I'm sad about it, but I know it was the right thing to do."

We sat there for a moment, looking at each other. It was almost as if we were seeing each other for the first time, or maybe just in a new light. I was single again. So was he. I knew we were both thinking that same thing. Neither one of us could turn away until the waitress interrupted to take our order.

"Well," he said, after she'd disappeared, "I'm sorry it didn't work out. I knew you guys were having some problems, but—"

"*Some* problems? That's an understatement." I laughed sadly and shifted back into the platonic slot we both knew and were comfortable with. "All we did was argue. And isn't it coincidental that every time we had a really big fight, I just so happened to have had a piece in the paper that got some attention? I could have set my watch to it."

"He was just jealous, insecure," he said.

"It wasn't so much jealousy as it was competition. I felt like he was always measuring his own accomplishments against mine, and if he didn't do better, it upset him. And then there was his family."

"But I thought his family was one of the things you loved about him."

"It is. Or it was. But the more time I spent with them, the more I realized it was really just the idea of them that I loved. Except for his father. I'm still crazy about him."

"Isn't he a judge? Traffic court?"

I nodded.

"I've had a few cases with him. Seems decent enough."

The waitress came back with our order. Scott folded back the top of his bun and inspected his hamburger. "So are you *really* okay? You seem okay. But I can't tell if you're just putting on a brave front."

"For you? Please." We locked eyes again like we had before. I smiled and looked away, fiddling with the napkin holder. "Okay, enough of this talk. How are *you* doing?"

He scrunched up his handsome face. "It's a whole different ball game being on the defense side."

"I'm sure it is. I remember when you wanted to be the one who put the bad guys away."

"Yeah, and now I'm the one helping them go free." He tried to smile, but there was too much regret in the way.

"Why don't you quit? You were talking about doing that before."

"It's not that easy."

"Why not?"

He wouldn't say. Instead he shook his head. "The legal system's not perfect. Doesn't matter which side you're on. People think it's about finding the truth and dispensing justice, and sometimes that happens, but it's more by accident than design.

It's really not about being right. It's about being more persuasive. And honestly, it's about money and power."

"But c'mon," I said. "Are you really that surprised? You always knew the justice system was flawed. Even when you were a prosecutor."

"I at least had a little faith back then. Now I don't know what I have. I don't even know what I'm doing."

"Then quit. You can practice a different kind of law. Join a firm."

"I can't. Someday. Soon. Maybe. I hope. But I can't right now." He took a sip from his drink. "I'm just trying to get through the day. Putting one foot in front of the other . . ."

As we were leaving the restaurant I remembered I had something for him. "Here—" I reached in my bag and handed him my copy of *Profiles in Courage*. "You said you hadn't read it yet."

He balanced the book on his open palm and ran his other hand over the cover as if he could feel the words rising up off the pages. "I'll get it back to you."

"You'd better." I smiled and gave him a peck on the cheek like I always did. Only this time I wanted him to hold me again like he had earlier.

As I watched him walking away, his broad shoulders disappearing into the crowded sidewalks, I questioned what had just come over me. Was I really feeling all this for Scott, or was I merely trying to mask my pain over Jack? I forced myself to clear them both from my mind and headed back to the city room.

Benny was at my side as soon as I reached my desk. "I heard about you and Jack," he said.

"Wow, that was fast. How did you find out?"

"This is a city room—we're always the first to hear *anything*." I smiled.

"Maybe you and me, you know, maybe you'd let me take you out sometime?"

Dear sweet, young Benny. I looked at him and sighed. Even if I had been interested in him, office romances were generally frowned upon. "Thanks anyway, but I think I'll need some time before I'll be ready to date anyone."

Chapter 24

• • •

I recognized the voice on the telephone immediately and dropped down into my chair. I'd been sure that Ahern had all but written me off. I hadn't spoken to him since last October, when I'd let the D'Arco story get away. Before that it was the insurance-fraud scoop that Walter had run with. It was February now and I already had two strikes against me as far as he was concerned.

"Can you meet me in thirty minutes?" he asked.

He said it was important, and I knew I couldn't afford to mess this one up—whatever it was—and there was a lot happening out there. As of January 1957, Eisenhower was back in office for another term and there were plenty of changes in Chicago. The biggest news was that Benjamin Adamowski had been elected the new state's attorney. He was a Democrat turned Republican who, in a local upset, shockingly defeated Daley's man, John Gutknecht. I remembered talking about Adamowski with Judge Casey. Adamowski had run on the promise of cleaning up the corruption in Cook County and that was bad news for the Daley machine.

All this was running through my mind when I met Ahern at Union Station. It was a big station, a place where we could get lost in the rush-hour crowd. I spotted him on one of the long wooden benches in the main terminal. He saw me, stood up and motioned for me to follow him. I lagged a good distance behind while he led me down to one of the tracks for the Milwaukee-bound trains. It was cold, dank and dark down there, and I smelled the heavy scent of creosol wafting up from the ties.

One of the conductors called out from the train steps, "Boarding now. Doors closing on the Milwaukee North."

"I've got a bit of news for you," Ahern said, pulling a cigarette from his pack and cupping his hand around his lighter as if blocking an imaginary wind. "I'm leaving the mayor's office."

"What?" I watched my breath cloud up in the frigid air and dissipate. "What are you going to do?"

"I'm going to work for Adamowski. I'll be one of his aides."

"So you're becoming a Republican now?" I was incredulous.

He drew down on his cigarette. "I don't think of it so much as Democrat versus Republican. I see it more as a chance to do some good in this city." He watched the train bound for Milwaukee ease away from the station. "I like what Adamowski stands for. I like what he's trying to do. I've seen too many dirty dealings inside the Daley administration. I don't want to be a part of that anymore."

He looked at me, and through a haze of cigarette and train smoke, I saw something different in his eyes. He'd dropped his political mask just long enough for me to see the real Richard Ahern. All this time I'd thought he was feeding me stories because he had an ax to grind. It never occurred to me that the things he'd seen and condoned inside the mayor's office had stayed with him, possibly keeping him up at night. For the first time since I'd met Ahern, I considered the possibility that he might actually be a decent guy after all.

"Well, thanks for letting me know." I thrust out my hand to

shake his. "I wish you luck in your new role. It was good working with you."

He laughed, ignoring my gesture. "This isn't good-bye, Walsh." He dropped his cigarette to the platform and ground it out with a twist of his heel. "Far from it." He laughed a little harder. "Hell, we're just getting started."

The penny dropped, and my heart started racing. I may have been losing my source in Daley's office, but I was gaining something better: a direct line to the state's attorney's office. I'd heard the accusations Adamowski had been making; Daley was looking the other way while traffic courts fixed tickets, while police officers ignored bordellos and even patronized them. Daley washed his hands of any wrongdoing even while his precinct captains were under indictment for various crimes. Adamowski didn't let a day go by without claiming Daley was involved with one scandal or another. Adamowski had a mission to bust the Daley machine wide open, and apparently Ahern planned to leak their attacks step by step to the press, specifically to me—and for reasons that I still didn't understand.

A fter our meeting at Union Station Ahern's tips came rapidly, and by the spring of 1957, four months after Adamowski took office, I had scooped half a dozen front-page stories.

I was the one who broke the story about the postmaster general taking kickbacks, followed by the one about a brothel that hosted a police chief's bachelor party. I brought Mr. Ellsworth and Mr. Copeland articles on political fixers, on parking ticket fixers, tax evasion and all kinds of dirty politics down at City Hall.

My parents were well aware of my accomplishments, though they didn't say much about them. Still, I was pleased, despite my colleagues—especially Walter, Henry, Peter and Randy—being unhappy about this development. Even Marty, who'd once been my greatest supporter, was cagey around me, secretive about his stories. The others had always been that way.

Now, instead of Benny, they picked on me. Mercilessly. I was the target, the source of their amusement, the butt of their pranks. I did a good job of laughing it off—like the time they hid my attaché case just for grins. I smiled each time they gave me a phony set of revisions for one of my stories or called me up from across the room, disguising their voices, pretending they had a hot tip for me. I was a good sport. Tough. I could take it.

But I admit that one day it got to me. Unbeknownst to me, Randy had started up an internal comic strip featuring me, the ruthless reporter, with my high-heeled shoes and a sword in one hand, my briefcase in the other, trying to get the scoop on crime and injustice in the streets of Chicago. He'd left the cartoon sketches on his desk where he knew I'd see them. Randy had turned my fingernails into talons, my nose into a beak. He had turned me into a vulture.

I remember how I was still laughing for all to see just before I slipped into the ladies' room, locked myself inside the last stall and sobbed into my fisted hands. I pressed my forehead against the marble wall, the coolness soothing the heat coming off my face.

Never cry in the city room. Never. Ever. Marty had gotten away with it, but that was because he was having a nervous breakdown. I'd seen Gabby and M and some of the other sob sisters fall apart at their desks in front of the men, who sat back and snickered or else showered them with pity. I swore I'd never let them see me cry, and yet here I was bawling my eyes out.

I had to question if this job was worth it. What was I trying to prove? The guys were never going to show me any respect as a reporter. My parents were never going to change just because I got a couple of stories published. They were too far gone, and I had to accept that I couldn't do for them what Eliot had done. I couldn't be my brother. Maybe I wasn't cut out for the life of a journalist after all. But even as I said that, I knew they were just words. I couldn't walk away. Not after I'd come so far.

I must have stayed in that bathroom stall for twenty minutes. I was exhausted by the time I unlatched the door, relieved that no one else was in the bathroom. I splashed cold water on my face and wiped the mascara from underneath my eyes with a brown, scratchy paper towel. Forcing a smile on my face, I went back out to my desk, acting as if everything were fine.

Chapter 25

• • •

It was late in the day. All the windows were thrown open and fans were planted on the desks. It was unusually hot for May, a portent of what the summer had in store for us. I had just finished reading something that had come off the wires, the ruling in a case involving white and Negro schoolchildren. "Separate but equal public schools," said the wire. It was groundbreaking, and if this was happening for Negro children, could equality for women be that far behind? I was completely absorbed when M called to me.

"Hey, Jordan, do you have time for a drink?"

"Sure." I set the wire report aside, switched off my desk lamp and placed the cover over my typewriter. "The others are over at Riccardo's. Want to meet up with them?"

M bit her lip and looked around the city room. "Would you mind if we went somewhere else? Just the two of us?"

We ended up at Boul Mich and sat at a booth toward the back. We recognized a few people in there, including Mike Royko, who was at the far end of the bar. We kept our backs toward them and placed our orders, two Beefeaters up, dry with a twist.

"So what's going on?" I asked after our martinis arrived. "Is everything okay?"

She shook her head and began chewing off her lipstick.

"What is it? What's wrong?"

"I'm in trouble."

"What kind of trouble?"

She lowered her eyes. "What kind do you think?" She rested her hand over her belly.

"Oh. How?"

"How do you think?"

"No, I mean, I—I didn't know you were seeing anyone. I know you go on dates all the time, but I didn't know there was anyone you were, you know . . . serious with."

She laughed. "Then maybe you're not as good of a reporter as you think you are." She planted her elbows on the table and braced her head in her hands. "I always said it wouldn't happen to me. And, well, here I am." She gave off another sour laugh. "I'm so damn scared I can't think straight."

"What about the father?"

She shook her head.

"Does he know? Maybe he could . . ."

"He's not an option. Believe me. I'm on my own on this one." She closed her eyes, her band of false lashes creating a strange shadow on her face. "It wasn't supposed to happen this way. Everything's so out of order. I was supposed to meet the man of my dreams. Get married. Make a home for us. And then—*then* I'd have children."

"Have you thought about what you want to do?"

"Pretty damn obvious, isn't it? I'm not going to have a child on my own. I can't do that. And I can't disappear for six or seven months and have a baby and come back acting like nothing happened." She leaned forward and grabbed my hand. "I need your help."

"Me? What can I do?"

"Remember that piece you wanted to write about doctors who were performing abortions?"

"Oh, God. M, no. I don't know . . ."

"Were any of them safe?"

"They're probably all in jail by now. Besides, are you sure that's what you want to do?"

"Please, spare me the lecture." The martini was trembling in her hand. "I've tried everything else. I've punched myself. I drank half a bottle of gin in a scorching-hot tub." She took another sip from her drink, her hand still shaking. "I even contemplated a coat hanger, but I lost my nerve."

"Oh, M." I grew sick inside.

"I know, but what choice do I have?"

"How far along are you?"

She shrugged. "About eight weeks."

"Have you been to a doctor?"

"I don't need to go to a doctor. I know I'm pregnant." She cleared her throat and reached for my hand. "Will you help me? Please?"

"It's not for me," I said to Ahern the next day when I met him for lunch at Beefy 19, an out-of-the-way place that sold burgers and hot dogs for nineteen cents apiece. Beefy 19 was on Berwyn and Western and catered to motorcycle riders and hot-rodders, and neither one of us was likely to know anyone there.

"It's for a friend," I said. "She doesn't know where else to turn."

"And you figured I would?" Ahern closed his menu, stuffed it into the metal holder and signaled the waitress over.

Originally I'd thought about asking Scott only because now that he was a defense attorney, he'd been rubbing elbows with the types of people who probably needed a doctor like that every now and again. But in the end I couldn't bring him in on something so messy. Besides, Ahern and I were the keepers of each other's secrets, and I figured this would be just one more to hold in our pockets.

"Okay," Ahern said after the waitress had disappeared with our orders, "there is one guy I know of."

"Do you have an address? A telephone number?"

"He never gives that information out. I'll have to take you and your friend."

So it was arranged.

The following Saturday morning M and I waited outside her apartment on Lincoln Park West until Ahern pulled up in his Chevrolet. I introduced him only as Richard and explained that I'd met him while conducting research for the abortion piece I'd never gotten to write. M didn't ask any questions. She didn't say a word on the way there. She just smoked cigarettes, pushing the live butts through a crack in the window before lighting another one.

While Ahern fiddled nonstop with the radio, I wondered how I'd gotten myself in the middle of all this. We drove on until finally, somewhere up on Irving Park, we came to an old limestone building with three small windows just above ground level. It looked like the sort of place where ominous things occurred. I held M's hand as we went inside while Ahern waited for us out in the car.

There was nothing medical about this facility. No canisters of cotton, no tongue depressors, no shiny silver trays of instruments. Instead we were in a little room with a couple of folding chairs and an opened box of wafers on a metal table. There was a dirty cat box resting in the corner. A door off to the side was cracked a hair. The doctor—if he even was a doctor—never gave us his name. He wore a white coat, but that wasn't enough to convince me.

"I'll need the money up front," he said.

M pinched the clasp on her Kelly bag and handed him a hundred dollars. She'd told me she had to borrow the last twenty from a neighbor. She was tapped out. I had a mind to grab M and run back out to the car, but he had already opened the door and gestured for her to go inside and change into the gown on the table. He asked me to wait in the outer room, but before the door closed, I got a good look inside. No overhead light, no windows, just a table and a stool.

I expected screams. I expected blood. I expected it to take longer than it did. But soon M was dressed again and joined me in the outer room. She seemed fine, almost a little too fine, and I had to wonder if she'd even gone through with it.

"Are you okay?" I whispered as we were walking back to Ahern's car.

"Yeah. He said to expect a really bad period. Said probably sometime this afternoon, but that I'd be good as new by Monday."

So that was it? That was an abortion?

We drove M home, but before Ahern dropped me off he said, "Could you use a drink? I know I could."

We went to a little place off the beaten path on Diversey Parkway called Mackerel's. They had mounted fish on the walls and photographs of boats everywhere. Neither one of us had been there before, and it was unlikely that anyone we knew would have wandered in.

Ahern twiddled the speared olive in his glass and thanked me for agreeing to the drink. "I wasn't ready to go home yet. My wife, she . . . Well, we've been trying to start a family. I don't think I could look her in the eye right now. You know, given what we did today. A woman who wants a baby more than anything in this world would never understand . . ." His eyes misted over, and he looked away, placing his thumb and index finger over his eyelids. "Sorry," he said. "It's just that we've been trying for so long. I hope your friend doesn't regret this for the rest of her life."

I was always surprised when Ahern gave me these occasional peeks at his vulnerable side. He really was a good guy. I reached across the table and squeezed his hand, which seemed to choke him up all the more.

On our second drink he told me about his days in law school. "I was working three jobs and taking a full course load. All I wanted was to be a lawyer. I came from a family of steel workers. I saw what that kind of physical labor does to a man. My father was old before his time, arthritis in his back. His feet and hands were like sandpaper. . . . I knew I had to do better for myself. I was going to make my money with my head, not my hands." He rattled the ice in his glass and grinned. "Didn't mean to talk your ear off like that." He shook his head and redirected the conversation. "So what about you? I never had the chance to ask what happened with the fiancé."

"How did you know?"

"The ring. You don't wear it anymore. So I figured . . ."

"Oh"—I waved the matter aside—"it just wasn't meant to be."

"Well, I'm sorry it didn't work out for you."

"It's okay." I shrugged, avoiding his gaze by staring at a mackerel on the wall above his head. It was crazy how the sadness still sneaked up on me. Just when I thought I was completely over Jack, someone would say something, or a song would come on the radio, or I'd see something and my entire body would fill with pain. Suddenly I'd be longing and aching to be with him even though I knew it would never work.

"You really don't like talking about yourself, do you?" said Ahern.

"I'm better at asking the questions than answering them."

"You really are tough, aren't you?"

I had just taken a pull from my drink and ended up half laughing, half choking. "Hardly," I said, catching a trickle of gin running down my chin. "I only look tough."

"I'm serious. Aren't you ever off your guard?"

"Apparently, according to my ex-fiancé, I'm a bit cold. But really, it's not that. I just don't like to burden people with my problems."

"But you're not burdening them if someone asks." He cocked his head to the side and smiled. "So is that what happened with the two of you? He wanted you to *burden* him?"

"Oh, please. No, what he wanted"—I paused, a finger raised to accent my forthcoming correction—"what he *needed* was a nice Irish-Catholic girl."

"And what are you?"

"I might have an Irish name, but that's where it ends. I'm not Catholic. I'm not anything."

"So it was religion that got in the way?"

"Sure, we can blame it on religion. It's easy to say that mixed marriages have disaster written all over them. But really, our problems ran a lot deeper than that." I raised my glass and realized that not only had I already finished my drink but that I'd been babbling. "Oh, God, don't listen to me. I don't know what I'm talking about."

Ahern didn't say anything, but he seemed wholly invested in my every word. Maybe it was that, or maybe it was that second martini, but for whatever reason, I kept talking.

"Jack couldn't handle me being a journalist. But he knew I was serious about my career when he met me. My God, I come from a family of journalists. Did you know that? Did I ever tell you that my father was a newspaperman and war correspondent? My grandfather was a newspaperman, too. And so was my brother.

He was a reporter. He worked at the *Sun-Times*. . . ." I was drunk and no longer in command of my words, and I realized that I was making Ahern uncomfortable.

He shifted in his chair and fidgeted with his cuff before he gestured to the bartender for the check. He turned back to me, consulting his wristwatch. "It's getting late. I hate to do this, but I have to get going."

"I'm sorry. I'm afraid I was rambling."

"Don't worry about it." Ahern gestured again for the bartender. "Check."

Suddenly I was very drunk and it seemed like neither one of us could get out of there fast enough.

Later that night, after I sobered up, I telephoned M to see how she was doing.

"It's like he said. Just a really bad period."

She sounded tired. I asked if she needed anything, and she assured me she was fine. And she did sound all right, but as the evening wore on, a nagging feeling crept up on me and I couldn't shake it. Finally, I broke down and telephoned her again. This time there was no answer. Maybe she stepped out to get a bite to eat, or she was sleeping? When there was still no answer half an hour later, the nagging feeling grew more persistent. Two more hours passed without an answer from her, and I grabbed my handbag, flagged down a taxi and went over to her apartment.

I rang the doorbell and knocked until I heard footsteps padding across the floor inside. She cracked the door, and even through that sliver I could see how pale she was. As soon as she let me inside, I gasped. Even before she opened her mouth, I knew she was in trouble. She was standing in a pink negligee soaked from the waist down in blood, and there was a crimson trail leading from her bedroom to the front door.

"Help me," she said, her voice weak and strained. "Something's wrong. I think I'm dying."

I hoisted her in my arms as best I could and got her back into bed, her blood-soaked hands faintly clutching to me. I called a doctor I knew who wouldn't have performed the abortion, but he wouldn't have reported it to the authorities. M was feverish, so I fed her aspirin and placed a cool washcloth on her forehead. It seemed to take forever for the doctor to arrive. While we waited for him, M slept and I cleaned up the trail of blood on the floor with a pile of rags and a bucket I found beneath her kitchen sink. The water turned scarlet after just a few wipes.

When the doctor showed up, I waited outside her bedroom door, pacing. Fifteen minutes later he came into the hallway, looking at me with such grave disappointment.

"Who did this to her?"

"I don't know." It was the truth. I didn't know the guy's name. Hell, I didn't even know who the father was. "Is she going to be okay?"

"She's lost a lot of blood. She'll recover, but if you'd waited any longer, she could have died. You girls, you." He shook his head and handed me a prescription. "Get this filled. Make sure she takes it. All of it."

I stayed with M that night, preparing cold compresses for her forehead and forcing tea and dry toast on her. It was the first time I'd ever seen her without makeup, without the false lashes, the penciled-in beauty mark, the painted-up lips. It was surprising just how truly beautiful she was as herself.

She moved in and out of sleep during the night while I kept watch from a chair parked in the corner of her room. There was a stack of movie magazines on the floor next to me. I leafed through issues of *Photoplay* and *Movie Life*. I was reading about

Ava Gardner when M began muttering. More cool compresses, more medicine and she fell back asleep.

I got up to stretch my legs and wandered out to the living room. M's place was nearly twice the size of mine. I couldn't imagine how she afforded it and I knew now that her father really had died, so he wasn't the one paying for it. I wondered if it belonged to the baby's father.

Big as it was, the place was a mess. There were more movie magazines strewn across the couch and floor, dirty glasses and coffee cups on the tables, lampshades hanging cockeyed. I straightened up the stack of magazines and set them on a bookshelf next to the fireplace. I couldn't help but notice that most of the titles she had were romance novels. One book, *A Certain Smile* by Françoise Sagan, was resting on her coffee table. As I picked it up a bookmark—or what I thought was a bookmark—fell to the floor, facedown. When I reached for it and turned it over, I was speechless.

I was holding a strip of photographs, the kind taken in a photo booth. What I found shocking was that the people in the photographs were M and Mr. Ellsworth. Together. Smiling. Cuddling. Kissing. I studied the shots one by one. There was no mistaking what I was seeing and yet I was confused. Mr. Ellsworth was married and M seemed to always be dating other men. She had a string of them, a dinner or two with this one or that and then she'd be on to the next.

I looked again at the photo strip. M was seated on his lap, an arm thrown over his shoulder, her face nuzzled into his collarbone, then his neck and finally it was her mouth on his. A new picture of my own was forming inside my head. I thought back to Christmas Eve and the shocked look on Mr. Ellsworth's face when he saw M all dressed up, and how he'd questioned me about her plans later that night. This was not just some fleeting affair. I realized Mr. Ellsworth must have been the father. He was the one paying for this apartment.

I studied the first shot. I'd never seen Mr. Ellsworth smile before. I'd never even seen his teeth, always hidden by his beard. For an older man, he was handsome. So where was he now? She needed him. He should have been there with her now, not me.

I heard M stirring in the bedroom and went to her. I didn't say anything about Mr. Ellsworth. She had enough on her mind as it was.

But the next day, when I went into the city room, her secret was eating me up inside. As the day wore on I became aware of Mr. Ellsworth passing by M's desk, looking for her, for signs of her: a cigarette burning in the ashtray, a steaming cup of coffee, a sweater tossed over the chair—anything. Surely he knew why she wasn't at work.

It took all my will not to scream at him to get himself over to her apartment. I knew I couldn't say a word. He was still my managing editor and this was none of my business, despite M having dragged me into the middle of it.

I went back to my typing, unable to look at Mr. Ellsworth.

Chapter 26

• • •

I knew it would happen sooner or later. After all, there were only so many bars the newspaper gang went to and I'd already run into Jack at most of them. Short, friendly encounters, quickly forgotten after the next drink.

But there was that one night in October when I glanced across the hazy, smoke-filled room at Andy's on Hubbard Street and saw Jack Casey with another girl. A beautiful girl with long dark hair that reached her rear end. I sobered up. It was like someone had just thrown ice on my heart.

I had to turn my back to them, but M was with me, reporting the details.

"They're laughing about something," M said. "Sitting pretty close together. But they're not holding hands or anything. . . . And don't worry, she may have that hair, but you're much prettier than she is. . . ."

Honestly, I didn't know why it bothered me. It wasn't like I wanted him back, and of course I would have expected him to move on. After all, we had split up more than a year ago. But still it stung because this girl was the first after me. Or at least the first one that I knew of.

M and I left our drinks on the bar and slipped out of Andy's undetected. We grabbed a bottle of vodka at the liquor store around the corner and went to her place.

From the very beginning I considered M a friend. But after everything we'd gone through with her abortion, we had formed an even tighter, almost sisterly-like bond. And yet as close as we were, we both guarded our secrets, refusing to share them with each other. She never told me about Mr. Ellsworth and I never told her about Ahern. She never spoke about the abortion and never questioned who the mysterious Richard was who'd accompanied us that day.

When we keyed into M's apartment, she went right over to a little bar cart in the corner and poured us both a healthy splash of vodka. After dropping some ice cubes in as an afterthought, she said, "I know exactly what you need. Come with me."

"What are we doing?" I asked, following her into the bathroom, which sparkled with glass shelves filled with perfumes and decorative bottles. A little pink fringe area rug matched the towels.

"You'll see." M opened a drawer and pulled out hairbrushes and combs, clips, bobby pins and God knows what else. She closed the lid on the toilet seat and gave it a pat. "Come over here." I went and sat while she draped a bath towel around my shoulders. "Trust me," she said. "A new hairdo will cheer you up."

"But I don't need cheering up."

"Nonsense. You just saw the love of your life with another woman."

Funny, but I didn't consider Jack the love of my life. Actually, it was Scott who popped into my mind when she said that. It surprised me. *How deep do my feelings for him really go?*

I cleared my head and sat quietly while M slathered my hair

with setting lotion, making the bathroom smell like a beauty parlor. I lit a cigarette to keep from choking on that sweet, powdery scent.

"You had such a cute hairstyle when I first met you," M said, holding a curl in place while prying open a bobby pin with her front teeth. "Why didn't you keep it up? Why did you let it grow out?"

"For the same reason I stopped wearing my new dresses. I wanted the men in this business to stop looking at me like a woman and start treating me fairly."

"Well, honey, you still look like a woman." She scissored her fingers, and I handed off the cigarette to her. She took a puff and returned it with a big red lipstick smear on the filter. "It's not like you're Gabby. She's about as plain as they come." M wound the last pin curl and secured it with a clip. "That poor girl hasn't been on a date since I've known her."

"She probably doesn't have time for dating. She helps her sister out a lot." I stood up and looked in the mirror, patting the metal clips and bobby pins in place, making sure they were secure.

"Well, I think that's a big mistake, if you ask me. How's she supposed to meet anyone when she spends almost every Saturday night babysitting her sister's children?"

"Maybe she likes doing that," I said, turning my head to the side. I looked like I was wearing a metal helmet. "I know you'll find this hard to believe, but a man isn't always the answer."

She didn't like hearing that and changed the subject. "Oh, before I forget, stay right there. I want to show you the new dress I got."

While she went into the bedroom for the dress, I went out to the living room and sipped my vodka as I glanced around. My eyes landed on a pair of crystal candlesticks on her dining room table with wax stalactites hanging off them, suggesting a recent romantic dinner. I looked at the stack of records next to the record player: the recordings of the Everly Brothers, Sonny James and Bobby Darin all pulled from their cover sleeves. I was sure I detected the lingering scent of a man's aftershave and I knew who the man was.

A few moments later M appeared in a low-cut black satin dress that hugged her hourglass curves.

"Ta-da!" She set her hands on her hips.

"It's stunning. You look gorgeous."

She smiled. She didn't need me to confirm how she looked in that dress.

"Did you get that for a special occasion? Do you have a big date coming up with someone?"

"I saw it at Field's and just couldn't resist."

"C'mon, you had to have someone special in mind when you bought that."

She gave me a coy shoulder shrug and I rolled my eyes in response. I don't know why it bothered me that she wouldn't tell me about Mr. Ellsworth, but it festered, and I found myself dropping more and more hints, hoping to make her confess.

"Wait till you see the shoes I got to go with it." She disappeared back into the bedroom.

I called out to her, "How are you affording all this?" She made even less money than I did, and I thought she was tapped out from the abortion. "You told me you were broke."

She never replied because the telephone rang. M answered on the extension in her bedroom. "It's not a good time," I heard her whisper. "I can't tonight. . . . I have company over. . . . Don't worry—it's a *she*. . . ."

When M came back into the living room I asked if everything was all right.

"Of course." She reached for a cigarette and a marble and gold lighter.

Something about that lighter—that lighter that probably cost more than I made in a month—set me off. "Who was that on the phone?" There was an edge to my voice.

"Just a friend."

"Oh, c'mon, M. I know who it was." I blurted it out. "I know about you and Mr. Ellsworth."

She nearly dropped her cigarette. "Who told you?"

"No one. I just put the pieces together."

"I see." She drew hard on her cigarette and exhaled toward the ceiling.

"M, he's a married man."

"Yes, thank you. I'm well aware of that."

"So what are you doing?"

"Waiting."

"Waiting for what?"

"For him," she said matter-of-factly. "He's going to leave his wife, and then we'll be together. And don't look at me like that. He's my soul mate."

"So he's going to get a divorce? Are you in love with him? Is he in love with you? How old is he, anyway? How long has this been going on? And where was he when you were so sick after the abortion? Hell, where was he during the abortion?"

M looked at me, exasperated. "Easy with the questions." She sat down hard and cradled her forehead in her hand. "Yes, he's going to divorce his wife. Yes, I'm in love with him. Yes, he's in love with me. And if you must know, we have a plan."

"What do you mean, a plan?"

"A plan. The plan." She said it louder the second time, as if that would make me understand. "He's going to get divorced and then we're going to start courting openly. Then we're going to get engaged and get married. And then—after we're married— then we're going to start a family."

"Why didn't he just get a divorce when he found out you were pregnant?" I had shifted into reporter mode and was prepared to challenge her.

"He couldn't do that. Think about it. He's the managing editor of the *Chicago Tribune*. He's an important man. He has a reputation to protect—"

"So do you."

She discounted that with a wave of her hand. "He can't afford to have a scandal like that on his hands. I know what I'm doing, Jordan. And I don't need a lecture about married men."

"But what about that one guy from Ogilvy? He's not married and you were seeing him."

"We had two dates." She took a puff and ground out her cigarette. "That was nothing. You know me—I'm a big flirt. Besides, I only went out with him to make Stanley jealous. Sometimes I get angry with him and so I go out with other men just to get back at him. But they don't mean anything. He knows it, too."

Stanley. I had almost forgotten that was Mr. Ellsworth's first name.

Now that I knew about the two of them, it seemed so obvious. I remembered the times he'd slip out of the city room, announcing a bit too loudly that he was heading down to the composing room, and sure enough, five or ten minutes later, M would disappear as well. They'd stagger their returns to the floor, her cheeks still flushed, his hair ever so slightly rumpled. I was aware of the lunch hours when they were both gone, returning one at a time. I

saw the joy in her eyes when he walked by her desk or acknowledged her in some small way.

But I also saw the pain grip hold of her at his slightest rebuff,
and I knew all about her restless nights. It had gotten so bad
lately that her doctor had prescribed sleeping pills for her. How
had I not noticed the two of them before? I was supposed to be
observant. It made me question what else I had missed.

Chapter 27

♦ ♦ ♦

I was standing in the cold, covering a ribbon-cutting ceremony for a new wing of the Michael Reese Hospital. The November winds were gusting while all the reporters huddled together. The mayor was there for the event, proudly saying to the press, "We are here today to commiserate that Chicago is becoming a leading disease center. . . ."

I watched his press secretary slap the sides of his head while we all chuckled, writing down the mayor's latest gaffe.

I was still laughing about that to myself when I went back to the city room. I hadn't even gotten my coat off when Benny pulled a chair over to my desk. He wanted to finish up a piece we'd both been assigned to the day before on a bridge fire. He leafed through his notes while I did the typing, my fingers still stiff from the cold.

"Oh, wait—" He'd stop me every few lines to insert a thought or change a fact. "That was the fire commissioner who said that."

"I know, Benny. I got it. See?" I pointed to the line. It was a routine story. I could have written the piece with my eyes closed.

The entire time Benny and I were working, Randy was singing *He's Got the Whole World in His Hands* and improvising

with bits like, "*He's got the printers and the slot man in his hands /
He's got the printers and the slot man in his hands. . . .*"

That past summer Randy had won a singing contest spon-
sored by H. C. Schrink & Sons, the owners of Eskimo Pies. Crooner
that he was, Randy brought down the house with his rendition
of *Some Enchanted Evening* and walked away with the grand prize,
a six-month supply of Eskimo Pies.

Ever since then he'd been talking about leaving the paper and
pursuing a career in music. Not that he didn't appreciate being
able to make a living as a cartoonist. He did. But as he put it, "I'm
tired of scraping by. Music is where the money is. I'm talking
serious money. So what I'm gonna do now is," he'd told us all,
"I'm gonna go talk to Pendulum Records and I'm gonna sign a
record deal with them."

"Would you listen to him?" Walter had laughed. "Our boy
Randy here's gonna be a big recording star. A regular Sinatra."

"You might not believe this, Walter," Randy had said, his
voice taking on a ferocious volume, "but I've got talent. A real
God-given gift. And I'm gonna be rich someday. Filthy rich." He
was trembling. I don't think he'd ever stood up to Walter—or
maybe to anyone—before.

The Eskimo Pies had run out, and as far as we knew, Randy
still hadn't spoken to anyone at Pendulum Records. The last time
I asked him about it, he said his wife was having gallbladder
surgery, as if that should have explained it. She still hadn't had
the operation, and according to Randy, she was feeling fine.

I was remembering all that when Henry came rushing into
the city room. He twisted out of his overcoat and tossed his hat
on his desk. "Ellsworth around?" he asked.

"You looking for me?" Mr. Ellsworth had been over by M's
desk before he appeared in the aisle.

Henry rushed to his side. "I got something big. You're not

gonna believe this. I just got an earful from my buddy at the Bureau."

"Well, are you going to tell me or just make me stand here and guess?"

Henry lowered his voice and said, "Can we go somewhere private?"

The two of them disappeared into one of the conference rooms, and through the glass panels I watched Mr. Ellsworth stop stroking his beard, which probably meant that Henry had given him something good. A few minutes later Henry returned to his seat and started typing, not saying a word to the rest of us.

My curious nature took over and I couldn't help but glancing over Henry's shoulder, reading as he typed: . . . *FBI sting operation* . . . *Probing corruption in the Cook County judiciary system* . . . *Undercover mole planted inside the system, posing as a corrupt lawyer* . . ."

At lunchtime I slipped out of the city room and went around the corner to call Ahern at the state's attorney's office. It was bitter cold, and I could hear the wind whistling through the glass doors on the phone booth.

"What do you know about the FBI's sting operation with the courts?" I asked.

He sighed loudly into the phone, as if I were annoying him. "The Bureau's handling all that. You probably know more at this point than I do."

I gripped the receiver and sighed louder than he had. I knew he was holding out on me. If the FBI was investigating the Cook County judiciary system, Adamowski and the state's attorney's office had to be in on it. Hell, Adamowski was probably the one who'd tipped off the Bureau.

"Well," I said, before hanging up, "if you hear anything, let me know."

The next morning I attended a press conference held by the Illinois Department of Transportation. They were presenting plans to reconstruct a bridge feeding into the downtown area.

The room was small and the radiator heat steamed up the windows and made me groggy. I fought to stay awake while a spokesman boasted about the thousands of vehicles that accessed the bridge daily and the estimated $5 million allotted for repairs. I stifled a yawn and glanced around the room. The reporter next to me was checking his wristwatch while the one on the other side was playing a solo game of tic-tac-toe. It would be another twenty minutes before we'd be out of there.

Afterward I stopped into a Peter Pan Snack Shop for lunch and sat at the counter. I ordered a burger and a malted, my reward for having sat through the press conference. I reached inside my attaché case for the *Tribune*. It was the first chance I'd had that day to read the paper.

I sipped my malted as I read through several articles, one of which was Henry's story about Operation K, which was what the FBI was calling it—*K* as in *Kangaroo*, as in *Kangaroo Court*. It was clear that the Bureau had strategically leaked information to the press, probably wanting to make people nervous so they'd come forward or else slip up under the stress.

For some reason Mr. Ellsworth had buried Henry's piece in the Neighborhood News section. He probably figured that a couple of crooked cops, a bribe here, a fixed parking ticket there wasn't exactly front-page news for Chicago. More like business as usual. No one paid much attention to that sort of thing.

But there was something else on that page—something completely unrelated that caught my eye. It was just a three-inch piece that Peter had written about a butcher shop on Ashland

Avenue accused of selling horsemeat and passing it off as beef. Just the word *horsemeat* alone made me stop. I was stunned and reread the snippet. My brother was the only other person I knew who'd been looking into this matter, and I could never understand why the *Sun-Times* had dropped the investigation. But given what Peter just reported, I figured this racket was still going on.

I looked at my burger resting on the plate and removed the bun to inspect the meat. It looked normal, like any other burger, but because of Peter's article, I questioned the color, the texture, the way the fat pooled and congealed on the lettuce leaf. I hadn't even taken a bite yet, and now I couldn't. Instead I pushed it aside, finished my malted and asked for my check.

When I got back to the city room, I went straight over to Peter's desk with my newspaper in hand.

"What do you know about this?" I asked, slapping his article down before him.

"Oh, that?" Peter adjusted his eyeshade and glanced at the paper. "What about it?"

"How'd you find out about this?"

"I don't know—got a call from some disgruntled customer, I think—"

"Do you have any more information on this? Do you think there are other butcher shops doing the same thing?"

"Whoa, slow down there, Walsh. What's this all about?"

"I think maybe there're more butcher shops doing this."

"Oh, I doubt that." Peter adjusted his eyeshade again and squinted at me. "This was just a butcher, down on his luck, looking to cut corners. There's nothing more to it. The authorities closed down the shop."

"How about if we team up on this?"

"On what?" Peter shook his head. "There's nothing to team

up on. I already told you, it was an isolated case. There's nothing more to it."

"So you don't want to look into this any further?"

He laughed. "No. I don't want to look into it any further."

"Then do you mind if I do it myself?"

He rolled his eyes. "Suit yourself. But wait—" He reached into his drawer and pulled out a file—"you might as well take these with you." He handed me a few sheets of paper with his notes scribbled down. "Knock yourself out, Walsh."

I went back to my desk and read through everything Peter had given me. I immediately followed up with the customer who had discovered the problem.

"It just didn't taste right," she said when I reached her on the telephone. Turns out her son, who taught biology at Francis Parker High School, took the meat down to the lab. "That's how we found out it was horsemeat."

According to Peter's notes, the butcher said it was his horse, an old mare that he'd recently put down. The butcher, who was falling behind on his bills, had the horse ground up and packaged and sold as beef. That was the end of the story for Peter, but there had to be more to it. I knew Eliot had spent two months investigating this very subject. He'd told me once that he suspected there was horsemeat sold throughout the city, even to school cafeterias and fine restaurants. I was tired of covering bridge repairs and road closures, fires and car crashes. The horsemeat scandal had reinvigorated me. And I thought maybe, if I learned more about it, I would know for sure if that article Eliot had been working on had anything to do with his death.

After work that day, I went back to my parents' house to try to locate Eliot's notes on the horsemeat scandal.

My father was in his office, working, and my mother was

visiting with the poet Delmore Schwartz, who happened to be in town. My mother was sitting with her legs crossed, the top one swinging back and forth. She was laughing, smiling and chatting. I hadn't seen her like that in so long. She knew how to shine, truly sparkle. When she was like that, you could see what it was about her that had captivated men like Hemingway and possibly Schwartz.

I said a quick hello, slipped upstairs and went into Eliot's room. I sat down at his desk, running my hands over the curve of the wood, the cigarette and water ring scars along the top. The typewriter I'd once wanted so badly was right there, ominous and forbidding, like a flashing red *don't touch* button. How could I resist? I placed my fingertips over the keys and thought about the horsemeat article. *I can do this*, I told myself. *I can do this.* I pulled open the desk drawers, leafing through his folders and notebooks, the pages yellowing, the smell of aging paper and ink breaking down.

"What are you doing?"

I jumped at the sound of my father's voice and sheepishly tried to hide the papers in my hand. I felt like I'd just been caught stealing candy. "I—I was just looking through some of his notes. I—I was thinking of picking up one of his stories."

I expected my father to explode, but he only leaned against the doorjamb and spoke in a soft, calm voice. "Which story?"

"Huh? What?" I wasn't sure I'd heard correctly.

"Which story do you want to pick up?"

"Um, I was thinking about the last one he was working on. You know, about the horsemeat scandal and . . ."

My father began nodding as if he understood, fully on board, and yet the expression on his face was bewildering. I couldn't read him at all. "Well, then, by all means, you need to dig right in and do that, don't you? Here." He quickly stepped inside the room. "Let me help you. Let me give you a hand. Let me—" He reached over and yanked out the top drawer, flinging the contents about the room.

For a second I thought the drawer had slipped by accident, but then I realized he'd done it intentionally.

"Let me help you, Jordan." He threw the drawer halfway across the room and reached for another.

"Dad, calm down. Why are you doing this?"

"Couldn't let sleeping dogs lie, could you? Couldn't just let it be." With a sweep of his arm, he cleared a bookshelf and hurled another drawer of papers onto the floor. "That was your brother's story. You leave it alone, goddammit." He had started for another drawer when my mother and Delmore appeared in the doorway.

"Hank, stop it. Just stop it. What are you doing?"

Delmore grabbed my father in a straitjacket hold, tightening his grip the more my father twisted and turned, trying to get free. The only other time I'd seen anyone so out of control was the day Marty Sinclair had his breakdown. Seeing my father like that—and knowing that I'd set him off—shook me hard. My father was growling and cursing. If he ended up in the hospital like Marty, I didn't know what I'd do.

I'd started to panic, thinking we should call for a doctor, when at last all the rage burned itself out of him and my father calmed down. Delmore loosened his grip, and my father composed himself, shrugging out of his hold. He was breathing heavily, and sweat had collected on his brow.

"All right. All right." My father held his arms out to his sides, presenting himself in full surrender. "Everybody just relax." He muttered something else and walked out of the room, his shoulders sloped, broken, his head hung low.

After my mother and Delmore went back downstairs, I did my best to straighten up Eliot's room, put his papers back inside his desk and straighten the lampshade. Before I left the house that day, I drew a deep breath and went to see my father. He was in my parents' bedroom down the hall, sitting on the bed in the dark. I found him staring out the window, the only source of light in the room. His back was turned toward me.

"I'm sorry," I said, hanging in the doorway, not daring to step inside. I wanted to say more but didn't know how.

He raised one arm, letting it drop to his side, slapping the mattress. "That's an angry-looking sky," he said, still focused on the window. "Looks like snow. Freezing rain. You should go home now. Go on, before the weather turns bad."

"Okay," I said. "I'm leaving."

He nodded. "Okay, then."

That was all he had to say. I stood there waiting and willing him to turn around, to say something else. Anything. Didn't he know that I held on to his every word? Was it so goddamn wrong to expect that little bit from him?

Chapter 28

◆ ◆ ◆

Despite my father's orders to leave it alone, I was more motivated than ever to investigate the horsemeat scandal. I was ready to dive in full force when I got pulled onto more urgent matters. Chicago got hit with two big news items, one right after the other. On December 1, 1957, a TWA jet crashed just moments after takeoff from O'Hare and less than an hour later, the FBI started releasing names in Operation K.

It soon became apparent that the corruption was working its way up the judiciary food chain. It started with a prominent lawyer who was accused of paying off an even more prominent Cook County circuit judge to fix a drunk-driving ticket. That one captured people's attention, and day by day the story began moving closer to the front page. The leads came in faster than Henry could keep up with them, and I went to Mr. Ellsworth, begging him to let me on the story.

"Sorry, Walsh. I've already got Walter working on it with him."

"Walter?"

"Yes, Walter. Do you have a problem with that? Besides, don't you have your hands full with the TWA crash?"

It was true, I did. I'd been doing the follow-up reporting on

the engine failure that resulted in 119 fatalities. It was the ulti-
mate story of human tragedy that Mr. Ellsworth thought I handled so well. Even though I was technically still on society news,
still stuck on the women's pages and only given a *real news story*
here and there, I desperately wanted in on Operation K.

In the days that followed, page one was splattered with more
names and more courts were added to the list. There were police
chiefs, lawyers, assistant judges and judges in nearly every court—
traffic court, narcotics court, prostitution court. It was the story
everyone was talking about, speculating about.

We all spent many a night over at Riccardo's and Boul Mich
debating, guessing about who was the mole. So far there were
seven cops, nine lawyers and twelve judges all accused of taking
bribes, fixing cases. Something of this magnitude was hard to get
one's head wrapped around. It suggested that the entire Cook
County judicial system could be rigged.

I asked Scott about it one night over drinks at the Scotch Mist
on Rush Street.

"C'mon," I said. "You're in the thick of things. Tell me the
truth, what do you really think about Operation K?"

He took a pull from his beer and rapped his knuckles on the
bar. "This is the same shit I was complaining about years ago. It's
a mess. A real nightmare."

"Do you have any idea who the mole is?"

"Honestly, it could be anyone."

Scott got up and went to the jukebox. I followed him.

"Doesn't this whole thing make you mad?" I leaned against
the wall while he scanned through the selections. "I mean, you're
one of the good guys, just trying to do your job, but how can you
when the whole system is corrupt? And what about all the legit-
imate cops and judges out there? How does it make them look?"
I thought about Danny Finn and Jack's father. Judge Casey was

a man who had worked his way up from a clerk, put himself through law school and made it all the way to the bench. He believed in the system. I couldn't imagine what this was doing to him. "The whole thing has to infuriate you."

"I got mad years ago." He slipped a few coins in the slot and made his picks. Tennessee Ernie Ford's *Sixteen Candles*. "The sad part," he said, "is that none of this really comes as a shock to me anymore. The whole system is dirty. Even dirtier than I ever suspected." He jangled a few coins in his pocket and headed back toward the table. I followed close behind. "As soon as I can swing it," he said, "I'm getting out of it. I'm going to move away and start over."

"You're going to leave Chicago?" I was stunned by how panicked this made me.

"I don't want to practice law in this city anymore."

"But . . ." I didn't know what to say other than *Don't leave. Don't leave me.*

"I'm not even sure I want to practice law anymore at all. Oh, c'mon," he said. "Don't look so surprised. Don't you ever feel that way about reporting? Don't you ever go home at the end of the day and feel like you're covered in nothing but shit? Don't you ever feel like you want to wash your hands of the whole mess?"

"I don't know . . ." I shrugged. "I guess some stories have been harder to shake than others. Like the el car derailment. That got to me. But at the same time, I feel like I have an obligation to tell the truth—to get the word out."

His lips parted ever so slightly before he burst out with a laugh. "Oh, listen to you. Still so idealistic about it all." His laughter subsided to a smile. "I guess I was, too, once upon a time, wasn't I?"

"That's the Scott I always knew."

"I kinda miss that guy. And you know what I really miss? I miss feeling like what we did made a difference. Now I don't know how I feel. Tired, I guess. Tired and dirty."

About a week later I was still thinking about the horsemeat scandal and wondering when I was going to find the time to get back to it. Lately I'd been getting all kinds of other assignments. This was on my mind one night as I was heading home from work. Making my way down the subway stairs, I noticed a tall, slender figure following me, his face partially illuminated by the streetlamp. A warning signal traveled down my spine and I picked up my pace. When I reached the bottom step, he called to me.

"Jordan. Come here."

"Ahern? Ahern, what are you doing?"

"Is there someplace quiet we can go to? I need to talk to you. Off the record."

My blood began pumping a little faster. "What's this about?"

"Let's go somewhere private first. Then we'll talk."

There was a diner a few doors down from the el stop, so we went there. It smelled like burned onions inside. The waitress was putting up Christmas decorations and stopped long enough to come by with a pot of coffee and a platter of day-old dough-nuts. "Two for a nickel," she said as she filled our cups.

I shook my head and waved her off. My pulse was hammering, anticipating what Ahern had to see me about. "So what's going on?" I asked, after the waitress drifted back behind the counter.

"Your ex-fiancé—his father's a judge, right?"

"Yes."

"Judge Casey? Patrick J. Casey?"

"What's happened to him? Is he okay?" A sinking feeling set-tled in my gut. I lifted my coffee cup and set it back down as if it weighed too much.

"His name just came up in the Operation K investigation."

"What? That's ridiculous."

"I hate to be the one to—"

"No, no. It's not true. I know him. They got it wrong this time." I shook my head and reached for my cigarettes. "Judge Casey is one of the good guys. Really, he is."

"I'm afraid it's not looking that way." He leaned in closer and said, "I'm telling you this off the record because I consider us friends now. I don't want you to be blindsided when this hits."

"Oh, c'mon." I fumbled with the pack of cigarettes. My hands were shaking so I couldn't get one out.

Ahern fished out a cigarette for me and lit a match. "I'm only telling you what I know. What I've heard."

"Well, you've heard wrong." I leaned in toward the flame. "You know, this whole investigation is starting to turn into a witch hunt."

"There's a lot of corruption in the court system. And I hate to be the one to tell you this, but Casey's on the chopping block."

"I don't believe it. Judge Casey's not like that. I know him, and that man would never take a bribe." I glowered at Ahern as if this were his fault.

"Okay, I wasn't going to say anything, but"—Ahern lowered his voice and leaned in closer—"the mole got him on tape."

"What? What are you talking about?"

"I heard it myself, Jordan. It's Judge Casey saying he could fix any case in Cook County that came his way." He looked at me and reached for my hand, but I pulled it away. "I'm sorry. I listened to the tape myself."

I dropped my head to my hands. My fingertips were pressing into my skull to keep me from exploding.

"Are you okay?"

I shook my head. "And you're sure about this?" I asked, raising my eyes. "Absolutely sure it's him?"

"I'm sure."

I left Ahern and fled the diner with my mind spinning. I was trying to decide what to do. Should I call Jack? Should I call Judge Casey? Would it be a kindness to warn them?

I walked three city blocks, but in the end, with my fingers trembling, I ducked into a phone booth and dialed Jack's apartment. The line was ringing and I didn't know if I'd be able to get the words out or where to start.

When Jack answered his telephone, he sounded surprised to hear from me.

"I need to see you," I said. "We need to talk tonight. It's important."

There was a bar called Dayton's halfway between his place and mine. We met there fifteen minutes later. He was waiting for me near a shabby-looking Christmas tree. He seemed more annoyed than anything, as if I'd dragged him out in the middle of the night for no good reason.

"So what's wrong?" he asked after we'd settled in at the bar and ordered a couple Canadian Clubs on the rocks. "Is everything okay? Are you in trouble?"

"What? No, no. I'm fine. This isn't about me. It's about you. Really, it's about your father."

"My father? Did something happen? Is he okay?"

"Yeah, yeah, he's okay." I didn't want him to think he'd been in an accident or was hurt, but then I caught myself. "I mean no. Not really. Oh, Jack." I reached over and squeezed his hand. "I just found out that your father's going to be named in Operation K."

"What? What do you mean, *named*?" He pulled his hand away like a reflex.

"They're saying he's accepted bribes and—"

"That's ridiculous. My father's as straight as an arrow."

"I didn't want you to find out about it in the papers. I felt I owed it to you to let you know that they're going to be investigating him. I just found out—just tonight. Right before I called you."

"And what? You expect me to believe that you had nothing to do with this? You—who thinks my family's so perfect and thinks nothing bad ever happens to the Caseys—you've just been waiting for something like this, haven't you?"

"What?" I was shocked, and then I almost laughed. "Jack, I'm not even working on this story."

"Then how do you know so much about this? You might not be covering this, but your buddies sure as hell are."

"Every paper in the city's covering this. The *Sun-Times* has Operation K all over the front page."

"The *Tribune* broke this story. I'm sure it would have been very easy for you to say, *Hey, why don't you tell your pals at the FBI to run a check on Judge Casey.*"

"Jack, you know I wouldn't have done a thing like that. I love your father. I was devastated when they told me."

"Who's they? Who told you?"

I squeezed my eyes shut. "What does that matter?"

"You're not gonna tell me that part, are you?" He stood up, and the legs of his barstool screeched against the floor. "Whoever they are, they don't know what they're talking about."

"Jack, they have him on tape. The mole's been wearing a wire, and he got your father on tape saying he was fixing cases."

Jack gulped his drink and set the glass down hard.

"I'm sorry to be the one to tell you, but I wanted to let you know what I found out—and technically, I shouldn't even be doing this. But—"

"But we all know you'll do anything to get a story. You've already proved that."

His words clobbered me. "I'm trying to do you a favor."

"I don't need any favors from you. And tell your buddies they got this one wrong." He stood up and reached for his coat.

I sat there numb after he'd stormed out of the bar, pushing the door with such force that the bottom caught on the sidewalk and it stayed open. The bartender finally stepped outside and lifted the door so it would close again. I stayed and finished my drink, wanting each swallow to wash away what I knew. My mind pushed against it. I ordered another Canadian Club and went over to the vending machine in the corner for a pack of cigarettes. I pulled the knob on the Lucky Strikes. Nothing. I tried again. Still nothing. I tugged and tugged and tugged on it and pounded my fist to the side before I caught ahold of myself and tried another brand with success.

I sat back at the bar and smoked and drank until closing. I didn't want to go home. I felt horrible. And about so many things: for shattering Jack's world, for having been the one to tell him. And I was also disappointed in Jack's father. I expected better from Judge Casey. He'd let me down, and I couldn't have been more upset if it had been my own father.

I was hungover the next day when I went into the city room. The clacking typewriters and harsh overhead lights seemed to make it worse. So did Randy's impersonation of Elvis Presley singing *Heartbreak Hotel* and M dabbing nail polish on a run in her stockings, filling the room with noxious fumes. Add to it all that Walter was banging his pipe against his ashtray and jabbering away on his telephone, while Henry was doing the same, talking to someone at the Bureau. Every now and again, he'd place his hand over the receiver and shout to anyone passing by, saying, "You're not gonna believe this."

When Henry finally hung up, he turned to me. "Hey, Walsh? Walsh? Wait till you hear this. Got some juicy news about your ex-fiancé's old man."

I set my pencil down and closed my eyes, dreading what was coming. Some small part of me had been hoping Ahern was wrong.

Henry howled. "Oh, boy, is Judge Casey in hot water. He was just named in Operation K." Henry laughed some more, louder this time. His face seemed distorted and exaggerated like a grotesque's. The more he laughed, the more my insides churned. "Looks like Judge Casey has *got some s'plainin' to do, Lucy.*"

"Shut up, Henry." I pushed away from my desk, ran to the bathroom and threw up in the sink.

Chapter 29

• • •

Ink made it real. Ink made it echo, rippling through every corner of the city. I kept picturing that buttercup yellow phone
mounted to the wall in Mrs. Casey's perfect kitchen ringing
nonstop as the relatives, neighbors and friends picked up their
morning papers and saw Judge Casey's name on the front page of
the *Tribune* and the *Sun-Times*, the *Daily News* and the *Chicago
American*.

What would Mrs. Casey say to her callers? How would she
explain? How would Mr. Casey handle it? What did he say to his
wife, to his children? To Grandma Casey? I didn't know how they
were dealing with it because Jack wouldn't take my calls. But as
removed as I was, I found myself still caught up in their nightmare.

The next evening I met Scott for a drink. Lately we'd been
spending more time together. Mostly we got together to commiserate. I whined about my workload and how I couldn't find time
for the stories I really wanted to tackle, like the horsemeat scandal. And now there was this whole business with Operation K
and Jack's father. Scott had headaches of his own, too. He had
difficult clients and a leaking roof and a cat with failing kidneys.

He'd called earlier in the afternoon to say he needed a drink.

He suggested Fitzpatrick's, a dive bar known for their burgers and gravy fries. Turned out we were both going to be in that part of town so it made sense to meet there. I'd never been there before. It was off the beaten path, next to a vacant field on one side and an alley on the other. The bar was dark inside, smelled of stale beer and was overcast with cigarette and cigar smoke. I was surprised when the guy working the door knew Scott by name and the bartender knew his drink.

"You're a regular here?" I asked, somewhat amused.

He shrugged. "What can I tell you? The drinks are cheap."

"On a budget these days, are you?" I laughed. Scott was more the classy bar type, and this place served beer straight from the bottle and hard liquor in glasses that had a used, filmy look about them, not exactly dirty but not quite clean either. The jukebox was broken, so instead they had a portable radio on the bar. One of the guys on the stool at the end motioned to Scott with his drink and they exchanged nods.

"Who's that?" I asked.

"Just some lawyer I know."

I glanced back at him. He looked like a prime suspect for Operation K. He had two days' worth of graying shadow on his face and wore a wrinkled suit jacket that looked like it was two sizes too small for him. His gut protruded, hanging over his waistline. Even from a distance I could see he had a mustard stain on his tie. After we sat down, the man looked over at us before he got up and squeezed his way into the phone booth in the back, barely able to get the door shut.

While we waited on our martinis, Scott told me about his day and how he'd had to defend his client, a fellow lawyer who'd been caught with a male prostitute in a parking lot. As he spoke, I noticed that the guy from the phone booth settled his tab, set his fedora on his head and waddled out of the bar. I didn't think much of it and focused back on Scott's story. Our food came out, but I barely touched mine.

I asked Scott what he knew about Judge Casey.

"He seemed like one of the good guys, but then again, most of them do at first."

"Jack won't even speak to me. He thinks I set his father up. He thinks I'm responsible for destroying his father. Like I personally put the FBI up to this."

"Well, that's ridiculous. He was probably in shock when you told him. He's a smart guy. He'll realize you had nothing to do with it. Hell, you're not even reporting on this story."

"That's what I told him. I wanted to be on this story, but Mr. Ellsworth wouldn't go for it."

"Be grateful you're not on it. It's ugly and messy, and I have a feeling it's going to get messier." He looked at my plate. "You should try to eat something."

I picked up my burger, contemplated it and set it back down, reaching for my martini instead. I had no appetite. Especially for burgers. Ever since Peter's article ran, I'd been trying to avoid them.

It was getting late. There was just a handful of guys hovering around the bar and another table of men in the back. Scott and I stayed for that one drink too many.

Ricky Nelson's *Be-Bop Baby* came on the radio, and Scott set his glass on the bar and held out his hand. I giggled as I stood up, and right there in the middle of the bar we started to jitterbug. Scott knew what he was doing and made me look like a better dancer than I was. The liquor bottles on the bar blurred into a vivid prism of browns and greens and blues as Scott spun me on our makeshift dance floor. When he gave me that final twirl, I coiled back around and collapsed in his arms, my head resting on his shoulder. The two of us were laughing as the tempo changed and the Platters came on next, singing *The Great Pretender*. We looked at each other as the slow rhythm took hold of us and our bodies swayed in time, our arms still wrapped around each other, his eyes never leaving mine. He leaned in and kissed me and I kissed him back. We went on kissing in the middle of the room until the Everly Brothers came on singing *Wake Up Little Susie*. Scott whispered into my lips, "Let's get out of here."

It had started to snow and Scott stood at the curb, trying to hail a cab. I knew he was coming home with me that night—what would happen once we were back at my apartment I couldn't say, but I felt like a million el car rides and a million conversations had been leading us to this point. I smiled at Scott, vaguely aware of our surroundings, of a dog barking in the distance, of the group of men—maybe five or six of them—walking up the sidewalk. I was still in a dreamy haze, looking at Scott, thinking about being with him, when the group of men turned in our direction. They wore tattered coats, scuffed-up boots and dirty trousers. I took them for some regular working-class men and figured they were heading into Fitzpatrick's for a nightcap.

One of them pointed and called out, "There he is! Over there!"

The men came charging. My head whipped around to see who they were after. There was no one else on the street, and when I realized it was us they were coming for, my heart clenched into a fist. I tried to scream, but nothing came out. A man lurched at us and I jumped out of the way, but Scott was drunk, too slow to realize that they were heading toward him.

"You fuckin' rat!" The one guy grabbed Scott by the shoulders and drove his knee up into his gut. Scott doubled over, writhing in pain while another guy clobbered him over the back of the head. They struck him again and again.

"Stop it!" I cried. "Stop it!" I was terrified, and when I saw one of the men pull out a gun, I screamed and ran back inside the bar.

"Help! Help—they're going to kill him. Quick, call the police."
I was shaking, my pulse pounding. "Please, help! Please."

I followed two men as they rushed outside. Once they saw the
gun, they backed off, staying with me beneath the streetlamp in
the alley, watching helplessly. I trembled, my hands clamped over
my mouth, my knees turning to rubber. I'd lost sight of the one
with the gun. Had he already fired it? I couldn't tell because the
thugs were on top of Scott, kicking him, punching him, slam-
ming his head into the ground. I winced when I saw that his face
was covered in blood. He tried to get up, and that's when I heard
the gun go *pop, pop, pop.* I screamed into my hands as they
pounded him back down.

"You cocksuckin' rat," said the one as he reached down and
tore open Scott's shirt, revealing a thick band of silvery gray
electrical tape running across his ribs. The thug tore it clean off
the flesh. Scott screamed out, his skin left raw and bleeding.

I didn't get it at first. Scott had been wearing a wire? *A wire!*
But then I began to piece it all together, and my heart nearly
stopped.

"You fuckin' rat." Another kick to the gut.

"Lying sack of shit." A punch to the head.

I couldn't believe it. Scott was the one. He was the Operation
K mole. The man yanked the wire clean and threw the tape
recorder on the ground, stomping on it, cracking it into bits. The
man with the gun aimed it at Scott's head just as we heard the
whine of sirens in the background. The thugs threw their final
punches and spit on him before taking off, disappearing in the
dark as the police arrived.

I rushed over to Scott. He was bleeding badly. I couldn't tell
if he'd been shot or not. Each time he opened his mouth, more
blood gushed out.

"Don't try to speak," I said. "Don't try to move. Help is coming." I gripped his bloody hand and held on tight until he lost consciousness.

I was in a panic, riding in the ambulance with him, asking over and over again if he was going to be okay. Both his eyes were swollen shut and his lip was split open. The ambulance workers were crouched over him, working on him the whole way. One of them kept mumbling about how much blood he'd lost.

As soon as we arrived at the hospital, a swarm of doctors and nurses circled around and rolled him on a gurney through a set of double doors. I tried to follow, but a nurse blocked me with her clipboard. "You'll have to stay out here," she said, indicating the waiting room.

Here I was again, back in this waiting room at Henrotin Hospital. That same sense of helplessness returned from the day Eliot was brought in. It wasn't until I was alone in that waiting room that I allowed myself to think about my kiss with Scott. It was a kiss that was years in the making, a kiss that made sense of Jack and of the affair with my professor and every other failed relationship I'd had, because now I had my answer. It was Scott Trevor all along. He had to be okay. He had to live. I wasn't good at expressing my feelings, but I vowed to be bold and tell Scott exactly how I felt about him when he came out of surgery.

Surgery . . . I thought about Eliot and about Harley Jackson, the little boy in the el car derailment. They had come into this very hospital, had surgery and never came out. What if Scott died, too? My leg began bobbing up, down, up, down. A clammy sweat spread over my skin as the anxiety rose up inside me. The helplessness and bad memories overwhelmed me. I couldn't sit still any longer and began to pace like an expectant father, trying to stay ahead of the thoughts gaining on me. I was never one to dwell on my emotions. Many times I'd been accused of being cold and unfeeling, but the opposite was true. I was always on the verge of feeling too much. That was the problem. So following my parents' example, I had shut down a part of myself when Eliot died. And now if I gave in to my emotions—to everything I was feeling right then—I would have drowned. So instead, I did what self-preservation had taught me to do. I simply didn't think about it. Avoidance had always been my best defense, and like I'd done so many times in my life, I switched off my mind. I began memorizing the names of the doctors being paged over the loudspeaker: *Dr. Wesley to ER. Dr. Wesley to ER. Dr. Spangler. Paging Dr. Spangler. Dr. Norris, Dr. Eugene, Dr. Montgomery* . . .

And in between, the police came into the waiting room to question me. Once they started asking questions and I began retelling the events, I realized what I was sitting on. *My God!* This was the biggest scoop of my career. I, Jordan Walsh, knew who the Operation K mole was. The thugs who beat up Scott were no doubt hired by a group of crooked lawyers, cops and judges. They showed up tonight to expose him, possibly kill him and foil his plan. I couldn't prove it yet—I'd have to go back to Fitzpatrick's Bar and ask some questions, do some digging around—but I was certain that the guy at the bar with the mustard stain on his tie had been the one to tip them off. I recalled how he'd squeezed into that phone booth and probably called whoever was giving the orders. But the real news—the immediate news—was that the Operation K mole had been exposed. And I had a firsthand account of it all.

As soon as the cops were done with me, my reporter instincts kicked in. The phone booth was just three feet away. I walked over, fed a nickel through the slot and dialed the city room.

"Get me the city desk."

Chapter 30

◆ ◆ ◆

By the time Scott came out of surgery I had already spoken to Mr. Ellsworth twice and dictated my eyewitness account to Higgs on the rewrite desk. As I made my way down the hospital corridor to see Scott, the story was on its way to the composing room.

I'd been up all night but was still wide-awake at four in the morning. I stepped inside Scott's room and saw him lying in that hospital bed and my heart sank down in my chest. His arms and torso were wrapped like a mummy's; his eyes were swollen, reduced to slits. When he saw me, he attempted a smile despite the zipper of stitches along his lip—the lips that had kissed mine just hours before.

I pulled up a chair and sat by his side, reaching for his hand. "The doctor said you're going to be okay. They expect you to make a full recovery."

He nodded and faintly squeezed my fingers. We stayed like that, his hand in mine while a nurse came in to check on him. After she'd taken his temperature and his pulse and had given him a shot, the nurse left, and the first thing Scott said was, "Are you disappointed in me?"

"Disappointed in you? Whatever for?"

"You know, the whole informant thing."

"Are you kidding me?" Just the fact that he'd said that made me love him all the more. "Why would I be disappointed in you? I'm so proud of you. Look at what you did. You did it. You went after the bad guys. Do you realize that because of you, they're finally cleaning up the court system? My God, Scott, I think you're one of the bravest men I've ever known. How could I possibly be disappointed in you?"

"I wanted to tell you. God, you have no idea how many times I almost did."

"What I don't understand, though, is how you got involved in all this in the first place."

"Such a long story." He closed his eyes and struggled to swallow.

"Don't. Don't try to talk. You'll tell me later."

"No." He opened his eyes. "Let me. Let me tell you now." He paused and swallowed hard again. "Remember a couple of years ago? When I was an assistant state's attorney? A prosecutor? Remember how I told you I wanted to quit my job because I kept prosecuting guilty men who were walking away with barely a hand slap?"

He closed his eyes and paused for a minute, as if harnessing his strength to get through the rest of it. "Then after I bitched about it to enough people, out of the blue I got contacted by someone at the Bureau. And he asked me to go undercover. At first I said 'There's no way in hell.' I wasn't about to do it. But they stayed on me—I was getting dozens of phone calls from them and I'd find them turning up all over town, following me around. They'd show up in restaurants, on street corners—you name it. They were doing everything they could to try to talk me into it. Eventually they convinced me that I could do more to straighten out the justice system by going undercover than continuing to prosecute guilty men who just got off. Finally I agreed. So I switched jobs and went to work as a defense attorney, remember?"

"Yeah, and I was shocked when you told me. It just didn't seem like you, but now it all makes sense."

"I could have done it as an assistant state's attorney, but I didn't want this to touch anyone I worked with—not directly anyway. So there I am, taking on the sleaziest cases out there—drunk drivers, prostitutes, drug dealers. I reported back that I'd heard about some lawyers dealing out fifty-dollar bills to this one judge. The FBI said they needed more concrete evidence. And by then some of these guys are thinking I'm their buddy because I'm palling around with them, trying to get them to tell me what they know. I spent way too much time in dive joints like that place we were at last night. I got smashed with these guys, started sitting in on their poker games just hoping and praying that one of them would say something that I could take back to the Bureau. It was so damn hard keeping all the lies straight. There were days I didn't even know who I was. The whole thing made me sick. Especially in the beginning. Remember when I lost all that weight? Dropped about twenty pounds because I couldn't keep anything down."

"And I thought that was because you broke up with Connie."

"Connie." He winced. "I'm glad she walked away when she did. I didn't want to bring anyone into this mess. Especially not you. Why do you think I kept everything between us so casual, so platonic? And believe me, it wasn't easy. I just didn't want to get you involved."

I ran my fingers over the back of his hand. So he'd been feeling the same way about me all this time.

"Even my parents didn't know what I was doing," he said. "So anyway, I reported everything back to the Bureau, and again they said they needed more hard evidence. Something that would give them an open-and-shut case."

"So is that when you started wearing a wire?"

He attempted a nod. "They told me I had to get it all on tape. They wanted these crooks to incriminate themselves. They wanted to hear these guys saying they were taking bribes and manipulating cases. I said absolutely not. I'd be a dead man if I got caught. The thought of it terrified me. But I was already in so deep. And they kept saying that this was my chance to help put some of those lying, cheating bastards away. I got so in over my head. . . ."

I couldn't believe what I was hearing, what he'd been through and had been forced to keep to himself. He was still talking as I instinctively reached inside my purse for my pad of paper and pen.

"What was the name of that first agent from the Bureau who contacted you?"

"What?" Scott's eyes strained to open, looking at me in confusion. I followed his gaze as it moved down to the notepad, and with all the energy he could muster, he shook his head. "Whoa, wait a minute, Jordan. This is all off the record. I'm not giving you a story here."

"Why not? This is huge."

"Because I haven't even spoken to the Bureau yet. The FBI needs to find the guys who jumped me. They have to see if they can identify me. We have to try to find a way to salvage the investigation. If you say anything now, you could jeopardize the entire operation."

As soon as he said that, I went light-headed and dizzy. The presses were running at that very moment. The story was already out. And with Scott named in it and my byline on it. It had never occurred to me to hold back, to exercise some restraint. I'd already told the police what happened—I had to do that. And my eagerness to break this news before the police leaked it to the press had clouded my judgment, completely eclipsed my sense of decency. I believed in what Scott was doing—I thought he was a hero—and yet I could have just destroyed all his work.

I turned away and stared at my reflection in a chrome water pitcher on the bedside stand. My nose and mouth, my eyes and ears were distorted. I looked like an ogre and felt like one, too.

"You have to keep all this to yourself. You can't tell anyone anything."

I heard his words circling around my head. I still couldn't look at him. "Oh, Scott." I swallowed hard. "It's already too late."

"What? What's too late?"

"I—I figured the investigation was . . . I thought it would already . . ."

"Jordan, what's going on?"

I saw the alarm set in on his face.

"Jordan?" he pressed me, struggling to sit up.

"Oh, God." I blurted it out. "I made a terrible mistake. I did something and I wasn't thinking and now it's too late."

"*What's* too late? What did you do?"

"Please don't hate me."

"Jordan." His swollen eyes were filling with panic, as if he knew what I was about to say. "You didn't say anything to the cops, did you?"

"Scott, I had to. Those guys could have killed you. They're still out there—they could come after you again."

"Oh, shit. Jesus, no."

"And I already called this into the city room."

"You *what*?" Scott leaned back into the pillow and closed his eyes. "No, God. Jordan, tell me you didn't. How could you do that?"

"I'm sorry. I figured those guys already knew it was you and so . . ."

"And so, what? You figured it would be okay to let everyone else know? Please, dear God, Jordan, please say you didn't name me."

I covered my mouth with my hand.

Scott collapsed against his pillows, like he was sinking into himself. "I get that you had to talk to the police. I get that. But, Jesus—the city desk? Jesus Christ. I can't believe you ran with this without even asking me about it first. Not everything is fodder for your paper, you know! Whatever happened to friendship? To loyalty? I didn't think I had to preface *everything* going on in my life with a 'please don't print this in the goddamn newspaper.'"

"I'm sorry, Scott. I was just—"

"Just what? Doing your job? Everything I've been through, everything I've done for the past eighteen months could be for nothing." He reached up and pushed the call button. "And goddammit, don't look like you're going to cry. We both know you're not a crier, so don't you dare try to make me feel sorry for you right now."

I wasn't crying. I wasn't thinking of crying. I was thinking of how to fix this. "I'll—I'll make it right. Somehow I'll—I'll make them retract the story."

"It's too late. The damage has been done."

"Please don't hate me. I didn't—"

"Stop it. Just stop. I can't deal with your guilt right now, too."

"But, Scott . . ."

"Please." He closed his eyes, wincing in pain. "Do me a favor: just get out of here. Just leave."

The nurse came in. "You need something in here?"

"Could you get her out of here? Just get her out of here and don't let her back in."

That part did make me cry. It was still dark outside when I left the hospital, and the tears blurred my vision, stringing the streetlights together as I passed by. It wasn't even seven o'clock yet and the city was only half awake. More snow had fallen overnight. The el rumbled by overhead, the taxicabs and buses peppered the streets. Newspaper boys stood on street corners, surrounded by stacks of bundles bound together with string, selling their papers. I couldn't bring myself to buy the morning edition of the *Tribune*. I wasn't ready to face the damage yet.

I walked through the early-dawn streets, hoping to clear my head, but it was no good. I couldn't stay ahead of what I'd done, my mind replaying the scene inside Scott's hospital room. And yet I had to tell the police what I'd seen. I'd been a witness to a crime. I had to report it, and Scott knew that. But I shouldn't have called it in to the paper. That's where I went wrong. Scott's cover was probably blown anyway, but thanks to me, it was certain. I dragged my sleeve across my eyes and nose, making way for more tears.

Normally I wasn't one to talk about my problems, but I needed someone to tell me I wasn't a horrid, self-serving person. Ironically, Scott would have been the perfect person to speak to, but there was no Scott anymore. There was no Jack anymore or Judge Casey, either. M didn't deal with her own problems, so I couldn't imagine she'd be much help with this. There was only one place left to turn.

As soon as I stepped inside, I smelled coffee brewing and heard the ticking of the radiators. It was only then that I realized how cold I was, my fingers and toes numb from the walk. My father was still asleep, but my mother was up and surprised to see me.

She was at the sink when she saw me standing in the doorway. As soon as she caught the look on my face, she cast aside the dish towel, came over and cupped my face.

"What's the matter? Why are you upset? Look at what you've done." Her chin gestured toward the newspaper. She'd already seen the morning paper. The *Tribune* was resting on the kitchen table with my story on the front page, faceup. The photo editor had included Scott Trevor's picture—a shot taken back when he worked for the state's attorney.

Yeah, look what I've done.

My mother searched my face. "What is it, honey? Why aren't you pleased?"

"I went too far." I dropped into a chair. "This time I went too far. I was only thinking about myself. About my byline." I tried to keep my voice steady as I relayed what had happened with Scott at the hospital. "I should have never called that story in to the city desk."

"Why not?" My mother looked genuinely confused. "You had to do it. That's your job. The police knew what happened. The story would have gotten out anyway."

"But not with my name on it."

My mother reached for my hand. "You're a reporter and a reporter's job is to report the news."

"But isn't there a point where you stop being a reporter and you start being a human being? At the end of the day, isn't there *anyone* you're supposed to protect?" I asked.

"If your father and your grandfather were sitting here with us right now, I know what they'd say." My mother tilted her head and smiled. "You protect your family. Your family and the people you love like family. Everyone else is fair game."

This made me feel even worse because I did love Scott. I had always loved him. He was the one I truly wanted. It had taken me all this time to realize that, and now it was too late.

"And don't be so hard on yourself," my mother said. "You didn't ruin the whole investigation. Trust me on that. Your friend gave the FBI enough to go on. He's just upset because his cover was blown. But from what you've said here"—she indicated the paper—"they were already onto him anyway. That's why he was attacked in the first place. You had nothing to do with that."

A lot of what my mother said was true. Much of the FBI's sting operation had already begun to unravel, and that was not because of me.

"Sweetheart," she said, "all you did was give it ink."

After leaving my mother, I stopped by my apartment, washed up and changed my clothes. It was going on nine in the morning. I still hadn't been to sleep, and as soon as I walked into the city room, Mr. Ellsworth and Mr. Copeland circled around me, wanting to talk about a follow-up piece.

I looked at them, wondering if I had the stomach to do another story about this. Then I thought about what my mother had said. I realized that my friendship with Scott, or budding romance or whatever it was to be, had been destroyed. It was over. He'd never trust me again and perhaps rightfully so.

But all the same, if I walked away from the story now, it would have all been for naught. I'd already lost Scott, and now I could lose my chance at the story that could make my career. If it wasn't going to be my byline, it would surely be someone else's. The inside story on Operation K had landed in my lap. How could I turn away?

So, with my decision made for me, I sat down with a cup of coffee and told Mr. Ellsworth and Mr. Copeland the whole story, everything that I'd been told by the mole himself from his hospital bed about how he'd come to work with the FBI in the first place and the toll that going undercover had taken on him.

"Well, what are you waiting for, Walsh?" Mr. Ellsworth cracked a sly smile. "Get busy. You've got an exclusive to write."

Chapter 31

• • •

My work on Operation K started out like a locomotive, moving slowly at first but then rapidly picking up steam. Whatever misgivings I had about pursuing this story were gradually replaced with an all-consuming drive, pushing everything else off for a later time. Even the horsemeat scandal. And yes, I admit that in the back of my mind I was hoping I would uncover something—something unexpected—that might make this up to Scott.

I went back to Fitzpatrick's, the bar where he'd been attacked. It looked different in the daylight, and by *different* I wish I could say *better*. But with the sun streaming in through the windows, I saw just how grungy the place really was. Stale beer and smoke lingered in the air. I stepped over cigarette butts and dead matchsticks on the floor. The liquor bottles behind the bar that had sparkled like a prism the night Scott and I danced before them were now streaked with greasy fingerprints.

The bartender, a fellow named Mick, was reluctant to talk to me at first.

As soon as I said I was from the *Tribune*, he said, "I read all about it in the paper. I don't know what more I can tell you that you don't already know." He was alternating between wiping out

glasses and clearing the surface of the bar. I couldn't help noticing he was using the same rag for both jobs.

I ordered a bottle of beer and eventually Mick started talking.

"Trevor seemed like a decent enough guy," he said, futzing at
the cash register. "He would come in here a couple nights a week
with some of the others."

"The others?"

"You know, some of the cops, the other lawyers. There was a
whole group of them. You know, regulars."

It took another beer and a bit more coaxing before he began
giving me names, including Albey Riley, the man with the mustard-
stained necktie. I left Fitzpatrick's, and after two fruitless attempts
to track down Albey Riley, one of his neighbors on the South
Side directed me to Manny's Deli on Roosevelt Road.

"Do you mind?" Riley said when I approached him, giving me
a look of disgust while he tucked his napkin into his shirt collar.
"I'm eating here." He was even bigger than I remembered and
more than filled his half of the table.

"I just have a few questions for you," I said, slipping into a
chair across from him.

"Who the hell are you?"

"I'm Jordan Walsh. I'm with the *Tribune*."

He grunted. "And what's this about?"

I told him that I was looking into the incident with Scott
Trevor and began asking questions, some of which he answered
truthfully: Yes, he was a lawyer. Yes, he knew Scott Trevor. But
the rest of the time he was playing games with me.

"Gotta tell you," he said, in between bites, "I was sorry as hell
to read about what happened to him. But I'm glad this city's
finally doing something to clean up the court system."

"So you were aware of the corruption?"

With each bite, the guts of his sandwich leaked out, chunks

of corned beef landing on his plate. "I'm not saying that I was personally, but you know, you hear things here and there."

"What sort of things?"

He dabbed his mouth. "Nothing specific. You know, just talk."

I backed up and tried a different angle. "You were at Fitzpatrick's the other night when Scott Trevor was attacked. And you made a phone call before you left. Who did you call?"

"Huh? What are you talking about?" He acted as if I were mistaken.

I scooted in closer and squared my elbows on the table, looking at him head-on. "You went to the phone booth in the back that night and made a call right before you paid your tab and left. I was there. I saw you do it."

That's when he made a show of checking his watch and said he was late for a meeting. It was probably the only time he'd ever left half a sandwich on his plate.

Before the day was done, I had spoken to nearly a dozen lawyers, bar patrons and cops. I even spoke with Ahern and some other people at Adamowski's office. What I needed now was a source inside the FBI. Although given that I'd interfered with their investigation, I was probably the last person they wanted to talk to. Still, I wasn't giving up.

"Hey, Henry," I called to him when I returned to the city room. "Who's your guy at the Bureau on Operation K?"

"Why do you want to know?"

"I just need to verify a few facts."

Henry grabbed the pencil from behind his ear and threw it down on his desk. "You've got to be kidding me. You want my contact at the Bureau? You've got a lot of nerve, Walsh."

Walter rolled his chair over to Henry's. "We're busting our asses on this investigation," he said, "and the whole time you've been holding out on us, going behind our backs and—"

"Hey—" I stopped him right there. "First things first. I did not go behind your backs. I wasn't holding out on you. I had no idea that Scott Trevor was an informant. Read what I wrote in my article and you'll know exactly how the whole thing came about."

Henry waved me off. "Aw, forget you. I don't trust a damn thing you have to say."

"You got some balls, Walsh," said Walter, stuffing his pipe in his mouth before he rolled his chair back to his desk.

Peter adjusted his eyeshade and kept his head down, refusing to look at me. Randy avoided me, too, keeping his back to me while he chattered away on his telephone. Even Marty was decidedly cool toward me, telling me he was busy when I stopped by his desk with a question. M, Gabby and the other girls didn't really care, since I'd done nothing to infringe upon their territory.

And then there was Benny. He came over, leaned in and whispered, "I think it was a great piece that you wrote. I really do."

"Benny!" Henry snapped. "Did you get that quote for me yet? You're holding up the whole piece."

Benny's ears turned almost as red as his hair. "I—I gotta get back to work. But maybe we could get a drink?"

"Benny! I need that now!"

He practically sprinted across the room, and I went back to the notes from my interview with Albey Riley.

About an hour or so later, Mrs. Angelo stopped by my desk. "Here"—she plunked a sandwich down in front of my typewriter— "ham and Swiss on rye."

I shook my head. "Thanks, but I can't eat."

"Okay, then, fine." She reached down and picked up the sandwich. "Grab your coat and come with me." She gestured with a tilt of her head.

I got up and followed her into the hallway, onto an elevator and down to the lobby. "Where are we going?"

"Someplace where we can talk. This is where I go to get away from those clowns upstairs so I can think."

We went out the back door and down one more level to the loading dock on Lower Wacker Drive. Hidden beneath Michigan Avenue, Lower Wacker was the underbelly of the city. If you didn't know this underground world existed, you'd never find it. It was dark and dank down there, with water leaking through the ceiling. I looked up at the dripping pipes and cracks, wondering what would happen if the street above collapsed. We could hear the traffic rumbling overhead while the cars on Lower Wacker turned on their headlights, speeding and swerving around the curved streets, barely slowing at the stop signs. Flatbeds on the dock were piled high with stacks of newspapers bundled together with twine, waiting to be loaded onto the *Tribune* trucks and sent out for delivery.

Mrs. Angelo paused before the white brick wall and a wooden milk crate. Dozens of lipstick-kissed cigarette butts littered the ground. "Sorry I don't have an extra chair."

"*This* is where you come to think?"

Mrs. Angelo pulled out a pack of cigarettes. "It's the one place where no one comes looking for me." She lit her cigarette and offered me one.

I leaned in to the flame she produced, exhaling into a gust of wind that blew the smoke back into my face. "I didn't go behind Henry's and Walter's backs. I wasn't trying to do anything underhanded."

"Oh, *pffft*. Don't sweat it, kid." Mrs. Angelo unwrapped the sandwich she'd bought for me and broke off a piece of bread, tossing it to a group of pigeons. "The others are just good and sore because you stole their thunder on Operation K." She tore off some more bits of the sandwich and sprinkled them on the concrete. "And they're extra sore because they were upstaged by a woman." A pigeon landed at the pile of crumbs, pecking at the offerings.

"But you know as well as I do that given the chance, they would have done the same thing."

"Oh, they would have, and without a shred of remorse," she said, drawing down on her cigarette as a flock of pigeons arrived on the feeding scene. "So don't sweat it. Besides, you take your marching orders from Mr. Ellsworth and Mr. Copeland now. And I'll back you on that."

"You will?"

"Why wouldn't I?" She looked just as surprised as I was. "I'll do anything to help a woman trying to make her way in this world."

I could have cried. All this time I thought Mrs. Angelo resented me for wanting off society news, but now I could see that in her own way, she'd been rooting me on.

"It's hard enough in this business," she said. "We women have to look out for each other. I got further ahead than most, but it was a fight every step of the way. I'm getting too old for this game now. I'm tired. But you—you've got what it takes to give those men a run for their money. I know I was tough on you in the beginning. I didn't encourage a lot of your stories. But you've made a believer out of me, kid. And someday you'll be in a position to do the same for a young girl who comes to you wanting to be the next Nellie Bly." She gave me a wink, took a final drag off her cigarette and pitched it to the ground. "You're a woman, but you're also a reporter, and you're one of the best I've seen."

After Scott's identity was exposed—or rather, after I had exposed him—Operation K came to an end. But the FBI continued pursuing their case because Scott had already given them enough crucial evidence. My mother had been right. The Bureau had the information needed to either arrest and convict or at the very least investigate and ultimately ruin the reputations of twenty-seven members of the Cook County judiciary system, including lawyers, cops and judges. One of whom was Judge Patrick Casey.

So Operation K wasn't over for the FBI and it wasn't over for me, either.

One night, about six months later, while I was in the middle of making spaghetti, I heard a knock on the door.

"Just a minute. Coming." I pulled open the door and almost dropped the colander.

Mrs. Casey was standing on my threshold, glowering at me. I noticed a letter in her trembling hand and I knew exactly what it was because I had written it. I recognized my handwriting on the envelope. It was to Mr. Casey.

"Now, you listen to me," said Mrs. Casey. Her voice shook with anger. "I want you to stay away from my family. No more letters to my husband. Or to my son. They want nothing more to do with you."

"Mrs. Casey, please come inside so we can talk." I opened the door wider and stepped aside. "Please give me a chance to explain—"

"Explain? You can't explain what you've done."

I heard the spaghetti boiling over, the water hissing as it hit the burner. I resisted the urge to go turn off the stove.

Mrs. Casey didn't budge. "You've done enough damage to my family. You've broken my son's heart and ruined my husband's reputation."

"I had nothing to do with Operation K. I wasn't even—"

"You knew that rat, that mole. You knew him. You knew what he was up to. And my husband has done nothing wrong. You had him trapped."

"I didn't have—"

"And I don't want you writing any more letters to my husband or my son." She fisted up the envelope and raised it to my face. "Leave us alone—you hear me? Leave my family alone!"

She stormed off, and I stood there staring at a fly swatter resting inside the baby carriage across the hall. I heard my spaghetti continuing to boil over, and by the time I could move, there was starchy water and strings of noodles strewn across the stove.

I turned off the gas and went out to the living room. I sat on the sofa until the sun went down, taking the light out of the room with it. The only time I got up was to get a bottle of wine. After that I sat in the dark, thinking about the letters I'd written to Jack, to his father. Neither one of them had bothered to reply. I'd written to Scott, too, but he'd never answered, either. I could scarcely think about Scott without tearing up. The only other person I had ever missed with such intensity was Eliot.

I was hoping the wine would make me sleepy, make me pass out, but it only made me sadder. The seasons had changed twice since I'd last spoken to Scott. I missed the sound of his voice, missed talking to him, hearing what he had to say because I loved the way his mind worked.

I didn't even know what time it was when I snapped, reached for the phone and dialed his number. I had nothing to lose at this point. The worst he could do was hang up on me.

He answered on the fifth ring, sounding groggy.

"I'm sorry," I said, realizing that I'd woken him up. That's when I looked at the clock. It was after midnight. "I'm sorry," I said again, but this time the apology was for everything else. "I miss you, Scott."

He sighed.

I kept talking, afraid to let the silence build.

"I know you probably don't want to hear from me, but you have to believe that I never meant to hurt you."

Another sigh, deeper, louder. I could almost picture him lying in the dark, his hair rumpled from sleep. I wanted to be there, beside him. I wanted to hold him until he couldn't deny me. My eyes started to tear up.

"Oh, Scott—I feel horrible about what happened. I think about it—about you—every day."

"It's late," he said. "I have to get up in a few hours."

"No, wait." I gripped the receiver with both hands. "I miss you, Scott. I want you back in my life."

Another sigh. "C'mon, Jordan, you're just feeling guilty."

"Don't you care about me? Don't you miss me? At all?"

"It doesn't matter—it'll never work. Right now I don't trust that you're not using this conversation for your next byline."

That stung, and I squeezed my eyes shut as a tear leaked out.

"Look, it's late. I gotta go."

I held on to the phone long after he'd hung up.

Because of Operation K, I had successfully alienated my ex-fiancé and his family, Scott Trevor and the majority of my colleagues. The only ones who were pleased with what I'd done were my editors.

Chapter 32

◆ ◆ ◆

It was a beautiful autumn day. M and I were going to have lunch and go for a walk. That was what we'd planned. But then we stepped off the elevator in the lobby and came face-to-face with Marilyn Monroe.

Miss Monroe had recently starred in a new film, and had stopped by the *Tribune* to give interviews. None of us knew she was coming by the paper, but there she suddenly was, standing less than three feet from M.

I would have expected M to fawn all over her idol, but either she was too starstruck to speak, or else she was embarrassed by her impersonation, because she stood there silently, like she was in shock. Seeing the two of them side by side left no question as to who was the original. Try as she might, M's hair wasn't as glossy, her skin not as creamy, her figure not as curvy. She was a cheap imitation, a fraud. Her cheeks turned a shade of red I'd never seen before.

"Well, look at what we have here," Marilyn Monroe said to the men who accompanied her. "Isn't that just too funny? They sure do know how to make a girl feel welcome here, don't they?" She gave M a wink.

That was it. Marilyn laughed and brushed past M as one of

her escorts directed her toward the elevator. The doors closed and she was gone.

M was paralyzed, red-faced and speechless. Eventually she said, "I—I can't go to lunch right now. Would you mind? I—I have to take care of something."

I wasn't all that hungry anyway and went back upstairs to finish working on a story about a madam in jail who claimed that the arresting officer had walked off with $20,000 from her safe. Peter had reported on a similar story a month before, and I asked if he could remember the officer's name.

"He's busy, Walsh," said Walter. "Do your own legwork, would you?"

"Jesus, Walter. Back off," I said. "I'm talking to Peter, not you."

And that got Henry into it. He slammed his box of Frosted Flakes on the desk and glowered at me. "We're all sick and tired of doing your work for you."

"That's bullshit, and you guys know it."

Things were starting to escalate when M showed up at the city room and we all shut up. I couldn't believe it. On her lunch hour she had become a brunette. After recovering from the shock, I realized her new hair color was more flattering to her features, softer and more natural.

"You look *ehhhx*-cellent," said Peter.

While we were all focused on M's hair and admiring her new look, Mr. Ellsworth called me into one of the conference rooms. I don't think he even realized that it was M sitting there—that's how different she looked.

"Have a seat, Walsh," Mr. Ellsworth said, closing the door behind him. "We're going to be making some changes around here."

"I don't believe it." My heart shut down. "You're letting me go?"

He twisted up his face. "Hell no, I'm not letting you go. But I am moving you to the night shift."

"What?" I felt punched in the gut. This was a clear demotion. "Why?"

"In case you haven't noticed, I've got a hostile working environment around here. I'm trying to keep some semblance of peace among my staff."

"This is because of me? Because of Operation K? That was ages ago. Oh, c'mon."

"You're a good reporter, Walsh. You did good work on that, but now I've got a situation that I need to deal with and I've—"

"Now you've got to find a way to appease Walter and the rest of them."

He didn't deny it. "The decision's been made. You'll be covering the overnight police beat."

M r. Ellsworth threw me to the wolves. From that night on I began covering the shootings, stabbings and muggings that happened in the city's wee hours. I was on the desk from nine in the evening until five, sometimes six in the morning. I was exhausted, burning on two and three hours of sleep a night because my body refused to adapt to this new schedule.

Sometimes I thought Mr. Ellsworth put me on nights hoping it would make me quit. I wondered if he'd decided that I was more trouble than I was worth and that the extreme hours, and all the blood and gore of the night beat, would make me give up. And it was a challenge—that I couldn't deny.

One night was particularly tough for me. It was early December, cold and snowy. I was called in to cover a hit-and-run. I rode along in the squad car with my buddy Danny Finn, who was also often on the night shift. My leg was bobbing up and down, my neck and shoulders already tensing up. The victim, a young woman, was pronounced dead at the scene. The driver was caught less than a mile away.

When Danny and I pulled up to Milwaukee and North Avenue

and I saw that driver standing by his car with its shattered head-lights and smashed-up hood, I flew into a rage. To me he represented every driver who'd ever hit a pedestrian. I wanted to kill him, to personally make him pay for every victim, for every broken family he'd left in his wake. I was out of the car before Danny even turned off the engine.

I stormed over to the driver, slouched against his car with snow collecting in his hair and along his shoulders, his hands cuffed and the smell of booze emanating from him. "Who in the hell do you think you are!" I screamed. "You're a coward. Nothing but a coward. You killed that girl. You hear me? You killed her. You live with that just like her family has to live without her now. I hope you rot in jail. . . ."

I was still shouting at him when I felt Danny pulling me back.

"C'mon, now," he said, butting his forehead up against mine, his hands running up and down my arms. "Get a grip. You can't do that. Just calm down."

I nodded. I knew he was right. I caught my breath and went back to the squad car and smoked a cigarette while the other police officers took the driver down to the station. I gathered my notes and tried to compose myself when I went over to the phone booth. I was still shaking even after I called in my report to the rewrite desk.

When I went back to the squad car, Danny placed his arm around my shoulder. "Drink?" he asked.

"What do you think?"

There was a place we always went to—JJ's Supper Club, which was not a supper club at all. It was a joint that stayed open all night and we could get a bourbon or a beer while other customers were coming in for coffee and eggs.

Danny guzzled his beer, practically draining it in one gulp. I wasn't far behind him with my scotch. There was a dart game going on a few feet away.

"So what was *that* all about?" Danny asked. "I've never seen you get that emotional."

I didn't want to talk about it. It was unprofessional and I was embarrassed by my behavior. Danny had finished his beer, and I absentmindedly reached for his empty bottle, set it on its side and gave it a twirl. 'Round and 'round it went until the neck faced me and the base faced him.

He smirked and said, "Looks like you have to kiss me."

"I demand a respin," I said jokingly.

"Seriously," he said. "I'm worried about you. You really came unhinged back there."

I planted my elbows on the table and rested my head in my hands. "Sometimes it just gets to me."

"Yeah, working nights can be hard. I know what you mean."

I tried to smile. He didn't know what I meant at all.

It was the middle of January and bitter cold. The temperature was struggling to reach ten degrees and my heat wasn't working for the second day in a row. The radiators that normally hissed and clanked through the night and steamed up the windows had gone cold. After sleeping in two pairs of socks and a sweater, I surrendered that morning when I got off work and went to stay at my parents' until the super fixed the heat.

I sat at the breakfast table with my mother, warming my hands around a mug of coffee. The phone rang, and my mother got it on the first ring, not wanting it to wake my father.

"Oh, hi, Dad," she said. "You shouldn't be calling now. Why didn't you wait until Sunday, when the rates are cheaper . . . ?" She turned her back toward me and looked out the kitchen window. "Yes, we did get it. Thank you. . . . He *is* making progress. . . ." She set her coffee cup down hard. I could see her shoulders tensing up as she leaned her forehead against a cupboard. "How's Mom? . . .

No, I can't say for sure when he'll be finished. It's a novel, not a magazine article. . . ." She stood up straight, yanked the cupboard open and then slammed it shut. "I don't really know how much they'll pay him. . . ."

When she got off the phone she came back to the table and slumped into the chair. "They don't understand. They never did understand your father."

"Well, you have to admit, it *is* taking him a long time to finish his book."

She shot me a sharp look. "Are you going to start in on me about this, too? He's writing a novel, for Christ's sake. It takes time. Doesn't anyone understand that?"

Her reaction surprised me. I didn't expect her to jump to his defense, especially since I knew she was hurt that he hadn't let her read his manuscript. It made me wonder if she thought my father was really that fragile. More fragile than I knew.

She reached for the percolator and brought the pot over to the table. "More coffee?" She was herself again.

A couple days later, my heat was fixed and I was exhausted, looking forward to a good night's sleep in my own bed. I was finishing up my night shift when I got a call from Ahern.

"I'm at 11th and State," he said. "I need you to meet me here."

"Now?" I was tired, stifling a yawn.

"Walsh, do you think I'd be at police headquarters at this ungodly hour if this weren't important?"

I peered into a cup of coffee that had long since turned cold. "What's this all about?"

"Let's just say your presence has been requested by a very important arrestee."

Twenty minutes later Ahern met me in front of the station. The sun was coming up, sending streams of light poking through the clouds. Smoke was coming from a nearby chimney. Icicles were hanging down the side of the building next to a snowbank that was so dark and dirty it looked like a pile of coal.

"This better be good," I said. "I'm freezing my ass off and I've been up for twenty-seven hours straight."

"Believe me," he said, "this will be worth your while. You're in for a treat. Come with me. Mr. Richard Morrison wants to talk to you."

"Who? And why me?"

"He requested a member of the press. He's got one hell of a story, and I assured him I was bringing in the best reporter I knew."

I followed Ahern inside. Danny Finn was there, but Ahern didn't seem concerned that we all knew each other. After all, this was official police business, and I covered this beat for the night shift. What Danny may have questioned was why Ahern had called the *Tribune* and not the other papers. But that was Ahern's concern, not mine.

Danny led us down to a catacomb-like corridor in the basement that I didn't know existed. At the very end there was a private holding cell where a man, rather clean-cut, was perched on a bench, smoking a cigarette.

"And this," said Ahern with a great flourish, "is Richard Morrison. We call him the Babbling Burglar. Richie, this is your reporter."

He squinted and drew down hard on his cigarette before he dropped the butt to the floor. "Her?" He exhaled in Ahern's direction. "I thought you said you were getting Jordan Walsh."

"I *am* Jordan Walsh."

"Jordan is a dame?"

"Sorry to disappoint." I turned to Ahern and caught a glimpse of the guard in the corner snickering. "Does someone want to tell me what's going on here?"

"Richard here's a burglar," Ahern said.

"The Babbling Burglar," he corrected him, springing up from his bench. "And I'm not just some ordinary robber. I'm a master robber. A true professional. The best there is. In fact, I'm so good I even got the cops working for me."

I looked at Ahern as if to say, *Is this guy pulling my leg?*

"They arrested Richie last night," Ahern explained. "They told him he had one call, and he decided to call Adamowski's office. He said to bring a reporter because he was ready to talk."

"Okay, then, Mr. Morrison." I pulled a chair up to my side of the bars and removed my pad and pen from my bag. "What's your story?"

"You're gonna love this," Morrison said.

"I'm all ears."

Morrison lit another cigarette, clearly enjoying making me wait on him. After two leisurely puffs, he started to speak. Or really, it was more like he started to perform. "I'm a burglar, ma'am," he began as he paced. "I've robbed a lot of businesses. Yes, indeed, I have. Guilty as charged." He paused and placed a humbled hand over his heart. "But the best part is, I didn't do it alone. No, ma'am. I had plenty of help from the Chicago Police Department. Yes, ma'am, the police from the Summerdale station were my business partners." He howled with laughter.

I looked at Ahern and Danny, who were both grinning, nodding. "Go on, Mr. Morrison."

"It started a couple years ago. See, I got caught one night and the police went to arrest me. But when they saw the kind of loot I was carrying—brand-new set of golf clubs, some fishing equipment—they decided they wanted it for themselves. They said if I handed it over and kept my mouth shut, they'd be willing to let me go. So I did 'em one better. I said, 'Hey, why don't you partner up with me and together we'll make a killing.'"

I didn't know if he was telling the truth or not, but I was

taking down Morrison's every word, filling up the pages of my pad, front and back.

"So what we'd do, see," the burglar continued, "is, I'd case the joints ahead of time, and when I found the right place, I'd call the cops. They'd come out in their squad cars, acting like they were patrolling the place, but what they were really doing was keeping watch while I cleaned out the stores. When we were looting TVs and appliances—you know, the big, heavy stuff—they'd come in and help me load the goods into their squad cars. Even brought a paddy wagon a few times. They've got all the loot sitting in their basements and garages."

I looked at Ahern, trying to keep my jaw from hitting the floor.

"You should have seen this one time," said the burglar. "Someone accidentally set off an alarm, and when another squad car answered the call, the cops that were helping me told the other cops they were gonna take care of me. So what they did was they paraded me out in front of the other cops in handcuffs and all." He mimed out the whole drama. "They said they were going to take me down to the station and book me. But as soon as the other cops left, they took off my cuffs and we got back to looting." He threw himself into a half-laughing, half-coughing jag. "We hit three more stores that night and went out for beers afterward."

"And who were these officers? Can you identify them?"

"We have all the names," said Ahern.

"Unbelievable." I motioned for Ahern to join me out in the hallway, out of earshot. "Is any of this real?"

Ahern smiled. "Paul Newey—do you know him?"

"Adamowski's chief investigator?"

He nodded. "Newey and his men are verifying everything now. So far everything this guy's telling us has checked out. They're going to raid the officers' homes in about an hour."

On nothing more than adrenaline, I went back to the city room, and as the day shift was coming on, I went to work on the story. Mr. Ellsworth was surprised to see me at my desk in the daylight.

"What are you doing here?"

I handed him the first page of my copy and kept typing. "I've been up all night working on this."

"Holy Christ." After finishing the first page, Mr. Ellsworth leaned in, reading over my shoulder. "Stay with this, Walsh. Henry? Hey, Henry—"

"Aw, don't bring Henry in on this."

But it was too late. Henry turned up at Mr. Ellsworth's side.

"Henry, do me a favor: go get Walsh here a cup of coffee."

It would take another couple months before all the Summerdale details shook out, but by the spring of '59, eight officers at that station were convicted of robbery. And by then Mr. Ellsworth had moved me back to the day shift. He knew that next to Marty, I was the hardest-working reporter he had. Apparently, he'd had a change of heart and now decided I was worth the trouble. Walter, Henry and the others would have to get used to it.

As for me, there was certainly a sense of validation. I'd been tested and I had won. But my victory wasn't as sweet as I'd imagined it would be. In reality, it didn't change a thing for me in the city room. The guys still razzed me about my attaché case, still gave me grief when I complained about their locker-room talk and still tried to push their empty coffee cups on me, expecting a refill. It seemed I still had something to prove to them. And to myself.

Shortly after I started back on the regular shift, and in between other assignments, I finally carved out the time to start really investigating the horsemeat scandal. I contacted the Department of

Agriculture, which led me to Daren Bowman, the superintendent for the Illinois Division of Meats and Dairies down in Springfield.

After much pleading with my suspicious father, I convinced him to let me borrow his car and drove downstate to meet with the superintendent in his office at the State Capitol Complex.

Bowman leaned back in his chair, behind his oversize desk, and pressed the pads of his fingers together, bouncing the tips off one another. "What I can tell you quite honestly," he said, "is that Illinois has the safest food supply in the nation. Especially when it comes to beef."

"And what about horsemeat?"

"Horsemeat?" The bouncing fingers held still, and something flickered across his face. Barely perceivable, but I'd caught it. I didn't know what I was touching on, but this man knew something and he didn't want me to find out what it was.

I rephrased my question. "Have your inspectors come across any horsemeat?"

He shifted in his chair and shook his head. "Just horsemeat that's earmarked for cat food and dog food, that sort of thing."

"Are you positive about that?"

"Positive as far as this administration goes."

"So then you're saying that there *was* horsemeat in the—"

"No, no, no. Now, don't go putting words in my mouth. I didn't say anything about horsemeat getting into the food supply."

"Neither did I." I smiled. "But now that you just *did*, I have to ask if there's been horsemeat in the system be—"

"You're being very manipulative, young lady, and I don't appreciate it. I don't know what you're getting at, but I can assure you there's no horsemeat being passed on for human consumption."

He was jumpy now and only digging himself in deeper. He was hiding something, and as he spoke, alarms were going off inside my head. Bowman was fueling my worst fear—that this scandal was huge, even bigger than I'd thought—and I was suddenly convinced that the whole thing was connected to my brother's death. I felt sick inside. My skin began to prickle, my lungs couldn't get enough air. I knew at that very moment—yes, I could feel it in my bones—that my brother had been murdered.

I left Bowman's office, got back in the car and drove, going fast, trying to outrun the anger and fear churning inside me. *They killed my brother.* Would they kill me now, too? And who were *they*? I didn't even know who the enemy was, but I knew I was getting close. What to do first? Go to the police? Go to Ahern? Break down and cry? Should I tell my parents? No, I couldn't do that—couldn't say anything to them until I knew something definite. Accidentally being killed was one thing. Being intentionally murdered was another.

Chapter 33

◆ ◆ ◆

The next day I stood inside the Chicago Theatre. Ahern was on the other side of the lobby, standing at the foot of the grand staircase, dabbing his forehead with his handkerchief. He saw me and gave a nod before heading inside. I purchased my ticket and stepped into the theater. It took a moment for my eyes to adjust to the darkness, but then I spotted Ahern seated in the last row. The matinee had already begun, but we weren't there to see the show.

"So what's so urgent that you needed to see me about?" he asked, keeping his voice low.

"I need your help. And I don't even know where to begin. I've been looking into this horsemeat scandal and—"

"Horsemeat?" He gave me an incredulous laugh. "You had me cancel a meeting and dragged me out here to talk about horsemeat?"

"Not just that. Give me a second here." I was rattled. "I think horsemeat is being passed off as beef and—"

"Aw, c'mon . . ."

I clenched my fist and pounded the armrest. "Will you just listen to me? I'm trying to explain. This isn't just about horsemeat. It's about my brother."

The lighting in the theater changed and grew even darker. I heard Ahern shift in his chair, a burst of air escaping from him.

"Do you remember when I told you about my brother? He was a reporter, too, remember? And he was investigating a horse-meat scandal around the time he was killed. It was a hit-and-run—it happened six years ago—and now I'm convinced that it wasn't an accident."

"Oh, Jesus."

"I think someone wanted him dead. I really do. I think whoever he was investigating had him killed."

"Aw, Jesus. Oh, God." He reached over and grabbed my hand. "I'm sorry. I didn't—"

"I need to get to the bottom of this. I need your help."

An uproar of applause came from the audience.

"Who do you think is behind it?" he asked.

"I have no idea. I went down to Springfield and interviewed the superintendent of Meats and Dairies. He knows something— I know he does—but he's not talking."

"Jesus, Jordan." He let go of my hand and turned to me. "What are you getting tangled up in?"

"Honestly, I don't know. I just need to find out what really happened to my brother. I want whoever killed him to pay for it."

"Why?"

"What do you mean *why*?"

Someone in the row ahead of us turned and shushed us.

"I mean," he said, dropping his voice to a whisper, "is this about revenge, about seeking justice, or is this more about you wanting to be a star reporter?"

"Fuck you!" I was out of my chair and heading for the lobby. I had made it as far as the grand staircase when Ahern caught up to me and grabbed me by the arm to hold me still.

"I'm sorry," he said.

I was still trying to get away from him.

"That wasn't fair of me," he said. "I'm sorry. I shouldn't have said that."

"What the hell is wrong with you? And why are you getting so upset about this?" I asked, pulling my arm out of his grip. "It was my brother. This happened to me, not you."

"I'm upset because I'm concerned. Because I don't know what you're getting involved in. With the other scoops—the stuff I bring you—I have a pretty good idea of who we're dealing with. But this"—he shook his head—"this is beyond me."

"What if I take it to the FBI?"

"With what? What have you got? Did anything concrete come out of your meeting down in Springfield?"

"No. But my gut tells me that—"

"C'mon, you're smarter than that. You know you can't go to the FBI with a gut feeling."

He was right, of course. I knew he was right. But I was upset and groping for answers. I leaned against the banister to steady myself. "Can you just ask around the state's attorney's office for me? See if anyone knows anything."

"About what? Nobody's going to know anything," he said. "We're talking about something that happened six years ago. Believe me, if I thought I could do something to help you, I would."

"So you won't even ask around?"

"Jordan, I know this isn't what you want to hear, but you don't have enough to go on. And I'd tell you to keep digging, but . . ."

"But what?"

"But if you're right about what happened to your brother— and that's a *big* if—then are you next?"

That was the question I kept coming up against myself. I was scared, and Ahern had just confirmed that I had good reason to be.

"If you were my sister, I'd tell you to leave it alone. Don't go looking for trouble."

I tried not to let Ahern discourage me, but he'd scared me good and made me realize that I was going to need a lot more than I had for the FBI to open this case. I had nothing but suspicion, an uncomfortable interview with Bowman in Springfield and an unsolved hit-and-run that happened years ago. Once again I had come to a dead end. So all that spring and into the summer I did my best to put it out of my mind and focus on other assignments.

I was verifying some facts for a piece on a school fire when Gabby broke into my thoughts. "M's back. C'mon."

Five minutes later Gabby brought out a birthday cake and placed it on M's desk while we gathered around to celebrate. None of us knew how old M was, but now that she was a brunette, I thought she looked younger. I also liked that she'd stopped penciling in that beauty mark and had stopped wearing those Playtex cone-shaped brassieres. Now M dressed in a more refined manner. She'd started wearing a double strand of pearls and matching earrings, which I suspected were gifts from Mr. Ellsworth. She had also purchased a pink pillbox hat and a suit to match. It wasn't until we all saw the new issue of *LIFE* magazine with Jackie Kennedy on the cover and Senator Kennedy in the background that we realized that day by day, week by week, M, our former Marilyn Monroe, had been subtly and quietly morphing into Jacqueline Kennedy.

After a lackluster rendition of *Happy Birthday*, carried by Randy, M blew out the candles. She didn't have to say it; I knew what her wish was. I could tell by the way she opened her heavily lashed lids and locked eyes on Mr. Ellsworth. Maybe no one else noticed, but I found that look of hers impossible to miss.

Walter shoveled a piece of cake into his mouth and said, "So, c'mon, fess up. How old are you, Mrs. Kennedy?"

"And what'd you do with Marilyn?" Henry hooted.

The others laughed, and I saw M take the hit. She stood there in the middle of the city room in her Jackie Kennedy costume like a lost child, on the verge of tears. It was Mr. Ellsworth who told the guys to knock it off and get back to work. But by then M had already thrown her pillbox hat on her desk and rushed into the lavatory.

I could still hear the others laughing, even after I'd followed her inside. I stood outside the bathroom stall, gently rapping the door with my knuckles, asking if she was okay. I could barely make out what she said because she was crying so hard.

When she finally came out of the stall, I handed her a fistful of tissues. One of her false eyelashes had come unglued, and she looked in the mirror and peeled it away.

"What am I going to do now?" She stared at the lash resting on her index finger like a centipede.

"You don't need those," I said. "You have beautiful eyes."

"Oh, you're just saying that."

"Seriously, M, you're a beautiful woman. What's wrong with you just being you?"

She splashed water on her face, drying herself off with a stiff paper towel. "Because," she cried out, "I don't know who I am, all right?" She broke down in a fresh round of sobs. "I'm so miserable right now. I'm so tired of everything. And I can't sleep. Even those sleeping pills aren't helping. . . ."

I didn't know what to do for her other than hand her more tissues.

"I thought by now I'd be married with children," she said. "I'm acting like a career woman, but that's not who I am. You may be okay with that, but that's not who I want to be. I don't want to turn into another Mrs. Angelo."

She seemed terrified of that fate. I stopped and thought about it for a minute, and I realized that if ever I were going to impersonate another woman, it wouldn't be a Marilyn Monroe or a Jackie Kennedy. It would be Mrs. Angelo.

The following Saturday afternoon I was walking down Wells Street where I was greeted by banjo music flooding out of a nearby tavern. It was that time of year. The neighborhood was on display for its ninth annual Old Town Holiday—or was it now called the Outdoor Arts and Crafts Fair? I would have to verify that for the feature I was doing for the Neighborhood News section. I had convinced Mr. Pearson that I could give this piece a unique touch seeing as I'd grown up in Old Town. Normally I wouldn't have pursued something like this, but I saw it as my chance to interview my father, who had been one of the early organizers of the fair, and I suppose I was still trying to prove myself to him.

As I made my way up Wells Street, I waved to my neighbors sitting outside their homes with their paintings and photography, their jewelry and crafts set up on card tables and hanging from makeshift easels. Some items were for sale; some were there strictly to be admired.

From the time I was a young girl I recalled how all the neighbors—most of whom were artists of one sort or another— came out of their houses and studios to share their work. People offered up fresh-baked pies and cookies while others grilled chicken and burgers on nearby barbecues. And, of course, there was music coming from places like Orphans and the Earl of Old Town. This fair that had come to identify the neighborhood was changing all the time. The bohemian edge it was known for was blossoming into something even more progressive and colorful. Beyond Piper's Alley, with its cigar and wine shop, were a slew of new stores, one that sold nothing but candles and incense. Another sold only posters. There was a T-shirt store, a record store, a bookstore and a plant store mixed in among the clubs and taverns.

I came up to Wells and Eugenie and spotted my parents on their lawn chairs out front of the Painted Lady. They each had a cigarette going and a tumbler of scotch or maybe whiskey. A TV tray with a bowl of chips on top was parked between them. I sat down on the front stoop as a couple neighbors stopped by.

"CeeCee," said the woman, who was wearing a big floppy straw hat, "where's your poetry?"

"Oh"—my mother swatted at the air—"I don't need to drag those old books out anymore."

"But you're the neighborhood poet," said the man, who was sporting a Hawaiian shirt.

"Oh, no, I'm not. There're others. . . ."

My father had a smile locked on his face and I noticed he didn't say a word. I felt sorry for him. Whereas my mother shunned attention like this, my father craved it. He would have given anything to have his neighbors fawn over his writing. As soon as my mother's admirers left, I turned my attention to him.

"So," I said, pulling out my pad and pencil, "should we get started?"

I'd been looking forward to interviewing my father and was feeling sentimental, remembering our early days in Old Town. When we'd moved into the neighborhood we'd had a Puerto Rican family living next door on one side and a Gypsy family on the other. The Gypsies used to terrify Eliot and me; we thought they'd curse us if we dared to step on their lawn.

"So, Dad," I said, my pencil poised, ready to write, "do you remember the first Old Town Holiday Street Fair?"

"Sure." He pinched his cigarette between his tobacco-stained fingers and drew down hard, keeping one eye closed, shielded from the smoke, or maybe the sunlight.

"Well?"

"Well, what?" He shooed a fly buzzing about his head.

I had prepared so many questions, determined to show him how smart I was, how professional I was, but the stern look on his face struck me dumb. All that came out was, "What was it like?"

"Like this," he said. "Only smaller."

"Well, now, Hank," my mother said, uncrossing her legs so she could nudge his thigh with her foot. "Give her more than that."

He flicked his still smoldering cigarette onto the sidewalk.

I dug up another question. "So let's see . . . The first fair started back in 1950. You had just seventy exhibitors. . . ." I wanted to show him that I'd done my homework. "Back then anyone in the neighborhood could show their artwork, but now it's become more selective, hasn't it?"

He nodded. "There's a jury now."

"What's the criterion for the artists now? How does the jury make their selections?"

"You'd have to ask someone on the committee. I haven't been on the committee for years." He glanced into his cup. "I'm gonna get more ice." He stood up and turned to my mother. "You need some?"

As I watched him walk back inside I gave my mother a helpless look. "What is wrong with him? Does he want to see me fail?"

"It's not you, honey." My mother leaned forward toward me and set her elbows on her knees. "I assure you, it's not you."

I sat out front with my mother while more neighbors came by to talk with her. A good twenty minutes had passed since my father went inside for ice.

"Is he even coming back?"

"Hank? Hank?" my mother called over her shoulder. "C'mon back out here."

A few minutes later my father appeared with a ream and a half of paper tucked under his arm. In a ceremonial gesture, he slammed it down on the TV tray and declared his novel finished.

"*Finished*, finished?" my mother asked.

"*Finished*, finished," he said.

Almost in unison my mother and I asked if we could read it.

He rested his hand on the stack of paper and drummed his fingers tinged from carbon paper, the typewriter ribbon and tobacco. He wasn't saying anything.

"Well?" I looked at my father and then at my mother and then back at my father. "Aren't you going to let us read it?"

"*Oy*, forget it." My mother shook her head. "I've been asking forever. He won't even tell me the title."

My father had a curious look on his face, as if amused by my mother's frustration.

"Well, if you're not going to let anyone read it," I asked, "what are you going to do with it now?"

"What do you think?" My father thumped his fist on the title page. "I'm going to get it published."

Chapter 34

• • •

"Hey, you guys," Benny called to us. "Here it is. It's on. Come listen to this." Benny turned up the volume on his portable radio. We grabbed Randy and crowded in around Benny's desk as WCFL's Dan Sorkin announced, "And we're back with Chicago's own Randy and the Rockets and that chart-climbing hit *Little Dab'll Do Ya.*"

Randy stuffed his hands in his front pockets and rocked back on his heels, feigning modesty as Benny turned up the radio even louder and thumped his hand on his desk, keeping time with the music. Walter fired up his pipe and bobbed his head to the beat. Henry and Mr. Ellsworth snapped their fingers. Even Mrs. Angelo tapped her toes and Peter discarded his green eyeshade. M, still sporting her Jacqueline Kennedy look, did a sexy little shuffle in the aisle. For a few minutes we ceased being a city room, and it was all about the music. *Little dab'll do ya / Little dab of my love / Little dab'll do ya / Straight from heaven above . . .*

At the end of the song we all broke into a round of applause, and Randy beamed, soaking up all the accolades, the slaps on the back, the handshakes. He'd done it. About a month ago, right around the time my father sent off his novel, Randy had worked up the nerve to audition for Pendulum Records and ended up signing a recording deal with them.

"That song is *ehhhx*-cellent," said Peter.

"Looks like you've got a real hit on your hands," said Henry.

Randy nodded. "And they're telling me the flip side is going to be even bigger. Pendulum is already talking about signing me to another recording deal, and as soon as that happens, I'm outta here." He looked over at Mr. Ellsworth and reeled himself back in. "Sorry."

"Don't apologize to me." Mr. Ellsworth raised his hands. "I'm happy for you, Randy. Just don't count your chickens before they've hatched."

"I hear ya. I hear ya. But trust me on this. Between *Little Dab* and the next one, *Snap*, Randy and the Rockets are going all the way to the top."

"Well, until you get there," said Mr. Copeland, "might I suggest you finish up today's cartoon?"

Everyone had a good laugh over that before returning to our desks. I was on deadline but could hardly concentrate with Randy fluttering all around, gloating, singing and humming. Twice already M had told him to knock it off and she wasn't the only one getting annoyed with him. I could tell that Randy's good fortune had struck a nerve with certain coworkers. Jealousy traveled through the city room like a low-grade fever. Their jokes and snickers did little to veil their disappointment in themselves. You couldn't tell me that when Gabby was a little girl she dreamed about sitting at a desk all day, being scared of her editor, afraid to even make a phone call while writing about other people's glamorous lives. And what about M? No husband, no child, no house with a white picket fence. And did Higgs really want to be the rewrite man on the night shift at age fifty-three? Never seeing his wife and children unless he passed them

in the hallway when he got home at six in the morning? Surely
he'd wanted more than that.

I looked over at Randy, spinning 'round and 'round in his
chair like a little kid, his smile growing wider with each turn.

Later that morning, I was tossing my nickel into the collection
kitty after taking a cup of coffee when I saw a very pregnant
woman enter the city room. She had a green Marshall Field's bag
looped on one arm and a small child in tow, holding tight to her
free hand. The woman's auburn hair was pinned up, revealing a
high forehead and a long, slender neck. Even as pregnant as she
was, she looked spectacular. The only other woman I'd seen in
such stylish maternity clothes was Lucille Ball when she carried
Little Ricky on *I Love Lucy*. I'd never seen this woman before,
but it was clear the others knew her. Marty rushed over and gave
her a friendly hug and a kiss on the cheek.

"Is he around?" she said. "I need him to watch Tommy for a
few hours."

"He's in the conference room, Marjorie."

She thanked Marty and proceeded to where Mr. Ellsworth
was sitting by himself at a big round table. The kiss she gave him
on the mouth confirmed that she could have only been Mrs.
Ellsworth. I looked over at M. She'd lost all the color in her
cheeks. She wasn't even blinking as she watched Mr. and Mrs.
Ellsworth through the glass walls of the conference room.

"Are you okay?" I asked.

M shook her head. "She's pregnant?" She posed this as a question, as if I might tell her she was mistaken. "He said his marriage
was over. He told me he didn't love her anymore. And now look
at her. She's pregnant. Oh my God. This is a nightmare. I can't
breathe. I have to get out of here." She reached inside her drawer

for her handbag. "If anyone's looking for me," she said, staring back at Mr. Ellsworth, "I'll be at Riccardo's."

I asked if she wanted me to come with her, but she shook her head and scurried out of the city room. But even so, an hour and a half later, when M still hadn't returned, I went over to Riccardo's to check on her. It was going on two in the afternoon and the lunch crowd had thinned out. I found M at the end of the bar, slumped over on her stool, elbows on the bar, her head pressed to her hands with a cigarette burning dangerously close to the tips of her hair.

"M?" I slid onto the barstool next to her. "Are you all right?"

She looked at me in a haze, barely able to hold her head up. "He told me his marriage was over. He told me he loved me. He was going to leave her. I've been waiting all this time—eight years—and now I realize he's been lying to me all along."

"How many martinis have you had?" When she didn't answer, I looked at the bartender. "How many did you give her?"

"That's her second," he said, wiping down the bar. "I swear. That's all I served her. She was fine one minute and then this."

"I can't believe he lied to me," M muttered. "I tried so hard. I didn't pressure him. I didn't give him any ultimatums. I was a good girl. I was patient—just like he told me to be. I waited and waited and waited and now this. . . ."

"M, c'mon," I said, hugging her around the midsection, trying to help her to her feet. She didn't fight me, but she was deadweight in my arms. "Let's get in a cab and get you home."

As I hefted her up, her handbag slid off the bar and opened, scattering its contents across the floor. M slumped back over the bar while I retrieved her wallet, her keys, her compact, her lipstick and an empty bottle of phenobarbital. I held it up and looked back at M. Her eyes were closed, her lips lax and hanging open as if it were too much work to close her mouth.

"M—what did you do?" I held up the empty bottle. She opened her eyes, rolling her head from side to side. "How many did you take? M? How many?"

She couldn't formulate the words. Couldn't hold her head up or keep her eyes open.

I motioned to the bartender. "Help me get her into a cab. Hurry. I need to take her to the hospital."

I got M to the hospital in time. While they pumped her stomach, I stayed out in the waiting room and drank bad coffee and leafed through outdated magazines. The one good thing about how many times I'd been to Henrotin Hospital in the past few years was that I no longer associated it just with Eliot's death. Now it had taken on other memories, other ghosts. Like Harley Jackson and the other casualties from the el derailment. There was also the night Scott was brought in. And now this.

It was about forty minutes later when the doctors let me back to see M. She was pale and weak. Her lips were dry and cracked, and the whites of her eyes were veined red. Now she was asking for Stanley, and it took a moment before I realized she meant Mr. Ellsworth.

"I need him. Please, Jordan. Tell him I need to see him."

It was going on six thirty. I made it back to the city room just as Mr. Ellsworth was about to leave. I caught him in the hallway by the elevators, fedora in one hand, briefcase in the other.

"Can I have a word with you?" I said. "In private." When he stalled, I added on, "It's about M."

We went into one of the conference rooms and he closed the door behind him.

"So what is it?" He was impatient as usual, and I could tell by his nonchalance that he hadn't a clue that I knew about his affair. "Well"—he planted his hands on his hips—"what is it?"

I thought about M lying in that hospital room because of him. It was the second time this man had nearly cost M her life. I became infuriated. "She's in the hospital."

"What? What happened?" He almost sounded more curious than concerned, and this further irritated me.

There was no delicate way to say it, and I was no longer interested in making this easy for him. "She tried to kill herself this afternoon."

"What?" His eyes opened wide, and his cheeks went pale. This was more the reaction I'd been expecting. "Good God, what happened?"

"She took half a bottle of sleeping pills and chased them down with a couple of martinis."

"Oh, Jesus. Is she going to be okay?"

"They pumped her stomach in time. She's been asking for you."

"For me?" He put on a confused face.

"Oh, please. Don't be coy at a time like this."

"Now, wait a minute, Walsh—"

"I've known about the two of you for a long time now. Who do you think she turned to when she was pregnant? Who do you think helped her after the abortion? You sure as hell weren't around."

He stammered and dropped back in his chair. His face went even whiter. "When was M pregnant?" He looked like I'd knocked the wind out of him.

"You didn't know?" Now I clutched a chair myself. "Oh no. You mean she didn't tell you?"

"She had an abortion?" He was still piecing it all together, his fingers pressed to his temples.

I nodded, afraid to speak for fear I'd say something else. He shouldn't have heard this from me. I just assumed that she'd told him about the baby. This wasn't any of my business, and yet I'd gotten myself in the middle of it. Even though I was still angry with him because of what he'd done to M, I hadn't meant to level him like this.

"It was mine? I was the father?" He dragged his fingers through his hair, then planted his elbows on the table and leaned his face into his hands. "What hospital is she at?"

"Henrotin."

He nodded into his hands. "Give me a minute alone, will you, Walsh? I'll go see her. I just need a moment to gather my thoughts."

Chapter 35

· · ·

With M in the hospital, I was covering her assignments in addition to my own, working on "Ways to Set a Stylish Dinner Table" with one hand while reporting on a firefighter who'd been injured in an eleven-alarm blaze with the other.

A week later I was still doing double duty, my fingers moving over the typewriter keys as if by their own command. When I got to the end of one typed line, a tinny chime sounded. I swatted the carriage return and went on to the next. Around four o'clock that day, I stuffed my attaché case with fashion and movie magazines and boxes of M's favorite candies—Good & Plenty and Milk Duds. They rattled around in my case as I headed to the hospital.

All week long I'd been making daily visits to see her. Especially since Ellsworth—as I'd taken to calling him, no longer feeling him worthy of the honorific *Mister*—hadn't been back since that first day. His wife, Marjorie, had just given birth to a little girl, Sheila.

I pulled up a chair close to M's bedside and handed her the magazines and candies. She didn't look through them and set the candy next to the water pitcher by the side of the bed. We talked about *things*, innocent things with no sharp edges to get caught on. She never once asked about Ellsworth, never said his name. Never mentioned the baby or asked if she'd been born yet.

"Randy is still insufferable," I said, shaking out a handful of Milk Duds, trying to add some levity to the mood. "If I hear him sing *Little Dab'll Do Ya* one more time I think I'm going to scream." I popped a candy into my mouth and offered her the box. "And if he's not singing, then he's going on and on about how he's going to become a millionaire."

M struggled with the box of Milk Duds and I resisted the urge to help. "Well, good for him. Good for him." She managed to pour a few candies into her hand. "It's about time someone's dream came true."

It was only as I was getting ready to leave that M finally mentioned Ellsworth. In a flat deadpan voice, she said, "I thought he loved me. I mean really loved me."

"I know. I'm sorry, M."

"I wasted so much time on him. Eight years. I sacrificed my child for that man. And what have I got to show for it? Not a goddamn thing." Her eyes went glassy, and she stared off into nothingness. "I don't know who I am or what I'm supposed to do without him."

"You'll be fine. I promise you, you will. You don't need him, M. And you don't need Marilyn or Jackie, either. You're enough, just as you are."

"You're saying that because you're my friend."

"M, it's the truth. You've put too much stock in Ellsworth. All that energy you poured into him, you need to start putting into yourself." I thought back to the conversation my mother had had all those years ago with Simone de Beauvoir. "If there's one thing I've learned, it's to never ever put a man first."

As those words left my mouth, I realized I hadn't really learned that lesson myself. I fiddled with the buckles on my attaché case, thinking about how I'd groveled for my father's love, how I'd kept myself small for Jack's comfort and had put Scott and Marty on pedestals. Even my dream of being a journalist had belonged to my brother first. At times like this I had to question what I truly wanted for myself.

When I left M that day, I felt depleted. The smell of disinfectant penetrated my nostrils and followed me outside of the hospital. I felt for her, I did, but I had to get back to my life. After caring for M all week, I realized that what I needed now was for someone to take care of me. So I went to the only place I could think of, to the one person who had once felt my head for fevers, bandaged my knees from scrapes and cuts, removed my every splinter. I went home to my mother.

She was in the kitchen, sifting through a drawer of S&H Green Stamps. This was the most bourgeois pursuit I'd ever seen my mother partake in. But, like most things, she did it with gusto. She'd been collecting Green Stamps for as long as I could remember, always coming in from the store and tossing the loose stamps into the kitchen drawer below the knives. Every few months or so, like now, she'd pull out the entire drawer, set it on the table and adhere the individual stamps into the saver booklets. When we were little, Eliot and I had taken turns licking the stamps and affixing them to the pages. I used to love the sweet residue the stickum left on my tongue. Through the years my mother had already redeemed previous booklets for a steam iron, a blender and a speed slicer, which was still in its box in the basement. This time she was saving for an electric frying pan. She had visions of making fried chicken from her grandmother's recipe.

"Want to help me here?" she asked, dabbing a stamp on her tongue, then making a face as she swallowed. Clearly she didn't enjoy the taste that I remembered.

I pulled out a chair and dropped into it like I weighed three hundred pounds. That was how I felt. I'd hoped she would notice how depressed I was, but she was too focused on her stamps.

"I just came from the hospital."

"You were there again? How's your friend M doing?" She had a cigarette dangling from her lips.

"Not good. I feel so helpless. I don't know what to do or what to say."

"She'll get through it. We all do." She filled a sheet with stamps and turned to a fresh page. "I think we only need one hundred and twenty-five more," she said.

"That's a lot of stamps for the electric frying pan."

"No. Not the pan. The power drill."

"Power drill?"

"Your father wants it." She shrugged. "I'm hoping it'll cheer him up. He's been such a beast lately. Just a real beast."

"Why? What's going on with him?"

"Oh, the editors at Scribner rejected his novel, and he's been impossible ever since."

"That was fast. He only sent it off about a month ago. And, besides, that's only one publisher. There're others."

"Of course there are. And that's what I told him, but he doesn't want to hear it. He's pouting. You know Scribner is Ernest's publisher. Your father was sure they'd take his novel, too."

"Did they explain why they rejected it?"

She shook her head. "He won't say. He won't even let me see the letter. I keep asking him to let me read the manuscript, but he won't let me do that, either." She reached for another stamp. "You know he used to always let me read his work—even if it was a magazine piece or a column for the paper. I was the first person he'd show something to." She paused to adhere a stamp in place. "I tell you, he's been a beast ever since he finished that novel of his. Now that he's sent it out to the publishers, the waiting is eating him up. I don't know what to do with him. He checks the mailbox every hour. 'Has the mailman been here yet?' He'll ask me that ten minutes after he's already gone outside and checked it himself."

"So where's the beast now?"

"Who knows? Probably down at Mister Kelly's. That's where he spends his time now that he's not writing. The drinking"—she shook her head—"it's not good."

"Well, that's nothing new," I reminded her.

"But it's gotten worse." My mother licked the last of her stamps. "There we go." She closed the booklet and ran her fingers over the cover. "Want to come with me to get the power drill? We have an hour before the store closes."

I went with her down to the S&H redemption store, not because I was particularly interested in shopping for power drills, but because I wanted to be near her. We moved up and down the aisle, and I saw the way my mother paused before the electric frying pans, running her fingertips along the black handle. It was only then that I realized how much she'd wanted that frying pan but how much more she wanted my father to be happy.

She saw me watching and smiled. "Really what I should do is hit him over the head with this."

"As if that would do any good," I said, and that got her laughing.

We both knew it wasn't that funny, but for some reason her laughter was contagious and I couldn't stop from joining in. It was like we needed an excuse—a reason to laugh, or maybe more correctly, we needed something to mask the sadness misting up our eyes. She was hurting for my father. I was hurting for them both. And for M, too. We couldn't cry outright. We didn't do that sort of thing. So instead, we stood in the middle of the aisle holding our sides while the tears trickled down our faces.

An hour and a half later my mother dropped me off at my apartment building and by then my troubles were off in the distance. It seemed like days since I'd been to the hospital to see M. It wasn't until I watched my mother drive away that I realized how she, in her own way, had ended up giving me exactly the kind of comfort I needed after all.

Chapter 36

• • •

I was worn-out, exhausted. It had been over two weeks since M swallowed that bottle of pills. No one but Ellsworth and I know about it. Everyone else was under the assumption that she had a bad flu. While she recuperated, I continued covering her assignments as well as my own. I still thought about the horse-meat scandal and how it tied into Eliot's death, but I had no time, and frankly not enough courage to pursue it. In some ways it felt like I was going backward, writing for White Collar Girl again, but I told myself it was only temporary until M was back, and at this point it was hard for me to say no to Mrs. Angelo for anything.

I was finishing up an article on "Secrets to a Perfect Gelatin Mold" when Randy hung up the telephone, pumped both fists in the air and let out a *whoop* as he spun his chair in a circle. "Yes!" He pumped his fists again. "This is it."

"What's going on?" I asked, my fingers on hold above my type-writer.

"That was Pendulum Records. They want to see me right away. What'd I tell you? What'd I tell you all? They're going to sign me to my next deal, and then I'm gonna make a pile of money." He laughed as he rose from his desk and gave us all an exaggerated salute. "So long, suckers." He put on his dark sunglasses—which he'd taken to wearing even on overcast days—planted his fedora on his head and practically skipped out of the city room singing, "*Snap, crackle, pop / That girl has what I want / Snap, crackle, pop / That girl has what I want. . . .*"

"What a goddamn blowhard," said Walter, puffing on his pipe. "If that guy can make it in show business, anyone can. Goddamn Randy and the Rockets. Sheesh."

"If I hear that *Little Dab'll Do Ya* one more time," said Benny, "I'm gonna smash my radio."

"You and me both," said Peter. "And just our luck, now Pendulum Records is going to give him a big fat recording deal and we'll never hear the end of it."

"No, I don't think that will be a problem," said Henry. "'Cause I bet none of us will ever hear from Randy again. He's gonna be a big fucking star. A millionaire, haven't you heard?"

Everyone was laughing, having fun taking shots at Randy. Though I couldn't say I blamed them. Without a shred of humility, Randy had spent his days gloating, telling us how he was expecting a huge royalty check from Pendulum Records and how he went and looked at Cadillacs one day, a new house the next. He was spending money like crazy, coming in to work every day wearing a new suit or a new pair of shoes. "Genuine Italian leather," he'd say. "Twelve bucks."

About an hour later, I was back into my work when I looked up and did a double take. There was M standing next to *Injun Summer*. I didn't know she was coming back to work yet. But that wasn't what I found so surprising. No, what captured my eye and made my mouth hang open was M herself. Her hair was straight and styled flat against the crown of her head, and aside from a little rouge and lipstick, she wasn't wearing any makeup. She looked fresh, and as far as I was concerned, even more beautiful than Marilyn or Jackie. Gabby and some of the fellows got up from their stations and welcomed her back, crowding in around her.

"It's good to see you back," said Mrs. Angelo, breaking through the commotion. "We could sure use your help." She handed M a sheet of paper. "Would you give this a quick rewrite? Poor Gabby," she said, lowering her voice. "The girl is drowning."

M hesitated.

"Well?" Mrs. Angelo planted her hands on her hips. "You're back, aren't you?"

"Give me a minute," said M. "I'll get to it in a minute. Right now I have to take care of a little business of my own."

"We're on deadline for this," Mrs. Angelo called after her as M walked down the center aisle and marched up to the horseshoe.

Ellsworth was on the telephone, his feet up on the desk, ankles crossed. He had his back toward M. I, along with everyone else, watched as she tapped him on the shoulder. He held up a just-a-minute finger while she moved around to face him, wagging her no-no-no finger back at him. Her jaw was set and her eyes said she was not fooling around. He must have realized that because he swung his legs down from the horseshoe, cut his call short and hung up the telephone. He was on his feet now, his back still toward us. He was saying something to her in a low voice when all of a sudden she pushed him away so hard that he dropped back into his chair.

"C'mon now, M," we heard him saying. "This isn't the time or the place. Let's not cause a scene. Let's—"

"'Let's not cause a scene'?" Her voice peaked an octave higher than usual, and she leaned over the horseshoe, her face just inches from his. "You want me to make this easy for you, you bastard? You don't want anyone to know what a cheat and a liar you are?

You're nothing but a fraud. I should have dropped you years ago when I first wanted to."

"M, c'mon, now. Let's go somewhere private and talk. I can explain." He tried to get up, but she shoved him back down again.

"You stay right where you are and don't you dare think of coming after me. From now on you stay away from me. We're done." She turned on her heel in a way that was not Marilyn or Jackie, but all M. She had arrived.

Right before my eyes I saw M come into her power. She had tapped her true core, and she owned the main aisle as she walked down the center of the city room. No one would have messed with her. She went to her desk, sat down, reached for a set of copy paper and spun it into her typewriter.

"Are you okay?" I asked.

"Never better." She began typing, rewriting Gabby's story.

A few minutes later Walter came into the city room. "Well, look who's back," he said with a sarcastic laugh.

I thought he was referring to M until I looked over and saw Randy, shoulders slumped, head down, feet dragging behind him.

"Randy, what's wrong?" I went to his side. "What's the matter?" He looked at me and shook his head.

"Yeah, what's the matter?" Walter asked, still laughing. "We didn't expect to see you back here now that you're a big recording star."

"Walter, knock it off," I said, guiding Randy over to his desk with the others following us.

A chorus of questions started up:

"Are you okay?"

"Did you meet with Pendulum?"

"When is your new record coming out?"

Randy looked dazed. He reached up for his hat, dragging it off his head and down the side of his face. He kept his eyes on me as he spoke to the group using short, staccato-like sentences.

"Kellogg's contacted Pendulum. They sent a cease-and-desist letter. They said my song violated their copyright. Said the words were too close. Even if the tune isn't. Pendulum thinks Beecham's going to do the same thing because of Brylcreem. They pulled my records off the air. They terminated my contract." He looked at the others with tears in his eyes. "What am I supposed to do now?" He clutched the sides of his head and began wailing. "I'm up to my eyeballs in debt. I went ahead and spent all that record money."

"Why in the hell would you have done that?" asked Henry.

"I was so sure it was going to happen. What am I going to do now?"

"Oh, Randy," I said, rubbing my hand along his shoulders. "You're a brilliant cartoonist. You still have a great job. You'll get yourself out of debt. You just have to cut back on your spending."

That only made him cry all the harder.

After work that night we all took him to Riccardo's for drinks, hoping to cheer him up. At about half past ten we had settled the bill and were filtering out onto Rush Street when the air-raid sirens began to whine.

"Holy shit," cried Randy.

We all went wide-eyed, turning instantly sober.

"Oh my God," said Gabby. "What is that?"

It was bizarre. Everyone was used to hearing the weekly tests of the air-raid sirens, but no one thought we'd ever hear them *for real*. What did this mean—the Russians were sending an H-bomb to kill us all? It didn't seem possible.

I watched people frantically pouring into the street, screaming, looking for a place to hide. The shrill of the sirens filled the air and deafened me.

"Anyone know of a shelter around here?" asked Benny.

"Fuck the shelter," said Walter. "I'm going back to the paper. We need to find out what's going on."

I was with him.

We raced back to the *Tribune*, darting in and out of the panic along Michigan Avenue. The sirens were still going, and we could hear their shriek even as we entered the city room. I made a beeline for the horseshoe where Ellsworth and a group of night reporters were clustered around a radio that was blaring *Jailhouse Rock*.

"Where the hell's the CONELRAD system?" I shouted over the din of the sirens.

"We can't find it. We've been searching for it on every station," said one of the night reporters.

"Give it here," said Walter, pushing him aside, twisting the dial up and down. Nothing. The CONELRAD emergency system that was supposed to instruct us in the event of a bomb had failed.

"Dammit. Anything coming over the wires?" asked Ellsworth, rolling up his shirtsleeves.

I went over to my desk and called down to police headquarters.

"We're going crazy over here, too, Walsh," said Danny. "We've got nothing."

And then, as I hung up, the sirens shut off. They died as abruptly as they had started. All was silent, and the quiet was even more disturbing. What now? Was this the end?

"We're a goddamn city room," said Ellsworth, pounding on the horseshoe. "How can we not know what the hell's going on?"

We sat and waited, just as helpless as the rest of the city. It was unnerving until the wire room bells rang. We all stormed over to the machines and Ellsworth reached past the copyboy and ripped the wire. I watched his expression change as he read it.

"Jesus fucking Christ." He dropped the sheet and shook his head.

"What? What is it?" I reached for the wire, but Walter intercepted it.

He looked at it and slapped his palm to his forehead. "Oh, c'mon. You've got to be fucking kidding me."

"What the hell is it?" I asked again. Walter handed me the wire, and as I read it I couldn't believe what I was seeing. "The White Sox? This was all because the White Sox won the pennant?"

Ellsworth dragged his hands through his hair. "Okay, people, let's get busy and write this up. We need to let the city know that the world hasn't come to an end and that our fire commissioner is a horse's ass for thinking it would be a good idea to set off the air-raid sirens to celebrate the White Sox's victory."

M moved out of her lavish apartment, which Ellsworth had been paying for, and into an efficiency. One fall evening, Benny, Gabby and I went over to help her move in. One look and I knew this was going to be a big adjustment for M. Her couch alone took up most of the living room. The place was tiny, but it was all she could afford now.

While unpacking we listened to music and drank rum and Coca-Colas. Gabby had one drink too many and when the *Peter Gunn* theme came on the radio, she got silly with the empty boxes and set one on Benny's head.

"Doesn't he look handsome?" She giggled.

"I don't think I've ever seen our little Gabby this tipsy before," M said, the two of us standing off to the side laughing. "It's nice to see her loosen up a little bit."

"And it's nice to see you in such a good mood," I said to M. The past few months I'd been accustomed to hysterical phone calls in the middle of the night and crying jags in the ladies' room at work.

"Aw, fucking Stanley," she said with a shrug. "Did I tell you I have a date next week?"

"You don't sound too excited about it."

"He's okay. He's one of those ad guys. I'm done with newspapermen." She clinked her glass to mine.

A Teenager in Love came on the radio and Gabby was on her feet dancing with no regard to the beat whatsoever. But she was smiling and looking happier than I'd ever seen her.

The next day we were all a bit hungover when we dragged ourselves into the city room. We took turns shaking out aspirin tablets and passing the bottle around. For lunch we all needed the hair of the dog and downed martinis with our sandwiches at Riccardo's.

I was starting to feel like myself by the time I made it back to my desk. I looked over and saw M shove a pink leather case— that no one would confuse with a man's attaché case—under her desk.

"What's that?" I asked, twisting out of my sweater.

"Oh, let me show you." M pulled the case back out and set it on top of my desk. She snapped it open, revealing bottles and jars of lotions, perfumes, cold creams, dusting powders, rouges and other makeup. "I'm an Avon Lady," she said proudly. "I've been so strapped for cash lately—I'm hoping this will help."

"Hmmm." I peered into her case. I wouldn't have known what to do with half the stuff in there. "So how's business?" I asked.

"Not too bad. I had a big order yesterday from Marty's wife. Can I interest you in a little something?" she asked, spiraling up a tube of crimson lipstick. "I'm hoping I can make enough money as an Avon Lady to quit working here and get as far away from Stanley as possible."

As if on cue, Ellsworth came over to my desk. M slammed her pink case shut and did a quick about-face.

"Excuse me," she said, brushing past him.

"Don't worry," I assured him. "I'm getting ready to head down to the press conference now."

He didn't respond. He stood there watching M walk away, looking like someone had stolen his favorite toy. Obviously he hadn't come over to talk to me at all. He'd just been trying to get close to M.

He hesitated for a moment, and I thought he was going to turn away. But then he stared down at his hands and said, "How's she doing? Is she okay?" I could see that it pained him just to say that much. "She won't even speak to me. I see her every day and she won't even look at me. She hates me now, doesn't she?"

"I don't think she could ever hate you. She was in love with you for a long time." I didn't tell him that M had a date with a new guy coming up, although I couldn't imagine why I felt the need to protect his feelings.

He nodded and dragged a hand across his face. "In case she's wondering, in case she ever asks, will you tell her that I miss her?"

Chapter 37

· · ·

It was official. On January 2, 1960, the handsome young senator from Massachusetts declared his candidacy for president. His opponent was Vice President Nixon. I was pleasantly surprised when Ellsworth put me on election coverage, working closely with Marty and Walter.

I did some preliminary reporting that spring and into the summer, and by fall the campaign began to heat up. On September 26, for the first time ever, a presidential debate was going to be televised. And it was going to be televised from Chicago and brought into the homes of millions of Americans.

While Marty and Walter were busy inside the studio with the candidates, Ellsworth had assigned me to cover the action outside WBBM. The streets were packed and the police were holding people back behind the barricades up and down McClurg Court. Cameras were flashing on every corner as people cheered and clapped. I saw the tail end of a black limo pulling up and that was about it. I didn't even know if it was Kennedy or Nixon arriving. I interviewed people who proudly displayed their Kennedy and Johnson buttons and others who waved their Dick Nixon flags. I asked questions and scrawled down the answers as people talked about what the election meant to them and to Chicago.

After I called everything in to Higgs on the rewrite desk, I had just enough time to make it over to the Lincoln Tavern to watch the debate with M and some of the others. The owner, Billy Sianis, had a TV in the corner. That night I met M's new beau, Gregory Bryant. Gregory was an account executive at Leo Burnett, working on Philip Morris. He sat with us, along with Gabby and Benny, waiting for the debate to begin.

The rest of the gang was at Radio Grill. It felt strange not being with everyone, but ever since M and Ellsworth had their falling out, there had been a split in our group. Now it was M, Gabby and the other sob sisters versus the fellows. For whatever reason, Benny and I managed to bop back and forth between the two sides.

It was clear to me from the moment I arrived that Gregory wasn't a newspaperman, because while the rest of us were glued to the television set, anxiously awaiting the start of the debate, he was telling us about his current advertising project.

"Right now we have a whole team of talent scouts scouring the country looking for an actress to play a cowgirl."

"A cowgirl?" I asked, barely turning away from the TV. "For a Philip Morris product? What happened to the Marlboro Man?"

"He's still there. But now we're introducing a cowgirl. The Marlboro Girl. We're testing a new ladies' cigarette."

"The Marlboro Girl?" Benny scrunched up his face. "That sounds like a dumb name."

Before Gregory could launch into his defense, the debate began and a hush came over the Lincoln Tavern.

"What's wrong with his face?" M pointed to the TV with her cigarette. "Nixon looks like he just got out of bed."

"He needs a better tailor," said Benny. "That suit doesn't even fit him."

Gabby laughed and playfully slapped his arm.

"Is he sweating?" I leaned in closer to get a better look. "Oh, God, he is."

"He looks terrible."

"What's the matter with him?"

"And would you look at Kennedy?" Gregory said. "Now, *he* looks like a president."

"Oh, you can't compare the two, can you?" said Gabby.

"No, you sure can't," said Benny.

It was true. Putting Nixon on the American stage next to Kennedy was like standing a plough horse next to a thoroughbred. Nixon was disheveled. He looked timid and lost in his chair, knees pressed together. He didn't look like a commander in chief, whereas Kennedy was well dressed, handsome and seemed at ease and confident.

It sent a powerful message, and the next morning as I sat on the el, I read the front-page coverage by Walter and Marty. According to their reporting, TV viewers thought Kennedy had won, whereas radio listeners thought Nixon was the victor.

About a week later I could feel a new season in the air. It was the beginning of October, and the autumn winds had shifted. Leaves peppered the sidewalks, sweaters and jackets were brought out of their mothballed chests, and collars were turned up. There was something electric in the air. It was like the city was waking up to something—and I wanted to find out what it was.

"We're running out of places to meet," Ahern said, as we walked through the Potter Palmer Collection at the Art Institute.

"I figured we could take in a bit of culture along the way," I said.

"So what is it that you wanted to see me about?"

"Well, we've got a presidential election around the corner." I paused before Degas's famous *On the Stage*. "And Adamowski's running for reelection."

"You don't say." He smiled.

"C'mon, I need an angle. I need something that'll give me an edge. We both know Daley will do anything to see to it that Adamowski is defeated. No way is he going to let him get elected to another term, right?"

"Right."

"So are you aware of anything the Democrats have planned?"

"You mean like is Daley gearing up to steal the election from the Republicans?"

"Voter fraud?" I almost laughed and start walking again. "C'mon, that's not news. Not in this town." From the corner of my eye I saw something come over Ahern. Subtle, but still I caught it. "Wait a minute—you know something, don't you? I can tell."

"C'mon, Walsh."

"I can help you," I said, grabbing hold of his arm. "I can give you ink. You know that. I just need to *know* what you *know*."

Ahern glanced around, making sure no one was within earshot. "I don't want to get you involved."

I laughed. "Now you *have* to tell me what's going on."

He stared at the ground and muttered, "I shouldn't have said anything. Should have kept my goddamn mouth shut. This could be dangerous, and I don't think this would be good for you. At all."

Now I was even more intrigued. "Why don't you let me be the judge of that?"

We were facing each other. A game of chicken. I wasn't backing down. And he knew it.

"Okay," he said finally, looking around again. The lines in his face were set hard and firm. "You're right. Daley will do anything to keep Adamowski from staying in office. So we have reason to believe that Daley is working with Kennedy *and* with the Mob to steal the election."

I got that chill that I always got when it was something big, and this was huge. "Holy crap. Go on. Go on."

"Kennedy's in on it. We've got it on record that Joseph Kennedy, the father, had a meeting with Sam Giancana. Daley knew about the meeting. Oh, and believe it or not, Sinatra arranged it for them."

"Sinatra? As in Frank?"

He nodded. "It's no secret that Giancana's got the labor unions in his pockets. He can snap his fingers and get all that manpower to do whatever he says. Including ballot stuffing. Including showing up to vote as the dead or as a comic-strip character, if you know what I mean."

"I get it." Chicago had a history of stuffing ballot boxes with bogus names. Mickey Mouse and Bozo the Clown were known to have voted, as well as a slew of people who had long been deceased.

"Joseph Kennedy's just as ruthless as Daley. He'll do anything to see that his son wins the presidency. We know they're going to try to steal the White House. Now all we have to do is prove it before they get away with it."

Ahern continued to talk while we made our way to the exit. I didn't say a word. I was already way up inside my head, figuring out how I was going to tackle this one.

"I want you to really think hard about this before you start looking into anything," he said. "This is the Chicago Outfit we're talking about."

I scarcely even remembered saying good-bye to Ahern. I just stood next to one of the lion statues outside the Art Institute and watched his tall figure disappear into the crowd on Michigan Avenue.

I thought about going after the Mob and wondered if I had the stomach for it. I regarded myself as pretty fearless when it came to reporting. I hadn't shied away from the story about D'Arco's auto-insurance scam. But this was Sam "Mooney" Giancana— the main man. The idea of snooping around in his business gave me pause. But only pause. I knew plenty of fellows at the paper who went drinking with members of the Outfit, gave them Christmas hams and attended their children's weddings. They weren't afraid. I could learn to play this game too.

I walked up Michigan Avenue weighing it all with each step. The sun was setting, the temperature dropping. Even before I made it back to the Tribune Tower, I knew there was no way I could turn my back on this story. This was a chance to hook the big one. I quickened my pace.

Ellsworth was already gone for the day when I got back, but I found Marty sitting around the horseshoe shooting the breeze with the slot man. It was late. The night shift was coming on, and I realized Marty was the perfect person for me to talk to. I asked if I might have a word with him in private and followed him into the conference room.

"I need your advice, Marty."

"Shoot."

"Well, I just got wind of something important and I'm not sure what to do."

"Okay, let's hear it." He unbuttoned his jacket and sat down.

I laid it all out for him, told him what had been secretly shared with me.

"The Mob, huh?" He adjusted his eyeglasses. "I can't say I'm surprised. What can you tell me about this source of yours?"

"All I can say is that I've got someone inside the state's attorney's office. I can't tell you anything more about the source."

He nodded. "That's all well and fine, but I'm telling you the *Tribune*'s not going to run a story about the mayor of Chicago and the Mafia stealing the White House unless you've got the goods to prove it. And now the big question is, are you sure you're prepared to go after this and go up against Giancana?"

"So you think I should pursue it?"

"I didn't tell you that. Listen to what I'm saying and not what you want to hear." He leaned back in his chair and removed his glasses, setting them on the table. "You know, there was a time when I was just like you. I would have gone after this. I remember when Robert Merriam ran for mayor in 1955. We suspected the Democrats were manipulating the vote. It was a mess. But that's Chicago for you." He laughed. "I used to be a lot like you. I used to think it was my personal responsibility to get to the truth and bring it out."

"But now?"

He rubbed his eyes. "But now I don't know. Maybe I'm getting too old for this business. Maybe I'm jaded. Or maybe Big Tony scared the hell out of me. But now I know you can't change certain things. Some things are bigger than we are, and I think some things are better left unsaid." He put his glasses back on and looked me square in the eyes. "I know you don't want to hear this, but if I were you, I'd cover the fraud—hell, George Thiem at the *Daily News* will be all over that—but I'd leave the Mob out of it."

"I appreciate what you're saying, but . . ." I shook my head because what he'd told me only made me want to go after it all the more.

"You can't do it, can you?" he said. "You can't leave it alone."

I shook my head. "Sorry, Marty, but I just can't."

The next day I set up an interview with Frank Durham and David Brill who were in charge of an operation called the Committee for Honest Elections.

"Have you looked into the Board of Commissioners?" asked Brill as we sat in a tiny office on LaSalle Street overlooking the Chicago Board of Trade. "They're practically all Democrats."

"Ask them about their polling lists," said Durham as he drummed his pencil against the edge of the desk.

Brill nodded. "They've got thousands of ghosts on there. People who've either died or moved away or got married and changed their names."

"And what's amazing," said Durham, "is how every name on that list—whether dead or alive—is going to *magically* appear as a Democratic vote."

I was writing all this down when Brill started telling me about their meeting with Daley.

"We sat in his office yesterday afternoon," said Brill. "He accused us of being a bunch of Republicans—"

"Can you imagine that?" said Durham with a smirk, still drumming his pencil.

"Daley said we wanted to suppress the Democratic vote."

"Although Daley said 'depress the Democratic vote.'" Durham chuckled. "Look, we're doing this for the good of the Chicago people and the nation. We all know Daley doesn't want Adamowski serving another term, and we know that if he can get Kennedy in the White House, he'll have some favors coming back around. It all comes down to power. That's how it works. You know it. I know it. We all know it. Now, the question is, how do we stop it?"

"Have you heard anything about the Chicago Outfit getting involved, using their muscle to sway voters?"

Durham set his pencil aside. "We don't know nothing about that sort of thing," he said. "We won't touch the Mob."

After I left Durham and Brill, I met with some members from the Joint Civic Committee on Elections. They echoed similar grievances and insisted they had no knowledge of the Mafia's involvement.

From there I canvassed various neighborhoods, speaking with Republicans and Democrats, anyone who would talk to me. I had a cup of coffee with Trey Nelson, a Republican election judge.

"What are your thoughts on Election Day?" I asked.

He gave his coffee a stir and tapped the spoon against the lip of the cup. "I don't trust the Democrats." He shook his head. "We're asking for extra security at the polls to make sure there's no funny business."

"What kind of funny business?"

"You know what kind of funny business I'm talking about. You know what those sons of bitches did? The Democrats sent out these postcards to every registered voter in Cook County telling them *the issues* and now they'll wait to see what cards come back as *address unknown* or *return to sender,* and they'll turn each and every one of those into a vote for the Democrats."

The next day, over a beer, I asked Sean O'Hara, a Democratic precinct captain, how he felt about the upcoming elections. He laughed. "It's gonna be a great day for Americans to exercise their right to vote. Tell the Republicans to quit their bellyaching."

After I left O'Hara, I went into a barbershop and talked to a couple of customers waiting their turn beside the red, white and blue helix pole. One gentleman chewed on his cigar and said, "I don't like any of 'em. Politics is a dirty business. Especially in this town."

"Does that mean you're not going to vote on Election Day?"

"I didn't say that."

Another man sitting in the barber's chair peeked around the side of his newspaper and said, "If a man's not going to vote, then he's got no right to complain."

I wasn't hearing anything new at this point and couldn't get anyone to discuss the Mob. They were all so tight-lipped about it, which only told me that Ahern was right. I needed to dig deeper. I went back to the city room and began writing up my notes. Walter was one desk over, working on his own election coverage, but he was focused on the candidates, whereas I was concerned about the voters. Marty seemed to be covering a bit of both.

I was typing hard, rattling all the pencils in my penholder, when Marty came up to me. "Did you see this?" He slapped a copy of the *Daily News* on my desk. "Told you Georgie would be all over this."

"Everyone in this city is expecting voter fraud," I said. "But I can't get anyone to even utter Giancana's name. Can you think of anyone I should talk to?"

"I've interviewed so many people, I can't keep them all straight," he said. "But I know for sure I never asked anyone about the Mob."

"I'm gonna go back and double check what we've got in the archives. See if I can find anything."

"Suit yourself, Walsh."

I went straight to the morgue and looked up Marty's recent stories. In one article he had interviewed an elderly woman named Gertrude Lammont, who said that her precinct captain told her he would give her a raffle ticket if she voted the right way. "And by 'right way,' I knew he meant Democratic. I don't need to win a turkey that badly," she said. I wondered who the precinct captain was and if he was connected to the Mob. I knew then that I needed to speak with Gertrude Lammont.

I reached for the telephone book and turned to the *L*s. I didn't find a Gertrude, but there were three G. Lammonts and a dozen or so other Lammonts in the book. I called them all and did track down a Gertrude Lammont, but her mother said she was only eleven years old. Next I ran a check with voter registration and was surprised that they didn't have a Gertrude Lammont on record.

I assumed the copy editor or someone else had gotten the name wrong. It happened from time to time, so I went back to Marty and found him hunched over his typewriter, clacking away on a piece. He sensed me standing there and looked up.

"Yes?"

"You wouldn't happen to have a phone number for Gertrude Lammont, would you?"

"Who?" He stopped typing and propped his eyeglasses up on his brow.

"Gertrude Lammont. She's the elderly woman you interviewed last week."

He steepled his fingers and leaned back. "Why do you need to talk to her?"

"She mentioned something about her precinct captain bribing her, and I want to track him down."

He mumbled something about having to go through his notes. "Give me till tomorrow. I'll see what I can get for you."

I went back to work on my article for that day about people complaining that their *Nixon for President* and *Reelect Adamowski* signs had been destroyed. After I turned that in, I focused again on the issue of voter fraud. And I wasn't the only one. A few articles here and there at the *Tribune* and other papers—mostly the *Daily News*—alluded to concerns about trouble at the polls, but no one said anything about Giancana, so I kept going down that path.

I went to see more precinct captains and spoke to election judges, the Chicago election commissioners, members of the city's election board and canvassers. After I gathered what information I could from them, I met up with a group of men from the Iron Workers Local #1 and had a drink with them at their favorite water hole on Southport.

"So, guys," I said, taking a swig of beer, trying to act like one of them. "We all know the union's backing Kennedy, right?"

"Yeah, I don't care for Nixon," said Smitty, who sat at the head of the table. "He doesn't impress me at all." Smitty had big beefy fingers and propped his arm up on his yellow hard hat resting on the tabletop. "And you can forget about Adamowski. He'll never see another term."

The others nodded.

I took a sip of beer and lit up a cigarette to bide my time while I thought through my next question. "What do you boys think about the allegations of voter fraud that are circulating?"

"I think it's horseshit," said Smitty as he shifted in his chair and took a long slug of beer.

"But you're aware of the rumors, right?"

"Rumors—that's all they are. No one's got any evidence."

"What about the rumors that the Mob is somehow connected?"

"That's bullshit, too. That's just the Republicans getting desperate."

"But don't you think—"

"I *think* I ain't interested in saying anything more about this." He stared me down, squinting one eye as he drew on his cigar.

The others were staring at me, hoping to make me squirm. I was trying to play it cool, trying to think of something to say when

Smitty began to snicker. They all found this humorous and went from glaring at me to laughing. It was the kind of laughter that gained momentum, growing louder and bolder until it became a raucous uproar. There was a nasty edge to it, and soon the whole table of men were howling and snorting and sniggering. A chill raced up my back, and I knew we were through talking.

Chapter 38

• • •

The next day it was Indian summer, nearly eighty degrees even though it was the last week in October. Ahern had his suit jacket hooked on two fingers and draped over his shoulder. We were walking down Maxwell Street, an open-air market that sold everything from produce to used appliances. It was a bargain hunter's paradise, where shoppers could haggle with the vendors. We passed tables butted up against one another and piled up with every kind of item imaginable: picture frames and old shoes, bolts of fabrics and secondhand lawn tools. Street musicians were stationed all around playing blues and jazz.

"You need to watch yourself," Ahern said to me.

"What do you mean?"

"We've heard some chatter that Giancana didn't like the idea of a reporter going around and talking to the unions. Even a female reporter."

The sharp smell of sausages and barbecued ribs hung heavy in the air. "What exactly did you hear?"

"I just know that he's aware of what you're doing. And he doesn't like it."

"How am I supposed to get the story if I can't talk to people? I'm just doing my job. Other people are reporting on voter fraud, too, you know."

"Yes, but they're not trying to tie it to the Mob."

"But that's what I'm trying to prove. Otherwise I'm just rehashing what every other reporter is saying."

"I think you need to back off."

"What?" I laughed.

"I'm serious."

"Is there something you're not telling me? Am I in danger or something?"

"It's the Outfit. C'mon—what do you think?"

"I think you're overreacting. Unless you know something that you're not telling me."

"No. I don't know anything specific. I told you all along that I was uncomfortable with this."

"So you really expect me to forget about this story? To just cover the election like everyone else? Speculate about voter fraud but not try to prove that it's going to happen? Or better yet, try to stop it? And if the Mob's behind it, how can we stop it unless people know they're connected to it?"

"As your friend, I'm saying—"

"Some friend."

"Goddammit, Jordan. I'm telling you to back off the story."

"I can't."

"I'm not trying to scare you, but this isn't worth it. I'm serious, Jordan. This is why I didn't want you to get involved in the first place. Please back off. I mean it. You have to let this go."

I'd never seen him so adamant. I could tell that he was genuinely scared for me. The sun was beating down. People were walking around in sleeveless shirts, and yet a chill came over me, turning my skin to gooseflesh. I hugged myself to keep warm.

Ahern pulled his suit jacket off his shoulder and held it open for me. "Here," he said, draping it over me.

"Okay. All right." I bit down on my lip and nodded. "Okay. I'll back off the investigation."

We left Maxwell Street, and by the time I made it back to the *Tribune*, I'd shaken off the chills and was now sitting at my desk, perspiring. It was balmy hot inside the city room, even with all the windows thrown open. The oscillating fans stationed about on file cabinets and desks did little good.

Benny came up to me, his shirt sweated through, half-moons forming beneath his arms. "Hey, Jordan," he said. "Guess what today is, huh? Guess."

"Ah, I don't know. Thursday?"

"No. No, well, yes, it's Thursday, but it's also my birthday."

"Oh, well, happy birthday."

"Twenty-three today." He tucked his thumbs up under his sweaty armpits.

"Twenty-three and he don't look a day over twelve," said Walter, laughing.

"Maybe one of these days he'll need to start shaving," said Henry.

"So anyway"—Benny ignored them and leaned in closer—"I was wondering if you'd let me take you out tonight. You know, to help me celebrate. I have reservations at Chez Paree. Nat King Cole's performing there tonight." His face was slick with sweat and all lit up, waiting for my response.

I could see it in his eyes. So much depended on me, and I felt horrible knowing that I was going to let him down. I could feel my coworkers watching us. M was glued to the situation.

"That's so sweet, Benny," I said. "But . . ."

"But, I know—you have other plans. Or another date. Or else you wouldn't be caught dead with me."

"No, Benny. No. That's not it."

He dragged his arm across his brow to clear the sweat. "I thought you liked me, Jordan."

"I do like you, but—"

"But?"

I looked into his downcast eyes and watched as he stuffed his hands in his pockets and hung his head.

Walter slapped Benny on the back, laughing. "Shot down on your birthday. Them's the breaks."

"Walter," I snapped. "Shut up. For once in your goddamned life, would you just shut the hell up?" I turned back to Benny and stared at him for a minute. Then I said, "You know what, Benny? Actually, I'd love to go to Chez Paree with you tonight."

That stunned everyone, including Benny. Including me. But I couldn't turn him down. Not on his birthday. Not after what Walter had said.

Gabby appeared out of nowhere, holding a flaming birthday cake. After everyone sang to Benny and had their cake, I went over and talked with Marty. I explained that I was taking his advice and the advice of my source and backing away from the story.

"I think you're doing the right thing," he said.

"But I just don't know how to turn it off. I'm not good at giving up."

"The only way is to get involved in your next story. Trust me, the only cure for one investigative piece is another investigative piece."

But still I couldn't let it go. I remembered one of Marty's pieces, which ran a few days before, that mentioned Simon Richter. I'd never heard of him before, and I thought by then that I knew all the key players. This Simon Richter was a gentleman whom Marty referred to as *a poll watcher with nonspecific ties to the Board of Commissioners*. Simon Richter went on record saying he suspected there would be voter irregularities at the upcoming election. "Without naming names," Richter was quoted as saying, "I know several *very connected* precinct captains who have a few tricks up their sleeves for Election Day." I wondered what he'd meant by *very connected* and *tricks up their sleeves*.

I wanted to ask Marty for a phone number, but he was in a meeting with Ellsworth and Mr. Copeland, so I dug in on my own. I searched the telephone directory, but couldn't find Simon Richter. Anywhere. And when I couldn't find him in the phone book or listed on the board of commissioners, a wave of nausea overcame me. The name *Gertrude Lammont* came to mind. Marty never did get back to me with a phone number for her. Initially I had chalked the whole thing up to fluke, a typo on the name. But this second time with Simon Richter made my heart pound faster.

I pushed away from my desk and looked around the city room. Marty was still in his meeting with Mr. Copeland and Ellsworth. Just as well because I couldn't have faced him anyway. All the chatter of the phones ringing, the typewriters going, the conversations volleying back and forth and the wire machines—all of it seemed to push itself far, far into the background, and I was left with an overwhelming sense of isolation. I was separated from everyone else by this *thing* that I'd just uncovered. I walked the perimeter of the city room, hoping this discovery of mine wasn't true, hoping it would go away, dissipate like a cloud of smoke from Walter's pipe.

Ten minutes later I was still pacing. I knew what I had to do— what everything inside me had been trained to do—but I didn't want to face it. The eerie quiet shattered and the noise picked up as alarms sounded inside my head. The din grew louder until I finally drew a deep breath, went into the morgue and began pulling Marty's stories.

I pulled all his articles from the previous month and went back to my desk and started to read. The hour grew later and the city room thinned out as my colleagues, including Marty, drifted over to Boul Mich for drinks.

I had forgotten about Benny. He was sitting at his desk waiting for me.

Finally, he said, "I thought we could get going soon. Nat King Cole goes on at Chez Paree at eight. We could still make it if we leave now."

"Oh, God, Benny." I looked down at my desk covered with Marty's clips.

"I know what that means." He stuffed his hands in his pockets. "You're not gonna come with me tonight, are you?"

I was thinking of what I could say, what I could do.

"I don't know why you don't like me." His voice began cracking. "I really like you, Jordan. I love you. I've loved you since the first time I saw you."

"Oh, Benny." I stood up and hugged him, his little boy–like body fitting into my embrace as I patted him and rubbed circles on his back. "I'm flattered. I really am. And I know you're going to find a wonderful girl who loves you every bit as much as you love her. You deserve that. You're a good guy." And then something took hold of me and I looked into his eyes and I kissed him. I kissed him long and hard right on his mouth.

"Happy birthday, Benny."

He looked stunned, his fingers pressed to his lips, his eyes sparkling wide and bright. So even though I didn't go to Chez Paree, I sent Benny on his way that night feeling happier than he had all day.

Meanwhile, I stayed at my desk and finished going through

Marty's articles. There was another *missing* person he'd quoted. No listing in the phone book, and when I called the restaurant at the address next door and asked about their neighbor, I was told there was nothing there but an abandoned storefront. I hung up and shoved the phone away, as if it were to blame. I was queasy, growing sick inside. I couldn't be sure, and I hoped that I was wrong, but my gut told me that Marty Sinclair, my journalist hero, had been fabricating his sources.

Chapter 39

$\bullet \quad \bullet \quad \bullet$

That night I left the *Tribune* in a stupor. I boarded the el, holding the ceiling strap with one hand, my attaché case with the other, and swaying along with the motion of the train. It was still unseasonably warm for that time of year and stale smells of the city poured in through the open windows.

I got off at the Armitage stop and headed down the platform, thinking about Marty, thinking that I should pick up something for dinner even though I wasn't the slightest bit hungry. I made my way down the station stairs and walked over to Lincoln Avenue. It was dark that night—for some reason the streetlamps hadn't kicked on yet. There were a few people around, hanging out in front of a pool hall and the taverns. I headed down a few more blocks and became aware of footsteps behind me. I didn't give it much thought at first, but when I turned onto Clark Street, the footsteps followed. My body tensed up. It knew something was wrong before I did.

I started walking faster. The footsteps matched my pace. Less than three feet later something inside me snapped and I broke out into a full-on run. So did my pursuer. With my attaché case banging against my knee, I ran, passing one darkened storefront after another. The dead lampposts and buildings whirled around me, disorienting me as I panicked. He was gaining on me, his footsteps growing louder, coming closer. I was about to scream when the man who'd been following me ran past me, waving his hand in the air, calling out, "Teddy? Hey, Teddy, wait up!"

I was panting as I watched my would-be assailant meet up with this Teddy person. I felt ridiculous. What had come over me? It was only my imagination chasing me. I was still shaking though, and I realized I was not okay. Everything was getting to me. Little flecks of light danced behind my eyes, like right before you're about to faint. I was scared of blacking out on the street, in the stairwell of my building, or on the floor of my apartment. Bottom line, I didn't want to be alone.

It had started to drizzle. The rain pelted my face and coat as I stood frantically waving to hail the first taxicab I saw. I jumped in, my hands shaking, my voice trembling as I rattled off my parents' address and stared through the windshield wipers swishing back and forth, back and forth. Slowly my heart rate returned to normal.

I looked out the window as we drove along, trying to distract myself. It was raining harder now. There were cars backed up on Wells Street, their headlights reflected in the wet pavement like an impressionist cityscape painting.

Finally the taxi pulled up to the Painted Lady. Even from the curb, through the sheets of rain, I could see the lights were on in the back of the house. As I made my way up the steps, the front door swung open, startling me.

"Where have you been—oh, God," my mother said, her hand clutched to her throat. "It's you."

"Yes, it's me. What's wrong? What's the matter?"

She looked around, stalling.

"Mom? What's going on?" I was still rattled by my own drama as I followed her inside the house, droplets of rain falling off my sweater, the tips of my hair. "Mom? What is it?"

"It's your father."

"Is he okay? What's wrong?" I twisted out of my wet sweater and set my attaché case down, the leather speckled from the raindrops.

"I'm furious with him. I can't find him."

"What do you mean, you can't find him?"

"He's missing."

"Missing?"

She hugged herself and chewed on her bottom lip. The smell of stale smoke and bookbindings hit me as soon as I got past the doorway. A bolt of lightning flashed through the front windows.

"He probably went for a drink," I said.

"I called around to the bars. No one's seen him."

"Why didn't you call me?"

"I kept thinking he'd be back any minute. I should have known better." She sighed and shook her head, her hands clenched in fists.

"What happened?"

"Oh, it's his damn book. Doubleday rejected his novel. They were his last shot. His novel has now been rejected by every publisher in New York."

"Oh, no. How'd he take it?"

"Not well. He was angry, fit to be tied. He said those editors didn't have any taste. And I thought, *Maybe he's right. Maybe it's just the wrong editors.*"

"It's possible. You hear all the time about great books that were rejected all over the place."

"So I finally convinced him to let me read the manuscript."

"And?"

"There it is." She gestured to a stack of paper on the floor next to her chair and folded her arms across her chest. "I wanted to fall in love with it. Really, I did. I wanted it to be brilliant, and I wanted to be able to look him in the eye and say, 'Yes, the editors were wrong.' But . . ."

"But?"

"*Auch.*" She unfolded her arms and swatted at the air. "The whole damn thing is about us. About Eliot. I'm so angry with him—how could he exploit what we've been through? How could he think it was all right to do this? And on top of that, the book's no damn good. It's self-indulgent and bloated. It's just no damn good."

"He wrote about Eliot?"

"I don't know how he could have done it." She brushed her hair up off her furrowed brow. "He had no right. I feel so violated. How dare he do that? He never should have sent it out. He should have let me read it beforehand. It's no one's business what happened. It's our business."

"What did you say to him?"

"Well, I told him how mad I was, and then I told him exactly what I thought of his goddamn book. I didn't do it to hurt him. I told him the truth. I've never lied to him—especially not about his work. I told him the book—regardless of what it's about—doesn't deserve to be published."

"Oh, boy."

"Oh, boy, is right. He flew into a rage. Wait till you see what he did to his office. I heard him in there throwing things, smashing things, and the next thing I knew, it was quiet. He was gone. I didn't even hear him leave."

"When was this?"

"Last night."

"*Last night?* And he hasn't been home since?" Now I was scared.

"I'm worried something's happened to him."

"Did you call the police?"

"Not yet. I'm still hoping he'll turn up."

I understood this. Bringing in the police meant that he had to be found, meant that she'd lost faith in his wandering through the front door on his own.

"If something's happened, I'll never forgive myself. I want to give it a little while longer before we call the police."

So we sat in the living room, our eyes trained on the bay window, our hearts leaping each time we heard a car go by or caught a glimpse of someone coming up the sidewalk. My mother was curled up on her chair, her eyes half closed. I finally convinced her to go upstairs and get some rest.

All alone in the family room, I drifted over to my father's manuscript, hefted it up—all twelve hundred plus pages—and sat with it in my mother's chair. I brought my feet up to the cushion, rested a stack of pages on my knees and began to read *The Lost Son*.

I shouldn't have been surprised that he would have written about Eliot and yet I was. I wasn't offended like my mother was, just stunned is all. The son's name had been changed to Edward and the surviving daughter was Georgina and the wife was Mimi. But it was all there, my broken family.

The prologue—forty-seven pages on its own—was a recap of the parents learning about the accident. I read the first twelve pages and had to pause and take a break. My mother was right about the manuscript. My father was a great writer, but this book was not well written. And subject matter aside, it wasn't fiction. It was more like a news article.

I couldn't believe he'd spent all this time on it and it was just plain bad. I tried but couldn't read any more. I set the manuscript down and went into the kitchen for a glass of water. The place was a mess and I needed to keep busy, so I washed the dishes, wiped down the counter, swept the floor. I bound up the trash and slipped into my shoes, still damp on the insides from the rain. I threw on the back porch lights and opened the door. Trash in hand, I started down the pathway where they picked up the garbage. It had stopped raining, but the air was damp with a faint misty drizzle.

As I headed toward the walkway, bathed in the glow of the porch lights, I saw the leaves piled up to the side of the fallout shelter door. I dropped off the garbage and as I turned around, I noticed a clearing in the leaves and a trail of footprints left in the soggy grass. They led from the back of our house, disappearing beneath the trapdoor to our shelter.

I rushed over through the leaves, the wet grass brushing against my ankles. I bent down and tugged on the hatch with both hands. "Dad?" My heart hammered, uncertain of what I was about to find. "Dad?" I called out again as I climbed down the steps, holding on to the handrail. "Dad? Are you down there?"

It was pitch-black down there. The darkness played havoc with my vision, and it took a moment for my eyes to adjust. When it did, I found my father on a cot, a bottle of bourbon at his side. His face had a white cast from his whiskers, a day or two's worth of growth. I'd never seen him looking so small, so old and broken.

"What are you doing down here?" I asked. "We've been worried sick about you."

He muttered something that I couldn't decipher. He was drunk and groggy. He must have been sleeping before I came down. He rubbed his eyes with the heel of his hand.

"Dad?" I waited. "Dad? Aren't you going to say something?"

He wouldn't look at me and that made me feel foolish for even trying to help him. All the years of his slights slapped me in the face. Every conversation he'd shut me out of, every achievement he'd refused to acknowledge—they all festered inside me. The longer I stood there being ignored, the more humiliated I felt.

"Would you at least say something, dammit? My God, what is it going to take to reach you? How long are you going to keep pushing me away? I know you're disappointed about the book. I know you're upset about what Mom said. But you can't just hide down here, scare the daylights out of us and feel sorry for yourself."

Still nothing. He stared ahead as if I weren't even there.

"Okay, that's it. I'm done. I'm not going to stand here and beg you to talk to me. You want to sit down here in the dark and pout, be my guest. I'm not going to be your audience. You want to self-destruct, then you do it on your own." I was shaking by then. I may have lost my temper in the past and raised my voice now and then but I'd never talked to him like I just had before. I was certain that I'd just destroyed what little was left of our relationship. I turned and made it halfway up the ladder.

"Jordan, wait—" His voice sounded strained, tinny.

I froze in place.

"Don't leave."

I slowly lowered myself back down and turned around. For a moment the two of us said nothing, but our eyes were locked on each other and I felt that for the first time in a long time he was seeing me.

Without a word, he made room for me next to him on the cot. When I sat down, he handed me the bottle of bourbon. I took a swallow, letting it burn the back of my throat, the heat spreading throughout my chest. I held out the bottle for him, and the touch of his fingers brushing against mine released the words I'd been holding inside all this time.

"What happened to us, Dad? Where did we all go? I miss us. I miss our family. You and Mom are all I have now. I need you, don't you understand that?"

"I—I can't . . ." He squeezed my fingers, his voice on the verge of cracking. "I can't find my way out of this one. I can't get past it." He took a pull from the bottle and composed himself. "When I was covering the war, I watched men die. Dozens of them. Right in front of me. I saw it all. I got past it."

"But that was different, Dad. This wasn't some soldier, some stranger. This was your son."

"I thought—I thought the book—I thought it would . . ." He shook his head, unable to finish his thought.

"I know what you were trying to do. You were trying to keep Eliot alive. Writing that book kept him with you every day. I know that because I do the same thing with my reporting. Every day I go into the city room and I think, *What would Eliot do?* Don't you see? We're all stuck and we all have to figure out a way to let him go. We're not abandoning him, but we have to find a way to move forward with our own lives. It's time."

He hung his head. "You don't know how tired I am. I'm tired of feeling miserable. Tired of feeling sad and angry. It's wearing me out."

"I know it is. Eliot wouldn't have wanted this for us. You know that, right?"

"I just—I'm just so . . ." He couldn't finish his thought, and I saw the frustration mount inside him right before he threw the empty bottle, smashing it to bits on the floor. Then he started to cry. I'd never seen him do that before. Not even at Eliot's funeral. But now he was sobbing like a baby as he reached for me, his arms pulling me in close, his head on my shoulder, his body shaking as he wept.

"It's all right," I said over and over again, or maybe I only thought I said that. I was delirious, my heart swelling and breaking all at the same time.

Chapter 40

◆ ◆ ◆

After I got my father out of the fallout shelter and into the house, my mother took him in her arms. It was late and I was exhausted. I ended up staying over that night in my old room still decorated with posters of Troy Donahue, Ricky Nelson and Fabian—a carryover from my youth. Everything seemed smaller than I remembered: the little bed and quilted headboard, the white eyelet curtains, the bookcase. I realized how much my world had expanded since I'd moved out, but still, I was an in-between. No longer a child, not fully a grown-up. I no longer fit inside that bedroom, but where did I belong? I always thought home was still an option, and now I realized it wasn't.

The next morning, after barely sleeping at all, I got up early, before either one of my parents was awake. I eased out the front door and headed toward the el. The sun was coming up, rising from behind the rooftops, its blinding rays poking through the tree branches. There was just a handful of passengers on the platform waiting for the train. Across the way, on the opposite platform, a southbound train was rushing through, and as the cars flashed by for a split second, I thought I saw Scott Trevor standing there among the commuters. I was forever thinking I saw him. It was the same way with Eliot right after he died. In restaurants, on a bus, across the way in a store, I imagined him. And now Scott had become another ghost. The southbound train rushed past and the platform was empty once again.

The northbound el was nowhere in sight and my head was crowded with thoughts of my father, my brother and Marty, my fallen hero. I was overtired and wondering how I was going to talk to Marty about his sources. I glanced at my watch. It was almost seven o'clock. I'd have just enough time to get home, get cleaned up and make it back to the city room by eight. The wind kicked up and a shiver took over my body. I hugged myself about the middle as I felt the rumble of the el approaching in the distance, drawing closer, closer and closer still. I was drifting toward the track when someone came up alongside me.

"I thought that was you."

I turned around. "Scott?"

He was breathing hard, and I realized that it had been him across the platform. He must have skipped his train to come to the other side to see me. With one look into his eyes, everything from the past day and night caught up to me, and I burst into tears.

"Hey, hey, c'mon now. What's going on?" He placed a hand on my shoulder but didn't go to hug me, to hold me in his arms.

"Sorry." I took a deep breath and composed myself. I realized then that I must have looked awful, my hair slept on, no lipstick or rouge. "Been a rough couple of days."

"Don't be sorry. How are you?"

"Not great. Obviously. How about you?"

He grinned but didn't say anything.

The train came barreling through, dropping off and picking up passengers. I couldn't bring myself to get on board and leave him.

"It's good to see you. I've missed you. I really have."

He nodded. "Yeah, I know. It's been a long time."

"You don't know how many times I prayed I'd run into you. It's like you disappeared off the face of the earth."

"I've been busy. Teaching. Back at Northwestern. An ethics class in law, if you can believe it."

I know I said something after that, but I couldn't remember what it was. I was so aware of his eyes staring into mine and my heart opening wide and wider still. I wanted him. I wanted to pick up where we'd left off. I wanted to take us back to that moment in that awful bar when we were dancing and kissing and ready to start something wonderful together. "Oh, Scott," I said, practically thinking out loud. "We should be together, you and me. You feel it, too. I know you—"

"No. Don't." He shook his head and brought his fingers to my lips to quiet me. "I can't. Jordan, it's too late."

"No, it's not. Don't say that. You wouldn't have come over here if you didn't want to be with me."

"I came over here because I wanted to see you. And I wanted . . . I wanted to tell you that . . . Well, I've met someone. I'm getting married."

"Oh." All the air left my lungs, and it was suddenly hard to breathe.

"I was actually going to call and tell you. I didn't want you to hear it from someone else."

I squeezed my eyes shut and willed myself not to cry. He was still talking, telling me about the girl, but I wasn't listening. I couldn't. I felt foolish and exposed. And abandoned. I was in agony. Thank God another train arrived because I couldn't have stood there and looked at him another minute.

We said good-bye and I disappeared inside the train and cried the rest of the way home.

————

The city room was a bundle of energy when I arrived. The floor was vibrating from the presses running in the basement, the phones were ringing and the wire machines were going like mad. We were less than twenty-four hours away from the vote.

Despite all that preelection excitement, I was still upset about Scott. I couldn't help blaming myself for ruining things with him. Strange, but even though we were never really together, losing Scott hurt more than breaking off my engagement with Jack.

I tried to clear my mind, focus on what I knew I had to do. Marty was shouting across the room to someone about exit polls as he ripped his latest pages from the typewriter, calling out, "Copy. Copy."

I thought about not saying anything to him, but I couldn't pretend I didn't know what he'd done. When I first met Marty he would have done anything to protect a source—including threatening to quit his job. Or so I thought. But I'd since learned that he was scared of going up against Big Tony, scared for his own safety rather than a violation of some ethical code. Maybe Marty had never been the hero I'd made him out to be. Maybe he was just as pragmatic as the rest of us, just getting the job done. And now here he was inventing sources out of thin air. He'd traded any sense of professional ethics he had at all for the sake of his byline. It hurt to think about him like that, but his fall from grace was turning one of the noblest professions into a sham.

As I looked at him, the only question running through my mind was, *Why?* Was he falling behind on his deadlines? Was there a mix-up with his notes? How could he have been that careless? I'd seen a lot of reporters do a lot of questionable things. I myself had even done a few borderline things to get the story, to get an interview, but doing this—and for no reason other than him being too lazy to do his job. It made my heart sink.

I watched him at work, feeding a new set of copy paper into his typewriter as he slurped his coffee and started pounding away. Benny came up to ask him something and Marty barked at him. "I'm on deadline, dammit."

I waited until he took a break and went over to his desk. I wanted to at least give him a chance to explain why he did it.

"Marty, can we grab some coffee or lunch? We have to talk."

He must have detected the seriousness in my tone, in my eyes. Perhaps he even knew what was coming. "Okay, Walsh, but we'll have to make it quick."

He backed away from his desk, reached for his hat and coat, and without saying another word, we went 'round the corner to Norm's Diner.

"I have to tell you, your timing stinks, Walsh," he said, as we took our seats at a table in the corner, away from everyone else. "We're gearing up for tomorrow's election returns, in case you haven't heard."

"I know, but I have to say something and I have to say it now before I lose my nerve." I leaned in closer. "We have to talk about your pieces."

"What about my pieces?"

"Oh, Marty, this is a painful conversation to have—and I hope to God you have an explanation, but—"

"What the hell are you getting at?" His brows knitted together. He looked genuinely confused. He had no idea what I was about to spring on him.

"Marty, some of your pieces, some of the facts, they're not checking out."

"What? That's ridiculous." He shoved his coffee aside, sloshing it onto the table. His cheeks grew dark as his fingers crumpled up his napkin. "I don't believe what I'm hearing. You've got some nerve, Walsh. I don't know what you're implying, but—"

"Your sources, Marty. Your quotes. C'mon, the jig is up. I know what you've been doing. You made them up."

The moment I said that, all his indignation evaporated. He looked like I'd punched him in the gut. The color drained from his face, and he brought his hands to his forehead. "Oh, God. Oh, good God."

"Why, Marty? Why would you do something like that? You're a brilliant journalist—you don't need to do something like that."

He dared to meet my gaze. "It was just the one piece," he said. "Just that one on Gertrude Lammont."

"Marty—"

"I just needed that one extra quote," he insisted. "I was on deadline and Ellsworth was breathing down my neck and . . ."

"Marty, I know it wasn't just that one time. I know what you've been doing. It's been going on for a while. What I don't know is why."

He squared his elbows on the table and dropped his head to his hands. His shoulders started to shake, and I realized he was crying.

"Marty—"

He raised his head as tears trickled down his face. "You don't know what it's been like for me. I don't care if Big Tony is in prison—you think I don't still worry about that? Ever since the hospital. Ever since I got sick. I can't take the pressure. The deadlines. The expectations. It's been too much."

"Then why didn't you ask for help?"

"A Pulitzer Prize–winning journalist doesn't ask for help, Walsh."

"Then why didn't you quit?"

"I have a family to support. And I only did it when I absolutely had to."

"No, Marty. You never *have* to do that. You're a journalist, not a fiction writer. The past three months your work's been full of holes." I reached in my bag and handed him a tissue.

He ignored it and continued to let the tears run down his face. "Are you going to tell Ellsworth?"

I sighed. That was the question I'd been wrestling with. "I don't want to do that to you. You know I don't. But you can't go on doing this."

"I promise. I won't ever do it again."

"Marty, you're tainting the whole paper, the whole field of journalism. If you were a doctor, it would be malpractice. If you were a lawyer, you'd be disbarred."

"This will destroy my whole career. My reputation. I'll never be able to work again. If word about this gets out, no one else will ever hire me. How am I going to support my family?"

My head was throbbing. I pressed my fingers to my pulsing temples and tried to steady my breathing. I took a moment and gathered my thoughts. "You're too good, too talented to take a shortcut like that." Despite what he'd done, despite how morally wrong it was, I looked across the table and I still saw the man who had inspired me, who'd taken me under his wing. I couldn't turn him in. I just couldn't do it. Swallowing past the lump in my throat, I said, "This'll stay between the two of us. I won't say a word. But—"

"But what?"

"But if I see it again, you know I'm going to have to say something."

"Oh, Walsh." He let out a deep breath and grabbed my hands. "Thank you. Thank you for understanding."

"I don't understand, Marty. I really don't. I just don't have the heart to bring you down."

————

Marty didn't come back to the city room with me. He said he needed to take some time, get some air. I watched him heading south, walking across the Michigan Avenue Bridge, with hunched shoulders and shrinking pride.

The rest of the day dragged for me. I finished up my workload and begged off when the others went across the street for a drink. I was exhausted from the night before and not in the mood to socialize.

I went straight home instead, poured myself a big glass of wine and wondered if I had anything besides eggs in the house for dinner. My body was stiff and ached to the bone, so I took a bath in my tub that never drained right.

I sat while the water lapped against my body, the waves slapping at my limbs. A ship lost at sea. My mind replayed the past twenty-four hours as the bath turned cold. I was so disillusioned and disappointed. Especially with myself. I wished I hadn't let Scott get away. I wished Marty hadn't let me down. And mostly I wished that I'd hadn't backed off my story about Daley and the Mafia stealing the White House.

I always knew that I would have had to tread lightly with the Mob, watch what I set to ink—but even that went against everything I believed in. Everything the press had been founded on. But the Outfit had won. They'd frightened me into submission. I had allowed them to intimidate and censor me.

I was toweling off when I heard someone out in the hallway. Maybe the lady with the mysterious baby buggy. As I slipped into my bathrobe, someone knocked on my door. I wasn't expecting anyone. It gave me a start, and Giancana flashed through my mind. Everything inside me clenched together as I tiptoed out to the living room. There was another round of knocking. And then

I saw the doorknob trying to turn. I had one sharp knife in the kitchen, and I reached for it, inching toward the door. I held my breath as I dared to look through the peephole.

I couldn't believe it. My heart nearly stopped. "Dad? What are you doing here?" I unlocked and unlatched the door, yanking it open.

"It's about time," he said. "This is heavy." He stepped inside, carrying Eliot's typewriter in his hands. "I thought you might like to have this."

"Really?" My eyes misted up.

"Really." He groaned as he set the typewriter down on the table. "Your mother and I started packing up Eliot's things. It's time." He said this as if he'd come to this realization on his own. I didn't mind though. I was just grateful that he'd gotten there at all.

He reached into his pocket for a handkerchief to wipe the sweat from his brow. "Next time, consider a building with an elevator, would you?" He did a quarter turn in the middle of the living room, assessing it all. "So this is where you live, huh?"

"This is it. Do you want to sit down?" I asked tentatively, composing myself, clearing my eyes.

"You got anything to drink in here?"

"Just wine. Sorry." I shrugged. "No whiskey, and I'm all out of vodka."

"Wine, huh? Well, okay, then wine it is." He hated wine.

I poured him a glass and asked if he was hungry. "I was just about to make some eggs."

"Eggs for dinner? You know how to live, don't you?" He laughed.

"So are you doing okay?" I asked, handing him his wine and perching myself on the arm of the sofa where he was sitting.

He took a gulp and winced. "I don't know how you can drink this crap."

"It gets the job done." I took a long sip, painfully aware of the silence mounting, interrupted only by the occasional creak of the building, the drip of the kitchen faucet.

"Oh, I almost forgot." My father got up, went out to the hall and returned with a box held together by twine, which he presented to me.

"What's this?"

"Your brother's files—his paperwork, his notes, his clips. I didn't have the heart to go through any of it, but your mother thought you'd like to have them. There're two more boxes out in the car."

I was speechless as I ran my hands over the box, blinking back tears. I took this offering as a sign, permission to finally talk about what really happened to Eliot.

"Dad, I know you never wanted me to look into his death. But I have a feeling some of the answers are in these boxes. . . ."

My father reached for the wine bottle and poured himself another glass.

"Dad?" I wasn't sure he'd heard me. "Are you prepared for what I might find?"

He gazed into his glass. "I always wanted to believe that it was an accident. Just a random, senseless act. That's what I told myself. That was easier for me. Easier for your mother. And for you."

"Me? Why me?"

"Because I knew you'd want to look into it and find out what happened. Hell, even that night at the hospital, you were questioning the police, the doctors." His chin began to crumple, and his eyes were clouding up. "I knew then that you had the family curse. You're a reporter, Jordan, and that's what we reporters do. We question. We probe. We go into those dark places that scare everyone else. They even scare us, but we still do it because we have to. We just have to." He paused and took a drink. "I didn't want that life for you. I wanted to protect you. In the back of my mind I always knew what happened to Eliot could have been tied to his work. I'm not stupid. But if it wasn't an accident, I didn't want you involved."

"But wouldn't you rather know what really happened? Wouldn't you rather seek justice for his murder? Doesn't Eliot deserve that?"

"But I—I can't do it."

We were silent for a long time. Then I said, "I know. I know you can't do it. But I can. I can do this, Dad."

For the second time in two days he broke down, his shoulders shaking. "I couldn't bear it if something happened to you too. You're all I've got."

"Then don't shut me out. Don't push me away."

With tears running down his face, he opened his arms and I fell into them.

A fter my father left and I'd dried my eyes, I untwined the boxes and began sorting through Eliot's notes. I understood his fears, but I also couldn't deny my brother the justice he deserved, especially if it was sitting in these boxes on my living room floor.

I sat in the center of the room, surrounded by piles of yellowing papers and tattered folders. All his early clips were there, and I grew nostalgic reading through them. After I emptied the last box, I noticed a folder dated 1952: *Butcher Field Work.*

I opened the folder and began to read through his familiar scrawl:

> *Willis Packing, Topeka, Kansas, verified shipment: 20 tons of horsemeat to Chicago each week. Chicago hamburgers contain up to 40 percent horsemeat. Illegal in Chicago and Illinois to sell horsemeat for human consumption. Multimillion-dollar horsemeat racket—traces back to Chicago Mob and Governor Stevenson's office.*

The Chicago Mob? Governor Stevenson? I looked up and reached for my glass of wine. I knew some powerful people were probably involved, but I had no idea it went this deep.

I went back to the file: *See Department of Agriculture. Get statement from mayor's office.* . . . No wonder the superintendent I met with got so jumpy.

I dug a bit deeper and found his appointment book stuffed in the very back of that file. It was peppered with birthdays, city council meetings, names and phone numbers jotted in the margins. There was a random street address here and there. A few doodles. Telephone numbers, hastily scribbled down. Lots of dates penciled in with Susan Hirsh. A star next to her name in one instance. These all meant something to him. All bits and pieces of his life.

I was about to close the appointment book when my eyes landed on something that bewildered me one second and made my pulse race the next. There it was, right in the margin, written in black ink and underscored: *Richard Ahern—BELMONT 5-9081.*

Chapter 41

◆ ◆ ◆

All it takes is one thing to shuffle your deck and reprioritize everything for you. The worries that had consumed me just twenty-four hours or even twenty minutes before had now sifted to the bottom of the pile, and an investigation that had been on the back burner for years was suddenly front and center. My world was tossed upside down, and my thoughts kaleidoscoped into a million fragments. Ahern. Eliot. Marty. My father. The Mob. A horsemeat racket that went all the way to the governor's office.

When I left my apartment early the next morning, it was breezy and cold. The wind blew up my collar and sent a chill from the base of my neck down the length of my body. The clouds were hanging thick and low in the sky, bathing the whole city in a grayish cast. I was weary from the night before, having stayed up till four in the morning, reading through Eliot's notes, trying to piece it all together and decide what to do about it. With everything that had happened, I'd almost forgotten that today was Election Day. I passed by the flags displayed outside the school where I voted. There were posters in the windows and people already lining up to exercise their rights.

I knew I wouldn't be able to vote or do anything else until I spoke to Ahern.

I telephoned his office. It was only a quarter past seven and he wasn't in yet. I went around the corner and had a cup of coffee. I smoked two cigarettes before I went into the phone booth in back, fished for a nickel from my handbag and dialed Ahern again. When his secretary said he was in a meeting, I hung up the phone and headed for Dearborn and Washington, to the state's attorney's office.

It was a huge building, home to some nine hundred lawyers and investigators. I rode up to the sixth floor, where the Criminal Prosecutions Bureau was located. As soon as I got off the elevator, I could sense the somber mood in the place, and I wasn't surprised. Adamowski was on the ballot for reelection that day, going up against Daley's candidate, Daniel P. Ward.

I saw the big gold letters stenciled over the frosted glass on Ahern's door and headed toward his office.

"Excuse me, miss?" his secretary called to me. "Miss, you can't go in there—"

But I already had my hand on the door before she could stop me.

Ahern was reaching for the phone but put down the receiver as soon as he saw me. "Walsh? What are you doing here?"

"I'm sorry," said the secretary. "I tried to stop her, but she—"

"It's okay," he told her, a hand raised, followed by a gesture motioning her out of his office. "Come on in, Walsh. What's going on?"

"You knew my brother?" I rushed over to his desk. "How did you know him?"

He looked sucker punched. His eyebrows hiked up on his forehead as his mouth dropped open.

"Why didn't you tell me you knew him?"

"Calm down. Have a seat."

"I don't want to have a seat."

"Just give me a minute and I'll explain it all to you."

"How did you know him?" My hands were clenched—my entire body was clenched. "Answer me, dammit."

"Okay. All right. Just calm down and I'll tell you." He rubbed his forehead and took a deep breath. "It was a long time ago. Eliot saved my career. He saved my life." He reached for a pack of Kools on the corner of his desk and lit a cigarette. "I was just getting ready to graduate from law school. I had my whole future ahead of me. I'd made it to the last semester of my final year. I was shooting pool one night with some buddies. We'd just come off of studying for the bar. We'd been drinking since noon." He took a drag from his cigarette, as if to calm himself.

"Anyway, we started shooting pool, and your brother showed up with another guy. We'd never seen them before. They seemed like good enough fellows, so we started playing a game of eight-ball with them. Then, I don't know—too many beers, too many shots of whiskey and things got out of hand. Somehow we got into a fight. I was drunk. I started the whole damn thing—it was my fault. The cops were called in. They cuffed me, threw me in the slammer. I was sure your brother was going to press charges. I know I would have. If he had, I probably wouldn't have gotten my license, and that would have been the end of my career. But for whatever reason, Eliot took mercy on me. He decided not to press charges. And because he did that, I went on to pass the bar and got my job, and I vowed that I'd do whatever I could to help him in his career." He got up and started pacing the room.

"So I landed a job working for Mayor Kennelly and I was privy to certain goings-on. Pretty heady stuff for a kid just out of law school, and so I started giving Eliot tips and leaking things about what was going on inside City Hall. I stuck my neck out to bring him information and he ran with it. He was a good reporter. Discreet. Smart. The way I saw it, we were doing each other a favor."

I pulled out the chair across from Ahern and dropped down in it. "You were Eliot's source? Before you were mine? You were Eliot's?" I felt kicked in the stomach. "I asked you—how many times did I ask you—why you came to me? Why didn't you ever tell me it was because of Eliot?"

He sighed and examined the tip of his cigarette. "Because I didn't want you to think of my help as a handout. Or charity."

"But it was. That's all it was." I'd always believed I'd earned Ahern's respect and trust. Learning now that he'd been my brother's source first undid all of that. It made me feel like a fraud. Like I hadn't gotten to where I was on my own. I'd been thrown a bone. "So what—you took pity on me?"

"No, I did *not* take pity on you."

"Jesus Christ . . ."

"Look, I knew Eliot had a younger sister. He said you would make a brilliant journalist. Said you were smarter than he was, and I found that hard to believe. Jordan, I may have come to you because of your brother, but you proved yourself. And that is no lie. I remember seeing you at the funeral. You didn't shed one tear. You just stood between your parents. You were a rock. And I'll tell you something else—you're a lot like your brother, you know. He didn't like me in the beginning either." Ahern laughed and ground out his cigarette.

It was still smoldering in the ashtray as he fished another cigarette from his pack, struck a match and inhaled deeply. "You know, I got into politics because I was naive and green and I actually believed I could make a difference. But once I got inside, it didn't take long for me to realize that it was futile. I could bust my hump and not even make a dent."

He reminded me of Scott just then. I could have cried.

"I admit that after Daley interfered with my run for the state senate, I had an ax to grind. All I wanted was to bring down the machine. But then, when I saw what was going on inside City Hall—all the corruption—I wanted to do something about it, and that gave me a chance to repay my debt to your brother. And after he was gone, I figured he'd want me to help you out, so I did."

"You did help me out," I said begrudgingly, my voice cracking on every word. It was true. I'd gotten ahead in my career in part because of Ahern. "Just tell me one thing. Did you know Eliot was investigating the horsemeat scandal?"

"Honestly, I'd never even heard about that investigation until you brought it up. I asked around the office here, too. No one has any information on it. I don't know who told Eliot about it, but I swear, I didn't tip him off."

I couldn't say why, but it made me feel better to know that Ahern hadn't had a hand in Eliot's death. I'd actually grown fond of Ahern through the years and I'd been disillusioned enough lately. I was glad that hadn't been spoiled.

As we sat in silence, the world outside his office began seeping back in: telephones ringing, voices chattering, footsteps walking across the marble floor.

"There is something else that I've been wanting to tell you. Can you keep a secret?"

"Can I keep a secret?" I laughed sarcastically.

"I'm leaving Chicago."

"You're what?"

"I'm leaving. Getting out of politics, too. My wife and I are moving to Vermont. Her father's got a business up there—a printing company—and I'm going to go work for him. My wife's pregnant. Finally. And she wants us to raise our child up there. Away from all the sin in the city." He laughed, but it came out sounding more like a choked-off sob.

"When? When is this happening?"

"I'm just waiting until after the election. I'm sure that by tomorrow at this time I'll be out of a job anyway. I realized we can't go up against the Mob. We tried—you and I—but we can't stop it. Or the machine." He glanced down at his wristwatch and offered me a gentle smile. "What do you say? Shall we go cast our votes?"

I left Ahern and went up north and stood in line at my polling station, wondering *What's the point of even voting?* The outcome was predetermined. But when my turn came, I went into the booth, drew the curtain closed and filled out my fruitless ballot.

Afterward, I hopped an el car and got off in the Loop. All my thoughts were twisted inside out and backward. Part of me felt like Ahern, like I was done with this racket, frustrated and convinced that I could never make a difference. And like politics, journalism had its dirty little secrets, and I had to ask if I still wanted to be a part of that. I'd already had a front-row seat for the demise of Judge Casey, and I'd seen what the system had done to Scott Trevor. Nothing felt clean, cut-and-dried. I knew Daley was stealing this election, if for no other reason than to kick Adamowski out of office. He needed that Democratic vote, and Kennedy was just along for the ride. Maybe if I'd been brave enough, I could have stopped it from happening. I could have broken that story. But instead, I'd let the story break me.

Walking over the Michigan Avenue Bridge, I had a view of the whole downtown. *Oh, the filth and corruption behind those white marble buildings.* I'd wanted to expose the Daley machine, but the powers that be still controlled the city and shaped the message. As much as the press tried to hold their feet to the fire, there was still so much deception that no one would ever know about.

I headed into the Tribune Tower and looked around the great lobby with those wonderful quotes carved into the limestone walls. Voltaire. Jefferson. Madison. I'd once aimed to live up to their words. But now I knew better. Or I thought I did. As I looked into those passages, something shifted inside me. Out of nowhere, a surge of clarity grabbed ahold of me, and despite my exhaustion, the adrenaline was already pumping. I wasn't a quitter. I was Hank Walsh's daughter. Eliot Walsh's sister. I wasn't ready to give up. The Daley machine and Giancana had beaten me up pretty good, but there was still one fight left in me.

I knew enough bits and pieces of what had really happened to Eliot, and I knew that the men who killed him were still out there. I had it in Eliot's notes that the horsemeat scandal went as high up as the governor's office, and if there was any truth to that, then those politicians down in Springfield would have known that some reporter at the *Sun-Times* was connecting the dots. Eliot had been getting close to running that exposé and they would have known it. They would have needed to stop him. So they did. I may not have had proof of this yet, but in my mind, that was how the puzzle fit together. It made me furious that they thought they could get away with it.

The fourth-floor city room was all abuzz. It was election night, and I could feel the pulse of the building from the presses in the basement to the composing room and straight up to the nerve center where I was. There was a giant map of the United States up on the wall with red and blue pushpins marking the states that had already been called. It was still early, but at a glance it looked like Nixon had a comfortable lead.

I saw Walter and Henry working the phones. Peter adjusted his eyeshade as he typed away, and Benny was running around verifying quotes and facts while Randy sketched the editorial cartoons for the next morning, humming softly to himself. Funny, but ever since his contract with Pendulum Records had been canceled he'd pretty much stopped singing in the city room. But that hum, that he couldn't suppress. Even the sob sisters were busy, as if recipes, leather gloves and home-decorating tips were just as important as electing a president.

And there was Marty typing away with one hand, the telephone receiver in the other, his eyeglasses pushed up on his head. With one fluid movement, like I'd seen him do so many times before, he hung up the phone, ripped the page from his typewriter, waved it in the air and shouted, "Copy!"

Despite all the excitement, in the time it took to ride the elevator up from the lobby, a bigger scoop—something more important to me than the election and stealing the White House—had hatched inside my head. It was bubbling up inside me and I knew what I had to write. I also knew that Ellsworth probably wouldn't be too thrilled about it. I was prepared for him to fire me because of it. And if he did, then so be it. I knew I'd still do this piece and I knew I'd find a home for it.

A reporter's job was to expose the truth, and that was exactly what I was going to do.

Chapter 42

• • •

It was half past seven, the local polls had closed and the city room was working itself into a white-hot frenzy. There were runners, who couldn't get through on the telephones, making their rounds to the wire services and the City News Bureau before coming to us and the other papers with updates and counts that the precinct committeemen and election judges had given them. According to the latest counts, Nixon had thirty-two percent of Cook County with more Republican votes pouring in from Will, Lake, DeKalb, DuPage and other counties across the state. The Democrats in Cook County—which was really the only county capable of changing the game—seemed to be asleep. By eight o'clock we were sending out for sandwiches and putting on fresh pots of coffee while the Republicans were whooping it up, thinking they had it in the bag.

We were all working like mad, trying to keep up, when the polls started slowing down. But still the Cook County Democrats were eerily silent. We hadn't seen a runner in the city room for nearly an hour and the phone lines were open. No one was calling in with numbers. I took advantage of the lull in the action and told the others I was stepping out to get some air.

Instead I stopped into a liquor store and headed down to 11th and State to see my old pal Danny Finn.

"Four Roses," he said, holding the bottle of bourbon. "What's this for? And what the hell are you doing here on election night?"

"You once said that Four Roses was your favorite." I grinned. "Oh, and I *do* need a favor."

He smiled. "You know I'd do anything for you. You don't have to ply me with liquor. Though I'm damn glad you did." He laughed and cocked his head to the side. "So tell me, what do you need?"

"It's—I—It's a . . ." A sense of vertigo welled up inside me. My head went fuzzy. I couldn't focus.

Danny sensed me struggling to get the words out. "What is it?"

I cleared my throat and started again. "Do you remember a long time ago when I asked you about that hit-and-run?"

He squinted as if trying to jog his memory.

"It was a few years ago," I said. "The accident happened back in '53? State and Grand, near the subway stop?"

"Oh, yeah. I think so. Yeah, I sorta remember something about that."

"Well, I need you to pull the police report."

"Didn't we already do that?"

"No, because you said it had happened too long ago. There was no point."

"So why pull it now? Now it's been even longer—we're talking seven years ago."

"I know. But I need to see the report for myself. Please? It's important."

He hesitated for a minute and grabbed his pencil and a pad of paper. "Okay. What's the name? I'll go take a look."

I paused. My heart was tight as a fist.

"The name?"

"Eliot. Eliot Walsh."

Danny started to write it down and then stopped, set his pencil down and looked at me. "Oh, shit. No."

I nodded. "The victim was my brother. I've never seen the police report," I said.

"Oh, Jordan, I'm sorry."

"They never caught the guy, and I just want to . . ."

"It's okay. You don't have to explain." He went to a shelf lined with thick binders, papers protruding, jutting out along the tops. He pulled out one with a tattered black cover and leafed through it, searching and turning pages before he closed that one and reached for another. He did the same thing with two other volumes before he found what he was looking for. "Okay. Here we go. Looks like they've got this case in the inactive files."

"What's an inactive file?"

"Well, it's not closed, but they're not actively pursuing it." He disappeared down the hall, and I lit a cigarette, drawing in deep puffs to keep me calm. The radio on his desk was crackling about the poll watchers stationed at more than three thousand precincts throughout the city. But the radio was soon drowned out by the commotion at 11th and State. From the open door at the stairwell I could hear scuffles from the floors below, thugs and prostitutes being brought in, shouting at the cops, the cops shouting back. I reached over to turn up the volume on the radio, and my fingertips came away dirty.

Eventually Danny came back with a manila folder. I had already started my third, or maybe it was my fourth cigarette. I set it in the ashtray and opened the file. There was a yellow copy of the police report. I could see places in the corners where the blue carbon had bled through from the original and saturated the tissue-like paper. I reached for my cigarette again and propped it in my mouth while I read. The detective who filed the report was Curtis Norton. I'd never heard of him.

"Do you know this detective?" I asked.

"He's not with the force anymore. He resigned a while ago. Before I started here."

I continued reading. The report mentioned that pieces of a broken headlight were found, but they weren't able to match them to the make of a car. There were tread marks, too, but they led to inconclusive findings. As I was grinding out my cigarette, I noticed that sections on the second page had been crossed out with a marker so black and thick it was impossible to see what was underneath. "What's this?" I asked. "Why did they cross all this out?"

Danny looked at the report and shrugged. "Probably somebody got some information wrong. It happens."

I held the carbon copy to the light, hoping to make out some of it. "Where's the original?"

He reached for the folder and leafed through the pages himself.

"I need to see the original," I said. My voice was getting shaky.

Danny kept going through the file. Finally he looked up at me and sighed. "I'm sorry, but that's all that's in here."

"They're hiding something. There's something in that report."

"Oh, c'mon." He gave off a slight laugh. "That's ridiculous, Jordan. That's just your imagination running wild. You see what a mess this place is. Things—papers, files get misplaced all the time."

I clasped both sides of my head, vaguely aware of other people in the station looking at me. "How can something like that just disappear?"

"I'm not sure what happened to the original. Maybe it got lost or someone spilled coffee on it, or who knows what happened, but it looks like it's gone. That's why they make carbon copies in the first place."

"It's got to be here somewhere. I need to see that report. You don't understand. My brother was investigating a story. A big

story that ran all the way to the governor's office. I know you're
going to think this is crazy, but I'm telling you, they did it on
purpose. They killed him."

"Shsssh. C'mon, now. You gotta get a grip." He reached across
the table and held my trembling hands. "I'll look again for the
original. I'll try to track it down, but . . ." He shook his head.

"But what?"

"But if what you're saying is true, that original report may be
missing for a reason."

I left 11th and State with my head spinning, like the cyclone
of dead leaves on the sidewalk formed by the wind. My mind was
swirling, wondering who or where I could turn to next. That's
when I thought of Susan Hirsh, the girl Eliot had been seeing at
the time of his death. I wondered if I could even find her. I wondered if she still lived in Chicago. What if she'd gotten married
and had a new name?

All this was heavy on my mind when I went back to the city
room only to find a sudden influx of Democratic votes pouring
in from Cook County. Now the scales were tilting toward Kennedy. Still, though, they hadn't called the election. We waited
up half the night while more Democratic numbers came in, mostly
from Cook County precincts.

Morning came and Americans still didn't know who their new
president was. It wasn't until almost noon on Wednesday that it
became official. John F. Kennedy had won. Illinois—more specifically, Chicago—had turned the tide. But within an hour the
Republicans were whispering and then outright crying foul play.

While my colleagues were covering the post-election round-
ups, I went to the telephone directory and looked up Susan
Hirsh. I was shocked by how easily I found her. She lived at
Fullerton and Clark, not far from my apartment. Susan and Eliot
hadn't been dating for all that long when he died, and my parents

and I had met her for the first time at the funeral. None of us had seen her since. She was understandably surprised to hear from me but agreed to have lunch with me the next day.

I almost didn't recognize her when she first came into the Blackhawk. She actually spotted me first, hovering near the bar and cigarette machine.

The first thing she said was, "You look so much like him."

I smiled. People always told me that.

The maître d' showed us to our table, a booth toward the back. Susan and I made small talk about the elections. Then I asked how she was, and she told me she was a secretary for an executive at an insurance company. Until I mentioned it, she'd had no idea that I was a reporter.

Susan Hirsh was a striking woman, meticulously dressed in a smart suit. She had glossy brown hair and pronounced dimples. I could understand my brother's attraction to her. She seemed a bit fidgety though, worrying her strand of pearls while gazing about the restaurant. The waiter at the next table was preparing their signature spinning salad bowl, and she seemed captivated, watching the server turn the bowl on a bed of ice while pouring in dollops of each ingredient with a showman's flourish. After he presented the salad, Susan focused her attention back on me, and I got to the point.

"So I've been thinking a lot about Eliot lately," I said. "You know they never did catch the guy who hit him."

"I'm sorry to hear that." She went back to worrying her necklace. "I always wondered . . ."

"I know this is going to sound crazy," I said, picking at my food, "but I don't think it was an accident."

Her fingers froze. "What do you mean?"

"I think he was murdered." The words stuck in my throat. It would never be easy to say that.

Her eyes grew wide. She didn't speak.

"I know he was working on an important story and I think that had something to do with his death. And I'm wondering if there's anything you remember that—"

"Me?" Her fingers started twitching against her pearls again.

"Did he say anything to you about the article he was working on?"

She set her silverware across her plate and dabbed her mouth with her napkin. "Eliot didn't talk to me about his work. You know we weren't seeing each other all that long. Honestly, I didn't even know him all that well."

"But you were together for four or five months, weren't you?"

"Like I said, Jordan, I didn't really know him all that well. It wasn't like he confided in me."

"Are you sure? Are you positive he didn't mention something about someone threatening him or if—"

"Listen, I can certainly appreciate what you're trying to do, but I don't know anything that would help you." She reached for her handbag and took out her wallet. "Let me get this," she said as she placed five dollars on the table even though we hadn't gotten our check yet. "I'm sorry I can't help you." She got up and rested her hand on my shoulder. "I know you want answers, Jordan, but sometimes there's no explanation for what happens. Sometimes an accident is just an accident."

I was disappointed that nothing more came of my lunch with Susan, and I didn't buy what she'd said. Maybe an accident was sometimes just an accident, but I was more and more certain that wasn't true in this case.

I sat at my desk and contemplated my assignment. Now that people were questioning the election results, I was looking into the voting machines that had recently been introduced. People were coming forward, saying they were confusing and difficult to use. I made some calls, talked to some election judges and poll watchers. Some claimed their voters, especially in the poorer precincts, were actually afraid they'd get stuck inside the booths.

While I was waiting for some callbacks and confirmations, I opened my attaché case and pulled out the list of names and numbers I'd jotted down after going through my brother's notes. I made some calls, getting one wrong number, one hang-up, one deceased. Finally I reached Dale Merkin. Merkin was a former meat inspector with the Department of Agriculture. Now he ran a dairy farm over in Rockford. He agreed to see me.

The next day I borrowed my father's car and drove two hours west of the city to meet Merkin at his dairy farm. He was wearing a plaid peacoat over his bib overalls, along with thick rubber boots. It was cold that day, and I wished I'd dressed a little warmer. He walked me through the dairy farm, with its silos and big red barn, the pungent scent of manure in the air. A wooden fence enclosed an endless pasture that I imagined was lush and green in the summertime. The cows occasionally stuck their heads through the wooden slots, straining at the grass on the other side. I'd never seen so many cows before, and he had all different kinds—red and white Ayrshires, brown and white Guernseys, and the black and white Holstein-Friesians.

"So you say you want to talk about horsemeat being pumped into the system. Well, I'm afraid you're a little late."

"What? What do you mean?"

"That was going on back in the early 1950s. 1951, '52, even up to '53. But not anymore. Not since Governor Stratton took office seven years ago. His hands are clean. But Stevenson"—he laughed as he reached through the fence to give one of the Holsteins a rubdown—"his office knew what was going on. We called him *Adlai Horsemeat*. Yeah, his office was in on it. And they weren't alone. And you can quote me on that."

"Who were they working with?" I was writing as we walked, trying my best to avoid the piles of cow dung.

"Without naming names, let's just say this one had Mafia written all over it. They were behind the whole thing."

I got a chill deep inside my bones. "How did it work? Do you remember?"

"Most of the horsemeat came in from Kansas. From an outfit called Willis Packing in Topeka. I can't say for sure how many tons, but I know for a fact that the amount of horsemeat coming into this state more than doubled from 1951 to 1953. It was turning up in restaurants, in kids' lunches at the schools, housewives were serving it to their families. People were lining their pockets, being paid a whole lot of money to look the other way. We inspectors were even paid—and I'm talking good money—to keep our mouths shut. I couldn't stomach it anymore. That's why I got out. That's why I called up the newspaper and told 'em what was going on."

"You?" I almost dropped my pencil. "You called this in? Do you remember which paper?"

"It was the *Sun-Times*."

My heart nearly stopped.

"Do you remember who you spoke to?"

"Some young reporter. I can't remember his name right off the—"

"It was Eliot. Eliot Walsh."

He turned and looked at me. "That sounds about right. I think that's who it was."

My skin turned to gooseflesh, and it wasn't from the cold.

"Well," Merkin continued, "we set up a time to meet, but I never did get to see him in person."

I was expecting him to tell me the meeting never took place because the reporter had died.

Merkin scratched his jaw. "Somehow it got out that I was talking to the press and they shut me up fast."

"They? Who was *they*? Who shut you up?"

"A couple young guys—they roughed me up pretty good. Broke my arm and a couple of ribs. They said that was just a warning and that if I said anything else to the press, I'd never talk to anyone again."

"Were they with the Mob? Were they Stevenson's men?"

"No. I think they were a couple of guys from out of state. I remember they were driving a car with Kansas plates on it. And like I said, most of the horsemeat was coming from Topeka. After that I was good and shook up. I wasn't about to call that reporter back. He kept trying me, but I wouldn't talk. Wouldn't say another word about it."

My heart about stopped again.

Merkin grabbed hold of the fence with both hands and gave it a tug. "Actually, that's not true. I did talk to that reporter once more after that." He dropped his hands to his sides, kicking dust up off his overalls. "He caught hold of me on the phone one day and I remember I told him to be careful. Said he was dealing with some very powerful people. Dangerous people. I remember I told him straight out, if I were you, I wouldn't mess with 'em."

As I drove back from Rockford, it was all I could do to focus on the lines in the pavement. It was hypnotizing, and I was scarcely aware of the cars passing by me or the exit signs along the interstate. By the time I reached Elgin, I had decided not to share what Merkin said with my parents. It would only upset them, and I knew it would be best to hold off until I had pieced this all together.

After I dropped off my father's car and dodged his questions, I went back to the city room to finish up another piece about voter fraud allegations. While some people were coming forward to say they were offered money for their votes, others flat-out denied it. It was a mess. I was sorting through it all when I got a call from Danny Finn.

"Why don't you meet me at the Gold Star when you get off work tonight?"

The Gold Star was an old dive on Division and Wood. A fleabag hotel was on the upper level. I arrived before Danny and took a seat at one of the tables, the Formica top scarred with cigarette burns and knife carvings. Some believed the Gold Star was haunted, and while I didn't necessarily believe in ghosts, the gargoyle above the bar always gave me the willies.

I ordered a J&B on the rocks and about ten minutes later Danny appeared in a pair of jeans and a flannel red and black checked shirt. His cheeks were tinged pink from the cold. It was one of the few times I'd ever seen him out of uniform, and I was aware of the women inside the bar watching him as he walked my way. He had an oversize brown envelope tucked under his arm.

"Sorry I'm late," he said, sitting down, setting the envelope on the spare chair.

He ordered a beer and we made small talk for a few minutes before he set the envelope on the table and nudged it toward me.

"What's this?" I placed my hands on top of it.

"I'm gonna hit the head," he said. "You've got ten minutes with that"—he nodded toward the envelope—"and then I need to get it back to the station."

As soon as Danny got up, I lifted the flap on the envelope and pulled out a file. The label on top read: *Walsh, Eliot, June 9, 1953.* My heart raced as I opened it up. And there it was. The original police report, written by Detective Curtis Norton.

I scanned the report and noticed that a few items had been crossed out on the original, too. But other than that, it looked like any other police report I'd seen countless times, especially back when I was working the night shift. But then something caught my eye. Under the investigation section I read: *According to the witness, James Harding . . .*

Witness! What witness? My head suddenly felt too tight, like my skull was about to explode. We were told there were no witnesses. I had questioned that over and over again. I kept reading.

> *According to the witness, James Harding, a black Packard with Illinois plates drove up onto the curb and struck the victim before steering back onto the street and driving off, heading south. The driver was Caucasian, in his mid-thirties. There was significant damage to the front of the grille. A broken headlight was found on the ground at the accident site.*

When Danny came back to the table, I was shaking.

"You got what you need?"

All I could do was nod.

The next day I tracked down Detective Norton. I found him living in the quiet suburb of Oak Lawn, running a private surveillance business. One train ride and two buses later, I met him at his office in a small nondescript building on 95th Street. The sign on his door was stenciled in gold lettering: NORTON INVESTIGATIONS.

He was in his early forties and had a slight frame and a nasty-looking scar running from the base of one ear to the center of his neck. He invited me to have a seat in a rickety chair and offered me burned coffee in a paper cup.

"So what is it that I can help you with?" he asked, pouring himself a cup.

"I'm looking into a hit-and-run accident."

"Uh-huh." He grabbed a pad of paper and jotted something on the top.

"It took place several years ago. When you were a detective with the Chicago Police Department." I paused when I saw the way his expression changed. "I was looking into the police report and—"

"Look, miss, I'm sorry, but I—I can't help you with this. I don't do that kind of work anymore."

"Listen, I'll come clean with you," I said. "I'm a reporter, but I'm not trying to trip you up. I'm not here as a reporter. I'm here because I need answers. My brother was the victim of that hit-and-run."

Though his face softened, he didn't say a word.

"All I'm trying to do is find out what happened. What *really* happened to him. I don't believe it was an accident. I think he was murdered. I know they altered the police report. I just don't know why. But I have a feeling you do. You were there. You filled out the report. Do you remember the accident? Back in June of 1953. A young, promising journalist was—"

"I left the force around that time."

"I know you left the force. You left right after it happened. Why did you resign?"

He set his coffee down and fidgeted with his wristwatch. "I didn't resign. That's what I told everyone. That's what they told everyone. Truth was, they fired me."

"Why?"

He shook his head and looked at a stain on the carpet. "Look, I have a wife and three kids. I'm not putting myself in this position. I'm sorry about your brother—I really am—but I just can't help you."

The following day Chicago got an early blast of winter. With six inches of snow on the ground, I trudged up to Rogers Park to meet with the witness, James Harding.

"I told the police everything I know," Harding said as he hefted another log into his fireplace, setting off a burst of sparks. The air around us was filled with a smoky hickory scent, and my toes were still frozen after the walk from the el. Harding replaced the fireplace grate and dusted his hands along his back pockets. "I remember I kept waiting for someone to come talk to me some more about it. I even called the police department and they kept saying someone would get back to me. I guess you're that someone. I just don't know why the *Tribune* would be interested in a story like this after all these years."

"Actually, the *Tribune* isn't. But I am. The victim was my brother."

"Aw, no." He dragged a liver-spotted hand through his white hair. "That's terrible. I'm sorry."

"What else can you tell me about that night? I want to hear everything."

"So long ago. Let's see . . ." He lifted his eyes toward the ceiling, as if trying to recall. "Mostly what I remember is the car. A '52 Cadillac—"

"Cadillac? Are you sure? The police report said it was a Packard."

"Nope. I'm sure. It was a Cadillac, all right. Tan with a red interior. 1952. I remember because the emblem on the hood— the *V*—was in gold. They did that on all the cars in '52 because it was Cadillac's fiftieth anniversary. See, I used to be a mechanic," he said. "So I pay attention to all that sort of stuff. Plus, it was a convertible, and I always wanted a Cadillac convertible."

"A convertible? It was June. Was the top down?"

"Oh, yeah, that's how I knew it had a red interior."

"And what about the driver?"

A spark shot out of the fireplace, through the grille and onto the wooden floor. Harding got up and stamped out the ember and then started poking at the fire.

"About the driver?" I asked again, thinking I'd lost him.

"There were two of them in the car. Both white boys. I remember thinking they were young to be driving in such a fancy car," he said, setting the poker down before he came back over to his chair. "And they weren't from around these parts."

"What do you mean? How do you know?"

"The plates. I didn't get the license number, but those were Kansas plates."

The following morning, on next to no sleep, I sat at my desk, trying to decide what to do. All the puzzle pieces were coming together and at a speed that made my head spin. The answers had been waiting there inside Eliot's file all this time. That was all that was needed to set everything in motion. It was like I'd pulled a thread and the whole hem had come undone. I didn't know whether I was ecstatic or scared to death. I only knew that I was overwhelmed.

"Did you get anywhere with Earl Bush on Daley holding back votes?" Marty asked. He was suddenly looming over my desk, although I hadn't seen him approach me.

"Huh? What?"

"Did you get a reaction from Bush? The allegations that Daley held back votes until they knew how many they needed to put Kennedy over the top."

"What?" I heard the words, knew he was talking about the assignment I was working on, but I couldn't understand.

"Jesus, Walsh. What the hell is wrong with you?"

I looked up at Marty and stared into his dark eyes until I felt myself starting to shake. "Oh, Marty, I'm—I'm . . ." I brought my hands to my temples and squeezed my eyes shut to keep from crying.

"What the hell? You okay? What's going on?"

"I've gotten myself in the middle of something. It's a cover-up. They killed my brother. I'm going to need help. I'm . . . I don't know what to do."

I knew he could see me shaking, but I hadn't cried. I wouldn't let myself cry in front of him. Or any of the others. Without a word, he took my hand and led me across the city room to Ellsworth.

Marty explained to him what I had said, and then Ellsworth asked me what I meant by a cover-up.

I took a deep breath and began to tell the story. "I've . . . I've been looking into a horsemeat scandal. Something that was going on a few years ago. I've found out they were selling horsemeat, passing it off as beef. Everywhere. All over Chicago." I was speaking like a robot, just concentrating on laying the facts out and keeping the emotion at bay. Oddly, Marty was still holding my hand. "I think the Mafia was behind it. Adlai Stevenson's administration was in on it, too. My brother tried to prove it years ago. Back in 1953. And they killed him before he could finish the—"

I felt Ellsworth's hand on my shoulder. "It's okay, Walsh. Peter? Hey, Peter, grab Walter and Henry and meet us in the conference room. Hey, Copeland," he called across the room. "I need you over here."

I followed them and sat at the far end of the table, facing Ellsworth, Mr. Copeland, Marty, Walter, Henry and Peter. The whole team. They asked questions and I told them what I'd learned about Detective Norton, about what James Harding had said, about the doctored police report, about my meeting with Dale Merkin. I was calmer by the time I finished. It helped to share all this with my colleagues. Collectively, they were a powerhouse, the very people who decided what *was* news. Looking at their faces, I heard Henry's words from long ago echoing in my head—it was a hard truth, something not to be challenged: *You can't fuck with a member of the press.*

"It's okay," Ellsworth said, handing me a glass of water. "We're going to get these bastards. We're going to nail them to the wall."

I drank the water down, feeling it hit the pit of my hollow stomach. A calmness came over me, as all my scattered thoughts and fears, the swirling of uncertainty that had nearly overwhelmed me, resolved itself into a settled, solid feeling. I was coming to a new place within myself. I was not the same. I would never be the same again. I was stronger and more determined than ever.

I went back to my desk while my coworkers rallied for my cause. I watched Peter reach for his phone. "Yeah, it's me. I need a favor," he said, cradling the phone between his ear and shoulder. "I need you to run a check for me. I need the names of everyone in Topeka, Kansas, who purchased a 1952 Cadillac convertible. Tan with red interior." Peter was the best crime reporter in the business. He had contacts in places that I couldn't begin to fathom. "And check if you have any records of someone selling a car like that in June of '53, with possible damage to the front grille, a broken headlight, anything suspicious. . . ."

Across the room, I heard Henry on the phone with a buddy at the *Capital-Journal* in Topeka. "See if you can find anything for me about Willis Packing being investigated for a horsemeat scandal back in '51—going up to '53."

Walter banged his pipe and turned his swivel chair toward me. "Walsh, I've got someone down in Springfield who worked for Stevenson. I always got the sense that he didn't like the governor. I think he knew he was up to something. I'm going to track him down, see if we can get him to talk, and then I'll call my source over at the Bureau. . . ."

I looked around the city room and watched as these men— the very men who had sabotaged and resented me and had ridiculed me for being a sob sister—took up my cause. They were following my lead and helping me investigate the most important scoop of my career.

My eyes filled with tears and I allowed one, just one, to leak down my face before I cleared it with the back of my hand.

Epilogue

◆ ◆ ◆

Chicago, November 22, 1963

It was the first time my parents' television set had been on for more than one hour at a time, and I knew my father was concerned about what all that extra viewing would do to the electric bill.

The day the president was shot I'd been having lunch with M, Mrs. Angelo, Gabby and Eppie Lederer. It was something of a bridal shower for M, who was getting married that weekend. Turned out she met and fell in love with Gregory's boss. We girls had knocked off early and decided to make this sort of a last hurrah for her at Riccardo's. We were talking about the wedding and what we were all planning to wear. Gabby was worried that her shoes would make her taller than Benny, whom she'd been dating for the past year. Not that any of us were surprised—the two had been inching their way toward each other for ages.

We were sitting at the bar, talking about Gabby's shoes, when we heard the news. Benny had been back in the city room when it came over on the wire, and he raced over to tell us. We tossed our money on the bar and fled back to the city room.

Ellsworth had a portable black-and-white TV set up on the horseshoe where I now sat, too. CBS was making a half-assed attempt to return to *As the World Turns* before Walter Cronkite broke back in with an update. Mr. Copeland adjusted the rabbit ears to clear the snow and static from Cronkite's face as he reported on blood transfusions and an unconfirmed report that the president was dead.

Dead? Dead!

Randy accidentally knocked over his coffee, and M and Gabby and even Peter seemed more concerned about offering up napkins and shoving cigarettes and lighters out of the way than accepting the possibility that President Kennedy was dead. I couldn't say I blamed them. It was just too much to fathom. The rest of us were hovering around the horseshoe, waiting until the confirmation came through. It had been an hour since we first learned that three shots had been fired.

It took a lot to shock a city room filled with jaded reporters who had seen it all, but when they announced that Kennedy was dead, we were speechless. But just for a minute. Then all at once we jumped into action. We had news to report.

I must have gone through a pack of Lucky Strikes that afternoon, contributing to the haze of blue smoke accumulating above our heads. It was several hours later when Ellsworth sent me home to get some rest, not that I wanted to leave.

I started to protest, but he said, "Get the hell out of here, Walsh. I've got it covered for now. But I hope you didn't have any plans this weekend, because I expect you back here at seven o'clock tomorrow morning. And pack a change or two of clothes—you won't be leaving anytime soon. I'll need a break by then, so you'll have to be fresh. I'm depending on you to help me cover this. Now, go."

I packed up my attaché case, thinking how much had changed over the past three years. After I broke the horsemeat scandal—which resulted in public outrage and a fifty percent drop in beef sales, despite the fact that our coverage assured everyone that the food supply was now clean—my status at the paper completely changed. It proved to be one of the most important stories the *Tribune* had scooped in years. There were countless indictments that followed. Department heads down in Springfield who had managed to keep their jobs under the new governor were fired. And that was only the beginning. The work I'd done on my brother's murder resulted in the authorities reopening the investigation. That past summer two men, junior executives from Willis Packing in Topeka, Kansas, were convicted of the murder of Eliot Walsh.

Finally, my family had a sense of justice and relief, and closure. My mother planted flowers again and even picked up her pen. My father cut back on his drinking and started working on a new novel. My grandparents came to town and no one stormed out of the room.

As for me, I was floundering. I'd spent more than a year on the story, but once all the investigating was done and meetings with detectives and lawyers were over, the case was closed. And none of it had brought Eliot back. I found myself left with a different kind of void to fill. So I threw myself even harder into my first love, my work. And the next scoop I discovered shocked even me. Because it had been sitting right under my nose for years. Turned out my neighbor across the hall, the one with the mysterious baby stroller, was actually running a black-market adoption ring. She was pulling in anywhere from $100 to $1,000 per child. I'd never actually seen her because she lived up north in a big house and just used the shoddy apartment across the hall from me as drop-off and pickup point.

Anyway, by this time, my big investigative articles had captured a lot of national attention. I began to develop a reputation as one of the top investigative reporters in Chicago and was even

honored with a few awards. After that Ellsworth and Mr. Copeland called me into the conference room and announced that
they were promoting me to deputy city editor. I was the first
female to hold that post and take my seat with the men at the
horseshoe. Since then I've hired on two female reporters and am
currently fighting with Ellsworth to bring on a third. Like Mrs.
Angelo said to me that day on Lower Wacker, now I'll do anything I can to help another woman.

It was raining when I left the *Tribune* the day Kennedy was
shot, but the temperature was unusually warm for the end of
November. Last I heard it was a clement sixty-one. I had an
umbrella with me but couldn't bring myself to open it. I was just
that numb.

Out on the street, it was too quiet for a Friday night. The city
had that eerie deserted feel, like on the eve of a holiday when
businesses and stores close early. There were cars on the road,
but no one honked. Everyone seemed to be moving carefully,
solemnly, respectfully. The few people I did see walking looked
as though they were in a trance, rain pelting their faces and over-
coats. It was either that or they went out of their way to make
eye contact, to hold you with a glance that seemed to say, *It'll be
okay. We'll all get through this.*

Suddenly the thought of getting on the el and going home to
my empty apartment was too much. Instead, I turned up my collar, flagged down a cab, and gave the driver my parents' address.
The cabbie's radio was tuned to WGN.

"Do you believe this?" said the driver. "What's this world
coming to?"

I hadn't noticed the driver before. He was a burly man with
matted-down hair, balding slightly in the back. When I shifted
my gaze to the rearview mirror, I saw tears in this big man's eyes.

"I was in the Loop when it happened," he said. "I had a

passenger running late for a lunch meeting. He's in the backseat telling me, 'Go this way; take that street.' I had the radio on. I was listening to *County Fair* when they broke in with the bulletin. I tell you, I had to pull over. I was shaking. I couldn't drive. The guy in the back was still worried about getting to his damn lunch meeting. 'Go! Go!' he's telling me. 'Why'd you pull over?' He didn't get it. His lunch didn't matter anymore. The world had just changed."

I looked into the rearview mirror, into his teary eyes. When he pulled up to my parents' house, I handed him two dollars for a fifty-cent fare and he clasped my fingers and I in turn held on to his.

Moments later I found my parents in the family room with the lights down low, their faces illuminated by the ghostlike flickers coming off the Westinghouse TV set. My mother had abandoned the ironing board in the corner and was perched on the edge of her chair. My father was in his recliner, his manuscript resting on the floor at his side. I could see my mother's handwriting all over it. She was editing it for him as he went. About a month before he'd even let me read the first fifty pages. It was a mystery, and it was good. Really good. I'd been begging him to give me more ever since.

My mother got up and hugged me, cupping my face in her hands. She was fixing herself a fresh drink. "You need one?"

"Sure," I said. "Give me whatever you're having."

My father could hardly look away from the TV set as I leaned down to kiss his forehead.

"This is the biggest news story since Pearl Harbor," he said. "Oh, what I wouldn't give to be back in the city room right now."

I stayed and had a drink with them, feeling antsy as I sat on the sofa and watched the news unfold on TV. A static *CBS News Bulletin* art card filled the screen before Walter Cronkite reappeared with reactions pouring in from leaders throughout the world. I had such a feeling of being abandoned. I wondered if my parents felt it, too. It seemed like we were all children whose father had just been killed. Who would take care of us now? We had Vice President Johnson, who was sort of like a distant uncle you didn't know very well. It didn't feel very comforting.

The evening wore on and we halfheartedly picked at dinner while seated in front of the TV set. Dan Rather, down in Dallas, was now reporting that they had a man in custody. A new layer to the story was unfolding. I closed my eyes and pictured everyone in the city room scrambling to find out what they could about this twenty-four-year-old Lee Oswald. I could hear the din of typewriters, the wire machines, the phones going and people racing up and down the aisles as the presses rumbled from down below.

I couldn't wait to get back there.

Author's Note

♦ ♦ ♦

As with my previous novels, *Dollface* and *What the Lady Wants*, I've woven many real-life people and historical events into the fabric of *White Collar Girl*. But unlike my previous novels, which were set in the 1920s and the Gilded Age, *White Collar Girl* takes place more recently, in the 1950s, and because of that I was able to meet and interview many people who were alive and vividly remember the time and events included in this novel.

White Collar Girl was the name of an actual column written by Ruth McKay, which ran in the *Chicago Tribune* during the 1940s and 1950s. And while the main characters, from the editors to the reporters, are all fictional, many of the events they covered in *White Collar Girl* are based on actual news stories and political scandals.

The el car derailment in *White Collar Girl* was based loosely on a similar derailment in the Loop, which occurred in 1977. However, the CTA scandal and the people and circumstances surrounding it in *White Collar Girl* are completely fictional.

Operation K in *White Collar Girl* was based on Operation Greylord, a major scandal that shook the Cook County judiciary system in the 1980s. The FBI conducted a three-and-a-half-year investigation in which one man, Terrence Hake, posed as a crooked lawyer on the take and went undercover to expose widespread corruption in the legal system. Operation Greylord resulted in countless arrests of police officers, lawyers and judges.

Richard Morrison, better known as the Babbling Burglar, was a real robber who ultimately helped Chicago police crack down on what became known as the Summerdale Scandal. As portrayed in *White Collar Girl*, several police officers were working in conjunction with Morrison in an elaborate robbing spree.

The air-raid sirens blasting after the White Sox won the 1959 pennant was a true event and one that many Chicagoans living today recall.

While Chicago has a long and notorious history of voter fraud, none was more notable than the 1960 Kennedy versus Nixon election, which is depicted in *White Collar Girl*. Though it was never completely proven, accusations of voter fraud significantly tarnished Daley's reputation.

The horsemeat scandal in *White Collar Girl* is also based on an actual scandal that rocked Chicago and Illinois from 1951–1953, in which horsemeat was passed on to consumers as beef. It turned up everywhere, from grocery stores to fine restaurants. Governor Adlai Stevenson's administration and the Mafia were involved in the scandal.

Please note that the Peterson-Schuessler murders actually took place in October 1955 rather than June 1955, where I have it here.

While I was conducting research for this book, my dear friend and former *Chicago Tribune* staff photographer Charles Osgood invited me to a *Chicago Tribune* reunion party. It was there that I met Marion Purcelli, who started at the *Tribune* in 1949 as a "copygirl." Marion served as a huge inspiration for the characters Jordan Walsh and Mrs. Angelo. Many stories Marion covered found their way into the pages of *White Collar Girl*, including the story on the Dwight Correctional Facility for Women and her article, "So I'm a Girl and I Carry an Attaché Case."

The *Tribune* city room of today looks nothing like it did during the 1950s, but still I'm grateful to Rick Kogan for giving me a look inside the Tribune Tower. It was also through Rick that I met Old Town historian Shirley Baugher, who was extremely generous with her vast knowledge of one of Chicago's most fascinating and charming neighborhoods.

In addition to personal interviews, I read countless 1950s issues and articles from the *Tribune* and am very grateful to the Chicago Public Library for making these archives available. I also did a great deal of reading in order to educate myself not only on Chicago politics of the 1950s but also on the field of journalism. For those interested in learning more about either subject (which tend to go hand in hand), I highly recommend the following books:

At Home in Our Old Town: Every House Has a Story by Shirley Baugher. Chicago: Old Town Triangle Association, 2005.

Hidden History of Old Town by Shirley Baugher. Charlestown: History Press, 2011.

Our Old Town: The History of a Neighborhood by Shirley Baugher. Chicago: Old Town Triangle Association, 2001.

American Pharaoh: Mayor Richard J. Daley: His Battle for Chicago and the Nation by Adam Cohen and Elizabeth Taylor. New York: Little, Brown and Co., 2000.

The Third Coast: When Chicago Built the American Dream by Thomas Dyja. New York: Penguin Books, 2013.

After Visiting Friends: A Son's Story by Michael Hainey. New York: Scribner, 2013.

Front-Page Girls: Women Journalists in American Culture and Fiction 1880–1930 by Jean Marie Lutes. Ithaca: Cornell University Press, 2006.

Don't Make No Waves . . . Don't Back No Losers: An Insider's Analysis of the Daley Machine by Milton L. Rakove. Bloomington: Indiana University Press, 1975.

Boss: Richard J. Daley of Chicago by Mike Royko. New York: Penguin Books, 1971.

Women in American Journalism: A New History by Jan Whitt. Urbana: University of Illinois Press, 2008.

Courthouse Over White House: Chicago and the Presidential Election of 1960 by Edmund Frank Kallina. University of Florida Press, 1988.

White Collar Girl

• • •

RENÉE ROSEN

Questions
for Discussion

1. A major theme in *White Collar Girl* is women in the workplace and the challenges they faced in trying to break through the glass ceiling. How do you see the challenges facing career women in the 1950s as compared to those found in today's workplace? In what ways have we advanced and in what ways do you feel we are still stuck? Are there advantages women have now that they didn't have then?

2. At various points in the book, Jordan is confronted with moral issues over what she is willing to do to get a story. In some cases she even bends the law. Do you think she's justified in going to these lengths in order to expose the truth? Do you think her drive is based more on her feeling she's a public watchdog, or do you think it's her ego?

3. How do you see the other women in the story? Do you see M as a tragic figure or as a woman coming into her own? What about Gabby? Do you think Mrs. Angelo is a mentor, and did you feel like she was helping Jordan advance or holding her back? In what ways do you feel each of these characters were typical of their time, and in what ways were they not?

4. Jordan's mother, CeeCee, was an unusual woman for her time. Do you think she was a good mother? How do you think CeeCee shaped the woman Jordan grew up to be?

5. If you were of working age in the 1950s, would you see yourself more as a career-minded woman like Jordan or a traditionalist like M? What did you find most interesting about each woman? What did you find most frustrating about them?

6. Marty Sinclair, Pulitzer Prize–winning journalist, is Jordan's hero at the start of the novel, but as the story progresses he falls from grace. How do you think she handles the situation? What would you have done if you had been in her shoes?

7. When Jordan falls in love with Jack Casey, a fellow journalist, he seems threatened by her professional accomplishments. Do you think that was the major reason they didn't get married? What do you see as the other obstacles in their relationship? Were you glad that Jordan decided to walk away from him?

8. Scott Trevor was the love of Jordan's life. When she called in the story about the Operation K mole, it put an end to their budding romance. Do you think Scott's reaction was understandable? Do you think Jordan made a mistake in putting the story before her loyalty to him?

9. As we all know, sadly newspapers no longer play the role in our lives that they did even a decade or two ago, let alone one as important as they did in the 1950s, when they were everyone's primary source of news. Do you think in general we are less informed about local, national and world events due to the decline

of newspapers? Or do you think we are better informed due to the immediacy of things like Twitter and 24-7 cable news?

10. Many of the scandals in *White Collar Girl* were based on actual events. Do you think we are more aware of political scandals today because in the digital age, social media and camera phones make it harder to conceal them? Or do you think we are less aware today because daily city newspapers play less of a role as a watchdog?

Photo by Charles Osgood

Renée Rosen is a freelance writer and the author of *What the Lady Wants, Dollface,* and *Every Crooked Pot.* She lives in Chicago, where she is at work on her next novel.